Catherine Greer is a Canadian–Australia nonfiction. She writes a weekly newsletter a where everyone is welcome. *The Bittersweet Bakery Café* is Catherine's first novel for adults.

Praise for
The Bittersweet Bakery Café

'Life-affirming and joyous . . . Audrey will inspire you to raise a glass to a bigger, better, brighter future.'

        Josephine Moon, bestselling author of *The Cake Maker's Wish*

'Funny, heartbreaking and rich with characters, grit and determination. A page-turner.'

        Susan Duncan, bestselling author of *Finding Joy in Oyster Bay*

'A sparkling novel with a tender heart, *The Bittersweet Bakery Café* offers a delicious take on reinvention. Who would have guessed that a fortune cookie could transform your life?'

        Sophie Beaumont, bestselling author of *The Paris Cooking School*

'I want to move in next door to the Bittersweet Bakery Café so Audrey can become my best friend. Every woman deserves a bestie like Audrey. This is the coming-of-middle-age, feel-good fiction we all need. A delectable feast of a novel!'

        Tess Woods, bestselling author of *The Venice Hotel*

'Get reading, be inspired, then get ready to cook!'

        Catriona Rowntree, television presenter and author

CATHERINE GREER

the bitter sweet bakery café

Sometimes losing everything is the only way to win

ALLEN & UNWIN
SYDNEY · MELBOURNE · AUCKLAND · LONDON

This is a work of fiction. Names, characters, places and incidents are products of the author's imagination or are used fictitiously. Any resemblance to actual events, locales or persons, living or dead, is entirely coincidental.

First published in 2025

Copyright © Catherine Greer 2025

All rights reserved. No part of this book may be reproduced or transmitted in any form or by any means, electronic or mechanical, including photocopying, recording or by any information storage and retrieval system, without prior permission in writing from the publisher. The Australian *Copyright Act 1968* (the Act) allows a maximum of one chapter or 10 per cent of this book, whichever is the greater, to be photocopied by any educational institution for its educational purposes provided that the educational institution (or body that administers it) has given a remuneration notice to the Copyright Agency (Australia) under the Act.

Allen and Unwin
Cammeraygal Country
83 Alexander Street
Crows Nest NSW 2065
Australia
Phone: (61 2) 8425 0100
Email: info@allenandunwin.com
Web: www.allenandunwin.com

Allen & Unwin acknowledges the Traditional Owners of the Country on which we live and work. We pay our respects to all Aboriginal and Torres Strait Islander Elders, past and present.

 A catalogue record for this book is available from the National Library of Australia

ISBN 978 1 76147 122 3

Set in 13.5/17pt Granjon Std by Bookhouse, Sydney

With love and deep gratitude to Australia—thank you for letting my Canadian family call this country 'home'. And to the Koori people of Booderee: thank you for sharing the white sand of Hyams Beach. It's the most beautiful place in the world, and the home of my heart.

CHAPTER 1

Audrey Sweetman-Brown hustled up the steps of the Sydney Opera House, its sails gleaming white against the orange and mauve dawn. With each stride, she checked off a mental list of everything she'd done. She'd created a groundbreaking ad campaign. She'd selected the most diverse and gorgeous group of midlife models in the country. She'd given them a gruelling four a.m. call time for the shoot. She'd hired the city's top beauty photographer and called in a favour with Klint Marsden, an award-winning director of television commercials. Audrey waved her coffee at Klint now. Dressed in black from his boots to his scarf, he lifted his takeaway cup in salute. Or so she thought.

'Audrey!' he roared. 'Where's your assistant? I need another coffee.'

But Summer was nowhere, late again, and Audrey was left doing the work of two. She hiked up the steps faster, sweating in her trench coat and wool dress, texting Summer as she went. The director could easily get his own half-soy half–oat milk double shot decaf latte—Audrey had run down the steps to the catering truck for her long black—but like many men, he preferred to be served. She sighed. Klint's ego was the size of a small planet, and like every woman she knew, she'd wrangled egos similar to his for years.

For example, to convince her boss, Colin, that her ad campaign pitch would work, it had taken four strategy meetings, a twenty-page customer validation research paper and a complete set of financials . . . even though at fifty-three, Audrey knew first-hand that midlife women had the money to splurge on luxury cosmetics. But. But! Every chirpy, aspirational ad aimed at them was anti-ageing and Audrey was sick of it. You're sixty? *You should look thirty-two!* You're fifty? *Jennifer Lopez pole danced at the Superbowl at your age!* Audrey questioned briefly what it would take to hoist her own backside up a stainless-steel pole in white boots and a sequined bodysuit. Answer: she was finding it was hard enough to race up the two hundred steps to the Opera House. She inhaled the tang of sea air and kept climbing, scattering a flock of brooding gulls back to the harbour. Where was Summer? Probably sleeping in again. Audrey's temples throbbed, and she wished she'd slept better herself. By midnight Wyatt had given up on her ever settling and had escaped to the guest room.

She paused outside the Opera House and took a deep breath. Then she gazed at the stunning expanse of mottled orange sky and sent up a silent wish that it would be a successful day for everyone on her shoot. She'd done this since she was a little girl—looking at the sky, thinking of the people she cared about and tossing joy over them like imaginary confetti. Audrey smiled at her own silliness. But the models, the support staff, the difficult director, everyone needed a little positivity, didn't they? She knew a shoot like this one was never just about winning over the client. It was about the people—all the creatives and techs and talent—and giving them their moment to shine. Ad campaigns could be manipulative, but they could also change lives: they had the power to influence people and make the world a little better, and in the end, that's why she'd stuck with the industry all these years.

If, if, if . . . Audrey's brain cartwheeled with exciting possibilities. If her shoot was exceptional, and if she nailed her pitch at Monday's meeting with Hayes Corp, her age-positive ad would run country-wide and the agency would get every cent of the cosmetic company's advertising budget for the next three years. Audrey would help empower women, the agency would score a huge win, and Colin would promote her to creative director. At last.

She wrenched open the heavy double doors of the Opera House. In the cold concrete foyer, five models with white bathrobes over their dresses were huddled together. Behind them, pop-up tents overflowed with tangled clothes and shoes, a stylist ironing frantically next to a rack of alternate clothing in case anyone had fudged their measurements. She nodded at the stylist, willing her to hurry up. The foyer smelled of hairspray, cloying, sweet.

'Nearly ready?' Audrey asked.

'Yep, just a sec. Hair and Make-up's spraying the last two with sunscreen. He says winter sun is just as bad as summer.'

As the models gathered around in their bathrobes, Audrey smiled at five women who looked just like herself and her friends—older bodies, yet beautiful all the same, their faces lined with warmth and intelligence. In the industry, they were called classic models. They were gorgeous and highly sought after, but Audrey had been surprised listening to their self-deprecating banter on the audition tapes; even classic models had trouble seeing themselves clearly, as if they couldn't recognise their own loveliness. She set her takeaway cup firmly on the ironing board.

'Thanks for making the early call time, ladies. I'm Audrey Sweetman-Brown, senior executive at the ad agency. We're celebrating women and selling some make-up, but we're going to use a radical tagline to do it.' Audrey paused. They looked at her expectantly.

'Love Your Age. Live beautifully.'

'That's fabulous!' one of them said.

'You could join us, Audrey,' another called.

Audrey laughed. 'Today's all yours, ladies.' She adjusted her glasses and smiled. 'You're going to take back the power. From fifty to seventy, all we get is anti-ageing, but this campaign is different. You're going to tell the world we don't have to look young to look good. And you do look fabulous.'

The models straightened their shoulders and shifted together; they were a gorgeous pack of midlife women. Mei, Simone, Fatima, Priya and Kelly: different sizes and heights, different cultural backgrounds, and every woman with a unique beauty. Expressive eyes or silver hair, smile lines, generous curves or athleticism. Audrey almost wanted to break into a victory dance. She loved the look of them; it'd taken her three days to sort through headshots with the casting agency until she'd found the perfect ensemble for Love Your Age.

'Simone, you're up first,' Audrey said. 'Let's go.'

Audrey hurried out the door and across the concrete landing outside to Klint and the rest of the crew, searching for just the right compliment for the city's most sought-after and belligerent director. They were racing against the sunrise, and she needed exquisite shots. With creativity, a precipice yawned between mediocre and remarkable; in retrospect, the leap looked effortless, obvious even, except it never was.

'Talent ready?' Klint asked.

'Almost. I'm excited to see your work, Klint. Your shoot with American Express was amazing.'

As Audrey spoke, Simone opened the doors of the Opera House and stepped into the light. Even from a distance, her blue eyes and silver hair, her finely lined brow and graceful stance made her look more like an athlete than a model. She was tall and muscular, vibrant and healthy. And older. Though she hadn't been asked to reveal her age, only her height, Simone had proudly told Audrey at the casting callbacks that she was turning sixty-four.

Klint whistled. 'Good casting, Audrey. Gorgeous.'

'She is,' Audrey said. 'I'm thinking low angle. Could we shoot down here, grab the sunrise do you think?'

'Got that?' Klint asked the photographer. Then he turned and called to the model, 'Raise your arm, uh . . .'

'Simone Grant,' Audrey whispered.

'Simone. Lean back. Perfect. Hair and Make-up! Give her more colour. Stylist, the skirt is caught. Can you make it swirl around her feet? I need movement.'

The photographer snapped some initial shots as the hair and make-up artist rushed forward, his cross-body bag bulging with hairbrushes, cosmetics and sunscreen. The stylist adjusted the hem of Simone's dress and backed out of the frame.

'I've only directed a commercial here once,' Klint said. 'Must've been tough to get.'

Audrey nodded and peered into the monitor, then had to catch her breath. It had taken months to convince the city to agree to a sunrise shoot at the Opera House, but it was worth it. On screen a woman with silver hair was caught mid-twirl, elegant in a black sleeveless turtleneck, her billowing maxi skirt constructed out of floating layers of silver tulle—majestic faerie queen meets corporate chic—with the Sydney Opera House sails rising behind her, and beyond that, orange and aqua sky.

Audrey shivered in the winter dawn. Her campaign would be incredible. It was her idea to dress the models in shades of silver, and the stylist had sourced the tulle skirt from Zimmermann, with additional pieces from Zara and H&M. High end mixed with high street, that was the magic: beauty and light, location, uniqueness. Women would love it; she was sure of it.

Behind her, someone tapped up the steps in stilettos.

'Who's the senior citizen?' a young woman called as she tossed her hair behind her shoulder. 'Jokes!' she added, but didn't laugh.

Summer. Her beach-wave hair and heels made her look more like an influencer or a socialite than a junior exec who should've spent the last two hours running around in sneakers and jeans, helping to manage the models and the support staff. Colin thought Summer had potential, but their boss didn't have to deal with her perpetual rudeness. Irritation gathered in Audrey's chest, and she hoped Simone hadn't overheard. One insult could shift the entire direction of a shoot.

'You're two hours late, Summer, and that wasn't funny.' Audrey raised her voice. 'Simone! You look great—thank you!'

Summer shrugged a thin shoulder as if she'd never received similar reprimands. 'I was kidding. Obviously. We all know how much you love your granny idea, Audrey.'

Klint scowled. 'Is there a problem here?'

There was a petulant silence, and Audrey could almost hear his ego waiting for a pat. She exhaled carefully, and her voice came out warm and strong. She couldn't afford to let Klint slide into a sullen mood. 'There's no problem at all, Klint. Your work is exceptional. It'll be groundbreaking, just like I said.'

'I've heard you're good, Klint, but the thing is . . .' Summer waved a manicured hand at Simone, who was still standing in front of the Opera House, 'this model? She's not exactly aspirational.' Summer wrinkled her nose. 'Like, would I want to be her?'

Audrey swallowed her frustration, a knot in her throat. 'Well, you're going to be her, Summer. You don't get to stay twenty-five forever. No one does. Now go call the rest of the talent outside. And next time, text if you're going to be late.'

Summer rolled her eyes so far back Audrey wondered if she could see inside her own skull. Teenagers did that, not agency professionals. 'Whatever you say, Audrey. It's your shoot.' Summer turned and stamped up the steps towards the foyer. 'People! Get a move on!'

'Audrey.' Klint paused dramatically. 'She clearly doesn't like it. And she's killing my vibe.'

It was all about to unravel, but Audrey was ready to stitch it back together. Klint, his vibe, the unstoppable sunrise, Summer's rudeness, the relentless fight to stay relevant at the agency: all of it made her feel like having a cup of tea, a chocolate croissant and a lie down. But not today. She believed in this campaign, and she'd worked nights and weekends for months to pull it together.

'Klint. All this . . .' Audrey swept a hand towards the Opera House, the silver-haired model, the support crew, the dark sea churning in the harbour, 'is your work.' Actually, it was her work. Well, most of it, anyway. She couldn't take credit for the dawn and the sea. But she needed preliminary stills before Monday's meeting with Hayes Corp, and she needed Klint to stop talking and start directing. *And guess what, Klint? Work is a verb!* she wanted to yell. Instead, she smiled calmly. The sky was beginning to lift from orange and mauve into yellow, the sun about to push above the waterline of the harbour. She was losing the light. 'We couldn't do it without you, Klint. You know that. You're an absolute legend, here and overseas, and it took months to secure you. We need you. Summer's just a junior. I'll handle her.'

The models filed into position, and the stylist collected their robes.

'How about those two alongside Simone, the contrast . . . ?' Audrey waited for Klint to appropriate her idea as his own.

He nodded grudgingly. 'Well, that's what I was thinking.'

'Good, let's shoot. Summer!' Audrey called. 'Klint needs a half-soy half–oat milk latte, no foam, decaf, with an extra shot. Summer?'

Audrey looked up. But mysteriously, infuriatingly, Summer had disappeared.

CHAPTER 2

At 7:25 on Monday morning, Audrey stepped sideways in the queue, making room for the cyclist in Lycra who pushed in front of her to order his coffee. When she took a purposeful step forward, he turned around. 'Didn't see you,' he said with a shrug.

Really? her raised eyebrows said back. *I'm standing right here.* But it didn't seem to matter whether she was ageing gracefully or disgracefully, she was somehow becoming invisible. The thought made Audrey want to pull her hair out by its secretly grey roots. Instead, she pulled her coat closer and waited for her long black in the chilly June morning. It was the start of winter in Australia, and Sydney was petrol fumes, a queue for coffee, a cerulean and bright white sky. She stepped forward briskly. Her age didn't impact her work at the agency, but grey roots that had once galloped away from her every six weeks, then four, and recently, two? She flushed. Last week, she'd caught Summer staring at her—the kind of pointed stare that sent a woman skulking to the Nice'N Easy aisle in the supermarket for a box of 9.5a Baby Blonde. She'd been too busy working on her pitch to Hayes Corp to waste three hours in a salon, and as she'd furtively coloured her hair herself that night, she'd rehearsed plausible excuses to give her hair stylist who was, of course, bound to ask. Every woman knew just how dicey it was lying to a hair stylist, especially one who was known for wearing skintight leather pants, overcharging and saying *But, darling, roots are for trees.*

Wyatt had barged into their ensuite, sniffing. 'Did you . . . dye your hair?'

For the past twenty-five years, he'd been on a need-to-know basis with her grooming, even though Audrey knew full well she had nothing to be ashamed of. Grey hair was fashionable now. In fact, she thought it was *gorgeous*—particularly on other women.

'Um,' she'd said, waving a hand, 'deep conditioner.'

The cyclist in front of her in the coffee cart queue swung his bag over his shoulder and Audrey leaned back to avoid it. It had been silly hiding her hair colour from Wyatt. Getting older didn't matter one bit; it made her wiser, like a slightly rounder and smarter Russian doll sheltering all the younger women she'd ever been. Wyatt loved her, and she'd built a respectable career. No matter what a random cyclist might think, or even a ruthless younger colleague like Summer, Audrey was in her prime and ready to charge ahead. The only thing missing from her life was the promotion she'd been working for, and today she was going to get it.

She lifted her chin and stepped forward. The queue was always too long at Jacked Up, but the business reminded her of Audrey's Cookies, the cookie cart she'd run in university. She'd loved that fledgling business. Her speciality had been spicy orange cardamom biscuits and vanilla sugar cookies iced with a thick layer of fresh buttercream frosting and sprinkles. Jacked

Up was painted a similar hot pink to Audrey's Cookies, but the coffee cart transformed into a mobile prosecco bar every Friday afternoon, a temptation Audrey resisted weekly. Behind Jacked Up rose the blue glass and steel office tower that housed, among other businesses, the corporate head office of a major bank, a co-working space, several floors of startups and UDKE. *U Don't Know Everything.* It was an aggressive name for a ruthless advertising agency, but Audrey had survived there for over two decades, and if her pitch to Hayes Corp this morning went as planned, she'd be creative director at last.

But first, coffee.

'Same, same, Audrey?'

'No croissant, thanks. I baked.' She held up the container with the delicate raspberry macarons she'd made for the pitch meeting. Behind a hiss of steam from the espresso machine, the barista nodded. Audrey reached into her briefcase for her wallet and flushed. Her laptop! She'd left it in their car in the parking garage, and that was two blocks away. While Wyatt drove, she'd rehearsed her pitch, holding back motion sickness until finally giving in and setting her computer at her feet. She glanced at her watch. Twenty-eight minutes—plenty of time to collect it, get to the boardroom and set up her presentation.

Audrey hustled against the tide of office workers as she made her way through the crowded streets. Reaching the carpark, she jabbed the button for the lift. Surely her pitch would clinch the promotion. She rummaged in her bag for the extra set of car keys, then stepped inside the mirrored lift and squinted at her reflection. She looked tired and more than a little frazzled. She hadn't slept well. At two-fifteen, Wyatt had trailed off to the guest room, while her brain unhelpfully served up hopes and catastrophes in equal measure. How she'd wow Hayes Corp with her brilliant pitch. Whether Colin would promote her on the spot or announce it later. Her recent weight gain. A suitable fitness regime. Her avoidance of all fitness regimes. Her favourite raspberry shortbread cookie recipe, the one with the white chocolate drizzle. People she was sure hated her. People she secretly hated back. Weird pains in her left hip. Cancer. Her mother. Funerals. The best songs for funerals. Leonard Cohen's 'Hallelujah'. And on and on her brain galloped for hours while she rolled alone in the sea of their king-sized bed.

Audrey took a careful sip of scalding coffee as the lift slid down to B4. What was that thing her best friend, Emma, always said? *LOL, none of us are sleeping, Audrey. It's menopause—that's why we act like Beauty AND the Beast.*

The doors slid open. Wyatt had parked in a different section than usual that morning, in a more secluded spot near the fire escape. There it was, their black SUV. Audrey clipped across the concrete and clicked the lock button; the Volvo headlights flashed twice.

A movement from the car.

A muffled scream.

And Audrey saw what she couldn't unsee.

CHAPTER 3

Wyatt jumped from the Volvo with his left hand outstretched, gold wedding band glinting under the fluorescent lights of the carpark.

'Audrey, I can explain . . .'

Behind the windshield, Wyatt's personal assistant tugged at her blouse. Shock whooshed through Audrey so fast it was either sit on the concrete carpark floor or faint. She stumbled to her knees and hid her face in her hands, while the other door opened and slammed shut. She heard Charmaine—the Charmaine she'd spoken to a million times on the phone, the one who'd dropped off papers to sign at their house on a Saturday in full yoga gear, the tiniest pink workout bra and matching bottoms—calling Wyatt's name as she scrambled out of the car.

'Just go, Charmaine,' Wyatt said, but no one moved. He rubbed Audrey's back in irritating circles that made her want to scream. In fact, someone was screaming, and it took Audrey a moment to realise it was her own voice. She leaned over. She was going to be sick, and then she was, and when she was done, Wyatt lifted her into the driver's seat of the car and set her handbag beside her. He stood near the open door and Charmaine crowded next to him. Audrey's head lolled on her neck. Shock. Spit. Blood thumping in her ears. She'd trusted Wyatt all her adult life.

'Birdie,' Wyatt crooned. He leaned into the car and his fingers dug into her shoulders.

'Don't . . .' Audrey tried to breathe but air wouldn't fill her lungs. 'Get away.'

'Birdie, you need to calm down.'

'Don't call me that!'

Wyatt's white face distorted into concern. 'I—look, this isn't what you—'

Not thinking, not anything, she shoved his chest, and Wyatt rocked back into Charmaine, whose cute face twisted into a surprised, slack-jawed O. Audrey yanked the door shut. She fumbled at the lock with shaking hands until it clicked. It felt like a victory.

The ads were right, she thought calmly, gripping the padded steering wheel; the Volvo was good in an emergency. That was what this was, wasn't it? She inhaled, light-headed, and her body felt as if it were buzzing. Exceptional marketing at Volvo, excellent Unique Selling Proposition. It was quiet inside and smelled of leather. She could barely hear Wyatt's voice from the safety of the car. Time stretched out and wobbled, seconds or minutes—she wasn't sure which—and she remembered this was what shock felt like. She'd felt just like this when Wyatt had woken with chest pains one night, and she'd driven him to Emergency. After a night in hospital, he was diagnosed with acid reflux and was told he was fine, and then it was as if nothing had happened.

If only this day could be like that one. She shook, disbelieving. Wyatt was having an *affair*? He stood next to Charmaine, staring at Audrey through the car window. Even the word 'affair' was ludicrous, too flamboyant for her calm, dependable husband. Her head throbbed and her phone pinged. With shaking hands, she pulled it from her bag. Meeting reminder. In twenty minutes, she had to deliver the pitch that would get her promoted to creative director. The boardroom at UDKE would be full of people waiting for her. But she couldn't face them. Not today, not like this. She groped for a tissue and wiped her mouth. She'd cancel, text Colin she was sick.

But then the meeting would go ahead without her, and Summer would deliver Audrey's pitch for her.

Wyatt smacked his palm against the window.

'Audrey! You're not capable of driving!'

Audrey jumped and dropped her phone. *No.* She was capable. The pitch had taken months and months of work—her work, not Summer's. Her stomach rolled over. She couldn't get out and walk past Wyatt and Charmaine. She'd drive the two blocks to the office and park somewhere, anywhere, out the front. She stuck the key in the ignition and twisted to the right. Lizzo blared from the speakers about feeling good as hell, and the engine revved. Gripping the steering wheel with both hands, she forced her foot on the accelerator and moved forward, towards the ramp, away from her husband and his lies. She was a professional. And she was a woman. She would go to the office and pitch. Like *this*.

Sixteen minutes later, Audrey yanked open the doors of UDKE. Her legs moved because she told them to. She'd parked illegally in front of the building and forced herself to breathe. In, out. Again. Pressed the heels of her hands into her eyes to stop crying. Shock helped. She'd bit her lip so hard it had bled, wiped it off, and reapplied lipstick over the stinging cut. *Wyatt is a liar?* She scrubbed at her smeared mascara and spread a layer of Skin Illusion foundation over her red and blotchy face. The chair of Hayes Corp and her boss, Colin, would be on their way to the boardroom. Wyatt and Charmaine would be—*Don't go there. One hour, one minute at a time.*

She stumbled to her desk and, hands shaking, arranged her raspberry macarons on a white porcelain platter. Small and fragrant, filled with freshly whipped buttercream, the tangy scent calmed her down, like baking always did.

The door swung open, and someone laughed sharply.

'Colin! You're terrible!' Summer pressed her chest against the boss's arm and Audrey blanched. Since the moment Summer had arrived eighteen months ago as UDKE's new junior account executive, she'd done everything she could to ingratiate herself with Colin. She was as young as Wyatt's personal assistant—*don't go there.*

Colin's mobile buzzed. 'Yep, Matthew, on my way.' He nodded in Audrey's direction and mouthed, 'See you up there.'

'Still killing us with sugar.' Summer glanced at the macarons and bit into her protein bar. 'Colin invited me to sit in on your pitch. I hope that's okay.'

It was not even remotely close to okay. 'Of course,' Audrey said.

Summer chewed and squinted. 'Have you been . . . crying?'

'Hay fever.' Audrey pushed a shaking hand through her Baby Blonde hair. She gathered her laptop and the tray of macarons. If she didn't move, she'd start sobbing. She was the first to arrive in the boardroom, but there was a new projector and she couldn't get it to work. Heat rose up her neck, and she tried again. Nothing. Bluetooth? Airplay? Cable? What?

Summer flounced into the room, followed by Colin.

'Oh God, Audrey. Tech problems?' Summer yanked out the adaptor and plugged in a different one. Her black nail polish matched the mess of electrical cords, the manicure giving her fingers more than a passing resemblance to talons. Audrey exhaled and squeezed her own hands together to stop them shaking. She had to focus. Her pitch would take less than thirty minutes. Afterwards, she could tell Colin she was ill and needed to go home, and then . . . *one minute at a time.*

Audrey forced herself to look at the huge screen, where a silver-haired model, strong and athletic, twirled on the steps of the Sydney Opera House at dawn. Power and beauty, one of the world's most iconic buildings, and a woman of age. The image was breathtaking. It squeezed Audrey's heart with a kind of recognition and longing. Underneath ran her tagline. *Love Your Age. Live Beautifully.*

'Who's this stunner?' The older man at the door lunged a kiss at Summer's cheek. Audrey watched her step back, expertly, and stick out her hand.

'Mr Hayes, lovely to meet you. I'm Summer.'

'And who's the granny in a tutu?'

Audrey inhaled sharply. Granny? Matthew Hayes looked at least fifteen years older than the model did. Her head throbbed and bile rose in her throat. She groped for words, but nothing came.

'Audrey?' Colin said, frowning at her. 'Are you—'

She forced herself to smile. 'Mr Hayes. It's good to meet you. I'm Audrey Sweetman-Brown, and this is our cosmetics campaign targeting midlife women.'

'We thought we could do something that stands out.' Colin poured a coffee as he spoke. 'Everyone else is doing anti-ageing.'

Matthew Hayes reached for a macaron and leaned back in his chair. 'Hmmm. Sell me.'

Audrey spoke fast, then faster to convince Matthew Hayes Senior, titan of business, husband to four wives—each one ten years younger than the last, according to the tabloids—that Hayes Corp should invest in a campaign celebrating positive ageing. But three minutes in, Matthew Hayes was reading emails on his phone, and by the time Audrey had run a succession of classic models posing before the Opera House across the screen, he was staring out the window.

She raised her voice. 'How many midlife women do you see in the media? Women who role model what fifty or sixty really looks like?'

Silence.

Summer shrugged. 'There's Jennifer Aniston. Nicole Kidman. Jennifer Lopez is over fifty—'

'Most of us don't age like that. Those women all look thirty.' Audrey's voice wobbled. 'Love Your Age features women *ageing* beautifully.'

Matthew Hayes leaned closer to Summer and glanced where he shouldn't. 'Does it grab you, Summer?'

Summer wrinkled her nose at the silver-haired model on the screen. 'Um, honestly, Matthew? It's not that relatable.'

Audrey bit her lip to stop herself from screaming. Summer would age eventually, just like every other woman! And she was meant to be loyal; they were on the same team. But Summer was ambitious, and young. In fact, she was the same age as Charmaine. *Don't go there.* She ignored the lump in her throat.

'Summer's not the target demographic. I am. We're inviting women to rethink ageing.' Audrey thought guiltily of the Baby Blonde Nice'N Easy box she'd hidden in the recycling the week before. 'What's the alternative—fight it forever?'

Matthew Hayes shrugged. 'Women don't have a problem with ageing. They either look good, or they look old. Why would you advertise looking old?'

Audrey's face flushed. She raised her chin and stared at him, blinking fiercely. 'Have you ever heard a woman say she feels invisible?'

'Nope.'

'Well, they do say it, all the time. It's because society tells us we shouldn't age. Men can, but we can't.' Audrey took a quick breath. 'Brad Pitt. George Clooney. It's sexy to be an older man. We call them silver foxes. But Jennifer Lopez is pole dancing at fifty-two, and she looks twenty-five. So do her peers. Then we see no one until Helen Mirren in her early eighties, or Judi Dench. Midlife women feel invisible because we *are* invisible, especially in advertising.' She clenched her fists, dug her nails into her palms.

'Bit shrill, isn't she?' Matthew rolled his eyes at Colin, who wouldn't meet Audrey's gaze.

Audrey swallowed her fury. Matthew Hayes didn't care. He didn't care about women and representation. He certainly didn't care about feminism or ageism. But he cared about money.

Audrey clicked through to the spreadsheet she'd spent hours perfecting. She'd even checked her calculations with Wy—*do not go there*. She forced her voice to remain calm. 'Your corporation will profit from this campaign. Here's a snapshot of the projected financials.' She took a breath. 'Midlife women spend *fifteen trillion* dollars a year, but eighty-two percent of them say their favourite retailer no longer understands them. And over seventy per cent of British women in a recent survey said they're afraid of becoming invisible. A campaign like this will make women feel seen.'

'I don't buy it.' Matthew Hayes reached out a liver-spotted hand to Summer's. 'What do you think, little lady?'

Audrey looked up as Summer raised an eyebrow at Colin. He nodded. What was happening? What had they done?

'Well, it's one approach, but you might find this a little fresher.' Summer yanked the adaptor from Audrey's laptop and plugged in her own. The boardroom filled with the pulsating rhythm of African drums. A stream of leggy adolescent models in suede bikinis strode across a beach boardwalk, eyes painted in gorgeous neon stripes—scarlet, chartreuse, mandarin, aqua, violet—with Summer's headline running like a ticker tape: *Beauty Beats. Beauty Beats. Beauty Beats.*

Matthew Hayes Senior sat up. 'Now this! This is the one.' The music thumped as the teenagers shimmied on the screen.

Colin shot an apologetic look at Audrey. He cleared his throat. 'I'm glad you like it, Matthew. I wanted to give you a couple of options.'

'I love it. Look at those girls. Can't take your eyes off them.'

Audrey's stomach clenched. When had Summer done this? Why did Colin approve it? The strategy and brand positioning were wrong. It wouldn't sell the product. Summer's models were beautiful, of course they were, but they were *so* thin and *so* young. Children, really, barely even teens. All her work, the years of it at UDKE, shimmered in front of her. Audrey took a ragged breath. 'I agree it has visual appeal. But it ignores the demographic fit for sales. Older women won't love it, and teens can't afford these cosmetics. Love Your Age is—'

'I know what I like, and I always pick a winner.' Matthew Hayes lifted his chin.

Colin pushed back his chair and avoided Audrey's eyes. 'That's good to hear, Matthew. I was planning to wait to make my announcement, but since you're going to be working with her . . .'

Audrey stared at Colin and willed it not to be true, but he kept his gaze on Matthew Hayes.

'Summer's our new creative director.'

CHAPTER 4

An hour later, Audrey huddled on her best friend Emma's sofa, a mug of tepid Earl Grey in her hand, a full box of tissues on the coffee table next to her. She'd resigned, and Colin had simply let her go. No arguing to keep her. No retrenchment package. Nothing. She couldn't bear to tell Emma—who always seemed to be successful no matter what she attempted—about her failure at UDKE. Not yet. Instead, the story of Wyatt and Charmaine tumbled out like a cliché daytime movie starring some clueless woman Audrey didn't recognise.

'You're in shock,' Emma said. 'You need sugar. And I'm not going to say a word about that bastard Wyatt. I'm here to listen.'

'Things were good for us. I just—'

'Didn't see it coming? Sweetie, it's the oldest story in the book. Middle-aged man gets bored and screws his secretary. That's part one. Part two is when he comes crawling back and asks you to forgive him, after she maxes out his credit card and tells him she wants babies.' Emma set down her mug on top of the new issue of *Vogue* and cracked off a piece of Fruit and Nut. Her gold bangles clanged together, and she waved the chocolate at Audrey. 'Sorry. I didn't mean to bring up babies.'

Audrey blinked and looked away. It still hurt, of course, but thankfully the pain had lessened as the years passed. She always thought Wyatt had dealt with their disappointment better than she had, but maybe not. 'He was trying to explain,' Audrey said. 'Maybe it was just once. A mistake.'

'And he thinks you'll forgive him?' Emma flicked her French manicure as if she were shooing a mosquito. 'He doesn't deserve it. But I know you. You'll be okay whatever happens. You're strong and smart. You can do anything.'

Strong. Smart. Do anything. She'd always believed it was true before today. But hours later, after a dinner of quinoa and chicken salad she could barely eat, Audrey had said everything she could and had cried too much to cry anymore. 'I need to sleep, Emma.'

'You're sure you don't want the guest room?'

Audrey shook her head. 'I'll sleep here, on the sofa.' The guest room reminded her of New Year's Eve, when Emma had insisted they stay over. Wyatt, naked and snoring, had held her in that bed. Was it only six months ago? She shuddered. Surely Charmaine was a mistake, an impulse he didn't check. He'd never been unfaithful before.

Emma glanced at the tray of Scotch and heavy crystal glasses on the console table. 'Should I move this before I go?'

Probably. Maybe?

'No, it's fine.' As Emma left, Audrey took a sip of water, and another one. She lit the freesia candle on the coffee table and it bathed the room in an orangey glow. She breathed in the scent of money, hard work and good luck. Emma had it all, plus she was loyal. She'd been there for Audrey's miscarriages, and had never criticised her for the secret nightly drinking they'd led to. When Audrey had finally started her recovery journey, she'd found thousands of women online who had a life problem and reached for a wine solution. It was often the same story: life was stressful, and wine helped them sleep. Wine helped many, many women sleep—until it stopped helping. The recovery movement was filled with successful women who performed admirably by day, and coped quietly at night.

Emma hadn't judged her; in fact, she'd encouraged Audrey as much as the women in the online support groups had. It wasn't strictly necessary to go to local AA meetings anymore—you could do so much recovery work online. Some recovery influencers even felt like friends to her in real life, and Audrey could hear their podcast voices in her head on repeat. *One day, one hour, one minute at a time. Progress, not perfection. Don't go there. Take good care.* Help was always as close as her phone, and for a little over eight years—two thousand nine hundred and forty-two days—she'd managed to leave drinking behind her.

Her mum, Joyce, had turned to baking whenever she was worried, and she'd encouraged Audrey to do the same. Cakes, pies, macarons, bread, cinnamon buns, all of it. Audrey had baked for as long as she could remember. She'd loved her Audrey's Cookies cart in university, with the paper bags she'd hand-lettered at night with famous Audrey Hepburn quotes.

Life is a party—dress like it!
I believe in pink.
Forgive quickly, kiss slowly, love truly.

The memory of a young, flirting Wyatt standing in front of Audrey's Cookies, her first and only business, gave her a pain so strong she almost doubled over. She'd wanted to keep going, turn her cart into a proper business; it was Wyatt who had convinced her a corporate career was less risky. But after all those years of climbing the ladder and paying her dues, she'd been replaced by Summer in a single morning.

She picked up a book on the coffee table, one of Emma's new self-help releases with a blue feather on the cover.

Are you fun to live with?

Was she? The question made her tear up, and then flush with something deadly. Fury. Disappointment. It used to be an unreserved *yes*—Audrey Sweetman was fun! But what would her colleagues at the agency say now? And what would Wyatt? She squeezed her water glass until she thought it might crack in two. Wyatt, her rock. They'd been married for twenty-five years and had dated for just fourteen weeks before that. His Catholic family never would've countenanced a noticeably pregnant bride, but all she could do was start a baby, never have one. Audrey winced and stared again at the Scotch. She threw down the stupid book and sobbed into her hands. It wasn't self-helping her enough. Nothing could.

'Did you open a bakery while I was sleeping?'

Audrey shrugged. 'You had butter and eggs and flour. I was up early.'

'Cinnamon buns? Shoot me now.' Emma pulled one apart and sniffed. 'It's making me gain weight just smelling it.' She took a bite. 'Oh my God, you can bake. Did you sleep at all?'

'Some.' This morning, sipping coffee, Audrey could breathe again. The shock of yesterday had worn off and left a dull thud in her heart. If only she could rewind or fast forward. She lowered herself into a wicker chair and breathed in the warm sea air. From Emma's verandah, she could see snippets of the beach and ocean.

'I'd love to have this view,' Audrey said. 'I thought one day we could get a beach house somewhere. You know I've always loved Whitehaven Bay. We were nearly ready for our second act.'

Emma handed her the tissue box. 'I know, Sweetie. But there's a way through this. You've got your health, and you've got your job—'

'Nope.'

'What do you mean?'

Audrey closed her eyes. She couldn't quite believe what she'd done. Raising her voice in Colin's office, throwing down her briefcase. Cringing while Colin explained that UDKE was looking for a more 'modern' approach anyway.

'I resigned yesterday. Summer was promoted, and I couldn't report to her. I'll have to look for something else.'

'Do you think that was hasty?' Emma asked kindly. 'You know how tough it is out there.'

Audrey sighed. Emma was right. 'I couldn't stay. It would have been too humiliating to have her as my boss.' Audrey had been so certain of the promotion. Her shoulders slumped and she set down her cup. 'Right now, all I want is a bomb shelter. Part of me wants to run away, and part of me wants Wyatt, the old one, the good one, but he's . . .' Audrey took a ragged breath and stopped.

Emma reached up, adjusted a pearl earring, and this time, waited. 'I'm listening.'

Two hours later, against her better judgement, Audrey pulled up in front of their North Shore home. Raspberry bushes lined one side of the front garden; jasmine climbed a trellis on the other. In between them was the lawn Wyatt mowed and fertilised like it was his religious duty. She hoped with all her heart he'd be at the office by now. Her eyes ached and so did her stomach. Tension crept up the base of her neck, and even worse, she was filled with an urge to run to him and demand he make her feel better. She wanted a hug from the Wyatt she thought she knew.

She was gutted.

She was furious.

Her heart ached, a physical pain that slid across her chest and up into her clenched jaw.

She clicked open the garage door and slid from the seat, still dressed in Emma's cashmere sweater and track pants. She'd driven home in bare feet and felt the light grit on the floor as she walked into the house. The kitchen lights were off, the dishwasher hummed, and her shoulders relaxed. She reached for her favourite saltwater-blue mug, dropped the strongest coffee pod she could find into the machine and waited for a hot cup of hope, or maybe strength or wisdom. She inhaled the comforting scent of the long black and tried to relax into the empty house.

Normally, she'd be at the agency by now. But today, everyone would be gossiping about her, and all the other agencies would soon know that she'd—

'Birdie?'

Wyatt stood in the doorway in his suit, no tie. His hair was mostly grey at the sides, distinguished, and he was still in good shape for fifty-five. He worked out four times a week at the gym and rode the stationary bike at home in their garage too.

'You were gone all night,' he said. 'I didn't know where you were.'

She looked past Wyatt's shoulder, out the French doors. His cherished flower beds were full of winter bloomers, pristine. Even the treasured Daphne plant he'd taken years to establish was blooming. Next to the pool were the only flowers she'd ever wanted: a wild bed of paper daisies. Wyatt kept them green and growing but he hated them. He said they were more like weeds, but they reminded her of growing up in less fancy suburbs, in a succession of tiny two-bedroom units with her mother.

'Audrey, I . . . I don't even know what to say.'

'How about the truth, Wyatt?' She held her breath. Maybe it was a mistake: maybe it had happened just once, and he was flooded with regret. He was guilty of betrayal, but surely he still loved her?

'I waited up for you.' He squinted in confusion at her, as if his gesture had been huge and she should appreciate it. She knew that look. He wanted her to explain herself and apologise.

'Are you saying I *inconvenienced* you?' Audrey's throat was closing, a tube crushed by a fist. She forced the words through gritted teeth. 'I didn't come home because you're having an affair, Wyatt.'

Wyatt's face turned red. 'I just . . . fell into it. It sort of . . . happened. I didn't know it was going that way. Charmaine wanted to ha—'

'Don't say that name to me.' Blood pulsed in her ears. She wanted to scream and keep screaming, to hit him, to sweep every coffee cup from the shelf beside her, to break everything they'd ever built. She wanted him to beg for forgiveness, to swear that he loved her.

'Audrey, please. I feel bad enough already.'

No. No, he didn't. He didn't feel nearly bad enough. She hugged herself and tried to stop shuddering. She knew from far too many friends that they would spend weeks of purgatory like this. The crying, the attempts at forgiveness, remorse sex with bile and tears, anger so powerful that her friends had thrown things, and furiously 'decluttered' anything their partners loved—golf clubs, first-edition books, and in one instance, a new laptop and an entire case of sixty-year-old Kaesler Old Bastard Shiraz. They couldn't stop themselves. And they would scream at their partners, scream inside their heads. Scream at life, at everything. Audrey knew—with the tired knowing of a woman who'd lived more than five decades—that she would go through the useless cycle of shame and fear and hope and confusion and come right back to where she started: the truth. His lies. What was that thing her mother said about how the truth had legs and would always stand, so you might as well start there to begin with? She squared her shoulders, her heart clenched like a fist.

'Do you love her?' Asking the question filled her with a fresh, nauseous wave of doubt. Her knees began to shake, and she couldn't stop her trembling. There was too much silence, and Wyatt didn't meet her eyes.

'I don't know.'

And just like that, Audrey's world blew up in her own fifty-three-year-old face.

She scrubbed the perfectly clean benchtop and threw down a package of frozen blackberries, bruised like her heart. Her mother had always told her, *When the world hands me garbage, I toss back something good.* Devona from next door had home care on a Thursday, and Audrey always took her a cake to share. She exhaled and measured flour and baking powder into her favourite English porcelain bowl. Maybe it was insane baking a cake when her world had collapsed, but it was less insane than smashing all the dishes from their kitchen cabinets on the floor.

There was a knock on the door. Impatient. Persistent. Audrey stumbled across shining timber floorboards towards the elegant front hall. Probably an Amazon package. They'd got into the habit of ordering so much online that Wyatt said he wouldn't be surprised if there was an alpaca at the door—he'd just assume Audrey had ordered it and lead it right on in. But the old Wyatt had said that, not this new version who . . .

She yanked it open.

Char-bloody-maine.

'I thought it was more mature to communicate like *adults*,' Charmaine said. Audrey's stomach dropped. The hide of her! Her hair was in two thick plaits, she wore denim shorts, a cropped pink jumper and cowboy boots. Her well-muscled yoga legs were burnt orange. Audrey moved to slam the door, but Charmaine stuck a boot inside. 'Really, Audrey, I know this is challenging, but—'

'Challenging?' Audrey's hand shook on the doorknob. 'You need to leave.'

Charmaine tried to frown but her forehead didn't budge. 'You may not get this, but I feel bad for you, Audrey. I do. I'm an empath!'

Audrey stared at her. Charmaine waved her mobile. 'I'm practically mainlining my meditation app to cope with the stress.' She pouted suspiciously puffy lips and held up a cake box. 'Vegan brownies, but with dates. Sugar kills.'

She was exactly like Summer. Young. Lethal. Audrey's voice shook. 'You need to leave, or I'll call the police.' She wanted to slap Charmaine, cut off one of her plaits, spit on the brownies. And yes, kill her with sugar if only she could figure out how.

'But poor Wyatt—' Charmaine started.

Audrey pushed Charmaine's foot out the door and slammed it shut. Poor Wyatt? Poor him? She could hear Charmaine continuing to talk behind the cheery bumblebee yellow of the door. An unusual choice, but it had been her mother's favourite colour. Wyatt had helped her paint it eleven months ago, the Saturday after Joyce had passed away, and he had insisted they go to Chinatown for dinner at Happy Lucky Go-Go. He said Joyce would've wanted them to celebrate at her favourite restaurant, with fortune cookies all around, and Audrey knew it was true. For her impulsive, free-spirited mother, every new experience was a chance at adventure, and an opportunity for luck to find her. Joyce had saved every fortune she'd ever got. Now, whenever Audrey and Wyatt ate at Happy Lucky Go-Go—especially when she cracked open her fortune cookie—Audrey felt loved.

'Audrey! Wyatt and I need to make plans!'

Audrey twisted the deadbolt and backed away from the door. She wanted her mother more than anything, ridiculous for a fifty-three-year-old, but true. She'd always relied on Joyce during a crisis, but out of nowhere on a rainy Wednesday afternoon, their team of two had gone. Emma had worked hard to fill that spot and so had Wyatt. But nothing compared.

'You can't ignore me,' Charmaine sang out in a voice that belonged to a teenager, not a . . . how old was she, exactly? Maybe twenty-four or twenty-five? How could Wyatt stand it, the narcissistic self-centredness of her, the huge lips, the plastic everything? More knocking. Her girlish voice grew louder. 'I'm here to set boundaries, Audrey. I'm concerned.'

Audrey bit back a scream. Boundaries? How dare she. And Charmaine was concerned? Well, it was worrying when you slept with your boss, and he happened to be someone else's *husband*. The thought of it made her hands shake with fury. Charmaine pounded the door again. Audrey tried to breathe, but her knees wobbled, and she felt light-headed. Was it murder if an adulteress was strangled by her own two plaits? Had anyone got away with it on Netflix? Her mind backflipped. No, no, she'd never do that—but a chat with Human Resources, or an anonymous email? She could make one ugly phone call to Wyatt's boss and torch both his and Charmaine's careers. Her body screamed for escape, a long sleep and a way to forget everything. She needed time to think. She wanted her mother, with her sensible hug and the smell of her inexpensive chemist-shop perfume, her level head, her cookies. As if cookies could solve anything.

Behind the closed door, Charmaine yelled, 'You can't run away from your problems!'

Audrey took another step back and stared at the deadbolt. She listened to Charmaine's pounding and remembered her mum telling her about the day she was born.

'Back then, my parents thought my life was ruined,' Joyce had said, snuggling beside Audrey and the pile of library books in her narrow bed. 'When I was five months pregnant, I couldn't hide it anymore and I escaped to Whitehaven Bay. They wanted me to give you up, but I walked that beach and promised myself I'd do whatever I could to keep you. I had you in a tiny hospital in a nearby town and then I moved us back to the city. That's why I'll always love Whitehaven. It reminds me of you, and how strong I was to run away.'

Charmaine's knocking stopped, then started again. Audrey could barely hear it. She strode to the cold, elegant bedroom she shared with Wyatt, yanked her weekend bag out of the closet and started packing.

CHAPTER 5

As she crested the hill leading down to the tiny beachside village—the Pacific Ocean unfurling across the horizon—Audrey's shoulders relaxed for the first time in days. Whitehaven Bay. She remembered its sugar-white sand and calm, turquoise waters, but it looked even more stunning now.

Her mother had always saved for a getaway for Audrey's birthday weekends when Audrey was a girl, and they'd driven the three hours from the city to Whitehaven. They'd go off-season for her winter birthday and walk the cold stretch of sand. It was more than three kilometres long, completely deserted save for a few dog walkers and locals. Whitehaven was a place so far removed from Audrey's childhood of tiny city apartments and gritty streets, and as a girl, she'd fallen in love with it. But it had meant even more to her mother. Audrey rolled down a window and breathed in. Salt air and hope, that's what Whitehaven reminded her of, and it was exactly what she needed.

A kind of peace settled over her then, a strange coming home feeling. The winding road was lined with scrubby grevillea bushes and elegant gum trees, and on either side nestled modest beach homes built in the fifties and sixties, as endearingly tatty as she remembered. She drove further down the hill, and on the beachfront ahead several newish mansions rose, majestically facing the sea. Painted dark charcoal or fashionable navy with crisp white trim, the gigantic houses had the look of city money, but even they couldn't spoil the ocean views she glimpsed between their fences. Audrey could feel herself falling under the village's spell. It was as if the sea were beckoning her down the hill towards the beach, whispering she was home.

Audrey's head throbbed and so did her heart. She pulled her worn-out Lexus into an empty space in front of the General Store and cut the ignition. She'd run away, but what would she do now? She'd returned to the beach village, but she couldn't bring her mother back. The only family she had was gone, and Wyatt was a traitor. Her legs and arms felt leaden; she wanted to curl up and sleep in the back seat, but that was ridiculous. She was a fifty-three-year-old woman, not a child. She rested her throbbing head on the steering wheel.

Audrey tried to relax her aching jaw. She'd been clenching her teeth on the three-hour drive without even realising. What was there to do now but keep moving forward? She'd shelter here for a week, and then go back and start her job search. She needed to eat something, but the thought of food made her sick.

She forced herself out of the car and walked towards the General Store. On a low bench on the porch perched a woman in an enormous blue fur coat, drumming on the railing with matching royal blue fingernails. Her gold hoop earrings were the size of oranges.

'Love the eyebrows,' she called as Audrey walked past. She took a sip of coffee. 'Stick-ons?'

Audrey stopped. 'Pardon?'

'Good choice. Eyebrows speak louder than words.'

'I'm sorry?' Audrey said, squinting.

'Oh, never apologise! Just say thank you.' The woman shrugged and waved blue nails in Audrey's direction. 'I blame the patriarchy. Makes it impossible for women to accept compliments, especially for falsies.'

'Well,' Audrey stuttered, 'my eyebrows are . . . real.'

'Sure.' The woman glanced down at her own chest. 'It's *all* real.' She winked a fluttery lash at Audrey. 'I'm Shez. Chief Executive Officer of Sherry's Holiday Flats. Welcome to Whitehaven.'

Shez wandered off the porch and Audrey stared at the back of her blue fur coat. CEO of some holiday flats? She wasn't at all like Colin at UDKE, and definitely not like the self-obsessed Matthew Hayes, but she certainly had the same air of confidence.

Audrey straightened her shoulders and stepped into the warm interior of the store. The windows of the long, narrow building faced the street, as if the store were somehow indifferent to the spectacular water views behind it. The white plank walls looked recently painted and the timber floorboards were varnished and clean.

'G'day! Something for you?' a stooped gentleman called out from behind the counter. His blue eyes seemed used to smiling.

'Coffee, please.'

Audrey glanced at the piles of dusty groceries stocked haphazardly on the shelves. A fridge with fizzy drinks and chocolate and strawberry milk was pushed against the wall, a few cartons of regular milk stacked along its bottom shelf. Beside it sat a cooler for ice creams. 'But maybe you only do cold drinks?'

'Nah, love, I do it all. I'm the whole shebang here. I'm Robert. Not Bob or Bobbie, mind.' Robert smiled at her. 'White, is it? Sugar?'

He unscrewed an oversized jar of Nescafé crystals and Audrey tried not to grimace. Something would be better than nothing. While he boiled the kettle, she glanced around the shop. She'd packed a cooler with a few things before she left, remembering that the village only had one store—at least, she'd guessed it would still be that way. She was comforted to see that it really hadn't changed much since her last holiday with her mother decades ago, other than the row of new waterfront mansions. Wyatt hated the beach—the sand bothered him, and also the sun—and he often mocked people for being uneducated or provincial, so she'd never taken him to Whitehaven. She didn't want him to spoil her memories. He was easier to manage when he was happy, and they'd spent their weekend escapes in the country, further inland.

'You here for the weekend?' asked Robert. 'If you are, you're in luck. Stock-car races are on down at the Speedway, lots of action. Sea's still too cold for the tourists, of course, but come summer, bam! We'll be busting at the seams. Can't even park when the tourists come, drives Ruth crazy. Ruth Hickson, head of the Community Association, she practically runs the place.' Robert brushed away a fly. 'She'd love to ban the tourists.'

'Oh,' said Audrey. 'Well, I guess I'm a tour—'

'Doesn't matter,' Robert went on cheerfully. 'Now, personally, I enjoy seeing the tourists coming in, stirring things up a little. Shez loves them, naturally, you likely saw her when you walked in. Blue buffalo coat? Furry? Talk your ears off, Shez does, considers herself a CEO entrepreneur but she inherited the flats when her auntie and uncle passed.' Before Audrey could stop him, he had poured milk from a jug on the counter into her instant coffee and added a huge spoon of sugar, then another. He handed her the white Styrofoam cup, unstirred.

'Yes, I met her outside.' Audrey sipped the sickly sweet coffee and cleared her throat. 'It . . . it really hits the spot, thanks.' She set down her cup. 'I'm hoping for something to rent. Maybe the holiday flats?'

'You could ask Lem. He runs the estate agent's—had trouble making a go of things in the city, did our Lem. But he's a good bloke, he's hooked up with Shez now, spends all his time hanging around with her. He'll fix you up. Shame that her holiday flats are closed just now.' He gestured to a screen door on the inside of the General Store, to the left of the entrance. 'That's his office. He's just stepped out for smoko, but he'll be back soon. We'll get you all sorted.'

'Thanks, Robert.' Audrey set down a container of yogurt and grabbed a package of rice crackers from a shelf that also held Tim Tams and Mint Slices. She felt an almost overwhelming sense of tiredness, and with it a strange detachment. She'd left the city and Wyatt didn't know where she'd gone. She'd turned off location-sharing on her phone, called Emma on the road, and blasted her Spotify playlist to stop herself from crying. She'd driven three hours to her favourite childhood holiday spot, thinking she'd magically figure out her next steps when she arrived, and here she was, getting compliments on her eyebrows and drinking bittersweet instant coffee with a stranger who seemed determined to be her new best friend. The kindness astounded her.

'Do you take cards or cash?' Audrey asked.

A teenager sloped into the store, banged the door carelessly, and leaned against the counter. 'He takes anything you got. Don't you, Bobbie?'

'G'day, Billie. What can I get for you?'

'Pack of smokes.' Billie shrugged.

'No can do. You don't have ID.'

'I do, Bobbers. I have the best ID money can buy.'

Robert threw back his head and laughed. 'Oh, boy-o, I will not be accepting that, or your mother'd kill me. And I'm too old to die at the hands of Ruth Hickson.'

'Told you, Bobbie. Not everyone identifies like that. You can't call people boy-o.'

Audrey glanced at Billie. Denim overalls, a black t-shirt covered in skulls, heavy boots and a shaved head. A nose ring. A girl's face or a boy's? Audrey wasn't quite sure, but those clothes could use a wash.

'Takes some getting used to, all this *they* business. I'm an old man. I forget. And you shouldn't be calling me Bobbie, so we're even.' He bagged Audrey's groceries and pointed a thumb in Billie's direction. 'This here's Billie Hickson, up to no good most of the time. They,' he said, and winked at Billie.

Billie was doing a decent job of pretending that Audrey wasn't there. Audrey pulled out her wallet and took a step forward.

'I didn't get your name,' Billie said, deciding at last to notice her.

'It's Audrey. Audrey Sweetman-Br . . .' She paused. Did she want Wyatt's name? Did he want her to have it? Her stomach twisted. She rubbed at a smear of mascara and blinked to stop the tears. 'Audrey Sweetman. Look, if I could just pay you, Robert, I'll go see about somewhere to rent . . .'

'Sure.' Robert held out the merchant terminal and Audrey tapped.

'You don't wanna forget this,' Billie said lazily, holding up Audrey's plastic bag of yogurt and crackers. Audrey took it from their outstretched hand. As she walked to Lem's office, she heard Billie laugh. 'What the hell's wrong with Tawdry Hepburn?'

'I can show you three other ones like this, luxury beachfront, but you say no one's joining you at the weekend?'

Audrey and Lem stood in the middle of Main Street, Lem in his too-tight suit proudly gesturing at a row of beach mansions—all gorgeous and obviously owned by wealthy people from the city. His voice was a deep baritone, comforting, and he stood with his hands in his pockets. Audrey thought he looked to be in his late thirties, and he seemed like the kind of laid-back bloke who'd like a pint on a Friday afternoon and an easy sort of life.

'No, thank you, I . . . well, like I said, I'm looking for something small. For the week? It's too bad Sherry's Holiday Flats are closed.'

'Ruth Hickson was behind that, for sure. Fire hazard, my arse. Those flats are made from cinder blocks, like the guts of a prison. Shez's Auntie Patti and Uncle Bruce built them themselves back in the sixties—that's why they lean sideways—but no, they wouldn't ever catch on fire. Shez told me she'll be back up and running soon, once the inspector comes. She's my girlfriend. Quite a talker, is Shez.'

'Yes, I met her.' Audrey's forehead puckered.

'Shez is impossible to miss.' He straightened proudly. 'She told me Ruth Hickson used to be a bigwig in the city, with an office in Macquarie Street. Retired judge of the Federal Court of Australia, do you mind.'

'And now Ruth lives here?' Audrey tried to keep the impatience from her voice. It was nearly five o'clock and her head throbbed. She did not care about village gossip. All she wanted was a clean place to sleep, to text Emma that she was okay, and then shut off her phone for days. She'd kill for a drink too, but she was trying very hard not to think about that.

'Ruth moved down to her beachfront when Billie got expelled last year. She's homeschooling Billie now, but you met them, right? You can guess how that's going. Damn little devil brought me a Coke last week with a Mentos stuck in the cap and it exploded on my new suit. Sixteen and a little shite, as my dad would say, but Shez got out the stain. Shez says all the best suits are machine-washable.'

Audrey nodded in a way she hoped seemed appreciative of Lem's washable suit. She glanced at the row of beach mansions, their two-storey facades facing the stretch of white sand. 'So, Ruth and Billie live in one of these?'

'Big blue one at the end, with the pool and pergola. I'm surprised Billie hasn't decorated the fence. They like a can of spray paint when they can get their hands on one.'

'Listen, Lem, these are all lovely but also . . . too big. It's just me. Is there anything smaller?' Audrey glanced at the modest houses on the hill a little way back from the beach. There were at least two hundred of them. How could they all be unavailable? Some of those houses must be suitable for a single person. Her heart ached at the description, and she inhaled sharply. That's what she was now, wasn't she? She barely needed any space at all.

'Most places here are on our Holidays Away! website, but I reckon you didn't book prior, did you?'

Audrey could feel her impatience rising like a scream. She needed to get somewhere, anywhere, with a bed and a door. And a lock.

'No, Lem. That's why I'm asking.' They had stopped walking, and now stood in front of the General Store. She couldn't let him disappear back inside his office.

'Well, everything's big, suitable for sleeping up to twelve, and pricey. Anywhere from eight hundred to two grand a night. Same prices as the city.'

Audrey's skin flushed. She thought she'd come to the beach village and find everything was the same—peaceful, low-key, quiet—but all that had changed. Her and Joyce's refuge had moved on, along with everything else. She'd have to drive to the nearest town and find a motel, but then what? Head back to the city in the morning and stay with Emma? Deal with the fallout before she had any time alone? No. She'd come this far; surely there would be something for a night or two. She did her best to smile.

'Is there anything at all, Lem? I don't care what it is, just as long as it's smaller than those places.'

Lem paused and glanced over Audrey's shoulder. 'Well, there might be something, but I don't think you'll like it unless you love cockroaches.' He snorted at his own joke.

'Show me.'

Lem led her to a crumbling grey two-storey building on the corner of the main street, one of its broken bay windows held together with cardboard and packing tape. She looked up at a plywood sign hanging precariously over the battered front door, the lettering barely legible beneath the peeling paint. *BITTERSWEET BAKERY—EST. 1988.*

CHAPTER 6

Audrey followed Lem into the dim interior of the derelict building. It smelled of dust and was lit by sunshine that struggled through dirty bay windows at the front of the high-ceilinged room. A glass-fronted bookcase ran the length of the wall, with a few tattered hardbacks shoved inside. Three square Formica-topped tables, pale yellow, stood forlornly beside several broken chairs. The floorboards had wide gaps and Audrey shuddered at the mouse droppings. She saw a glint of brass between the boards, kneeled and wedged it out. It was a lapel pin, white enamel, scratched and worn, with VIETNAM stamped inside a red cross. She set the pin on the bookcase.

'It was a bakery? When?'

'Dust gets me.' Lem coughed. 'Back in the eighties. Before that it was a ladieswear store of some sort, and before that, a chemist. Mostly just one disaster after another, as far back as I can remember. The baker left for Byron Bay. Heard he made it big up there, with the yogis and all.'

Audrey walked across creaking floorboards. The kitchen was separated from the front of the bakery by an old-fashioned marble-topped counter. On the counter perched an ancient cash register. There was a disused oven along one wall, a chipped porcelain sink, a double glass-fronted commercial fridge and a dented dishwasher. In the middle of the room sat a large rectangular timber table—oak? jarrah?—its four stout legs painted a peeling off-white. Stairs led from the back of the kitchen to the second floor.

'Up there's the apartment. Course I'll have to check with Buddy first.'

'Buddy?'

'The owner. He lives out back in the cabana. Rude old bugger. Sometimes he lets the upstairs flat to backpackers if there's an overflow in the summer. It's not the best up there. Rough as guts.'

Audrey tried not to frown. All she wanted to do was curl up and end the day. Her head pounded, and she hadn't drunk enough water. The coffee from the General Store had been so terrible that she'd dumped it, surreptitiously, into the flower bed in front of Robert's building.

'Should I wait here?'

'No, you go on up and take a stickybeak, and I'll ask Buddy.' Then Lem was gone.

She picked her way through the kitchen, trying not to notice the dead cockroaches and the stench of rubbish. Lem was right about the bugs. Something thumped overhead. Audrey jumped and squinted up the staircase. It was dark and narrow, but someone had painted each riser in rainbow hues, from crimson to indigo and violet. Maybe it had been a well-loved home at one time? She didn't remember seeing the building when she was young, but it was possible that, boarded up and derelict, it had held no interest for a little girl who only wanted to run on the sand, chase seagulls and share beach picnics with her mother.

She strained to listen. Nothing.

She walked up the staircase to a lemon-yellow door that creaked open into a dirty kitchen. Sunlight and dust motes streamed from the bay windows into the large living and bedroom area. The apartment was open plan, spacious and surprisingly bright and airy. The ceiling was more than three metres high, painted a grubby white, with plasterwork designs of daisies and leaves surrounding an ornate, dusty chandelier hanging in the middle of the room. The scent of dust and something pleasant—timber floorboards heated by the sun—made her shoulders relax. Even in its unloved state, the apartment felt like someone's home. Except for the graffiti. Down one long wall, someone had spray-painted *Question everything*. Underneath was scrawled a single word: *Why?*

The bay windows were identical to those on the ground floor, but these were unbroken. Cobwebs hung in the corners like a shroud, and an insistent fly hurled itself against the glass, again, again. Beneath one window sat a massive wooden chest. Audrey set her handbag on the kitchen benchtop and walked across the timber floorboards towards the insect's useless buzzing. She unlocked the centre window, and after four hard tugs, it groaned open and the chilly June afternoon air flooded in. She cupped the fly with her hand and pushed it outside, then spun around. The quiet settled over her. She unclenched her jaw.

Against one wall leaned a broken bedframe, no mattress, with a watercolour of a seascape hung crookedly above it. She reached out and straightened the frame.

'Not bad,' she said, and thought she heard a tiny click. She strained to listen while waves rolled over, faint in the distance. The room was silent. Audrey stood, waiting, until her nerves settled. She needed to sleep so badly, but could she, without the wine? Her stomach dropped and she gritted her teeth. Yes, of course she could. She'd recovered from those times, step by difficult step, and she wouldn't waste it now. She walked across the wide planks of the floor and peered into the tiny bathroom. It had a shower, a pedestal sink and a grubby toilet that she flushed once, then again. She twisted the taps, and after several seconds of a rusty dribble, hot water flowed onto her hands. She wiped them on her jeans and pulled the door closed; a few bottles of bleach were needed, but it seemed to be in good repair.

The kitchen had a gas stovetop and a wall oven that looked newer than the stove. A cheap black microwave perched on the benchtop between the fridge and the sink, and behind the counter was a cheerful splashback the shade of Granny Smith apples. Charming if a little grimy, the tile was laid in a complicated herringbone pattern. The kitchen had been renovated at some point; so many beach communities had cashed in on the influx of overseas visitors before the 2000 Sydney Olympics. Even she and Wyatt had considered having a granny flat built in their garden like their neighbours had done, but ultimately they decided it would be too much work to gain council approval. Audrey sagged against the kitchen sink.

That life, their marriage, her job at the agency, how could it all be ruined? Her mind rolled on to the cycle she'd been avoiding since she got out of her car: the Volvo, her discovery, Summer's promotion, her resignation. Wyatt's and Charmaine's guilty faces. Colin avoiding her eyes. Shame and failure flooded her body, and she took a shaky breath. She forced her gaze up, towards the large window overlooking the back garden, and beyond that, the sea.

The sea.

Aquamarine, churning slowly over and over in the quiet bay, the sea was as beautiful as she'd remembered. And the sand: white as sugar, the bay extending down to her right as far as she could see. The beach was empty. Breathtaking. It was the most beautiful ocean view she'd ever seen. Her mother had always said Whitehaven Bay had the whitest sand in the world. Audrey unlocked the window and tugged on it, but it was stuck with layers of cracked and yellowed paint.

Her hands shook. She had to be closer to the sea. She needed to take a deep breath and let the thrum of the waves roll through her. She walked to the back door, twisted the deadbolt and stepped onto a tiny balcony that ran the width of the building. It was only a metre wide, a little too narrow for furniture, but a rickety set of stairs led down to the garden. The view from the balcony was not close enough to the ocean. She wanted to walk on that sand again, feel it under her feet. She'd hurry down to the beach just for a moment, and then come back to wait for Lem.

Audrey inhaled salt air and closed her eyes. She felt her whole body relax and her limbs soften with relief. No one knew she was here. Not Wyatt, not her colleagues from the ad agency (a hot wave of embarrassment washed over her), not even Emma. She was alone and free from having to explain anything to anyone. She didn't have to consider their thoughts, their needs, their constant suggestions and hopes and demands. Her own failure hadn't caught up with her here. It was just Audrey and the Pacific

Ocean, a few hundred houses, and this expanse of pristine sand. For the first time in two days, she was saf—

'Tawdry Hepburn!'

Audrey shrieked. She whirled around, shaking, and stared through the back door into the flat. The mouthy teenager from the General Store stood in the open chest near the windows.

'No need to get your knickers in a knot, Tawdry. Didn't you hear me breathing?'

Audrey exhaled. How dare they? It was breaking and entering! She could've had a heart attack, might have fallen from the balcony. She cleared her throat. The teen grinned at her.

'Of course I heard you,' Audrey said.

'Liar!' Billie loped through the flat and onto the balcony.

'You're trespassing. How did you get in here, Billie?'

'Oh, I can break in anywhere. Just when you least expect me, bam!' Billie bumped a hip into Audrey, throwing her off balance. Audrey shuddered and grabbed the railing as Lem emerged from the cabana. His face had settled into a frown.

'Nope. No can do. Sorry. Buddy won't rent it,' he said.

Audrey's heart pinched in her chest. It was a no. This place, this view, another no.

'I said I didn't give a flying rat's arse who wanted the place!' An old man wheeled his red walker out of the cabana's front door. He yanked the frame onto the path running from the granny flat to the steps and shuffled forward in striped pyjamas, a straw fedora tipped rakishly, with a string dangling beneath his chin. Audrey noticed he had a phone strapped to one arm with one of those armbands that runners use. For safety? Certainly not for exercise. He craned his neck and seemed to size up Audrey and find her wanting. 'It's a goddamn no to you, missus! NO thank you. I don't need some sheila from the city bothering me.' He waggled a crooked finger at Billie. 'And you! You goddamn brat! I told you before. Get outta my place.'

'Old turd!' Billie pushed Audrey aside and thundered down the top steps, then jumped to the ground and ran.

Audrey's eyes ached. She'd barely eaten and there was clearly nowhere to sleep, but she knew one thing: she'd do anything for this view. Just for a few days. Just until she felt like herself again. She'd walk the beach and sleep, she'd remember her mother and her own childhood, and somehow she'd gather her thoughts before she faced her tattered life in the city. She gritted her teeth and set them into what she hoped looked like a friendly grin. She felt like a hyena, desperate to win.

'You must be Buddy. I'll come down.' She gripped the railing and hustled down the steps to the garden. Both Lem and Buddy moved towards her, arms outstretched at the same time.

'No, no, no—' yelled Lem.

'Can she hear us?' a growly voice above Audrey asked. 'Is she dead?' Her head throbbed and her stomach felt sick.

'Well, she's certainly a problem.' A woman's voice. 'We should slap her! Give her a sharp smack!'

Audrey heard Lem, his voice worried and high-pitched, ridiculously girlish now. 'Reckon we call an ambulance? I'll get Shez! She'll know what to do.'

'Stupid jackasses. Couldn't fight your way out of a wet paper sack. I texted Doc Flood. Don't know how the pair of you think you can run this town. Not a brain cell between you.'

'I'll remind you that I was a judge of the Federal Court!'

'See what I mean? Stupid *and* crooked!'

The voices were loud. Too loud.

'I'll ignore that because you're a pensioner and you don't have all your faculties. She could be bleeding internally. Justin will know. She's probably got a concussion.'

A car screeched to a stop and, after a few moments, Audrey felt someone kneel beside her. A quiet voice, then a cool pair of hands pulled open one eye and then the other. More murmuring. She let herself fall down, down, further down the staircase and into the blackness. It would be lovely to be asleep for good and be done with all of it and see her mother. She could escape everything she'd been carrying. Oh, her mother! She could see Joyce's crinkly eyes and the seventies hairdo she couldn't bear to relinquish, zipping through the salon carrying a big can of aerosol hairspray, clouds of optimism following her. Her mother liked to think she could look like Farah Fawcett forever.

Get up now, Audrey, she heard Joyce whisper.

'I'm . . . fine,' Audrey said, and opened her eyes. 'I just tripped down the steps, that's all.' She struggled to sit up but was helped by two strong hands. Audrey glanced down at the arms holding hers. Her fall might have interrupted his golf game: that was what the man seemed to be dressed for. He had grey hair and a dimpled chin covered in neatly trimmed grey stubble.

'Do you know what year it is?'

She told him.

'And the date?'

'Seventh of June.'

He smiled at her. His eyes were a soft blue, close to the colour of his jumper. Kind eyes. 'That's right. Do you know where you are?'

Audrey tried to smile back but her mouth felt dry. 'At the most beautiful beach in the world.' She sat up and looked behind her. She'd broken the treads of the last few steps, and her shoulder felt sore, but that was it. Other than her aching heart, she really was fine. 'I caught myself on the railing. I didn't fall that far.' She rubbed her shoulder.

'Do you think you can stand? I'm Justin Flood. Doctor. Retired.' He squinted at her kindly. A woman with a short black bob crowded next to him.

'I was parked at the store when I heard someone scream,' the woman said.

Lem shrugged. 'That was me.'

Dr Flood held Audrey's hands and pulled her up. She was near enough to him to smell the bergamot and cedar scent of his cologne. She brushed at her jeans and attempted a laugh, but it came out warbly and strange. 'I must have been a bit unsteady on my feet. I—didn't sleep much last night, and need to eat, that's all. Are my glasses somewhere?'

The woman handed them to her. 'I've known for years this building should be torn down! Buddy, it's well within her rights to litigate—'

'I'm fine,' Audrey said quickly. She walked a few steps to show everyone just how fine she was. Her shoulder throbbed, and she'd torn the seat of her jeans.

'She wouldn't call the law. She's my tenant,' Buddy said. 'Lem is fixing up those stairs tomorrow, aren't you, Lem?'

Audrey stared at Buddy. He raised a pair of unruly grey eyebrows back at her.

The black-haired woman snorted. 'Tenant! In this death-trap? You know what happened last time you rented it out, Buddy, and it wasn't—'

'Shut yer yap, Judge Judy!' Buddy snapped. 'A deal is a deal, right, lady?'

Audrey's head throbbed, and she desperately needed a drink, water, anything. What she wouldn't give for a—*don't go there*. But it didn't matter. She had the apartment. She'd have the view, for a few days at least. She'd feel closer to her mother. 'Right. I'm renting it for . . . the week.'

'Well, if that's settled,' Dr Flood said, 'I recommend a trip to your doctor tomorrow. You shouldn't stay alone tonight. You'll need to go to Emergency if you have any vision problems, headaches, anything like that. Are you here with someone?'

Audrey shook her head in what she hoped was a capable way. She had a place to stay; now all she had to do was get up there and go to sleep. There was no bed, no mattress, but she'd bring in her clothes from the car, use her puffer jacket as a pillow and just curl up and bring an end to the horrible day. 'I'm fine. I didn't hit my head. I'll just go back to the flat and—'

'I'll put you up for the night.' The black-haired woman made this pronouncement with a slightly pained voice, as if she were the Mother Teresa of Whitehaven Bay. 'I'm Ruth Hickson. President of the Community Association. We have five bedrooms and Billie and I only take two.' Over Audrey's head, Ruth grimaced at Buddy. 'Lem, you get her handbag and her luggage from her car. Justin, you can drop us off, and stay for a cocktail.'

'Oh, I couldn't possibly—' Audrey began.

'Don't be ridiculous,' Ruth said. 'Justin said you can't be alone. Where else are you going to stay?'

CHAPTER 7

Audrey washed her face in the marble sink in Ruth Hickson's guest room and rubbed in the anti-ageing face cream she found in the vanity. It smelled like peonies and weekends away in a luxury resort and made her stomach churn. Love Your Age, all right. She'd been foolish even to suggest it. From the looks of Ruth's ink-black hair and 'age-defying' face cream, Audrey could see she was busy fighting ageing like everyone else. She sighed. Ruth was a former judge and likely to initiate the career conversation over dinner. And what would Audrey say? That she'd recently resigned from her corporate job and run away from her life?

She shouldn't have agreed to stay over, but it had all happened so fast. Dr Flood had helped her into the passenger seat of his car and Ruth had hopped in the back, chatting all the while. Audrey suspected Ruth's generosity had more to do with impressing the handsome Dr Flood than helping a stranger, and she'd noticed how Ruth had laughed a little too loudly, leaning over the back seat and even patting his shoulder. Audrey could've slept on the floor at the apartment, or driven to the nearest town to a motel, but the doctor was insistent: she was not to drive or be alone. In the end, too exhausted to argue, she'd given in. It was only one night; tomorrow she'd sort out a bed and be sleeping above the old bakery. She set down Ruth's cream and stared at her hands. Her wedding rings, the thin gold band, the carat diamond she'd loved. To her, they meant something but to Wyatt they—

Someone rapped on the bedroom door.

'Dinner's ready!'

Billie. Why were they so good at breaking and entering? The family obviously had money. 'Coming,' Audrey called. She pulled off her diamond ring and wedding band and threw them into her make-up bag.

'Well, if it isn't Tawdry Hepburn,' Billie said when Audrey walked in ten minutes later, her hair slicked back in a ponytail. 'Just in time for our fight.'

Ruth had changed into a cream linen dress and pearls. Behind the wide table and leather dining chairs, floor to ceiling windows faced the now-dark sea. The table was set with three placemats and wineglasses, Ruth sitting at the head. Billie sat to Ruth's left and had also changed for dinner: into a different hoodie. This one was black, printed with a photograph of an open palm, fingers splayed, with a spike through it. Audrey shuddered. The cutlery gleamed, and next to Audrey's soup bowl was a large cloth napkin. She pulled out the chair across from Billie.

'We weren't fighting.' Ruth took a sip from one of the elegant wineglasses. 'Soup was getting cold, so we started without you. It's a shame Justin couldn't join us.' She handed Audrey a breadbasket that contained what looked like some very hard rolls and sighed. 'Always something to do.'

'Sorry I kept you waiting.'

'So rude, Tawdry Hepburn.' Billie winked.

'It's *Audrey*.'

They half-shrugged and continued chewing.

'I hope you didn't go to too much trouble.' Audrey sipped a spoonful of pumpkin soup. It was lukewarm and tasted of metal.

'Wine, Tawdry?' Billie asked, grabbing the bottle and sloshing pinot gris into Audrey's wineglass. The wine looked innocent. Delicious. Audrey avoided it and glanced at the soup: bright orange, with the scent of nutmeg and possibly tarragon. Then she stared at the smooth rectangle of butter in the dish, the placemats, the darkness outside. All the while, the pinot gris sat like a little shimmering pond, calm and round in the delicate crystal wineglass. So pretty. One sip would be fine. It would calm her nerves. Audrey tried to drag her eyes away.

Billie laughed. 'You got a drinking problem? You look like a dog with its tongue hanging out, Tawdry.'

Audrey's face flushed. The nerve. Billie was out of control and completely out of line. Rude, mouthy and obviously indulged by Ruth Hickson, and ready to be taught a lesson. Audrey raised her eyebrows. 'No, but I do have a problem with people trespassing in the apartment I'm renting.'

The look on Billie's face—guilt, then worry and fear—was surprisingly rewarding for a split second. Fear? But why—

Ruth slammed her hands on the table. The soup bowls rattled, and Audrey flinched. Ruth hammered her fists. 'I told you no more, Billie. I mean it! Go to your room!'

Billie jumped up. 'You old hag! You can't make me stay! You couldn't make Dad stay with you either. And I don't blame him. Why would he want to be with someone like you?'

Ruth's hand shot out and grabbed Billie's wrist, twisting it in her grip. Billie pulled free and ran. The front door banged, and the room was silent except for the ticking clock and Ruth's ragged breath. Faintly, through the wall of glass windows, the waves churned and fell against the shore.

Audrey cleared her throat but wasn't sure what to say. She hadn't meant to get Billie in trouble. Billie hadn't done any real harm, no more than a teenage prank. Audrey didn't want it repeated but surely it hadn't warranted the shrieking and banging, twisting Billie's wrist like that? She frowned. Ruth had almost looked . . . almost looked as if she'd *enjoyed* it. The clock ticked loudly in the silent room.

'Ruth, I'm sorry. I . . . it was just a teenage prank.'

Ruth took a sip of wine and tugged at her pearls. 'Billie has always been difficult. I'll make sure it doesn't happen again.' She reached for the bottle and didn't meet Audrey's shocked eyes. 'Billie's father was exactly the same.'

In the morning, the beach was deserted. Audrey had woken by six, stripped the sheets from her bed, packed her bag and written Ruth a thank-you note on a piece of paper she'd fished from the recycling. As a sort of apology to Billie, she drew a tiny cartoon of Audrey Hepburn from *Breakfast at Tiffany's* beside her name: beehive hairdo, pearls around the neck, long gloves, even a cigarette holder. Billie might see it and find it funny, and possibly it would cheer them up a little. She signed her name with a flourish that made the A in Audrey almost look like a T. Despite the beautiful guest room and the rhythmic sound of the sea, she'd had a hard time falling asleep the night before. Her shoulder throbbed from the fall down the steps, and she'd lain awake until one-thirty, but had never heard Billie come home.

It took only minutes to walk to Buddy's property, but she was sure it would be too early for anyone to be up. Audrey's car was still parked out front; she could drop off her overnight bag and have a beach walk, then a hot cup of . . . instant Nescafé at the General Store. She shuddered and considered driving back to the small country town on the highway to see if she could buy a decent coffee, but nothing would be open at this hour.

The sky was orange and pink and whipbirds whistled in the distance. Audrey hoped the beach would be deserted for a while. She rubbed sun cream onto her face, grabbed her hat and sunnies and locked her bag in her car. When she turned to walk down the path towards the cabana, she stopped. Buddy was ten metres ahead of her.

Or rather, Buddy's bare backside was.

Trundling down the path to the beach, a fully naked Buddy pushed his red walker ahead of him, a small striped towel draped over his shoulder, ready to take what Audrey guessed was his morning constitutional. Whatever the season, older Aussies swore by their daily swim. She turned and tried to walk back to her car silently, but hearing was one faculty that Buddy seemed to have no problems with whatsoever.

He wheeled his walker around, but Audrey couldn't bear to look.

'You!' he called out. 'Sweetman! What are you doing here so goddamn early? Suppose you'll be wanting the keys.'

'Oh, no rush,' she called out. 'I'm fine. I was just—'

'Just had to get away from Judge Judy, I bet. That old cow is a right pain in the arse, isn't she?' He stood in front of her in all his ancient, shrivelled glory.

Audrey looked everywhere but straight ahead. 'Uh—well . . .'

'And that larrikin of hers, Billie The Kid, a little too handy with a can of spray paint.' Buddy coughed. 'What's wrong with you? Got something in your eye?'

'No.'

'Well, come on in,' he said, turning back towards his property. 'I'll get your keys. You stuffed up my swim, but the water's not going anywhere.'

Audrey found herself following Buddy's naked bottom into his cabana. She suppressed a shocked giggle. She'd finally met a person who was fine with ageing. What would Summer think if she saw her with Buddy, baring all?

Buddy's home smelled of unwashed clothes, but it was tidy enough. A shelf overflowed with books, and an old-fashioned stereo cabinet was shoved against the wall, along with hundreds of vinyl albums. She'd never seen a record collection like it. On a low beechwood side table to the left of the stereo, Nina Simone, gorgeous in tones of indigo, gazed unsmiling from the album cover of *My Baby Just Cares For Me*.

Audrey looked everywhere other than at Buddy.

'You right in the head, Sweetman?' he asked as he squinted at her, dangling the keys in front of her. 'You one of those weird ones, the meditation yoga people? The self-helpers? The manifesters?'

She took the keys gingerly. 'Uh, no. No, I'm not. Thanks. Did you want an online transfer?'

'Nope. Cash. Three thousand a week.' Buddy coughed twice, then cleared his throat. The amount was ridiculous for the dirty apartment.

'I think we need to discuss this. It's very run-down . . .' Audrey started, and Buddy laughed.

'Just seeing what you'd do if I took the piss!' he cackled. 'You don't seem like you have a lot of backbone, but maybe there's more to you than meets the eye.'

She thought of the agency and her tattered marriage. She did have backbone, but at the moment, she didn't know where to find it. In less than three days, she'd lost her job and, possibly, her husband. Now, her biggest challenge was not running a creative department in the city's best ad agency, but negotiating reasonable rent with a naked senior citizen for an apartment so run-down it should be condemned. She took a deep breath and named a fair price. 'That's my final offer,' she said.

He coughed again, and she was afraid he might spit. 'Done, Sweetman. We have a deal.'

But what had she done? Her new landlord stood in front of her, stark naked. She was in a tiny community where she knew no one, had no friends, no support. No furniture. Nothing! She could get in her car and drive back, but drive back to what? Emma's sympathy and guest room would only remind Audrey of her own beautiful home and what she stood to lose. No. She would stay at Whitehaven Bay long enough to make a plan.

'I guess that's settled, then,' she said.

'There's no washer and dryer. Laundry's at Shez's holiday flats.'

'That's fine. I'll just—'

'Are you done jawing, Sweetman? I'm getting shrivelled over here. Woulda put on my budgie smugglers, but the goddamn things get tangled in my legs.'

Audrey spent the morning cleaning the apartment with a dishcloth, an oversized bowl she found in the kitchen cabinets, her travel shampoo and hot water.

'Keep moving, Sweetie,' she whispered to herself. For the most part, her encouragement worked. She was able to ignore the yawning hole in her stomach, the real ache in her shoulder and the even bigger heartache that spread across her chest. By ten-thirty she had distracted herself sufficiently, and become desperate enough for a coffee, to walk to the General Store. Robert was as cheerful as ever. She bought a bottle of lemon-scented dishwashing liquid, toilet cleaner, vinegar, a decaying packet of plastic gloves and a small bag of flour.

When she returned to the apartment, she sat on the floor in a patch of sunlight with the bay windows open, sipping the General Store's sweet, milky coffee from a Styrofoam cup. The ice packs in her cooler had melted overnight, but the butter and brie she'd packed in Sydney were still fine. The fridge was filthy inside and out, but it had hummed when she'd plugged it in. She'd given it a good scrub and unpacked her fresh food: three Royal Gala apples, a bag of carrots, the butter and cheese, some yeast and the package of flour, a jar of her homemade raspberry jam, a loaf of linseed bread, a package of smoked salmon.

Until now, she'd ignored her phone. She couldn't bring herself to look at it, but she'd have to deal with it eventually. Maybe she should do it. Of course she should! Emma would be wondering about her. And if any of her clients had called, Audrey would have to explain she'd moved on. Summer would've delegated all her campaigns by now, but not everyone would know. She frowned. Maybe Wyatt had left a message—but no, she couldn't bring herself to check in case he hadn't.

She picked up her phone and ignored Mail and Messages. Instead, remembering the album she'd seen at Buddy's, she searched 'Nina Simone Little Girl Blue' on Spotify. There. Play. The opening notes of a mournful Christmas 'Good King Wenceslas' began, picked out on a piano, one by one. Then slowly, like a poem on the keyboard, Nina Simone spun those same notes deeper, fuller, into a jazz ballad of a girl who was completely through with it all and counting raindrops. Audrey hunched on the floor in the sun, hugged her knees to her chest, and cried. When Nina finished, Audrey wiped her nose and breathed in the scent of lemon cleaner and sea. The apartment was quiet. No mattress. A broken bedframe. Cockroach corpses and cobwebs, dirt and not a single chair. Billie's graffiti—she had no doubt it was theirs—stared back at her. *Question everything.* That's what she would do.

She never wanted to leave.

She wanted to stay in this flat alone with no one bothering her, no ex-colleagues or Wyatt or friends, no need to think about her past or her future. Everything could be now, this moment, her private war against the dirt and the dead bugs and trying to make the empty apartment feel like home for a week or so. It's what her mother would've done: start over, make it liveable, do what she could with her own two hands. She'd live in the moment like Joyce always had. She'd drive to town and visit the hardware store; they'd be sure to have an air mattress and a sleeping bag, and for today, truly, a rest was all she needed. That, herself, and time.

CHAPTER 8

Later that afternoon, Audrey adjusted her sunnies against the glare. When she'd dropped in on Buddy to ask if she could fix up the apartment a little, he'd shrugged and said to go for her life. It didn't matter to him what she did, but he hoped she was handy with a paintbrush and bug spray. His laugh had then turned into a hacking cough, and he'd taken a swig of bourbon straight from the bottle to fix it.

The town nearest to the beach village was bigger than she remembered, or more likely it had grown since she was a girl. She slowed down and passed a library and a movie theatre, then parked in front of an ugly strip mall with a two-dollar shop, a liquor store, a hardware store and a Thai restaurant. She walked past the bottle-o and glanced at the ads plastered on the front window. Chardonnay was always on sale, all over the world, all the time. So inexpensive, handy by the case, excellent cold, even in a coffee mug. She forced herself to keep walking. The hardware store had pots of cheerful chrysanthemums in a welcoming queue beside the door, and Audrey picked up two blush pink beauties and set them in her trolley. The trolley had a wonky wheel, but she rattled her way inside the shop, which was surprisingly spacious, cool and dark. A lanky teen at the cash register nodded, not lifting her eyes from her mobile.

By the time the young woman had rung up all Audrey's purchases, she looked slightly happier. 'You've got a lot of stuff,' the teen said. 'Renovating?'

'Not exactly.' While the sullen teen watched, Audrey loaded her bags and tins back into the wobbly trolley. 'Is there somewhere I can buy bedding? Or at least a blanket?'

'Try the two-dollar shop. I think they've got sleeping bags. Or maybe the op shop? It's over by the theatre.' She went back to staring at her phone.

Audrey wheeled her trolley from the store. A used blanket was not what she was dreaming of. She'd only ever bought the softest and best bedding: the thousand thread count sheets, the duck feather pillows. It was a little indulgence that she and Wyatt—*don't go there.* A pain sliced through her chest. She forced herself to tick off the items in her cart to see if she'd remembered everything. Paint. Brushes. Two buckets. Double air mattress. Screwdriver, duct tape, spackle, a toilet brush and a flat pack table big enough for one person, two at a pinch.

For the first time in days, a flutter of what—hope? excitement?—unfolded next to the ache in her chest. She hoisted her supplies into the car, feeling grateful that Buddy was fine with a little DIY in the flat. It was unlikely he could even get himself up there with his walker. This is ridiculous, she told herself sternly, you're only going to be at the beach for a week, two at the most. Why bother? But even a week was a long time alone if all you were doing was beach walking and trying to avoid your own phone.

She'd learned all through her childhood how much nicer it made a rental if you put in an effort. When Audrey was ten, Joyce had found twenty-five metres of vintage fabric in an op shop and bought it with their grocery money. They'd spent the weekend transforming Audrey's bedroom into a tiny castle fit for a princess, with nothing more than floral fabric, fairy lights and a staple gun. By Sunday night, the entire room was hung from floor to ceiling in heavy white damask, dotted with the tiniest pink sweetheart roses. Her mum had even created a canopy around the lumpy single bed. Audrey's best friend at the time, who lived in a huge house with a pool and an intercom system and her own pink telephone, the same friend who had at least twelve pairs of jeans lying neatly on a shelf in her walk-in closet, told Audrey it was the prettiest room she'd ever seen. Audrey and her mother had eaten beans on toast for two weeks on a picnic blanket on her bedroom floor, with the fairy lights on.

It had been worth it.

The apartment above the bakery was dirty and needed paint, but it had good bones. Before she left, she'd checked the kitchen and added to her list: measuring cups and spoons, a small electric mixer, a good-sized bowl. Everything else was old, but not unusable. Tonight, she'd scrub up the lot of it and maybe bake a—

Her phone buzzed. Emma. Audrey closed her car boot and answered on the fifth ring.

'Sweetie! How are you? I've been trying to reach you.'

How was she? Numb. In denial. Trying to keep busy.

'I'm okay. I just . . . haven't felt like talking. I'm sorry.'

'Wyatt called me when he couldn't get through to you. I could barely talk to that cheating piece of rubbish, but I was civil. He wanted to know if you were okay. I told him you were as okay as a woman could be whose bastard husband had run away with a teenager.' On the other end of the line, Emma paused for dramatic effect, but not long enough for Audrey to say anything. 'I told him to imagine how that feels. Being dumped for a receptionist half your age. And I told him that you'd talk to him when you were good and ready, and he better not have his secretary in *your house*, and—'

'Oh, Emma, stop!' Audrey breathed in and tried to keep calm. Her brain slammed against her forehead. 'I rented a flat at Whitehaven Bay. I need a break from the city.'

'Of course you do. I'll drive down! I'd love a beach walk, and listen, I'll take you out for dinner. Give me—oh, four hours. Should I stay over?'

Audrey's head throbbed and she felt herself nodding. She'd go back in and grab a second air mattress and organise all the bedding with Emma. She'd find out if the Thai place did takeaway. Emma didn't love Thai food, but there didn't seem to be much else. Or should she go back to the grocery store? Audrey could throw together a salad and a chicken pie; it wasn't hard. Some indulgent ice cream for dessert, or Emma's favourite blackberry cake? All she needed was frozen berries. Then she stopped. Waited for her heart to catch up. She thought of the blackberries thawed and slushy on her own benchtop in her home where Wyatt was, probably with Charmaine. He'd have thrown them out by now.

'Sweetie? It'll be fun—two women on the loose!'

Audrey took a breath. 'I know, and I'm so grateful, but . . . I don't think so. Not yet.'

'Are you sure?'

Yes. The thought surprised her. All she had was this place, a room of her own to think things through, with no memories here but hers. She didn't need the comfort of a friend. She needed herself.

'I'm sure.'

Thirty minutes later, Audrey pulled up in front of the bakery building. Billie slouched against the wall, vaping, wearing a hoodie emblazoned with a severed head, the tongue sticking out. They puffed contentedly like Gandalf in *Lord of the Rings*. How could a mouthy, rangy teen look so confident? They acted as if they didn't have a care in the world. Billie truly had no idea what was about to hit them square in the face. Adulting. Oh, sure, the future was bright, but it was also a series of problems just waiting to unfold like backwards origami. Just when you thought you had everything figured out, you had zero. Career in tatters. A wrinkled, useless marriage certificate and a broken heart.

'Well, if it isn't Tawdry Hepburn. Is that a flat-pack table?'

Audrey yanked the potted mums from her boot and didn't answer. One chrysanthemum had spilled and she scooped the dirt back into the pot. Entertaining rude Billie Hickson was not on her to-do list. She breathed in and thought of Billie's furious mother, and her own lighthearted, fun one. What would Joyce do? *Be kind, Audrey: you never know the dragons someone else is trying to slay.*

'You could put away that vape and make yourself useful,' she finally said.

'You ratted me out to Ruth.' Billie inhaled sharply. 'The last time that happened to me, she tried to lock me in my room at night. Lucky I know how to climb the drainpipe and get out. But now Ruth is pissed, and it's your fault, Tawdry.'

Audrey knew how to deal with this: it was like having a junior in the office. Or maybe she didn't know, not anymore. She looked at Billie and sighed. 'You shouldn't be breaking and entering. You know better.'

Billie exhaled a stream of vapour and shrugged. Wouldn't look her in the eyes.

Audrey waited. 'And?'

'Fine. I won't do it again, Tawdry.'

Audrey set the two potted mums on each side of the front door. 'I'm an older woman. You could offer to help me carry something.'

'You look like you could run up those steps.'

'Not with this table.'

Billie laughed and picked up the box easily. When they'd carried up the last of Audrey's purchases, Billie sat on the floor and took a long drag from the purple vape.

'Absolutely not,' Audrey said. 'Does your mother let you vape inside?'

Billie slid the purple tube into the pocket of their oversized jeans. 'Ruth isn't the most easygoing. Not like Dad.' Their eyes moved from the scrub rag in the middle of the floor to the bay windows and across the graffitied wall. 'It's nice up here.'

Audrey nodded.

'Quiet,' Billie said. 'I like breaking into this one. I've done most places at Whitehaven, and the post office and op shop in town. Lots of good places to sleep.'

Why would they need to break into a building and sleep there? Audrey thought of Ruth Hickson, how she'd slammed the table. Hammered it. Twisted Billie's wrist. Ruth was so different from how her own mother had been during Audrey's rebellious teenage years. Joyce had usually laughed and made Audrey work off her rudeness. Chores and more chores. Sweeping hair from the salon floor. Folding towels. Cleaning the apartment.

Audrey gestured to the boxes. 'Well, if you're that resourceful, can you put this together? Building furniture is my worst nightmare.'

'Your husband always do that sort of thing? You that kind of helpless woman?' Billie pulled out the vape and pointed it at Audrey.

'No.' *Yes*. Yes she was, but couldn't afford to be that way anymore. All the optimism she'd felt at the hardware store left her, and she was suddenly more tired than she'd ever been. 'Look, Billie, I'll pay you.'

'How much?' Billie blew vapour in Audrey's direction.

'Minimum wage. You can put together the table and help me paint over the graffiti. You obviously know how to paint.'

'I do, Tawdry. You'd be surprised how handy I am with a spray can.'

While Billie built the table, Audrey turned on the oven. She didn't know why she didn't want Emma at the beach; she needed Emma! Didn't she? Emma was resourceful and successful and strong. Audrey, on the other hand, was numb. That's all. Like someone had stabbed a kitchen knife through her chest, and yet

... she lived. Breathed. She wanted to be alone, but somehow Billie didn't count. They were just a teenager, not an adult judging her and finding her wanting. She shuddered again, thinking of Ruth slamming her fists. Where had Billie been all night?

As the oven heated, the acrid smell of burnt pizza drifted through the room. Audrey took a bowl from the drying rack, and when she rummaged for a spatula in the drawer, she found a simple brass bracelet, tarnished, with markings cut into the sides. She set it on the benchtop. It reminded her of something, but she couldn't think what. She unpackaged the cheap hand-mixer she'd bought. She browned the butter in a pan, then creamed it with sugar, added two eggs, three cups of plain flour, baking soda and baking powder, poured in a teaspoon of vanilla and finished with her secret ingredient, an overly generous shake of Himalayan pink salt. Then she stirred in the chocolate chips.

Billie was whistling.

Audrey opened the back door. Lem hadn't fixed the broken steps, and her shoulder was sore. She could hear a tinny recording of 'Cry Me a River' from Buddy's cabana, and the wintry sea breeze rose to meet her, delicious and cool. Soon enough it would be sunset. The bracelet on the benchtop seemed so familiar, and then she remembered: she'd watched a documentary with Wyatt about Vietnam special forces, and the indigenous tribes—Montanegros? Montagnards?—who'd sided with the Americans and gifted them brass bracelets as a sign of trust. It looked like one of those. She turned back to the benchtop, heavy with memories of Friday nights with Wyatt and a documentary, popcorn for her, peanuts for him.

While Billie whistled, Audrey rolled cookie dough into balls and popped a tray in the oven. Twelve minutes in her oven at home but here, in this strange little reprieve of a makeshift sanctuary, where time didn't matter and real life wasn't happening, how long would this ancient oven take? She checked after eleven minutes. The cookies were done. Crinkled on top, the scent of warm, melted chocolate mingled with vanilla and butter: Audrey placed two on a yellow plate and added the tiniest scoop of cookie dough on the side. Kids always loved sneaking cookie dough, didn't they? She pulled a daisy head from the grocery store flowers she'd stuck in a jar on the counter and set the blossom on the plate beside the cookies. She carried it through to Billie, touched their shoulder and they jumped.

Billie tapped an AirPod to stop the music. They stared at Audrey and the warm chocolate chip cookies, the daisy, the small dollop of chilled dough dotted with chocolate chips.

'Uncooked dough can give you salmonella, Tawdry.'

Audrey shrugged. 'It's a little risky, but better than vaping, I think.'

'I always used to sneak it anyway. When we lived in the city.' Billie took a bite. 'Damn, Tawdry. Good. None of the nannies made cookies like these.'

'It's the chocolate and browned butter. My mum always said they taste like joy.'

'Chip, chip, hooray!' Billie waved a cookie at her. Billie was creative, almost effortlessly. It was the perfect name for Audrey's decadent chocolate chip cookies.

'How many nannies did you have?'

Billie waved a slim hand airily. 'Oh, years of them, all different ones, but only after Dad left. Before then, he took care of me. We did everything together until Ruth wrecked our family. Me and Dad, we were always . . .' Billie looked up and blinked. 'Thick as thieves. Ruth called us the Two Bandits, but we took it as a compliment. Anyway. The first nanny after Ruth kicked Dad out was from the Philippines—Ruth caught her using her La Prairie make-up, so she was gone. One from China, not enough English for Ruth, and Ruth got her deported, I think. I really liked her, Sui-Lin, her name was. One from Canada, that was sad, Ruth said she was a pushover . . . she caught her reading to me before bed like Dad used to. Ruth said children need to be independent. Especially at bedtime. Dark room. Door closed.'

Billie took another bite. Audrey remembered being squished beside her mother on the floral canopied bed, feverishly reading a Narnia book together, desperate to find out when Lucy's siblings would wise up.

Audrey bit into a cookie. Wyatt used to love them before he got into his latest fitness regime. Colin, her boss, had loved them, too. Her stomach knotted. Best not to think about that.

'What about when you were older?'

'Well, eventually I got tutors instead. By year six I had tutors before school and after school.' Billie ticked them off. 'Maths, Science, English. Those were the after-school tutors. Before school was a track coach and a French tutor. I ran cross country for a while, long legs, kinda fast.' Billie nodded their shaved head. 'But Ruth said I needed a private track coach because Hicksons have to stay ahead of the game.' Billie shook a fist in the air dramatically. 'We conquer the game. Until we don't.'

'Do you like high school?' Audrey asked.

Billie raised an eyebrow. 'I'm the first Hickson dropout. Ran away at the start of year ten but Ruth tracked me down, and then she moved us here to the holiday house. Homeschooling.

She tells everyone I'm recovering from glandular fever. So yeah, we're all first at something. I'm the first failure. Go, Hicksons.'

Audrey thought of her own high-school years, heading to the hair salon with her best friend, Emma, in the afternoons, the way Joyce would let them wander the shopping centre and sweep the salon floors and wash and fold towels for pocket money. Her mother had been genuinely surprised and thrilled when Audrey had applied to university.

'You're too young to call yourself a failure, Billie.'

'You're right. I'm a carpenter.' Billie knocked twice on the table. 'See? Solid as a rock. Thanks for the cookies.' They handed Audrey the plate and pushed up their sleeves. 'Gotta get going or Ruth'll spit the dummy.' They'd written GET LOST on one arm and LOSER on the other in what looked like black permanent marker. Billie loped to the door.

'Billie?'

They turned and Audrey caught a flicker of a smile. 'Yes, Tawdry?'

'Thank you.'

Audrey ate cookies for dinner, and they were delicious. She made a cup of Earl Grey and kicked herself for forgetting about the coffee. Even a coffee press would do! What had she been thinking? Robert would be seeing her again in the morning. She used the foot pump for the double air mattress—tedious, but after thirty minutes she was sure it counted as exercise for her thighs—and made up the bed with the new sleeping bag and the pillow from the two-dollar shop that smelled of factories.

Tomorrow she'd see about fixing the bedframe. As she washed her face and changed into her nightgown, she hoped fervently that she'd found all the cockroaches there were to find. Oh, God, and the spiders! Huntsmen, red-backs. She shuddered.

The air mattress was surprisingly comfy, and she was exhausted. Through the bay windows the night sky bloomed indigo, and slowly filled with stars. Somewhere a Peron's tree frog cackled, then another. She'd have to fix the kitchen window in the morning if she wanted to hear the waves at night and it would be good to find a screen to keep out the insects. Maybe Lem could help, or someone at the hardware store. Actually, she'd have to fix everything. Everything was broken. It was impossible to even make a list. She stared up at the ceiling, waiting for sleep to come.

On the floor next to her, her phone flashed. She turned it over. Texts from Wyatt.

Where are you?
I called your office. What the hell is going on?
We need to talk.
Audrey???

As she stared at the messages, three dots came up, swirled, then disappeared. Again. One more time. Then finally nothing at all.

CHAPTER 9

The dawn was overcast, with wintry clouds suspended mauve and grey, lowering the sky to touch the sea. Audrey walked across damp sand the colour of cornflour, so clean it squeaked with each step. She hadn't needed an alarm; she woke at four-thirty wrestling in her sleeping bag with an ache in her chest and night sweats. Her dreams were a tangle of Wyatt and one thousand thread count sheets, Colin with his arm around Summer at the agency, but a silver-haired Summer wearing Charmaine's cowboy boots. By five-thirty, Audrey had made tea, and by six-fifteen she'd layered on all her warmest clothes. By first light, she was on the beach.

The sand stretched three kilometres to the south, all around the bay. She was alone. Freezing. The sea breeze slid inside her collar and whipped down her jacket. She trembled from the winter morning and her own exhaustion. According to the weather app, the sun would rise at 7:01, but Audrey felt it could stay dark and quiet forever. She wished it would.

She wasn't a runner, but she'd always walked, and she walked even more when she'd started down the long track to not drinking. In the early days, she'd remembered a phrase from her high-school Latin class, and it had resonated deep inside her. *Solvitur ambulando*: it is solved by walking. For eight years, the walking had helped her calm down and avoid turning to wine, but it had been a long time since she'd faced problems like this. This was a life implosion, fast, impossible to grasp, a loss of confidence in every way, and her heart ached to talk to the old Wyatt, the one who loved to read the paper for hours on a Saturday morning, and drink as many cups of coffee as she did. They took their coffee the same way—hot and black, nothing else—and though Audrey had little interest in the news compared to Wyatt, she loved to flip through her cookbooks for inspiration or watch pastry chefs on YouTube make delicate creations out of almond flour, egg whites and time.

Wind.

The squeak of her trainers on the hard sand.

Her breath came in ragged bursts. Still, she kept walking. A return to wine never helped, but it was seductive, wine, so she always felt like it would. She heard a rustle to her right: a kangaroo lolloped from the bush, feminine face and brown eyes watching Audrey as if she were an intruder. The young doe balanced forward and hopped down the beach. There was kangaroo scat on the lawn at Buddy's, but she hadn't seen any does or boomers until now. The doe looked gentle, with a face similar to a deer, but she was wild, capable of rearing back on her powerful tail and attacking with her claws. Usually kangaroos struck dogs, not humans, but it was best not to get too close.

At one time, the *Guinness Book of World Records* said Whitehaven had the whitest sand in the world. Joyce had loved those books, the crazy lists, the stunts, the daring people. Every time her mother took Audrey to the library, she'd give Audrey a pull-trolley and told her to load up; she could have whatever she wanted up to the limit on both their cards. *Twenty items for four weeks, aren't we rich, Audrey, and lucky?* That's how they'd found Narnia together. When she got older, Audrey would choose Enid Blyton and Mary Norton and as many Nancy Drews as were left on the shelves, but her mum always slid a *Guinness Book of World Records* in the trolley. *The world's a big, unpredictable place*, Joyce always said. *You never know when the magic will find you.*

In the distance, a jogger ran along the shoreline. Audrey walked slowly, closing the gap between them, hoping she wouldn't need to start a conversation. Her head ached and she knew that anything could make her cry: thoughts of Joyce, a talk with a stranger, wondering where Wyatt was and what was happening in her home. The runner was closer now, and he looked familiar.

'Audrey?' he called.

She kept walking towards him and plastered a smile on her face. 'Hello. Dr Flood. I didn't get a chance to thank you the other day.'

He stopped in front of her, his grey t-shirt wet with sweat. 'How's that head? And your shoulder?'

'I'm fine. Feeling much better now. How are you?'

He squinted at her. He looked as if he could see right through her subterfuge, which made the tears come all the closer to the surface. She blinked twice and turned to the sea.

'Just trying to get my exercise done,' he said. 'I love these beach runs. Secretly? I think this is the most beautiful beach in the world.'

Audrey nodded. 'It's what my mother used to say. She brought us here when I was a girl.'

'She's a wise lady,' Dr Flood said. He shifted to stretch his calves, first one, then the other. Audrey was surprised that she noticed how strong his legs were, how handsome his face in the morning before a shave, his crinkly grey-blue eyes almost the colour of the water. 'Does she get to come back often?' he asked.

'No, she passed away last year.' Audrey hugged her arms and exhaled. She would not cry in front of a stranger, even if he was kind, and a doctor, and probably used to all sorts of human misery.

'I'm sorry,' he said. He reached out and touched her shoulder. His grip was gentle, and comfort flooded through her. 'It's hard to lose the people we love, but I've found they want us to keep moving forward.'

'You're right. But it does feel good to talk about them.'

'Yes,' he said, and his eyes had a faraway look that made her wish she knew what he was thinking. Was he a widower? He seemed interested in what she had to say, but somehow respectful of her privacy at the same time. Patient. She suspected he was a good listener.

Audrey's phone buzzed, loud on the quiet beach.

'I'll leave you to it, Audrey,' Dr Flood said. 'Have a good walk.' He turned and jogged towards the path leading to the village.

She pulled her phone from her pocket and glanced at the screen. It was a message from Wyatt. *You can't avoid this, Audrey. Call me at 3.*

A colony of gulls swooped from the sky to the water's edge. One seagull stood alone, stalking the beach, cawing at the others, cocking its head and staring at Audrey with green marble eyes rimmed in orange. The gull took three steps towards her and waited. The ocean rolled against the shore, exactly the way she remembered from her holidays as a girl.

'Mum?' Audrey whispered, and then felt utterly ridiculous. If only they could walk the beach together now, Audrey would find a way out of this mess. Joyce would give her the courage to start a job search. She'd tell her to call Wyatt and sort through her real life, the one she'd been avoiding.

In the General Store later that morning, from where she was hidden behind the back shelves, Audrey heard Robert greet first Ruth and a few minutes later, Dr Flood. She pushed aside the ancient packages of brown sugar and tins of peaches gone past their use-by date stacked on the bottom shelf. She was searching unsuccessfully for the one packet of raisins Robert insisted was there, along with a tin of pineapple he swore he had in stock.

'Surely you're free for dinner, Justin?'

'I'm sorry, Ruth.'

'How about a drink on Monday? Happy Hour! I make a delicious negroni.' Audrey cringed at Ruth Hickson's girlish laugh.

'Ruth, I . . . listen. It's better if I'm honest and well, I'm . . . seeing someone.' A low cough.

Audrey felt a strange tug at her insides and her cheeks burnt. This was not a conversation she wanted to overhear, especially because it was none of her business. It was obvious the handsome

Dr Flood would be seeing someone, and besides, why should that matter to her? She crouched and scooted behind the shelves towards Lem's office door. She flung it open and stepped inside.

'What the hell—' Lem said, and Audrey put her finger to her lips.

'Lem! Is there a back door?'

'No,' he whispered back. He glanced around his tiny office: the single desk, the printer on a stand, the rubbish bin and window with its plastic venetian blinds. 'Should I put one in?'

'No!' Audrey hissed. 'Ruth Hickson's out there and I don't want her to see me. She'll think I was eavesdropping.' More voices: the deep rumble of Dr Flood's and Ruth's embarrassed laughter.

Then a mobile rang, and she heard him say, 'Lucinda? Sure. I can pick you up at three.' Audrey caught a glimpse of broad shoulders in a navy wool jumper. Dr Flood walked out the door, banging it shut behind him.

'Audrey!' Robert's baritone was too loud for the tiny space. 'Coffee's up. Milk and two sugars, easy on the Nescafé, just like you ordered. Weak and sweet.'

Audrey threw a pleading look in Lem's direction and he shrugged.

'Coming!'

She took the warm Styrofoam cup and paid quickly. 'Maybe next time no sugar, Robert? And no milk?' She glanced in Ruth's direction. 'Hi Ruth. Lovely morning.'

'Audrey.'

Robert handed Audrey her change. 'Did you find the raisins and the pineapple?'

She shook her head and took a sip. Beside her, Ruth set a carton of milk on the counter with a thunk, followed by a loaf of bread and a jar of peanut butter. The bell above the door clanged and Billie pushed through. Blood ran down Billie's neck on both sides of their pinched face. A steel barbell earring covered in blood had been pierced horizontally across the top of each red and pulsing ear.

Ruth gasped.

'Look what I did! Ordered titanium barbells online. Hurt like a bitch, though. I froze the first one with ice cubes, but not the second. I think this one is crooked. I had to jab it a few times.' Billie tugged at an earlobe and winced.

'Oh my God, Billie!' Ruth's face was furious. 'What have you done?'

'My body, my rules, Ruth. You don't own me.'

'You're my responsibility!' Ruth's screech was too loud for the tiny store.

'You can't stop me.' Billie yanked at their earrings, hard, and Audrey winced.

Ruth's face flushed crimson. 'I'm taking you ho—'

'No!' Billie stepped back and rubbed a sleeve against the blood.

A car pulled up at the front of the store, and Robert shuffled to the door. Audrey took a step to follow him. She couldn't bear to be in the middle of a family drama featuring Ruth Hickson. But poor Billie. Audrey winced, imagining what it had taken Billie to pierce their own ears with a needle and no freezing. To hurt yourself, so you could hurt your mother.

'What about you, Tawdry? Do you hate it, too?' There was an edge to Billie's voice, and it was high-pitched like a child's.

Audrey turned back and tried not to think about the blood. She wasn't good with anything medical—accidents, pain, vomiting—and caregiving had never come naturally to her. It was probably best she'd never had a child. She exhaled carefully. No, she wasn't a mother, but she knew when someone needed her. Didn't teens rely on other adults aside from their parents, especially with a mum as volatile as Ruth? Billie's ears dripped with blood. Audrey forced herself to look at one, and then the other, her face deliberately calm. 'I used to watch the piercings in my mum's hair salon. A rinse with saline solution would help,' she said, her voice even. 'I have some for my contact lenses. It's a bit different from the one for wounds, but I think it will work.'

'Will it sting?'

'A little, but you don't want an infection.'

Ruth's voice was low, her hands balled into fists. 'You're interfering, Audrey.'

'I'm sorry.' Audrey nodded at Ruth and turned towards the door. Maybe Ruth was right. This was not her problem; Billie was Ruth's child. Besides, she had more than enough problems of her own.

'Billie,' Ruth said, 'you're coming home with me.'

'No, I'm going to get saline at Tawdry's place.'

'You're going home. Now.'

'You just don't get it, Ruth. Not like Tawdry does.' Billie wiped a sleeve across their face and followed Audrey from the store.

CHAPTER 10

'Oh, for Chrissakes, cover up that flabby old *arse*, Buddy!' Audrey heard someone cry early the next morning. She rolled over and tried to ignore it. Then she heard a loud cough. She tossed aside her blanket and stumbled to the balcony door.

'Mouthy young fella, I reckon yours isn't any better!'

'As if I'd show you. And how many times do I have to tell you, I'm not a fella. I'm non-binary.'

'You're goddamn mouthy. Yelling at an old fella who's trying to get fit, that's what you are! And I don't want to see your young arse.'

'Well, I don't want to see yours either!'

'Well, I don't want to see yours ei—'

'Enough!' Audrey roared from the tiny balcony. Buddy and Billie looked up. 'It's six-forty-five in the morning! What is your problem? Both of you?'

When they started to explain, loudly, Audrey threw up her arms and walked back inside. She rubbed them to warm up. A space heater was what the apartment needed, and a reverse-cycle air conditioning unit for the summer, but she'd never be here that long. She turned on the kettle and watched Buddy roll his walker to the beach, the same dirty striped towel slung over his shoulder, jiggly buttocks heading towards the sea. Billie stood in the middle of the lawn. They looked tiny. Lonely. Audrey sighed.

'You might as well come up,' she called through the back door. 'I'll make muffins.'

Instead of going around and knocking on the locked front door of the building like any adult would, Billie hopped up on the railing of the broken back stairs and balanced on red Converse trainers, leaped onto the first unbroken tread, and ran up the rest.

'Gotta get Lem to fix those steps, Tawdry.'

Audrey yawned and waved a hand in the direction of her phone on the kitchen benchtop. 'Recipe's on my phone. Make a start on the muffins. Don't overmix, though, and put in the frozen blueberries last. You roll them in flour first, so they don't sink. That's the secret.'

Audrey returned from the shower, wearing jeans and her warmest jumper, her wet hair wound up in a towel and Ugg boots on her feet.

Billie stared at the bowl. 'How does it look? Too lumpy?'

'Perfect. Let's get them in the oven. I'm starving.'

An hour later, the June winter air whistled through the open windows of the apartment. Billie and Audrey stood beside each other painting, and Audrey could see she was terrible at it. Her portion of the wall was uneven, and she'd dripped on the floor. Wyatt had always done the painting in their house, inside and out, while she cleaned up the mess he made.

'Why yellow, Tawdry? Why this softest hue of summer twilight sunset, the palest of pale yellows?' Billie asked, in the high-pitched voice of a Disney princess. Their ears looked much better today: less swollen, not so red. Audrey was afraid to ask what happened when Billie finally turned up at home. Ruth had been so angry.

'Reminds me of my mum, I guess.'

They brushed companionably, and Audrey noticed that Billie was especially careful at edging. In fact, their painting was better than hers. Much better.

'Was your mum like you, Tawd, all you know . . . excessively helpful?'

'What's that supposed to mean?'

Billie hooted. 'Relax Tawdry, no biggie. She's probably dead, right, because you're old? I just wondered, was she kind of all *let me help you* and *no, I'm totally fine with it* and *sure, I'll just people-please all the freaking people I know* . . .'

Audrey stared at Billie. 'Is that what you think of me?'

'Well, hate to say it, Tawdry, but it's a little bit true, isn't it?'

Audrey blinked twice. 'Look, maybe you should go.'

'I saw the texts from your husband,' Billie said. 'Wyatt, right? He's your dickhead husband? You need to stand up to him.'

Audrey frowned. 'That's private.'

'It was right there on the screen, Tawdry, when I was reading the recipe. Kind of. Anyway, I want to know about Wy-ass. Tell me the story.'

Audrey gazed out the bay windows to the empty street below. She hadn't eaten properly for days, and the paint smell was making her feel light-headed.

'It's nothing. I'm fine.'

'No, you're lying your freaking face off, Tawd. I can see it. A liar can always spot a liar.'

Audrey sighed. Billie sighed right back at her.

'My life is complicated just now, that's all.'

Billie kicked the toe of Audrey's Ugg boot with a sneaker. 'Unload a little. I can take it.'

Four muffins, two ruined paintbrushes, an hour of talking and half a box of tissues later, Audrey realised she'd just confided in a sixteen-year-old high-school dropout who hated their mother. Oh, God. Was she really that screwed up that she'd discuss her failed promotion and ruined marriage with a struggling teen? Everything was crumbling, all the good things she knew herself to be. She was the one who took care of people! She was the calm, sane, strong one: the giver, the good listener. Corporate exec! Baker of cookies! Healer of souls!

Billie helped themselves to another muffin. 'You got screwed over at the advertising agency.'

'You're pretty smart for a kid.'

'Yeah, well, I've been through a lot. I'm young, but I'm not stupid. You're old like Ruth, but you're cool. You get me. She doesn't. I'm just a problem she needs to whip into shape.'

Audrey frowned. Did Wyatt think she was a problem? Had Colin at UDKE? Obviously, both of them had been searching for a more 'modern' alternative. Her marriage, her failure to land the promotion at the agency, all of it came crashing in. She exhaled and made herself stop. Instead, she attacked the graffiti, rolling over *Question everything*. Maybe that wasn't the advice she needed after all. Maybe she needed to stand up and back herself. Keep going.

'I'll cut in around the windows. You'll be so much worse,' Billie said.

It was true: Audrey had paint in her hair and on her jeans. She'd have to use a scraper to clean the timber floorboards, but the apartment glowed like a buttery twilight. It was beautiful.

'You could do an IKEA order.' Billie's voice was tinged with an enthusiasm Audrey hadn't heard before. 'They deliver here. They have these gauze-panelled curtains; we could hang them in the bay windows. And then some of those chunky black frames? For art. If you're staying for a while.'

It was the first time Billie had sounded truly excited. Audrey wondered what it would take to give them a bit of joy in a DIY project. She smiled. It was exactly what Joyce would've done.

'It's a good idea. Let me think about it.'

Just before three, Billie grabbed the brushes and wrapped them in a plastic bag from the kitchen. 'I'll put these in turps. We could do the white wall in the kitchen tomorrow if you want.'

Audrey stretched her arms wide and spun around slowly. The room felt new with its fresh coat of paint and all the cleaning she'd done. 'It looks so much better in here. I almost feel like I can breathe.'

'Well, remember that when Wy-ass calls. Time to put on your big-girl pants, Tawdry.' Billie shrugged. 'I'll be back tomorrow. You can tell me how it went.'

It did not go well.

Audrey opened Favourites in her phone and stared at Wyatt's picture at the top. He was in a suit and tie, smiling innocently at the camera. She jabbed his face with her forefinger and sat down on the air mattress. He was far from innocent, but she would be calm. She wouldn't cry. She would ask him every question, every detail she wanted to know but also didn't want to know. She would not get sick thinking about what he'd done with Charmaine.

The rock in her chest wouldn't let her breathe normally so she forced herself: in through her nostrils, and out. Again. It was just Wyatt who would answer, but was it the Wyatt she knew? The man of a million breakfasts in the seasoned cast-iron pan, the one who left his socks turned inside out in the laundry, the one with the morning hair that made him look like a character from Dr Seuss? The Wyatt of twenty-five Christmases, the one in the waiting room after every miscarriage and those horrible, inevitable dilation and curettage surgeries, the one who cried with her after the first two and eventually stopped crying? The silent Wyatt who got her handbag and held her arm while she limped to the car?

He answered on the third ring.

'Finally,' he said. 'It's about time, Audrey.'

In her head, silently, she let out a string of expletives she'd never said before. She heard him exhale as if he were exhausted by waiting for her, but she would not say anything. She would not make this easy for him. He could speak next; there was no way she was going to give in, not this time, but obfuscating and logic were Wyatt's specialty. She could see that now. That and making her feel just a teeny bit lacking, no matter how hard she tried to please him. He would try to reason his way out of this, Audrey knew. It was his style.

Finally, Wyatt spoke. 'I'm trying to think this through. You're the one who left, Audrey.'

Her voice came out too loud. 'What did you even see in her? She's twenty-five! Was it the yoga pants? Did she wave burnt sage around our house and give you a Reiki session?'

'That's not fair. You don't know her, Audrey.'

'You want to talk about fair?' Audrey's voice tilted up dangerously high, until she was shrieking. She clenched the phone so tightly she felt she could crush it.

'It just happened, Audrey. I know she's young but . . .' The pause went on forever, and Audrey could imagine his face. Confused. Handsome. He'd be rubbing his right hand through his grey hair, his left elbow leaning on the granite benchtop while he pressed his phone to his ear. There would be a long black beside him in a stainless-steel coffee cup with no handle. Audrey hated those cups. Wyatt had four of them in the cupboard, collected randomly from the Nespresso shop. They bumped around and didn't fit and cluttered up the cupboard.

'What? What is she, Wyatt?'

His voice was petulant. 'She notices things. Me. She notices me.'

Audrey breathed in so sharply she thought the pounding in her forehead might break through her skull. She'd done nothing but notice Wyatt every day for the past twenty-five years. She noticed how he liked his eggs (over easy) and how he wanted silence after dinner so he could read the news on his iPad. How he preferred peanuts in the shell (not popcorn, her favourite) for movie nights. Noticed when his shaving cream (gel, not foam) was low, noticed that he needed new jeans (a thirty-two inseam, short and hard to find) and noticed when he no longer wanted to eat her macarons (when the affair started, and he was trying to lose weight?).

She bloody well took notice when he said her chocolate cake should only be made twice a year, for each of their birthdays, and when he said he preferred to go to the gym alone. How he found it irritating if she was in the garden when he was trimming or weeding, even if she was just sitting on the patio with a cup of tea. How he hated having dinner at anyone's house and would signal 'Let's go' by patting his knees twice. How he shot down every business idea she'd ever had with a stultifying, *Birdie, in the end, we both know an advertising job is your safest bet.* Everything she'd done for every second of the day was to make sure Wyatt was comfortable and content. Seen. Known.

And the one thing she couldn't seem to do, that her body wouldn't do, the thing she needed the wine for during those years of pregnancy tests dumped in the rubbish bin and bloody toilets and doctors' waiting rooms and two expensive rounds of IVF and failure, all of that was for him, too. For both of them, for a family. In an illogical way, even the drinking was also for him, so she could fall asleep at night and didn't lose her mind, and could stop asking him *why, why us, why me, why can't this work, what is wrong with me?* And finally, when she was strong enough to give up the wine, her recovery journey was definitely for both of them. Wasn't it?

'I noticed everything, Wyatt. Except *your affair.*'

'Audrey.' His voice was tired, but Audrey didn't care. He deserved to feel tired, to feel split in two, to realise what he'd done to their marriage and their life. 'You could stay with Emma for a while . . .'

'You want *me* to move out, Wyatt? No.'

'You'll struggle to get another job. You're ageing out. I called your office and Colin told me you resigned. That's a mistake and you need to face it, whatever we decide.'

'Who is we, Wyatt?'

He paused for so long that Audrey knew, even if he didn't. Wyatt wasn't hers. He was trying to choose.

She dropped her phone and wrapped her arms around her body. She trembled and bile rose in her throat. Then she pressed the red button to end the call, and lay shivering on the floor.

CHAPTER 11

It was past midnight when the jazz started. Nina Simone again. Audrey shifted under the sleeping bag and wiped her mouth. Her nose was so blocked from crying that she'd been snoring and mouth breathing. This was how failure looked, she thought: you curl up on an air mattress in a derelict building, cry yourself to sleep and wake up in wrinkled clothes, drooling. And you wish you could sleep forever.

Which she would have done, would love to do, were it not for Buddy's jazz in the middle of the night, blasting from his ancient stereo in the cabana. She listened to Nina Simone sing 'Love Me or Leave Me', her bouncy piano belying just how truly terrible this felt: to be loved, then left. But in a way, she was the one who left, who ran away, not Wyatt. She hugged herself, trying to get warm.

She'd lost faith in everything she believed she had; it was all an illusion, the job and promotion, being valued at work and at home. No one valued her. Wyatt had replaced her with Charmaine, as Colin had with Summer. Audrey struggled to take a breath. Her time at the beach was meant to be a haven, a small break where she could collect her thoughts and get stronger before she faced the ruins of her life.

She got up shakily, needing to pee, and when she finished, she stood at the kitchen window and looked down on the garden in the dark. The music was loud enough for a party. Then the door to the cabana opened and there was Buddy, fully clothed this time, leaning over his walker. The stupid old fool pushed it out the front door towards the beach. It was dark and rocky on the path, no moonlight, and she was sure he'd fall. Groaning, she grabbed her puffer jacket and slid into Ugg boots. She clicked the flashlight on her phone and headed down the internal steps, across the dusty floorboards of the disused bakery and let herself out the front door between the potted mums. She'd have to water them in the morning when she was done rescuing pensioners who couldn't behave and take care of themselves. She hustled towards the cabana.

'Buddy!' she called. 'You need to come back inside. It's too dark.'

'No damn way. I'm going for a walk.' He waved a bottle of bourbon in her direction. 'Need fresh air.'

He was drunk; she could smell it. 'You left your music on. You're going to wake up the neighbours.'

He snorted. 'Too late, already did.'

'Buddy, it's dark. You can walk in the morning. You don't have a jacket on. You'll freeze. Come on inside.' She reached for his arm. He swatted her away.

'I'm not a goddamn kid. Can't tell me what to do.'

Drunk Buddy was even worse than Regular Buddy, if that was possible. No wonder she hadn't seen anyone visit him but

Lem. She debated what to do. More often than not, food worked. 'Look, come inside. I'll make you a sandwich.'

He paused. 'What kind?' He took a drink from the bottle and waved it at her. 'Will you put pickles in it?'

'Sure,' she said. 'You can have pickles.' She'd have to magic up a reasonable facsimile of a pickle from what she could find in his refrigerator. Maybe he had cucumbers, but she doubted it.

He pushed his walker towards the door and, like a gentleman, stepped aside for Audrey to go in first. She turned Nina down to a reasonable level and glanced at the side table next to his recliner. Three empty beer bottles, a plate with a cold piece of toast and an open photo album. A woman wearing a sixties sundress leaned inside a car, her face hidden from the camera. Her dress was simple, yellow, homemade. So many women sewed back then, a lost art.

'Don't look at that!' Buddy pulled the album close to his chest.

'Sorry, I didn't mean—'

'Goddamn interfering women! It's private.'

Audrey picked up the empties and the toast and headed to the tiny kitchen. She'd get it done quickly and go back to the flat. She opened the fridge. 'How old is this chicken?'

'Don't know. Monday?'

Audrey reached for a package of cheddar instead and checked the date on his mayonnaise. Still okay. At the back of a shelf, she found a jar of dill pickles. She'd make a cheddar and pickle sandwich, toasted, slathered with mayo like her mum used to make.

Buddy sang with Nina—'Nobody Knows You When You're Down and Out'—while Audrey made his sandwich. The room was warm from the gas heater, and smelled comfortingly of beer and darkness, jazz and rue. She set down two plates of warm toasted cheese sandwiches cut into triangles, propped up on their crusts, and handed Buddy a folded paper towel. His plate had a sliced pickle. She watched him chew, then take a long drink of bourbon.

She was so, so tired of all of it. Her shoulders slumped forward. What would Wyatt be doing in the middle of this dark night after the conversation they'd had? He wouldn't be sitting with a drunk pensioner in a run-down cabana in the middle of nowhere. He would be holding Charmaine, she was sure of it.

Her heart ached, a dull thud. She couldn't trust Wyatt, and he'd thrown her away after all their years together. She'd lost her promotion to Summer. It was ridiculous to think anyone valued age or experience in a woman; where was the evidence? There was none. No one wanted her. She rubbed the frown line between her eyes, etched deep by years of concentration. Her roots were already showing. Her hair would grow greyer by the day: the real Audrey, the older her, emerging, all alone.

Buddy lifted his plate and sniffed at the sandwich. He stared at her, and picked up the bottle of bourbon. 'Whatever it is, this fixes it. Get a glass, Sweetman.'

She shouldn't. She knew it wouldn't fix a thing. But it was there, waiting for her, and maybe it could dim the throbbing in her head for a little while. She picked up a glass and he poured. She swirled the glass slowly, inhaling the unforgettable scent of vanilla and caramel. *Progress, not perfection* was what her favourite recovery podcaster said. But it was stupid to even attempt to change; there was nothing about Audrey that was perfect, nothing at all, and she hadn't progressed a thing.

She raised the glass to her lips. The bourbon was better than she remembered, welcome and sharp, sweeter than biscuits.

And Audrey drank. Regretting, forgetting, with Buddy and Nina Simone.

'What the hell, Tawdry?'

Audrey rolled over on a scratchy sofa and groaned. 'Too loud,' she whispered.

'Damn right! What's the matter with you two old geezers? Goddamn, Buddy, were you both pissed? Why wasn't I invited to the old-people party?'

Audrey sat up and her head thumped. Welcome to day one, she thought: again. Before her throbbing brain could even get to the next remorseful, spiteful, self-berating thought about the unbroken string of two thousand nine hundred and forty-six sober days wasted, Billie was whistling in the kitchen. Loudly.

'You need to wash these dishes, you old fart! Buddy! You dead?'

'Mmmmmm,' he said. 'Shut up, Kid.'

'Look, I'll leave you two to clean up,' Billie said, in a loud voice that sounded very similar to Ruth Hickson's. 'And when you're done, text me, Tawdry. I'm ready to paint. I put my number in your phone.'

Audrey nodded, shielding her eyes from the morning sun.

After she'd picked up the plates and glasses, tidied Buddy's tiny lounge room and told him to crawl into bed, she tottered to the flat. She took two headache tablets from the bottle in her make-up bag and forced herself to drink a glass of water. Then she sobbed in her tiny shower, soaping herself with lemon verbena body wash. She'd have to start the climb all over again. She pressed the heels of her palms into her eyes. What had she told Buddy? She remembered him calling Wyatt an arsehole and doing something that resembled a dingo call, like a wolf howl, except louder. And then she'd joined in. Oh God, she'd probably told him everything.

Audrey screwed her eyes shut and washed her face. The lemon verbena smelled too optimistic for this kind of morning. Billie was coming back to paint the white walls in the kitchen, but Audrey needed something to do that didn't involve thinking about her own stupid mistakes. She shuddered, and the sick feeling dropped into her stomach. How had she arrived here again? *One day, one hour, one minute at a time.* She needed to get out of the flat. Maybe they could go into town, do some shopping, see if there was any furniture at the op shop. She'd be able to fit a few things in her car, and Billie seemed keen on talking about design. They obviously loved it. It was the least she could do after disappointing herself so thoroughly: think about somebody else for a bit, help them, that was what she did best.

And what about you? a voice whispered.

It sounded like something her mum would've said, but Audrey just scrubbed her face harder. She didn't deserve anything. Or maybe she did deserve everything she got—she was weak enough to give in to Buddy's bourbon so maybe she deserved every terrible thing that was happening to her.

When she was dressed and brewing Earl Grey, she heard a scrabbling up the broken steps. Billie opened the back door.

'Brought you this,' Billie said.

Audrey winced at the Styrofoam cup of instant coffee but took a sip.

'Bobbie said you take it weak, white and two sugars. Which is gross, Tawd. Puke! Oh, and Lem said he's getting timber to fix your steps. It might take a while, though. Hey, the walls look good. I'll get the brushes.'

Audrey nodded. She had zero energy, but if anyone wanted some remorse and self-hatred, well, she had boatloads of that. She took another sip of lukewarm sickeningly sweet coffee as penance for her sins. The memory of Wyatt's words—*You're ageing out . . . That's a mistake and you need to face it, whatever we decide*—seemed to echo in the apartment. She wanted this place to be beautiful, not tainted with failure. She wanted her mother, and Joyce's special wizardry that turned a few bits of nothing into something lovely. But that wasn't going to happen if she sat wallowing in self-pity.

'Look, Billie, let's go into town first. I thought the op shop might have a few things, and I'd like to fix this bed. I can't sleep on the floor anymore. I just . . . can't. Won't.'

Billie laughed, too loudly for Audrey's head. 'I reckon. You're probably sleeping next to spiders. And yeah, sometimes the op shop has cool stuff. I got this old watch there once, and a velvet tuxedo from the seventies that Ruth hates. There's furniture, too.'

Audrey found her phone. She exhaled and clicked on the SoberUp app; her thumb hovered over the bright green Reset button. She wanted to slap herself, but she knew that wasn't how you got any better. Forgiving yourself was how you got better. A sunrise emoji floated on the screen with a large numeral one, and a chirpy motivational quote: *Every day is a new beginning.* God, that app. For all the years she'd used it she wished they'd had a better copywriter working on the quotes.

She picked up her car keys and suddenly stopped. Her face flushed red, but there was no alternative. 'Billie, um . . .' She took a breath and forced herself to say the rest. 'Can you drive?'

'You're still *drunk*, Tawdry?'

Audrey looked away.

Billie took the keys. 'Yeah, I have my Ls. As long as someone's with me, I can drive.'

CHAPTER 12

'Do these dishes make you feel sad?' Billie asked. They stood at the glass shelves near the front window of the op shop. Most of the sets were floral and fussy, with matching cups and saucers, butter dishes and side plates, dainty soup cups with a handle on either side.

Audrey leaned in to look closer. The eight-place setting of floral dishes reminded her of the mismatched crockery her mum used to buy in op shops exactly like this one. It was just the kind of shop Joyce would've loved. Treasure-hunting, she'd called it. 'Like they belonged to an old lady who finally realised no one was coming for tea? Absolutely,' Audrey said.

'You're old, Tawdry.'

'Thanks.'

'I mean, you know, grey roots, wrinkles et cetera. How old are you?'

Audrey sighed and felt her hairline. Grey roots. What did they matter now? 'Fifty-three.'

'Weird. You're the same age as Ruth, but you seem younger. Do you have kids?'

Audrey bowed her head, picked up a pink-blossom cup and turned it over. Derby Posies, Royal Crown Derby. The very best. It was sad to think of the woman who had collected these pieces so lovingly and had passed away, or worse, left them to a relative who'd chucked them in a box and donated the expensive dinner set as if it were rubbish.

'No. No kids.'

'Why not?'

'We couldn't. Or I couldn't. We tried a few things but . . . it didn't work out.'

'Sorry,' Billie said. 'I shouldn't've asked.'

Audrey set the fancy cup back on its saucer and gave Billie a small smile. 'It wasn't so bad,' she lied. 'In the end, I came to terms with it.'

'I don't think I want kids,' Billie said. 'But I might change my mind.'

Audrey looked at the slim body in the huge t-shirt and sloppy jacket, and wondered, just for second, then stopped herself.

Billie shrugged. 'You're thinking who am I, aren't you, Tawd? Are they a girl; are they a boy? I get it all the time. I can see it in people's faces. I don't care. People are curious. Whatever.'

'No, I . . .' Audrey paused. Billie was so open, so matter-of-fact. They were more patient than Audrey would've been under the same circumstances. With her imploded marriage and the gaping hole in her career, she felt like one of those frogs she'd dissected in high-school biology class: guts cut open, skin pinned down to a board, intestines bulging. People poking at her life and cringing. She frowned. She hoped she hadn't made Billie feel the same. 'You're right, Billie. I was wondering, and it's none of my business. I'm sorry.' She straightened and tried to put on a bright, teacherly sort of voice. 'But if you ever want to talk to someone about your gender identi—'

'No thanks, dumbass.' Billie's eyes rolled practically to the back of their head. 'I've got it sorted. I know who I am. Jeez, you old people! It's so *tiring* teaching you about this! I am who I am. I'm me. A regular person. That's all there is to it.' Billie shrugged. 'Let's go to the back, Tawdry. There's a room with furniture.' They picked up a red stop sign with the word LOVE written in huge white letters instead. 'Cool. I need this.'

In the back room, wedged behind a table, Audrey found a moss-green velvet love seat, perfect for the apartment. It was worn on the underside of the seat cushions and needed new foam inserts, but the springs were fine, according to Billie who bounced up and down. Billie lined up four mismatched timber kitchen chairs for Audrey to inspect. The back of one chair was carved with daisies.

'This one's yours,' Billie said, hoisting it above their head and setting it down in front of Audrey. 'I'll use the shaker one. The lines are perfect, look.' They flipped the second chair over like an expert. 'I could strip it down and sand it.'

Audrey traced a finger over the daisies carved on the back of her chair. 'How do you know so much about this?'

'I love Industrial Tech. Well, I did. That was the only class I topped. Timber, you know, carpentry. Not English. Not Physics. Ruth spat the dummy at that!' Billie laughed and raised an eyebrow. 'Then eventually she got me a carpentry tutor.'

Audrey couldn't help herself. She snorted. 'Are you serious?'

'I am, Tawdry, because you know . . . if a Hickson is going to love carpentry, they have to be the best carpenter there ever was at their private high school. So, I dropped it to piss her off. Then I left. I hated that place.' Billie bent down and inspected the elegant spindles of the chair.

'Do you ever think about going back? Trying again?'

'Don't get all therapy on me, Tawdry. Been there, done that, hated the t-shirt.' Billie hoisted the chair overhead. 'Let's go.'

Audrey sighed. 'Give me your LOVE sign, Billie.'

'I can pay for it, Tawd.'

'Nope. You're the driver. The love's on me.'

It took half an hour to unload Audrey's car. In the end, she bought the entire set of Royal Crown Derby (foolish, but too pretty to leave) and four timber chairs they'd puzzled into the car, along with a large rococo mirror and the cushions from the love seat. The volunteer cashier promised that her husband would drop off the sofa in his truck for a ridiculously small delivery fee.

On a whim on the way out, Audrey bought a newish fedora for Buddy, less grubby than his current one. Then she saw a yellow vintage shift dress hanging on a hat stand, the softest shade of creamy butter, a heavy shot silk fabric with short sleeves and a chain of white lace daisies sewn around the empire waist. It smelled like moth balls and was probably too small for her, but she picked up the price tag. Twelve dollars, a bargain. Her mother would've loved it, and Audrey couldn't leave it behind.

When they got back to the apartment, Billie and Audrey carried the chairs and cushions through the dirty bakery, up the staircase and into the flat. They were laughing too loudly to hear the first knock on the door, but then there was pounding, and it sounded urgent. They looked at each other and Audrey shrugged before heading over to it.

She opened the door to Ruth Hickson. Audrey followed her through the tiny kitchen and into the main room where Billie stood scowling. Ruth sniffed and set her handbag next to her on the floor. 'Well, it's a firetrap but at least it's clean.' She crossed her arms. 'I thought I'd find you here. We had a deal, Billie. Homework during the day.'

'Screw your deal,' Billie said.

'Would you like tea?' Audrey thought about all the reasons why tea with Ruth Hickson wouldn't go well with a hangover that followed a previously unbroken two thousand nine hundred and forty-six days of sobriety. She gritted her teeth and walked to the kitchen to put the kettle on.

'No, I wouldn't. Billie, you have schoolwork to do.'

'Except I haven't done any in two months, Ruth. And you can't make me. I'm not your shitty employee. But if I was your employee, or maybe, say, a husband, I'd leave you like everyone else does because you're such a domineering bi—'

Ruth screamed.

The sound—sharp, impossible—hung between them.

A whipbird whistled on the lawn below. Audrey ran from the kitchen and reached them as Billie shoved Ruth's shoulders, hard and fast. As if in slow motion, off balance, Ruth stumbled backwards, and Audrey grabbed for her hand. Missed.

Ruth landed on the floor on her backside. She rolled to her knees. Billie ran out the balcony door. There was a thump as they jumped past the broken steps.

The apartment was silent, except for the sound of Ruth's ragged breath.

'Here, you can sit here,' Audrey said quietly. She pulled over the kitchen chair, her new chair, the daisy one that Billie had found for her.

Ruth straightened her cardigan. 'I'm leaving.'

'Maybe you should sit, though? You just—'

'Maybe you should stop encouraging my child.'

Audrey stared at Ruth's mouth, a wrinkled line, the black hair, severe in its dyed bob. Her thoughts tumbled together. Billie blamed Ruth for the divorce, but it was never that simple. Ruth's husband had been a stay-at-home dad when Billie was little, and of course that would have made them extra close. Maybe Ruth had not been as present as Billie needed? How much time could a Federal Court judge spend with a child, especially when her husband was doing all the caregiving? A woman like Ruth would think the love and parenting were done; she'd assigned her husband to it and ticked it off a list. But Billie? Billie seemed to hate Ruth and blamed Ruth for forcing her husband to find another relationship, to go off and leave them both. Manipulative. Demanding. Always right, always the judge. Billie had said as much about their mother.

'You're so *unusually* interested in my child.' Ruth wiped her mouth with a tissue from her pocket. She stared at Audrey. 'Why are you spending so much time with a sixteen-year-old? Alone. The two of you.'

The insinuation washed over Audrey. She was astounded. She felt a shame that wasn't hers—it wasn't true!—but Ruth's ugly words were there, crouching in the room, and couldn't be unsaid. A tremor chilled its way through Audrey's body. What

Ruth was suggesting was impossible. Audrey would never hurt a child, never. She was only trying to help.

'What are you saying?'

'You heard me,' Ruth said.

It was ridiculous! Billie was a . . . what were they, exactly? Billie was a funny teen, more like a . . . child . . . the kind of free-spirited child Audrey might've had all those years ago if only she'd had better luck. But she wasn't Billie's mother. She felt sick. 'Billie needs a friend. I was trying to be kind.'

Ruth sneered. 'A stranger? So helpful to a teenager? You can see why I'm concerned. Go back to the city, Audrey. You don't belong here.' Ruth yanked her handbag from the floor and walked to the stairs.

CHAPTER 13

By late afternoon, storm clouds hung black and dismal over the beach. Audrey had walked the length of it four times after Ruth left, twelve kilometres of peace and quiet except for the hammering of her own thoughts. The ball of her right foot was sore, an old injury from her running days, but she ignored it and kept going. Most of the time she didn't feel her age at all, except for things like her foot, or her face in the mirror, which sometimes startled her with its loosening skin and hooded eyes.

Love Your Age, her innovative campaign: that should have worked.

Her marriage: that should have worked, too.

Having a holiday in a seaside town? Simple for most people, but not for her. She'd made the mistake of getting involved, always assuming she could fix everything, bake some cookies, bring some joy, interfere. In fact, all she'd brought on herself was the contempt of other people. She was old, jobless, betrayed in love, directionless and holding her breath in a tiny community when she should be dealing with her life in the city. And a retired judge had just accused her of being a danger to an unhappy sixteen-year-old she'd only been trying to help.

Emma would know what to do.

She took her phone from her pocket and tapped on Emma's picture, second under Wyatt in her Favourites, and probably soon to become first if Charmaine had her way. But reception was poor on the beach and the call didn't go through. She'd have to try from the flat. In fact, why not just go back, pack up everything, get on the road and then call Emma—explain that she needed to stay for a while and get help sorting out her life in Sydney. Emma was strong and capable; she'd probably have it all figured out and come up with a doable plan by the time they finished dessert.

The sky was ink where it touched the sea, layered with light grey and charcoal like a dark cake rising overhead. She could smell rain coming. The ocean rolled on, hypnotic, and the freezing winter wind buffeted her steps. *Go back, Audrey, and confront your mistakes*, she told herself sternly. That was what an adult would do. That was the plan of an adult woman in control of her life. Go back, retreat, regroup. But wasn't moving forward better somehow? She didn't know. She trudged up the path beside the cabana to keep ahead of the rain. The air was misty with the threat of it; she felt it in her hair, wild, silver roots with blonde, windblown. Buddy's door was banging in the wind. She stepped on the porch to pull it closed, hoping he wouldn't hear her.

'Sweetman!'

No, she didn't want to. She didn't want to talk, to help an old man who was all alone but seemed to be doing fine. She thought about the bourbon and the lack of visitors. Or mostly fine. She sighed, considering all the things no one knew about families and closed doors, and heard the scream all over again, sharp and dreamlike, coming from Ruth's howling face. Poor Billie. And Ruth? Billie had shoved her hard, knocked her down. It made Audrey wonder who was hurting whom, but she knew it was both of them.

Both.

Could it be that somehow, in some way, she had also been hurting Wyatt? The childless life, the truce, how different they were at the core of themselves, how she'd been absorbed with grieving her mother? It didn't excuse him, but it was there in the background, a simmering discontent.

Buddy shuffled forward with his walker. 'Goddamn deaf, are you, Sweetman? I said come in.' Buddy's eyes were bloodshot, and he hadn't bathed or shaved. He was wearing the same brown trousers and grey cardigan. 'Come have a drink.'

Audrey shook her head. 'No. I can't. I . . . shouldn't've last night.'

Buddy wheeled towards his recliner. He poured himself a bourbon from a mostly full new bottle. 'Ah, it's like that, is it? Well, I find it helps and just keeps right on helping.'

'I find the opposite, but I see your point.'

'Sweetman, you are one screwed-up lady, aren't you?' He waved at her with the glass, and it sloshed convivially. 'How old are you?'

'Fifty-three. Young enough to be your daughter,' Audrey said firmly. Buddy must be over eighty, maybe even closer to eighty-five. She didn't think he'd got the wrong idea, but she wanted to be clear about her intentions. Ruth's accusation! Preying on Billie! Her stomach clenched.

She watched Buddy take a drink, and then another. When he poured a third, she had to get out of the room, or she'd be in trouble. Again.

'Have you eaten anything?' she asked.

'Not hungry.'

'You need to eat.'

'Says who? I don't need nobody telling me! They all leave me alone, except that Judge Judy, well, she's a right nosy old cow. She hauled the doc over here before you came and *insisted* that he give me an assessment for the old folks' home. ACAT assessment for the senile oldies.' He took a sip and grinned. 'But Doc Flood's a good bloke. He talked to me for a bit and saw I could take care of myself. Got interrupted by a call from his girlfriend, Lorraine, or Lucinda somebody. Kept saying, "I'll meet you later, but I'm helping a mate first." See? Doc's a mate of mine. Checked my cupboards for food and everything, but Lem's got that sorted for me. I have a standing order and he delivers.'

'Let me guess—roast chicken and pickles and bourbon?'

Buddy raised his glass. 'Cheers!'

'I'm going to go make you a proper meal. It's the least I can do after your . . . after last night.' Audrey sighed. 'To thank you—'

'For listening to you crap on about that goddamn husband of yours, what's-his-name? Wippet? That was nothing, kid. Losing someone is a cruel, cruel business.'

'Give me thirty minutes,' Audrey said. 'I'll be back.'

She glanced out her kitchen window. The sea churned against the darkening sky and a cape of winter rain pelted down. She relaxed her shoulders in the kitchen's warmth, and reached into the fridge for eggs, cream, brie and the smoked salmon she'd packed when she'd fled the city. It had been less than a week since she'd left Charmaine at her own front door, but it felt like months. Thunder boomed, and she caught a glimpse of lightning. The thought of the clean spaces of her kitchen at home, her expensive mixer, her favourite glass bowls in various sizes, French whisks and a handmade bread hook, her double oven and thick black granite benchtop made her want to weep. While she preheated the oven for a cake, she chopped an apple, creamed butter with sugar, mixed the batter and sprinkled the top with a simple streusel of sugar, flour and cinnamon. As she worked, rain drummed on the roof of the apartment. Audrey let tears slide down her face. If only life were as easy as baking.

She scrubbed a two-place setting of the Royal Crown Derby in the scratched sink. It would be a shame to leave the dishes dusty and unused in the apartment but what would happen to them in Sydney? What would happen to all their things? Most men like Wyatt moved themselves and their girlfriends to apartments overlooking the water in Cremorne Point anyway . . . free from the roof and gutter-cleaning that was always required in the leafy North Shore, free from the lawn maintenance and the plumbing that was always a problem with the relentless tree roots. The wife—the *ex-wife*—rattled on alone in the big house with only quick visits from the adult children and grandchildren for comfort, but in her case: no one. Audrey would be as alone as Buddy, maybe even for the rest of her life.

No. They'd sell the house, and she could start over. As big as it was and in a good suburb, she knew it was worth a lot. But another job in advertising? That felt impossible. She'd been doing everything she could at UDKE to stay relevant, and in recent years she'd been given all the campaigns that the younger execs wouldn't tackle with any maturity or finesse. Audrey had believed she'd offered a depth of experience, a wisdom, a set of marketing and strategic insights that a younger person couldn't—but she was wrong.

And dating? An image of Dr Flood in his grey t-shirt, reaching out a tanned hand to touch her shoulder, crept into her mind. He'd told Ruth he was dating someone and taken a call from a woman at the General Store. But he'd been so kind to her on the beach, asking about her mother. He understood what grief was, and he was easy to talk to . . . but of course he was. He was a doctor and used to listening to people. Audrey shook her head at her own stupidity. She should be thankful to be standing in a kitchen that was warm with the scent of apple cake, and not outside in the rain. She had so much, even if she didn't have love. Anyway, everyone knew how hard it was to find a decent partner over fifty. Her divorced friends spent their girls' nights showing Audrey men's profiles on dating apps. No one seemed to be seeking a woman over fifty. Of course, women also partnered up with each other. Nowadays people loved who they loved, and Audrey didn't feel the slightest bit of interest in judging anyone. An image of Billie gleefully waving the LOVE sign made her breathe in sharply. She hoped they'd find the love they needed, a better kind of love than Audrey had in her marriage. No, Audrey didn't judge.

Except for cheating. Oh, she could judge that all day, any time, just ask her.

Her phone timer went off like a cricket chirping, but the wind had picked up outside and it was hard to hear. Audrey opened the oven door through sheer instinct. The scent of cinnamon and baked apple drifted through the kitchen, a smell of home. She transferred the warm apple cake to a cooling rack on the table, diced up the smoked salmon and the brie. She'd pack the dinner in a cardboard box from the op shop and keep the frittata hot in the cast-iron pan.

Her hair was damp from the rain and Buddy was dozing in his chair when she carried the box into the room. She set out the plates and cutlery, the cups for tea. As she cut the frittata, melted brie stuck to her knife and she thought about how nice it would be to grow herbs in the overgrown flower bed in front of the cabana, to toss some fresh dill in a frittata like this one. Dill, coriander, basil: surely she could keep herbs alive? Gardening was Wyatt's job, and she'd never been that interested in trying. He always said he didn't want her help. She placed a warm slice of frittata on Buddy's plate and touched his knee.

'Ready to eat?'

'Smells good,' he mumbled.

They ate in silence while the wind blew outside the cabana and the rain beat down on Buddy's tin roof. When he finished his piece of apple cake, he squashed the rich crumbs on the back of his fork. 'Been a long time since I had a cake like that.'

'My mum used to make them. We didn't have much money, but she always said if you had butter and an apple, you could make a decent cake.'

He held out his plate. 'She still around, your mum?'

Audrey slid another warm slice onto his plate. 'She passed away nearly a year ago. But this was one of her favourite places. She brought me here a few times when I was girl. I guess it was more affordable back then. It's why I came here when, well, you know.' Thunder cracked near them, and Audrey flinched.

Buddy nodded slowly. 'Mighta been her. The cake. Years ago, now. I was . . . a little worse for wear. Sittin' on the beach. Lady came up with an apple cake. Left the whole thing for me. The whole goddamn cake.' He shook his grey head.

'Sounds like something my mum would do. I don't remember it.' Buddy would've been exactly the kind of person Joyce noticed on the beach: alone, unloved, needing life to be a little sweeter. 'What about you, Buddy? Do you have any family?'

'No,' he said in a way that made it clear she shouldn't ask again. He slopped some bourbon into his tea and took a large swallow.

She watched the cup go up to his lips.

'If you want a dri—' Buddy began.

'No. I should clean up. And I came to tell you it's time for me to go back to Sydney. I'm only putting off the inevitable.' Audrey stood and collected the plates.

Buddy coughed until his thin shoulders shook. 'Shame. I thought maybe you could help me with Judge Judy,' he said. 'Someone like you from the big city might be better at dealing with her.'

Audrey exhaled. She wanted to wash the dishes, tidy up and leave the town to their own problems. How Ruth ran things in the tiny beach village was none of Audrey's business. But Buddy had let her stay in his flat. He was an old man, old enough to be her father, not that she'd ever had one. He didn't have much support in the village, from what she'd seen. And she was Joyce's daughter.

'Help how?'

And that's when he pulled out a letter from the Community Association.

CHAPTER 14

'Judge Judy's out to get me.'

Audrey flipped over the paper and scanned the second side. 'It's a quarterly meeting to discuss tourism and a few other matters. That seems okay.'

'She's got the local pollies on her side.'

Audrey nodded, reading. 'Politicians?'

'All those arse-wipes. She's got herself on the local council.' Buddy did a perfect Ruth imitation, enunciating every syllable. 'She wants me in an old folks' home, but I'm not going. Don't want to. Can't afford it, neither.'

Audrey poured him the last of the tea, too cold probably, but he'd only dilute it with bourbon anyway. 'I think there are some state ones—' she started cautiously.

'With those old people drooling and pissing their pants and watching TV? I don't want that. We all know how bad the free ones are. I'd rot in a place like that. I'd go barmy.'

Audrey gave him a tiny smile. 'You wouldn't have your jazz or your . . .' She nodded in the direction of his teacup.

'Right. Well, I'm not going, no matter what Judge Judy says.'

'Buddy, she can't make you move anywhere.'

He leaned forward and pointed at the cake. Audrey served him a third slice. 'She could if she got a council building inspector out here. She'd be going to the council meetings with the inspector. She told me this is an illegal dwelling because it has plumbing; it's supposed to be a cabana. The plumbing, according to Judge Judy, makes it a granny flat, but I'm not sure where the old cow expects me to sh—'

'Okay,' Audrey cut in. 'I get it. But if she orders an inspection, you may not have a choice. Could you move into the flat? I've painted it and cleaned it up.'

'Are you stupid, Sweetman? The stairs. Lem'd have to carry me up and I've got Buckley's of getting back down until I carked it. I'd only go out feet-first. And what about my fitness regime? I have to get to the beach for my swim. I'm committed to it,' he said, with a dead-serious expression.

Audrey rubbed her temples and tried not to remember the sight of his jiggly backside. 'It says the meeting is on Wednesday afternoon. That's four days from now.'

'You could go,' Buddy said innocently. 'And if Judge Judy attacks me when I'm not there, you could explain why I need to stay. You're a big city girl, aren't you? You could have a crack!'

'Buddy, I need to go back to Sydney. I'm . . .' She looked at his face, his grizzled beard, the unwashed clothes. Ruth might be right; it probably would be better for him to be in a community of older people, with regular care and hot meals and combed hair. But who knew what was better for someone else? Buddy seemed sharp, except for the drinking, and what would happen to him if he didn't have his morning swim and his jazz, his regular natter with Lem when he dropped off his groceries, the sea, the sky? He had no family and no other friends. What kind of life would it be to sit in a state aged care facility until he died? He might be old, but he still had the right to enjoy his life. Those places could be terrible, and the private ones were expensive. Even if he could afford it, if he sold his waterfront property, he'd probably hate a luxury retirement village with their craft rooms and chair yoga and retired bankers bragging about their golf games.

She sighed. 'I'll see what I can do. I'm not promising anything, though. Ruth's tough. She's got the law on her side. She'd probably love to see your property sold to a developer.'

The rain pelted down on the tin roof, making her nearly miss his reply. 'I have a feeling you could be tougher,' he said, 'and my gut's never wrong.'

Four days later, Audrey found herself standing outside the front door of Ruth Hickson's home. It made sense that the meeting was there—there was no community hall or any other space where the villagers could gather. The General Store was too small, and the only other public place seemed to be the launderette in a shed attached to Sherry's Holiday Flats.

Audrey had spent Monday morning washing her clothes and then Buddy's, plus all his bedding, his towels and kitchen towels. She'd even washed his well-used striped beach towel.

'You must be Audrey Sweetman.' Shez had tugged down the hem of her denim miniskirt. 'Remember me? CEO and entrepreneur.' Shez pointed a white gel nail sprinkled with diamantes at the striped towel. 'I see you've got Buddy's gear. Are you some kind of do-gooder?' Her large gold hoop earrings swung. 'Or are you after Buddy's money?'

Audrey held up a pair of saggy underpants. 'I don't think he has any.'

Shez threw back her head and laughed. 'Well, he owns that property. He bought it with insurance money back in eighty-eight, that's what Lem said. He got some kind of big payout from his insurance company for something, an accident maybe, but I don't know the details.' Shez raised a slim shoulder in a shrug. 'Lem overshares. That man's desperate to marry me. But I already had a starter-marriage, and it wasn't rated five star. I tell him, "Think, Lem, think! You've already got the milk. Why buy the cow?"'

Audrey tried to suppress a smile and kept folding Buddy's laundry. Shez looked young, but it might just be Botox and hair colour. It was sometimes hard to tell. There was no way of knowing how long Shez's starter-marriage had been. Audrey wondered if that's what she'd end up calling her twenty-five years with Wyatt. She'd planned for it to last a lifetime, but would it? She wasn't sure.

'Lem's a keeper, but not if he keeps on talking hollow matrimony. I'm too independent.'

Audrey frowned. 'Don't you mean holy matrimony?'

'Whatever you say, Audrey. Anyway, Lem helps Buddy a lot, takes him groceries, the dodgy old coot. No one else does.'

'How do you mean dodgy?'

Shez rolled her eyes. 'Think, Audrey!'

'Sorry?'

'Buddy's drinking himself to death in a granny flat. Why? What's his story? Why would anyone buy beachfront forty years ago with an insurance payout and leave it to rot? It isn't Aussie, is it? We're property-mad! Sydney house prices are higher than Manhattan. This shed, even. Lem says I could renovate it; it'd be worth a fortune!' Shez raised her dark, template-like eyebrows. They were perfectly symmetrical and had the look of being drawn carefully with a magic marker. 'So why would Buddy buy a place and act like he can't be bothered? He could cash in. He hasn't been upstairs for years.'

Audrey folded another plaid button-down shirt, a hole in the left elbow. If Buddy owned the building, he could sell anytime. It was waterfront. And Buddy selling was probably exactly what Ruth wanted. Bulldoze the building and the cabana, and the new owner would put up a nice big McMansion for a rich Sydney investor, another house in the long queue of beautiful holiday homes along the beachfront. It would increase the value of all their properties. Maybe selling was the best option for him. She'd have to give up her flat, of course (an unreasonable pain jabbed her heart), but she'd be leaving anyway. She'd come to chase a memory of her mother, but Joyce was gone forever. Whitehaven Bay was a hideaway and a refuge, but she needed to move forward. As she carried Buddy's folded laundry to the cabana, she reminded herself of all the ways the people of Whitehaven had been good to her and imagined tossing joy over them like imaginary confetti. Billie and Buddy, Shez and Lem. Even Dr Flood.

But now, standing at Ruth's door ten minutes before the Community Association meeting was due to start, Audrey had to force herself to knock. The door swung open. Billie stood in front of her, dark circles under their eyes, drowning in a huge black hoodie printed with a realistic photo of a man's torn-open chest, revealing the bloody heart and ribs. Audrey blanched. Ruth must hate every choice Billie made.

'How are you?' Audrey asked.

''Bout as good as you could imagine, Tawdry.'

The scream and the push lay unmentioned between them. Billie looked away. Audrey heard the hum of voices inside.

'I brought you something.' She held out a Royal Crown Derby dinner plate piled with warm chocolate chip cookies. 'And this one's for the meeting.' The spicy scent of cinnamon buns with cream cheese frosting made Audrey's empty stomach rumble.

Billie opened the door wider and reached for the cookies. 'Ohhhh, I love these. Thanks. They're in there.'

Audrey hadn't been inside Ruth and Billie's lounge room when she stayed the night. It had a spectacular view of white beach and azure sea, with lovely oatmeal-coloured overstuffed sofas, huge abstract art and an expensive-looking wicker patio set sprawled on a large glass-fronted balcony. Lem and Dr Flood chatted near a table that held a few scant plates of cheese and biscuits. Audrey set down her cinnamon buns and glanced at Dr Flood. He smiled at her. Was he remembering her fall down the steps and how disoriented she'd been? Or maybe thinking about how sad she had seemed on the beach the last time they met, when she confided in him about her mother's death? She returned his smile awkwardly.

'Those smell good, Audrey. You want a cuppa?' Lem wore his shiny machine-washable suit with an orange and baby blue striped tie. 'This is a monthly. Only time we get a stickybeak at Ruth's property, so we all turn out.' He handed Audrey a cup of tea so steeped and black it would keep her awake half the night. She glanced across the crowd of strangers. Shez sat on Ruth Hickson's glass and chrome console table, swinging her orange, self-tanned legs. She smiled and waved magenta nails at Audrey. Audrey waved back.

'Looks like you're settling into village life,' Dr Flood said. 'It suits you.'

Audrey flushed. 'It's beautiful here, but I'm leaving next week. Buddy asked me to come to the meeting.'

'Is he worried about Ruth getting rid of him?'

Audrey nodded. She took a sip of tea and tried not to grimace. Absolutely terrible. 'I thought he might be overreacting.'

'Oh, everybody knows,' Lem said. 'Lots of people are keen on getting Buddy out. Only thing that stops Ruth is what Doc Flood would think.'

'I'm not so sure about that, Lem, but Buddy seems fine for the time being.' Dr Flood looked around the room and his eyes settled back on Audrey. 'What do you think, Audrey?' He waited, gazing at her. She felt her cheeks burn.

'He's a survivor,' she said. 'There's a lot more to him than meets the eye.'

Dr Flood nodded. 'You're not wrong there. It's good to see you, Audrey. You're a breath of fresh air around here.' When he moved away to chat with Robert, she realised with a start that part of her wanted him to stay.

Ruth stepped in front of the windows and rang a tiny brass bell. People took their seats, and Audrey found herself squashed on a small sofa between Lem and Robert. Lem leaned in. 'Ruth acts like the doc's her best friend, but he hasn't been here long. Anyway, I think she's out of luck. I saw him FaceTime some lady just before you got here. He sure seems to like you, though, Audrey.'

'The first order of business,' Ruth said, 'is the environmental impact of tourism.'

Robert groaned. 'She's acting like a greenie, but I don't think she cares. It's just the cars come summer, and the fact that they park on the street in front of her place.'

'Tourists are *loving us to death*,' Ruth said in a voice more like a hysterical Instagram influencer than a retired judge of the Federal Court of Australia. Audrey assumed Ruth had dreamt up the slogan and was planning to repeat it all summer long. As far as advertising taglines went, Ruth's was pretty good; it certainly incited rage and was easy to remember. 'Every summer, there's more rubbish and traffic, the beach will be spoiled, and there are too many holiday renters. We don't need renters! And the noise from that biker gang. They rode motorcycles through the village two weeks ago, dozens of them, tearing up the streets! We need restrictions on weekend traffic, or tariffs, or both. I'm proposing a task force to investigate. We need to protect the environment!'

'Yeah, if only it was that, Ruth,' Billie called from the back of the room, 'and not just you protecting our driveway.'

There were a few laughs and Shez snorted, but Ruth cleared her throat and kept on. She'd chosen people for the task force; she, Robert and Justin Flood were the logical choices. The two men agreed, but Audrey thought she saw Dr Flood grimace. Then Ruth moved on to new business about resurfacing the main road and how to approach the local council, especially since there was a massive pothole in front of the General Store.

Lem's stomach growled, a low rumble.

'Hey, Ruth, let's wrap it up and have some afternoon tea,' Shez said. 'I brought lamingtons . . . my cousin Kylee made them so they're drier than dust. But Audrey baked for us too.'

'Shez loves lamingtons,' Lem said to Audrey in a stage whisper, 'but I reckon she'll change her mind when she tries your cinnamon buns.'

'There's one more important matter,' Ruth said, looking around the room. 'It's about Buddy and his property. As you know, the bakery's derelict, the back stairs are broken, completely unsafe—'

'I'm fixing those, Ruth. Just haven't got around to it yet.'

'You're a bludger, Lem!' Billie called. 'Too busy getting facials with Shez at Curl Up and Dye!'

Lem blushed. 'Men get facials.'

'Too right,' Shez said. 'Trixie does more than hair. She's giving Lem and me Full Frontal Dermal Invasion. It takes a battery of sessions. Don't knock it till you've tried it.'

Across the room, Billie snorted.

'You should get on that yourself, Billie,' said Shez.

'I'm sixteen,' Billie said.

Shez shrugged sadly. 'So, a little late for you, but better late than nev—'

'Enough,' Ruth roared. 'That's irrelevant. Buddy's alone, without any caregiver. There's also the issue of the illegal cabana he's living in. He's elderly and obviously not of sound mind. How many of you visit him?'

There were murmurs from the back of the room, and Lem and Justin Flood raised their hands, but no one else stirred. Audrey flushed, thinking of just how lonely Buddy must be.

Ruth cleared her throat. 'And how many of you have seen Buddy completely nude in the morning?'

Every hand shot in the air. Audrey raised hers gingerly.

'Well,' Ruth said. 'What will we do about it? Nudity? Dementia?'

'I'll get him some budgie smugglers,' Shez called from the side of the room.

'Shez, you know how goddamn hard it is to get those swimmers on. So tight I can barely do it, and I'm only seventy-three,' Robert said.

'A bigger towel!' Billie called out from the back. 'One that hides his butt cheeks. Or a mankini!' Laughter erupted across the room.

'Could work,' said Lem, getting up to demonstrate, 'what with the mankini straps and all hoisting up his business. Or if he's facing forward, then the bigger towel could cover his butt crack if he just sorta draped it more—'

Robert started to giggle, and Audrey fought herself to keep from grinning. From across the room, Dr Flood winked at her. It was crazy, but true: Buddy was Buddy, and he entertained the entire village with his big personality.

'This isn't a joke. It's indecent exposure.' Ruth frowned.

'Aw, come on, Ruth, it's only indecent if you think his old doo-thingy's worth looking at,' Shez said. 'Buddy's been here forever, and he keeps to himself. Well, mostly . . . aside from the public indecency.'

'Shez is right,' Lem said, and Shez threw a sweet smile in his general direction. 'He's not hurting anyone. If the doc says it's safe for him on his own, I'll keep getting his groceries.'

'He's a pensioner who needs professional care.' Ruth turned to Dr Flood. 'Justin, I'm sure you agree with me?'

'I can't discuss a patient,' Dr Flood said, 'but as his friend . . . the village is his home. For the moment, I think he's fine.'

'But he's completely alone! It's unsafe, and it's our responsibility to put him in care.'

Billie stepped forward. 'He's not alone, though. He's got Tawdry Hepburn. Right, Tawdry? You'll look out for him.'

Everyone stared. Audrey pushed herself out of the feather-filled sofa and cleared her throat.

'Hi.' She glanced around the room. Forty or more faces turned to her. 'Uh, for anyone I haven't met yet, I'm Audrey, Buddy's tenant. He, um . . . asked me to tell you he's fine. I know he's older, but he's not unwell.' She winced, thinking of the bourbon bottles. 'He gets around with his walker, and I cleaned up his place. He should be able to live on his own for a while yet. He's got all his faculties—'

'Not if I've seen him *naked*, he hasn't!' Ruth shrilled.

'She has a point,' Robert said. 'Who'd be dumb enough to show his willy to a judge?'

'Are you leaving, Tawdry?' Billie's chin was up, but it trembled like it had after Ruth had screamed at them. Audrey tried to smile. She wanted to reassure Billie, but no one deserved to be lied to. Not like Wyatt had lied to her.

At the front of the room, Ruth snorted. 'Don't be ridiculous, Billie. Of course she's leaving. Audrey lives in the city.'

'City girl.' Lem nodded. 'Not enough for you to do out here, I reckon.'

'It's not that.' Audrey took a deep breath. 'It's beautiful here, but I do have to leave soon.'

'Do you think he needs care, Audrey?' Dr Flood asked. 'You've seen him quite a lot these past few days.' He smiled at her, waiting.

'I think Buddy's fine. He still gets around and seems sharp. And he doesn't want to go into aged care. He doesn't think he belongs there,' Audrey said.

'I agree,' Shez said. 'Think of the oldies in assisted living staring at his bare butt. Would they *consent*?' She shook her head until her gold hoop earrings jangled. 'I wouldn't. Not in my indoor heated saltwater pool.'

'But his drinking,' Ruth said sharply, 'we could find him dead or worse, that he's fallen and can't get up.'

'Exactly how long are you staying, Tawdry?' Billie stared straight at her.

Their tone made Audrey think that even if Ruth and her child hated each other, the apple didn't fall far from the tree. She bit the inside of her cheek, her hands sweating. How could she suddenly be responsible for an isolated old man and for not disappointing a teen who had a terrible mother? She was supposed to be sorting out her tangled life! She thought of Ruth's scream and Billie's white face, that look of fear, and how she wasn't exactly eager to confront Wyatt in their huge home and start looking in earnest for a job. She took a shaky breath. Another week wouldn't hurt, and maybe she could help. 'I can stay a little while longer, but I have to go back soon.'

Shez hopped off the console table. 'All good then,' she said cheerfully. 'If Buddy carks it, Audrey will discover the corpse and let us know.'

'But Audrey can't p-possibly—' Ruth stuttered, her face red.

'She can for now,' Dr Flood said. 'We have faith in her. Meeting adjourned.'

CHAPTER 15

'Are you sure you should be here, Billie? Will your mum be okay with it?' Audrey asked.

'It's not like you're some weird old dude, Tawdry, who's going to chase me around and muscle me onto the broken bed.' Billie waved a paintbrush at the bedframe that Audrey hadn't managed to fix.

Audrey rolled her eyes. 'If you're so good with timber, why don't you have a go at fixing the frame? I'd murder someone to get this air mattress off the floor.'

'See, Tawdry? Murder. You are dangerous. Mother knows best.' Billie walked over and inspected the broken bed. 'I could do this, easy. I'll ask Lem when the wood for the stairs is coming. I could fix it so fast.' They avoided looking in Audrey's direction. 'I'm sure I can do it for you, and then you'll sleep better.'

Audrey touched Billie's arm. 'You know I'm not staying here forever, Billie.'

Billie stood motionless, staring out the bay windows to the street below. 'I know. I'm not stupid, Tawd.'

'I get that you don't want to talk about it, but . . . are things okay for you? And Ruth?'

Billie turned. 'You mean The Scream and me, uh . . .' Billie mimed pushing something heavy. 'Like, is our family dysfunctional and—quote unquote—"physically unsafe"?'

Audrey winced.

'In this instance, Tawdry . . .' Billie attempted a laugh, 'I think it's just a little bit of . . . I stepped over the line three months ago when we fought about going back to school in the city, and gave Ruth the tiniest shove, and whoops, it happened again.'

Audrey patted the sleeve of Billie's hoodie, a red one this time, with a dead cockroach upturned on the front. 'It's not good, Billie. Are you okay?'

Billie sighed. 'You're sounding like a mental-health campaign, Tawd. R U OK? R U OK? Well, no, I'm not freaking okay, okay?'

'Okay. You want to talk about it?'

'Fine. But I want cookies.'

Audrey filled a Royal Crown Derby plate with chocolate chip cookies from the container on the counter and put the kettle on for tea. She carried it through to the table and pulled out her chair with the daisies carved on the back and pointed. 'Sit. Eat. I'll get you some milk.'

'These are exceptional, Tawdry. You're the only way to get good cookies around here. Downstairs used to be a bakery when Ruth and Dad bought our place in the eighties. I saw some pictures. Ruth in red jeans with a perm this high. You young beauties used a lot of hairspray. And the fringe!' Billie laughed.

Audrey waited in the kitchen while the kettle boiled. If there was one thing every woman knew how to do, it was hold space for someone else to talk through their problems. She swirled the

Earl Grey tea bag in the pot, then carried two cups and saucers to the table, one with tea, one filled with cold milk for Billie. Audrey sat and crossed her arms.

Billie took a sip. 'Dad's an architect. He's in Sydney with his wife and new kid.'

'Ah,' Audrey said.

'Yeah, Ruth screwed that up. Dad and me were a team. He raised me, and Ruth was gone all the time, always in court. Whenever she was home, she was a total bitch, and just ordered him around. He wasn't successful enough for her. And anytime I wasn't perfect, she yelled at Dad. But now . . .' Billie bit a cookie, 'he has this cute teeny weeny tiny baby, a little tiny girl, a girly-girl, pink everything up the yin yang.' Billie shrugged. 'I hate that ugly baby. It's wacko. It drools.'

Audrey smiled. 'Kind of hard to hate a baby, huh?'

'Yeah, well, it's boring, Tawd. A boring old story like yours. You've seen what Ruth is like. Not exactly lovable.' Billie's jaw was set. 'Dad went back to work part-time, and then he ran off with Debra from his firm. Now he sends me these guilt gifts, except I hate them all. He sent me a drone and I hate that, for example. He gave me a new laptop and, okay, I don't hate that, but I did engrave the lid with skulls. Debra was so pissed! She's asked me to be, you know, not like this when I visit.' Billie swept a hand up and down in front of themselves and twirled it around their pierced ears.

Audrey nodded.

'I scare the baby, apparently. I scare Debra too, but she doesn't have the balls to say. Debs, he calls her. Or Debbie.'

'Hmmm,' Audrey said, and bit into a cookie. 'Sounds like a—'

'Primary school teacher? Yeah, she's very energetic and on the go, is our Debs. Mid-thirties, loads of Botox. She hates me. You'd hate her.'

Audrey sipped her tea. Of all the people she did not want to relate to on any level, Ruth Hickson was at the top of the list. But there Ruth was: another older woman replaced by a younger one. Wyatt had made Audrey a cliché.

'Debra gets Dad to listen to her music and be on Instagram, and wear trainers, and gel his hair, but it's all complete bullshit. And the baby is just a baby, but—you know, an upgrade on me. Version 2.0. Dad's probably hoping she works out better. And Ruth is stuck with me, and yeah, all she gets is child support for another couple of years, which she doesn't need, obviously. But she took him to the cleaners anyway. We got pretty much everything. He's living in an apartment he hates, so Ruth says that's something, at least.' Billie shrugged.

'And you and Ruth are here.'

'We are. Because . . .' Billie took a second cookie and waved it around, 'according to Ruth's story, I have social anxiety—which I don't, by the way, I just hated the dumbasses at my school.'

'You said she told everyone you had glandular fever.'

Billie snorted. 'That was yesterday's excuse, Tawdry. Now it's my fake anxiety. So: still homeschooling. We barely go to Sydney anymore.'

'Do you text your friends?'

Billie laughed. 'What friends? Private school pricks. Besides, I have you two geriatrics to take care of. And damn, I'm gonna go feed Buddy some of these.' Billie hopped up with the plate and was out the back door.

'How are you going to jump off the steps with the cook—' but Audrey heard the thud on the ground and Billie yelling at Buddy's door.

'Hey, you old fart, Uber Eats! Tawdry's biscuits!'

The voicemail from Wyatt came late on Tuesday night, a week later, when Audrey was reading in bed. She'd decided to let Billie loose on the IKEA website with a sensible budget, but no other constraints. Billie had been so desperate to fix up the apartment, and decorating took Audrey's mind off the miserable results she'd had from a quick and depressing online job search. Basically, every job was too junior, and the only creative director role going had asked for five years of director-level experience.

What did it matter, indulging Billie a little and letting them do something that brought so much happiness? Besides, it felt like the least she could do for Buddy—leave the place better than she found it. Any improvement made her feel a little less guilty about the inevitable fact that she would one day go back to Sydney and desert him, and the delivery had transformed the apartment. Soft white gauze curtains hung from new black curtain rods Billie had installed above the bay windows, and there was a velvet wing chair with a matching footstool in the corner beside a floor lamp, which made a perfect reading nook. Billie had insisted on several black frames in different sizes that looked elegant on the white wall beside the back door. When Audrey protested that she didn't have art to go in them, Billie had returned the next morning with three simple charcoal drawings, clippings from a magazine, and one black and white image of a seascape that looked suspiciously like it had been cut out of a coffee table book. The effect was artistic, beautiful. Best of all, they'd 'fixed' Audrey's bed by ordering a new wrought iron one and hauling the broken frame out the back and stowing it behind the cabana. Audrey chose white sheets and a white waffle duvet cover, then added European pillows and a soft throw blanket the shade of winter ocean.

She set down her paperback, a tattered copy of *The Alchemist* she'd found in the attic, and idly picked up her phone. It had been on silent on the bedside table, and she'd missed Wyatt's call. Her heart hammered when she pressed play and heard the familiar voice.

Birdie, can you meet me tomorrow? Please. I've booked us in at Happy Lucky Go-Go for dinner. I . . . we need to talk. A pause. *I . . . listen, I think I've made a mistake.* There was another pause so long she thought he'd finished, and then—*I miss you.*

She dropped her phone to the bed, her stomach churning. Did he want her back? Could she forgive him, or trust him again? Audrey stared at her shaking hands on the crisp white duvet, the book in her lap open to the title page. *To Clara, my treasure forever, Love Bernard—Sydney, 1988.* Bernard had written the inscription nearly forty years ago. Whoever they were, Bernard and Clara, she hoped they'd made it to forever.

'Been a while, stranger!' In her red Happy Lucky Go-Go t-shirt and black jeans, Bec leaned in and air-kissed Audrey first on one cheek and then the other. Her long black hair was parted in the middle and slicked into a ponytail. She raised her voice over the noise. 'Dad's been wondering where you two have been. Wyatt's at your table.'

Audrey nodded. 'Thanks, Bec. Business been good?'

'Chockers.'

'And how's uni?'

Rebecca led Audrey through the maze of tables. 'It's okay. I don't exactly love studying medicine but . . .'

Audrey raised an eyebrow. 'Your dad loves it enough for both of you?'

Bec laughed. 'Yep. You know how it is. He'd choke if I told him I'd rather run this place. I'd love to have my own business. Who wouldn't? Hey Wyatt! Here she is. Should I give you a few minutes before I bring your food?'

Despite the one-sided conversations Audrey had rehearsed in the car, her chest ached when she saw him. The old Wyatt sat at their usual table, as if everything that had happened was from a multiverse he didn't remember. This Wyatt beamed at her as if he'd forgotten their last terse exchange on the phone, and everything that had come before that. Charmaine. The Volvo. His lies. He stood. 'I already ordered. I got the usual. You look good, Birdie. Your hair. It suits you.'

She'd pulled her hair back, and the silver roots made her eyes bluer. But roots were the least of her problems. This wasn't about her age, was it? They were both in the middle of their lives, but he had jumped ship, sailed away with a younger woman. Audrey sat and took a sip of sparkling water. Her throat was blocked with rage.

'Why did you call, Wyatt?'

He began talking, a monologue filled with his innocence and regret. That he'd never planned on having an affair. That it just happened; he fell into it. That Charmaine convinced him! She did! That Audrey had seemed so distant for so long, wrapped up in her own world of problems at work and unable to notice him at all. Well, he was right about the work problems. Her stomach tightened. She wondered for the hundredth time what her former colleagues would be thinking of her.

Around them, the special Asian delicacies they loved grew cold and congealed. Audrey picked at her rice. After the first tense half hour, Bec avoided their table completely, and in the noise and the flow of patrons who came and ordered and ate and left, Wyatt talked.

It was endless.

Something about it seemed forced, off, but she didn't know why. Who was this man, apologetic and concerned, his brow furrowed with sorrow? Was it real? Could she trust him? Wyatt pleaded with her. He explained that he'd been rash, stupid and childish. He said he knew Audrey was the woman he loved. They had history, a life together, and they could start over. He raked his hands through his hair and looked earnest and charming and flawed. He was different, he swore he'd changed: he understood what he'd almost lost, and he was scared he was going to lose her forever. He seemed desperate for her to understand him.

Finally, he stopped. She struggled under the burden of his words, the weight of his repeated apologies. She trembled with cold and exhaustion. All she wanted to do was crawl into their king-size bed with her own familiar pillow and the thousand thread count sheets and go to sleep. She hadn't slept well in weeks.

She glanced down. Bec had delivered two fortune cookies with the bill. What was she looking for? Something to help her decide if she should give Wyatt a second chance. It was their life, and all their history together on the line. Her home. All they'd built. Wyatt said he wanted her back, but did she want him? She picked up a fortune cookie and cracked it in two. Foolishly, she looked at the broken pieces for a sign. Her mother had always believed in her fortunes and always saved them, even the silly ones. The paper was folded on one corner, the ink fuzzy and black. Audrey squinted at it.

Love will come back to you.

She shook her head, incredulous, and slid the fortune in her wallet, just as Joyce used to do.

'It's time to go,' she said, more weary than sure.

'Home?' His eyes pleaded with her.

'Home.'

CHAPTER 16

'Birdie. I'm begging you. Please.'

Their kitchen under the soft downlights was clean and modern compared to her ramshackle rental at the beach. Audrey set her handbag on the benchtop. She was so tired. In her chest, her stomach, her aching head, she felt pain for them both. She slipped off her heels and winced. Could they start over? Not unless they tried. Wyatt stepped closer and she shifted away from his body, so they weren't touching. He'd wronged her, but he'd also loved her for years before that. Hadn't he? Had she loved him? Of course she had. She'd loved faithfully, blindly, like she did everything else: expecting that if you were decent, if you were good, life would love you right back. Except it didn't always. Wyatt might be her only chance at love.

'I forgive you,' she said, and tasted the lie in her mouth like bile.

Mercifully, he stopped talking then, and she trudged upstairs. Wyatt followed her. Without looking at him, she pulled off her dress and bra, undies, everything, and slid into the familiar relief of her own bed. She felt the slight indentation on her side of the mattress, then Wyatt's heavy arm draped across her, his nakedness, his warmth. It was like thousands of nights she'd known before, and everything else—the recent months that, in hindsight, seemed just a little off, a little wrong, inexplicable, not her Wyatt at all, his weight loss, the nights of working late—she would forget about them, put them behind her. She would make herself want only this: peace and quiet, her home, his arms, mouth, familiar body this close to hers. Lying beside her was the old Wyatt she'd known since she was in her twenties.

Then he was on top of her, asking her if this was okay in that patient way of his she'd always loved, and then she stopped.

Stopped breathing.

Gasped. Searched. Trapped.

The air?

Gone.

'Birdie?' Wyatt rolled off. 'Birdie, are you okay?'

She sobbed, choking, tried to breathe and couldn't. Sat up. Heaved.

Air.

'You're panicking. You're having a panic attack. You need to breathe, Birdie. Breathe in, that's right.' He held her. Finally, she was able to take a long breath, her head pounding while she sobbed. He held and rocked her, cradled in his arms.

'Let me get you some water, okay?' He walked naked from the dark room, humming. She struggled to suck in air, to calm herself, while her brain rebelled against Wyatt's self-assured hum. Why was he humming at a time like this? She squeezed her eyes shut and focused on breathing. He'd gone straight back to being dependable Wyatt, good in a crisis. Making all the decisions for both of them. She could hear him in the kitchen, opening the cupboard, getting a glass. He'd put in an ice cube. He'd choose crystal, not an everyday glass that was battered from the dishwasher. And he would be smiling to himself, relieved she had changed her mind. Audrey thought about that hum and what it meant. It meant something . . . untrue, but she couldn't grasp what. Breathe, she told herself. Her body was trying to tell her something. *What was he hiding?*

She rolled over. His phone was on the bedside table. She picked it up and hammered in the pass code. It took four panicked tries to guess it. And there they were: texts to Charmaine. About meeting her tomorrow in the city. That he loved her. That he had to be careful and take it slow to get what he wanted from Audrey.

Her mind spiralled down, and the truth stood up on its own wobbly legs. That's what Wyatt was hiding: he wanted everything. He didn't want to split the little empire they'd built, and he didn't want to lose more than his half to a woman who was no longer employed and unlikely to find a new job, comparable to her last, at another advertising agency. Audrey knew from the divorces of her friends that the less financially stable partner usually got awarded more.

Wyatt didn't want her back; he just didn't want to lose anything.

In the meantime, Charmaine would be his mistress, and Audrey would be his fool. She flailed from the sheets as if she were drowning, reaching, stumbling to her chest of drawers. When he came back, she was dressed in a grey tracksuit, knees shaking, sitting in the chair.

'Birdie? What the—'

'I read your texts, Wyatt.'

'No! Birdie, I—'

'Don't. I know.'

He sat on the bed, put his head in his hands. 'You're imagining—'

'Go, Wyatt.'

His face was grey, and he was a liar.

It was after midnight by the time she heard Wyatt's car drive away. She stood in the middle of her beautifully renovated kitchen—the white cabinets with glass-fronted doors, the black granite benchtop, her expensive mixer on the counter, the state-of-the-art coffee machine. The liquor cabinet above the fridge. Wyatt had kept it empty during those early years, the grim ones when they'd tried and tried for a baby, but in the past few she knew he'd slowly introduced bourbon, which she didn't like, and then gin, which she did. She walked over and yanked it open. The bottles sat, innocent, half full . . . or were they half empty? Audrey stared for a long moment.

This was what she always did, wasn't it?

This was who she was, right?

A person who, with every yes and batch of cookies, with every drink, stuffed the truth down further and further and made herself smaller and smaller so other people could do whatever they wanted while she shrank back, trying to protect herself by being nice. Wyatt. Colin. Summer. Even Ruth Hickson. Even Buddy. Even her loving and slightly unreliable mother, who dragged them from unit to cheaper unit all through childhood. Audrey had been nice through it all.

Except it wasn't self-protection. It didn't work. Every *yes* was a lie.

Audrey had been lying to everyone her entire life. And lying to herself.

She slammed the door and backed away from the cabinet. She walked to the garage and found what she needed, then stepped into the pitch-black garden. Around the pool were Wyatt's winter bloomers: the polyanthus, the fairy primrose, the luculia and his favourite: the daphne. The daphne stood a metre high, full of white blossoms tinged with pink. It had taken him seven years to establish it and get it to bloom. The scent was beautiful, fresh vanilla, sweet in the winter darkness.

She hacked it down.

All of it.

Every plant, every flower.

She cut the precious daphne so close to the ground that her nails were caked with soil. Then she gathered heads from the bed of daisies he'd planted for her and carried them inside. She ripped paper from the printer tray in the study and whacked it on the benchtop. A pair of scissors. A fine black pen from her desk. Flour. Sugar. Eggs. Vanilla. Paper daisy petals. She searched for Joni Mitchell on Spotify but found Charlie Dée instead, and let Charlie into her wounded heart, let her sing on repeat about Canada and about life being both bitter and sweet.

Three hours later, her counters were filled with fortune cookies, but these ones told the truth. Delicate biscuits, pressed with flower petals and baked flat in rounds, each with a fortune she'd handwritten on blank slips of paper tucked inside. To shape the fortune cookies, Audrey had painstakingly folded each hot baked disc in half, crimped them over the edge of a glass and let them cool. Truth in a biscuit, honest and bittersweet.

Dear Karma: I have a list of people you missed.
The cavalry isn't coming. You need to rescue you.
Some things break your heart but fix your vision.

The more Audrey wrote, the more she cried over how foolish she'd been. By the time dawn filtered through the French doors and the kookaburras started chortling, she'd scrubbed the kitchen spotless and packed her fortune cookies in Tupperware containers for Billie. The back garden looked like a mob of kangaroos had burst through, trampling the cherished plants Wyatt had grown.

She walked to the bedroom and packed her clothes in every suitcase they owned. She carried the suitcases and her mixer to the car. She left a voicemail for Emma. Then she showered for the last time in their beautiful home, dressed carefully in a black cashmere turtleneck and wide-legged grey trousers and drove to the city office of Wainscot Smith Roberts and refused to leave until she got a morning appointment with the best divorce lawyer in the city.

'Eshana Patel can see you at eleven. Her rate is six hundred dollars for thirty minutes.'

'Fine. I'll wait.'

'But it's eight forty-five.' The receptionist stared at her. 'Do you want someone to bring you a coffee?'

'I'll get it myself,' Audrey said.

Hours later, when Audrey walked into the plush office on the thirtieth floor, she thought Eshana Patel looked slightly older than her photo on the law firm's website. Her caramel-coloured suit was elegant, her black hair carefully styled. She wore tortoise-shell glasses and had a huge diamond on her right hand. When she shook Audrey's in a firm grip, Audrey stared at the ring. Eshana shrugged. 'A gift for myself,' she said. 'To me, from me. I find it's more dependable that way. What can I do for you?'

'I need a divorce lawyer.'

'I'm the best. Well, top four in the city, probably. Tell me what you want.'

Audrey inhaled. 'A fresh start. As much money as I can get. Our house is in a good suburb; it should be worth a few million.'

'The usual—an affair?' Eshana Patel said, waving her phone. 'Mind if I record this so my PA can make notes?'

'Yes, that's OK.' Audrey waited for some sort of compassion, but Eshana simply clicked record.

'Kids?'

Audrey shook her head.

'What do you know about your finances?'

When Audrey finished, Eshana looked straight into her eyes without blinking. 'I'll begin making enquiries with Wyatt's legal counsel today, assuming he's signed someone. I warn every client that this could be difficult. There's no fifty/fifty split under Australian law. Usually the financially less able party gains a little more, which would be you because you're not working, but we'll have to fight. You have the stomach for it?'

'I do now.'

'Fine. You know my fees. I'll investigate and call you with a plan. I recommend you pull all the assets from any joint bank accounts now.'

Audrey nodded distractedly. Her chest ached, and her head. 'I will.'

'No. I mean now, as in, the second you walk from my office, you log in to internet banking in reception and do it.'

'Thank you.'

'Don't thank me yet. I haven't won.'

Audrey shook her lawyer's hand. 'Well, I'm going to,' she said.

CHAPTER 17

Their usual café in the Strand Arcade was packed at lunchtime, but Audrey found a tiny marble table for two. A cranky waitress dumped two warm glasses on the table and took Audrey's order for a bottle of sparkling water. Audrey pulled *The Alchemist* out of her handbag while she waited for Emma, and when she opened it, a photo strip fell out. A pretty teen in an acid-wash denim jacket and neon pink t-shirt smiled in the first frame, then poked out her tongue in the second, then had her eyes shut in the third. The fourth and final photo was blurry, where she'd thrown her head back and laughed, her silver hoop earrings tangled in curly black hair. Audrey turned it over: scrawled on the bottom was *S.T. 1986*. Her phone pinged and she set down the book.

Emma: *Do you want chocolates from Koko Black?*

Audrey sent back: *I'm a woman in distress. Of course I want chocolate!!!* She picked up *The Alchemist* and read for a few minutes. She stopped in her tracks when she came to a line about listening to your heart because you could never escape what it had to say.

Emma sashayed to the table, gorgeous in a black lace dress, tights, black winter coat with a fur collar and a more delicate version of combat boots with silver buckles.

'Sweetie!' she said, and kissed Audrey's cheeks, then set a Koko Black bag and a slim package tied with a bow on the table. 'Just a little gift for you. It feels like it's been ages. Tell me everything.'

Audrey cradled the gift box in her hands. It smelled like Chanel No. 5. 'I've missed you.'

'Me too.' Emma glanced at Audrey's roots. 'Should I call my stylist? I can muscle you in.'

'Not just now. I want to see what it looks like. The silver.'

Emma squinted at her. 'It looks . . . older, but good. I think it suits you.'

Audrey tore off the wrapping and saved the ribbon, grosgrain, thick and creamy. Inside the box lay a necklace with a heavy heart pendant.

'No more wearing it on your sleeve, Sweetie. So, catch me up. How did dinner go?'

Audrey took a wobbly breath and started talking. She'd cried too much to cry anymore. In between two hours of confession and strategising, they ordered toasted chicken and cheddar paninis with slices of avocado, drank mineral water, had two long blacks each, and split a crunchy Italian pistachio biscuit covered in flaked almonds for dessert. Emma squeezed Audrey's hand. 'But are you sure you want to go back to the beach? Why not chuck all Wyatt's stuff into the street and keep your beautiful house? Maybe it's better to dive in, Sweetie. No point in putting it off, is there?'

Audrey paused. It was difficult to explain. The beach was connected to her mother, to safety, and she needed more time. 'I can't stand to be in the house, and I can't keep it.' Audrey tilted her head to the side. 'I feel like the house was lying to me, right along with Wyatt. I'm going to sell. Plus, the mortgage, Emma. We're almost done, but I couldn't carry it alone, not even with my old job.'

'I don't mean to pry, but—are you okay for cash? Now that you're not working?'

Audrey shrugged. Her job search so far had yielded nothing. She'd been working towards the promotion to creative director for years. How would she ever find something comparable?

'I'm looking for work, but we'll get a lot for the house. My lawyer thinks I'll get more than half, enough for a townhouse, or a nice apartment—'

'Closer to me! I'll start looking. You know I can spot a good deal,' Emma said.

'Thanks. I have some cash in my own account but it's not a lot. A few thousand dollars. Eshana Patel told me to grab everything from our joint accounts, but we don't have any money there. We were both putting all our pay into the mortgage. The house was appreciating so much, it seemed the sensible thing to do.'

'You're lucky property prices are so high. You'll be fine, Sweetie.'

Audrey sipped her lukewarm coffee. The finances, at least that was one area where she could trust Wyatt. When they'd purchased their home, it had been a stretch and the mortgage was enormous, but Wyatt had insisted they buy a big house, suitable for a family, close to private schools. Another wave of hurt swelled in her throat. Like all the houses across the city and especially in their suburb, their five-bedroom, three-bathroom home had appreciated so much it would fund their retirement.

'Do you want to move in with me for a while?' Emma asked.

Audrey shook her head. 'Thanks. But I just . . . there's a few things I need to do at Whitehaven, a couple of people I need to say goodbye to.'

'Be careful, Sweetie. Is this you being agreeable again? Cookies for everyone? I know you.'

Audrey stared past Emma's shoulder at the shoppers rushing through the arcade, strangers everywhere. She thought of Whitehaven Bay. It seemed oddly *busy* for a quiet beach village, and somehow, she'd landed in the middle of it. She mattered there. Billie, Buddy and Shez dropped in. They were more than willing to tell Audrey exactly what they were thinking, and she'd seen enough of them to believe she could take them at face value. They were the polar opposite of Wyatt and her old life.

'I'll be back in a couple of weeks. Then I'll ramp up my job search and get the house on the market. But if you want to look for real estate . . . well, I'd love that, Em. It'll have to be modest, though. I'm starting over.'

'That's okay. Beginnings are good.' Emma reached over and squeezed Audrey's hand. 'We all get through our problems in the end. Sometimes they can be the making of us.'

'I hope you're right.'

Emma waved over the grumpy waitress and clicked open the real-estate app on her phone. 'Can you clear these and bring us another biscuit? No, bring two. I need sugar to work my magic.'

By the time Audrey pulled up in front of the old bakery building that evening, the sky was nearly dark. Upstairs in the unlit apartment, the gauze curtains floated in the bay windows, and she longed to crawl into bed. But she'd picked up a roast chicken and a Greek salad for Buddy on her way through town. First, dinner for Buddy, then bed. She knocked on his door and when he called out, let herself in.

'You're spoiling me, Sweetman,' he said gruffly. 'There's two plates in the kitchen.'

'I had a huge lunch with a girlfriend.'

'You all right? You look like something the cat dragged in.'

'It's over with Wyatt,' Audrey said. 'I'm filing for divorce.' She set down her bags and breathed in. The room still smelled of lemon polish.

'You don't want a . . .' He gestured to the bottle on the end table.

'Don't even offer, okay?'

'Rightio.'

Someone knocked on the door. 'You old farts in here?'

'Come in, but don't be a pain in the arse!' Buddy called.

'But I'm so good at it.' Billie smiled at Audrey, but their face was white and strained.

'Do you want dinner?' Audrey asked.

'Nah. I ate with Ruth. Got any biscuits?'

'I do, in the car, some special ones. Make yourself useful and put the kettle on. I'll get them.' As Audrey left, she could hear them arguing, something about smelly old man socks and comb-overs and who'd be dumb enough to wear a goddamn ugly jumper with a bleeding eyeball on it. Outside the stars were bright in the blue-black sky. Audrey inhaled the scent of eucalyptus and sea and exhaled to the rhythm of the rolling ocean. The waves were relentless but calming, and a peace settled over her. The street in front of the old bakery building was empty. In the houses up on the hill, lights shone, and Audrey imagined people tucked inside for a long winter evening. She couldn't wait to unpack in the flat, put on her warmest pyjamas, climb between clean white sheets and sleep. She'd need a wardrobe or a rack for her clothes, and now that she'd brought her winter things, there was no reason to hurry back to the city, was there? Beach life was simple. Manageable. She could look for a new job from anywhere, and in the meantime, she could rest. No chance of running into any former colleagues, no explanations needed. No Wyatt. No Charmaine. No Colin or Summer.

A Mercedes convertible drove up the street slowly, and when it got close, the passenger window slid open.

'I thought it was you, Audrey.' Dr Flood turned down his music. Motown. 'Thanks for speaking up for Buddy at the meeting last week. How are you tonight?'

How was she? Everything had changed in the past twenty-four hours. Her marriage had ended; she'd never trust Wyatt again. Her life had imploded, and she needed to start over. She fought the urge to sigh and instead lifted her chin. Being back at the beach should have felt like waiting in an airport for a delayed flight, an irritating hiatus to tie up loose ends before heading back to tackle her real problems in the city. But the night sky glowed with stars, the street silent save for the low hum of Dr Flood's car. Somehow the rickety life she'd created for herself at Whitehaven felt familiar, a bit like the home she'd shared with her mother as a girl. They'd only had a series of humble rented apartments, yes, but everyone was welcome there: friends and neighbours popping around for a cuppa, sticking their noses into Joyce's business, taking an interest in raising Audrey, sharing a slice of homemade cake and a laugh. Sugar, flour, butter, love.

'Buddy's waiting inside for me with Billie. He's been a good landlord. He deserves a little help.'

'A rescue from the Community Association, you mean?' Dr Flood chuckled. 'I don't think Ruth likes his swimming much.'

Audrey grinned back at him. 'No. But she should be grateful. I bet he keeps the tourists away.'

Dr Flood laughed. 'You're not wrong there. I should get going, but I'll see you around. Maybe at Robert's. He's a top bloke, but that coffee . . .'

'Terrible.' Audrey smiled.

'Absolutely the worst I've ever had,' Dr Flood said, shaking his head. 'And no matter what I do, I can't get him to change my order. He calls it a Depresso.'

Audrey laughed. 'Sad coffee, hey?'

'The saddest. Anyway . . .' he smiled up at her, 'they're probably waiting for you inside. Night, Audrey. See you soon.'

'Bye.' As he drove away, Audrey wondered if she should've invited him in for tea and a biscuit. It's what her mother would have done. He obviously cared about Buddy, and maybe he was lonelier than she knew, despite his dating and his comfortable lifestyle.

Nina Simone started singing from Buddy's record player in the cabana, a loud cover version of 'Here Comes the Sun'. *Next time I see him, I just might invite him in*, she thought, and despite everything, she started to hum along. After all, it was always good to make new friends. Audrey pulled the Tupperware container from the back seat. She'd see what Buddy thought of her fortune cookies; she hoped the snarky fortunes would make Billie smile.

CHAPTER 18

'God, Tawd, what were you thinking?' Billie said. 'Listen to this, Buddy: *Some people are such treasures that you just want to bury them.* I should've saved this one for Ruth!'

'You're cracking them all, you greedy bugger. Give me one.' Buddy reached out a hand and Billie tossed a fortune cookie across the table at him. He caught it midair. Billie gasped.

'What? I played cricket.'

Billie snapped another cookie and munched on half. 'How about this one: *What a year this week has been.* I mean, that one's old people funny, but still, pretty cool. You wrote these, Tawdry? I didn't think you had it in you.'

'What, being a sarcastic jerk?' Audrey sipped her tea and realised she'd found it refreshingly easy to be a writer of fortune cookies that told the truth. In her current mood, she'd be happy to do it again. Venting in fortune cookies was easy, especially after the night she'd had with Wyatt. It was simpler to tell the bitter truth on paper than it was in person. She turned a fortune cookie over in her hand, the petals from her daisies baked in beautifully on the outside of the biscuit.

Her floral fortune cookies were a strange hybrid, familiar and unique, prettier than any she'd ever seen, and she knew they tasted better, too. She inhaled like a seasoned baker; the cookies smelled delicious—like toasted almonds with a hint of vanilla. Most people loved fortune cookies and couldn't stop themselves from nibbling on them. Bec at Happy Lucky Go-Go had told her there'd been an investigation in 2005 when one hundred and nine people in America played the same lucky numbers printed on the back of a fortune and had to share the twenty-five-million-dollar lottery prize. She said customers were horrified anytime the restaurant ran out.

'People sort of believe in fortune cookies, even if they get a weird one,' Bec had said. 'And if you get a good one, you save it. You put the fortune in your wallet or something. It's tradition.'

Audrey could've used her laptop to type and print her fortunes properly, but she'd handwritten them with her favourite thin black marking pen, crying in her kitchen. Each bitter truth had forced its way out of her. She hoped Billie wouldn't open the ones she'd written about Wyatt and Charmaine: pithy little sayings like *All you need is love and a low IQ.*

Audrey set down her teacup and sighed. She knew what she had to do, but that didn't make it any easier. Until she heard from the lawyer, there would be no point in worrying. She could rest now, take some long beach walks, find a good realtor, keep searching online for her next agency job and figure everything else out after Eshana Patel called. She wanted to stay as far away from Charmaine and Wyatt as possible, and far away from the house, too. Away from the city, and all her failure there.

'Ruth's good at sarcasm, with a side order of bitchy.' Billie crunched a fortune cookie. 'But I didn't think you'd be, Tawdry. These biscuits taste amazing. Usually they're so stale.'

'You've only had factory-made, not fresh.' Audrey nibbled a corner of a cookie. They were delicate enough to melt on her tongue, the vanilla and sugar balancing each other out perfectly. The daisies made them just a tiny bit bitter, but the blend of flavours was lovely. 'How's it going with your mum?'

Billie half-shrugged, started to talk and then stopped themselves and folded their arms across their chest.

'Better out than in, Kid,' Buddy said.

'Fine, you old coot: she's threatening to send me to the city to live with my dad. She says she needs a break from "coping" with me full-time.' Billie made air-quote fingers around the word coping. 'She's given me a million rules and expects me to change, or she'll force Dad to take me. They were on a Zoom call fighting over who wants me the least.'

Audrey couldn't imagine her own mother not wanting her. They'd been more like friends than parent and child and Joyce's only rule was 'Stick together'. It had been just the two of them, the tiniest family, but Ruth and Billie were also two.

'What do you want to do?' Audrey asked.

Billie's voice was low. 'I want to stay here.'

Audrey leaned back and waited for Billie to say more. Billie wiggled in the dusty armchair and sighed. 'Dad doesn't want me. Debra hates me. They don't know what to do with someone like me. When Dad introduces me, he says: "Billie is *unconventional*."

It makes me feel like a warthog at Taronga Zoo. Ruth expects me to be a CEO or something and I'll never do it.'

Audrey looked at Billie's shaved head, bent over to read a fortune. It was easy to see the good in people, even if they couldn't see it in themselves: Emma's generosity, Buddy's naked swims that entertained the village, Shez's good-hearted enthusiasm beneath all her make-up, Lem's loyalty. Billie, with their energy and creativity, their fierce need for independence. Billie was strong and creative and funny, but they couldn't seem to see it. They were the kind of child Audrey wished she'd been.

She breathed in, her chest aching. *No.* Billie was the kind of child Audrey wished she'd had.

'They don't want me.' Billie shrugged and blinked. 'Nobody does.'

Audrey's breath caught in her throat. She held out a paper napkin and squeezed Billie's arm. 'That's not true, Billie. Buddy and I want you—'

'No, we don't. Well, I sure as hell don't.' Buddy poured himself another bourbon. 'I'd be afraid you'd be piercing my goddamn ears in my sleep, Kid.' Audrey paused for half a beat and gaped at him. Buddy sputtered and laughed at her until he coughed. He winked at Billie. 'Goddamn Sweetman's getting soft in her old age! The look on her face!' He laughed again. 'Imagine Judge Judy in her bed shaking her skinny arse and you leaning over to pierce her earlobe with a big needle and a drippy ice cube . . .' cackled Buddy, waving his bourbon in Billie's direction. 'Who in hell'd want that? I don't want ya.'

Billie hooted. 'Yeah, me wearing my hoodie with the severed hand . . . just a little drunk and shaky . . .'

Audrey rolled her eyes; Billie and Buddy crowed with laughter. She barely heard her phone ring inside her bag, and she reached in to grab it just in time. 'My lawyer,' she mouthed. 'Hello? Eshana? I thought you'd call in a couple of days.'

'I'm working late. I started investigating your case and I ran into a problem.'

CHAPTER 19

Audrey took a deep breath. 'What's wrong?'

'Your house has a first *and* a second mortgage, with a total of 3.4 million drawn down. Even considering the sales history in your suburb, you're likely to sell for a debt. I'll start mediation with Wyatt's lawyer.'

'What?' Audrey sank back into Buddy's couch.

'Do you need me to repeat it?' Eshana said. 'You have a shared debt you owe to the bank.'

'But that's not possible! We've been putting everything on the mortgage. Both of us. We should have that much in equity. We were nearly ready to discharge. Wyatt handled it, but he told me—'

'You weren't checking your mortgage account, were you?'

Audrey's hands shook. 'I didn't think . . .'

'Did he get you to sign papers?' Eshana asked.

Her head throbbed. 'Yes, a couple of years ago, but I thought—'

'Wyatt's drawn down funds to invest in a resort in Queensland, on a golf course. The developers were anticipating tourism from Japan, Japanese golfers, and the local airport tried to get international status for direct flights, but it didn't happen. The resort is failing, and investors have been asked several times to inject funds to keep it afloat but . . .'

'The investment's worthless.' Audrey squeezed her eyes shut.

'How could you not know?' Eshana sounded incredulous, and Audrey imagined her widening her principled brown eyes, as if Audrey was the stupidest woman she'd had the privilege of representing in her long and illustrious career as a divorce attorney.

'I . . . I've always transferred money to his account for repayments. We've done it that way since we got married. I thought . . .' What? That they were a team? Her stomach rolled over. That she didn't need to *monitor* him? A vision of Charmaine in cowboy boots made her wince.

'Well,' Eshana said severely, 'lesson learned. Unless you have funds elsewhere, I recommend you hire a more affordable lawyer. Or do you want me to continue representing you?'

'I—no, I . . . thank you.' Audrey's stomach churned. 'I'll take it from here.'

'I assumed. Good luck, Audrey. I'll have my PA email the invoice. It's due in seven days.'

With hands shaking so badly she could barely hold her phone, Audrey stood.

'What the hell was that, Sweetman?'

'Bad news. I need to go.'

'Sit,' Buddy said. 'We're nothin' but ears.'

Wyatt didn't return her calls. At three in the morning, nauseous and unable to sleep, she'd texted him a video-call link for noon the next day, along with a warning: *We need to talk, or I'll show up at your office.* She wanted it to be a serious meeting, not just a call he took on his phone. Audrey spent the ten thousand hours between three and five-thirty in the undertow of fear and fury, half-listening to old episodes of a sobriety podcast she loved.

'Who's taking care of you?' the host asked. 'It's *you*. You might as well get started.'

She got up and took a long beach walk: darkness and waves, cold winter wind, and eventually a bleak and rainy dawn. She walked until her hands were red and freezing, then headed to the apartment and made herself a cup of tea. She flipped on her laptop to look for work, and the search results were dismal. Junior positions at new agencies. It was the last thing she wanted to do, if they'd even hire her.

The lawyer's email slid into her inbox. Eshana Patel's invoice was charged in six-minute increments: she'd spent over four thousand dollars to learn that Wyatt had squandered their entire life savings. After paying Eshana's bill, she'd have less than five thousand dollars to her name. Audrey started shaking, the shoulds coming at her fierce and ugly: she should've stayed at UDKE and worked under Summer, she should've checked their mortgage account, she should've had her own nest egg, she should've known that something, everything was wrong.

At noon, when Wyatt logged in to the call from a meeting room at the office, his face looked older than she'd ever remembered seeing it.

'What were you *thinking*?' Her voice was strangled, furious.

He rubbed his hands through his hair. 'All the investors are in the same position. It should've worked. But then . . . the airport didn't qualify for international status. They asked investors for a second round of capital, and then another round, and . . . it just went belly up from there. I thought they'd get a bailout, maybe even from the government because it was connected to the airport but . . .'

Audrey swore, a string of words she'd never said together or out loud.

In his leather chair, Wyatt flinched. 'I thought I—'

'You thought what, Wyatt?'

'I thought I could fix it, but I couldn't.'

Audrey's mind raced. She stopped herself from screaming. He'd ruined their marriage and their finances. He'd ruined everything. Was that why he'd wanted her back? He needed her to find another job and keep on working to pay their bills? He wanted to buy more time until he could *fix it* and go off with Charmaine?

'Does Charmaine know you have *nothing*? That you've lied about everything? These stupid investments, too?' She pounded her fists on the table so hard that it rattled. She'd never done a thing like it before, and it felt absurd but also somehow powerful, like she was starring in a Netflix drama.

Wyatt glanced at something. Or someone. His voice wobbled. 'When you got pregnant, I did the *right thing*, Audrey. I married you. But all you did when we lost the baby was fall apart and drink. You barely pulled it together. I'm not the only bad guy here.'

Audrey froze. She saw Wyatt glance off-screen. Of course, Charmaine would be there, sending him comforting vibes and planning a detox to get rid of all the negative energy. They'd have talked about Audrey, probably endlessly. Raking over her faults, discussing her. Everything was draining away, like the feeling she got when her feet were in the sand and the waves rolled back. She was disoriented, falling. Had she ever loved him, this grey-faced man who'd just admitted he'd married her because he was trapped?

When her voice came out, it was barely a whisper.

'I did everything I could to make you happy. Everything. I gave up my business. I tried to have a family. When you asked me this week, I almost took you back.' She heard a gasp. Charmaine. 'But never again. You're a liar, Wyatt, and you ruined us.'

Other words came to her then, accusations she wanted to scream at Wyatt and Charmaine. But what was the point?

'You don't have a job, Audrey. You'll drink again. You might as well file for bankruptcy.'

'I know exactly what I'm going to do.' She had no idea what she was going to do.

'Really? What?' he sneered.

'None of your business. I never should have bet on *you*, Wyatt. I should've bet on *me*.'

Audrey slammed her laptop shut. Her thoughts tumbled together. She had enough money for a couple of months' rent, and that was possibly just enough time to do a job search. She rested her head in her hands. She knew how that would go: headhunters treating her like she was ancient, interviews where the other candidates were twenty years younger. But if she did get a job, she could save a deposit and buy an apartment eventu— Audrey stopped. Oh God. She was fifty-three. *Too old for a mortgage without a guarantor.* She'd never own a home again. And if she declared bankruptcy and started over? She wouldn't even have a credit card.

She heard a banging out the back behind the building. It stopped, then started again. Why had she trusted Wyatt with everything? The banging continued, louder now. She stood up shakily and walked to the kitchen. She looked out the window, and there was Lem. When she opened the back door, he waved and grinned.

Audrey stared at him.

'Were you taking a nap?' Lem's face crinkled in concern. 'You look a little crook. Shez told me to fix up these steps for you. "She's a kick-arse woman," Shez said, "so don't dick around, Lem."'

Audrey looked past Lem to the sea. Even if she worked for a hundred years in the city, she'd never have another view like this. Buddy was all alone and needed her, and Billie needed her too, no matter what Ruth said. If she could make enough money for rent, and negotiate a debt repayment plan with the bank after the house was sold, surely she could figure it out?

'I was wondering,' Lem said, looking up at her sheepishly, 'if you might have any biscuits, Audrey, or those cinnamon buns? I can't stop thinking about them. You sure do know how to bake.'

CHAPTER 20

In the cabana the following morning, Buddy was mansplaining to Audrey how the steps should have been fixed when there was a knock on the door. Shez pushed her way through, followed meekly by Lem.

'We can't come in,' Shez said, and sat down across from Audrey. 'We were on our way for date night breakfast at the Retired Service League in town, when Lem here told me that Robert told him that Billie told Robert your marriage was on the rocks,' she paused. 'It happens to the best of us, Audrey, so keep your eyebrows up.'

Audrey stared at her. Blinked.

'It's good you're not going around blabbing about it, Shez,' Buddy said.

Shez twisted her silver hoop earring. 'Her secrets are safe with me. My mind is shut like a steel vault. You'd be surprised how many strictly confidential things people have told me, right Lem?'

Lem nodded.

'So anyways. I was thinking, Audrey, you need some quick cash and since I hate my cleaner at the holiday flats, a real bludger, my cousin Sally who we call Sal, she never comes to work on time, totally unprofessional, I thought for a minute I could ask you if you wanted to be on my staff.'

Audrey's eyes widened. 'Thanks, but I'm an advertising exec—'

'Think, Audrey, think! I'm not offering. But then I asked myself, *Shez, would she want Sal's job?* Would a city woman like her want to work for a CEO and entrepreneur, underneath her?'

'They call them boss babes now, Shez,' Lem said.

Shez rolled her eyes in Lem's direction. 'I know I am, Lem, but Audrey's getting on in years. She might not want to work for a younger woman. Look at her roots. Grey as a badger. So I thought,' she said, pointing a hot-pink nail at Audrey, with the rest in every other neon colour, '*You* need a startup. Your own business. Think, Audrey! You can stand on the platform of my success, and I will raise you up. And what better place than the Speedway?' Shez smiled, triumphant.

'I love the Speedway,' Lem said. 'Are you thinking what I'm thinking, Shez?'

'I'm ten kilometres down the motorway ahead of you, Lem. You know I have an entrepreneurial mindset.' She shrugged in Audrey's direction. 'I was trained by Marie Forleo back in 2019. I did her online course, well, half of it because the internet got spotty when they put in the new road, and something happened with the signal. I invested in myself,' Shez jabbed a neon-green-painted thumb nail at her own chest. 'I cost a fortune.'

'You do,' Lem said.

'It's all mindset, Lem. Every entrepreneur has her challenges, but only the paranoid survive.'

'You two aren't making any goddamn sense.' Buddy waved a folded newspaper at Audrey. 'She's desperate! That's her problem. Her husband was a right git and ran off with the secretary and made his dodgy business deals, and now she's out here in Woop Woop with us—'

'Oh,' Billie said as they pushed through the front door, 'are we talking about Tawdry Hepburn again?' They hopped onto the armchair and balanced on the edge. 'God, Tawd, you get a lot of airtime around here.'

'We don't need to talk about me,' Audrey said. 'In fact, I'd appreciate a little privacy. I'll work it out my—'

'Sure you will, Tawdry. Like what have you come up with so far?'

Audrey stared at the faces that turned to her.

Shez tugged down her royal-blue pleather miniskirt and crossed her arms, Lem wouldn't meet Audrey's eyes and Billie was trying not to laugh. It was only Buddy who gazed at her with all the trust of an old Labrador.

'If my job search doesn't work out, I'm going to try e-commerce,' Audrey said.

'What sort of dodgy business is that?' Buddy asked.

'She's going to sell cookies!' Billie crowed. 'Right, Tawd? You're going to be like Mrs Fields without the shopping malls, or the Byron Bay Cookie Company, but less successful!'

Audrey coughed. 'I thought I'd start small. Do some market testing. Set up a website, and—'

'Now this is where you need a business plan,' Shez said. 'I'll read it over for you. You get it on my desk, say, by Thursday at five a.m., and we'll talk. Miracle mornings, critical. I hope you have a morning pages routine, Audrey: self-talk, journal, meditate, eliminate. Write it down, then rip it up. Works wonders.'

'Shez is a good writer.' Lem moved closer and draped his arm around her skinny shoulders. 'Turns all my real-estate ads into fiction.'

'*You are enough*, Lem. Remember that tapping video I saw on Instagram? You need to say it and tap your forehead hard, like you mean it. But listen, Audrey, this is exactly why you should check out the races at the Speedway.' She whipped out her phone. 'My cousin, Kylee, sister of my cleaner, Sal, she has a food stall but she's often crook with what's officially known as pica syndrome—'

'Kylee's a dirt-eater,' nodded Lem conversationally. 'It's a challenge for her.'

'We respect each other's mental health, Lem,' Shez said. 'It's a journey that lasts a lifetime. But he's right, and on those days it's best for Kylee not to be down at the track, what with all the dust tempting her, so her food stall will be unmanned next Saturday at the stockcar races. You could sell your baking, Audrey! A test market!' Shez beamed at her. 'Customer research.'

Audrey stared at them. She'd been ambushed by a pensioner, a teen, a small-town real-estate agent and a questionable CEO of some holiday flats. Did she need their advice? No, she did not. Audrey cleared her throat. 'I've already—'

'The kitchen!' Billie said. 'We could fix it up! Let's go look.' Everyone headed towards the door. Even Buddy raised himself up from his chair and wheeled his walker forward.

'What's your goddamn problem, Sweetman?' he said. 'You coming, or will you sit there like a goldfish and yawp at us? You gotta be in it to win it. Get a move on, girl.'

In the bakery, the broken glass in the bay window was duct-taped together, and the floorboards creaked as they followed Buddy pushing his red walker. Audrey had traipsed through the derelict bakery on the way to her apartment several times a day, but now she reconsidered it. Could she work in here? Maybe the timber floorboards could be scrubbed with sugar soap, and she could wash the walls and put on a new coat of paint. Paint was cheap and she knew from Billie's distant gaze that renovation plans were racing through their mind. Billie shoved aside a broken table. Buddy wheeled over to a bookcase propped against the side wall near the front door. He turned around slowly and sat on his walker, his shoulders slumped forward. He didn't follow them into the kitchen.

Billie got there first, and Audrey followed, taking in the dark forest-green walls, a depressing eighties colour, and the floor tiles that had been laid in a simple black checkerboard pattern. The tile was in good shape, retro and upbeat. Along the back wall was the oven, huge and grubby, made of stainless steel. It was old and disused but positioned well in the large kitchen. She wondered if it even worked, but when she turned the dial to the right it hummed to life. The oven was a couple of metres high, taller than she was, with a door that opened to reveal a series of empty racks. There were no baking trays, but maybe they were hidden in the depths of the kitchen cupboards, which were also painted forest-green, to match the walls. Audrey opened a door, and the smell of mould came from a suspicious-looking container. Glassware and more old books were stacked inside, but nothing of any use. She wiped a finger across the stone benchtop. The whole kitchen was covered in a layer of grease and over that, dust. A cockroach scuttled out of the ancient dishwasher when Billie opened the door.

'God, Lem!' Shez shrieked as she bumped into him. He'd been inspecting the broken shelves of the double fridge.

'Looks state of the art . . . from fifty years ago,' Billie said. The outside front panel of the fridge was rusted and there was a cheerful Bob Hawke bumper sticker on the glass, presumably stuck there by a supporter in the eighties when he was prime minister. In the middle of the room stood a timber table, an island that would have been useful when the bakery had been running. It was beautiful if dirty: the timber was soft and worn, and Audrey could imagine someone hand-kneading bread on it.

She made a quick mental list and it seemed never-ending: bomb for insects, wash the entire place down, possibly stain and seal the floorboards, but the kitchen—where would she begin? Paint over all that forest-green, and it would take several coats. She didn't know anything—anything!—about a commercial kitchen or food safety or what it took to bake in large batches, but she did know enough to realise there would be an enormous amount of work involved. She'd have to set up her own website, but that was easy with the website packages available now, and it would take her less than a day once she had photos of her products. Then marketing, social media, order fulfilment, probably delivering her biscuits by post, so it would have to be a cookie that had a longer shelf life, something unique—and what would that be?

She'd be working practically twenty-four hours a day; there was no way that she could do everything she needed to do in the few weeks before her money ran out if she stuck to regular business hours. She had almost no capital to fix anything, and the place was a ruin. There was nothing but work here, and potential failure, or no—more like certain failure. Audrey, a business owner? All those years ago, with her Audrey's Cookies cart, Wyatt had convinced her she'd never have the guts to do it.

'It's bad, isn't it?' Billie sighed. 'It's never going to work.'

Audrey turned and looked at their sombre faces. What if, just this once, she bet on herself?

CHAPTER 21

Audrey started with buckets and bleach. It took her two days to scrub the bakery from the ceiling down to the wide-planked timber floor, and Billie helped in the afternoons. Around mid-morning, Buddy would wheel in as far as the front door and sit next to one of the bay windows on his walker. On the second day, Billie dragged in an almost new leather armchair for Buddy to sit in by the window. When Billie carried in another bucket with hot water, Audrey reached out a hand to stop them.

'How about minimum wage for a part-time job?'

Billie frowned. 'What would I be doing? More cleaning?'

'A bit,' Audrey said. 'And maybe helping me set up Bittersweet Biscuits.'

'Hey, what about some interior design, Tawdry? I mean . . . if you're working in here every day, you want it to look good, right?'

'But it's an online business, Billie, and my budget's tiny.' Audrey shook her head, trying not to think of her bank account. 'I won't be serving customers here. Plus the building belongs to Buddy, so he may not want us to change anything.'

Across the room, Buddy snorted. 'I don't give a goddamn, Sweetman. Do what you want. As long as the Kid doesn't spray paint it with skulls or big willies on the walls.'

Billie laughed. 'You've been talking to Lem, haven't you, you old fart? That was only one giant willy anyway.' Billie squinted. 'I could design this whole space, and the kitchen, but I'd have to do it on the cheap.'

Audrey frowned. 'No stealing.'

'Course not. I'm a Hickson.'

Buddy coughed. 'Turning over a new leaf, are ya, Kid?'

'I'll get a few things from the council clean-up in town. People always throw away good stuff. But I won't steal anything. Obviously.'

'Where's the chair from then?' Audrey asked.

Billie shrugged. 'My bedroom. It just happened to get ripped yesterday with a steak knife. Ruth said chuck it out, so I did. I chucked it here. I'll come up with some plans for you, Tawdry. I was thinking maybe a black and white vibe, with plants and, I don't know, wicker . . . like outdoor furniture but indoors, and white walls instead of all this green? White paint's cheap and—'

Audrey handed Billie the pail of hot water. 'First, we clean. Then you can design anything you want to.'

An hour later, Billie announced they were starving and wandered upstairs.

'Bring a tray, please,' Audrey said. 'Earl Grey for me and a cinnamon bun for Buddy. Biscuits are on the counter.'

'I'll have a cuppa, too,' Buddy called out, but Billie was already running up the internal staircase. Thumping sounds came from overhead, but Audrey concentrated on the task at hand: scrubbing out the old MX Goldbake. Cleaning helped her avoid thinking about Wyatt and her problems. When she started ruminating, she couldn't stop, so instead, she forced herself to do what Joyce always had: fix things up, do what she could with what she had in her own two hands. She'd searched online for information about the old oven and found that it would've cost a fortune in the eighties. If it would still bake cookies, well, that was one less thing she'd have to pay to have repaired. Lem had kindly tinkered with the dishwasher and got that working, but it was so loud you had to shout over the top of the noise from the motor. The whole idea of resurrecting the old bakery, launching Bittersweet Biscuits seemed crazy, huge, impossible. She had no idea what she was doing, but it was bliss to shower and roll into bed at night, wet-haired and exhausted, and sleep for a solid seven hours without dreaming. Every muscle ached, but she had to press on and get the kitchen in shape in time to bake for her launch at the Speedway. She had a little under a week, as Shez dropped by and reminded her.

'Kylee normally does lamingtons and passionfruit melting moments if that's any help,' Shez had told her, supervising from her spot on the kitchen benchtop, where she sat cross-legged while Audrey scrubbed out the fridge. 'But Lem finds Kylee's baking a little on the dry side.'

Audrey had nodded and got back to work. The cleaning had been endless, but also satisfying. She could see the results from her efforts, and best of all, she was rarely on her own. Lem and Shez often dropped in for a chat, and so did Robert; Buddy was a regular fixture in his armchair, and Billie barrelled over to the bakery as soon as their homework was done.

A thump on the stairs made her turn around. Billie carried a tray with a teapot, cups and saucers and a plate of cinnamon buns. They were wearing strange old clothes, a green military hat and a corduroy jacket with wide lapels. Around their neck they'd wound a faux zebra scarf of black and white fur stripes.

'Look what I found in the attic!' Billie crowed. 'There's so much crap up there: clothes and books and all these—'

'Get it off!' Buddy roared and charged across the room on his walker. 'Get that off yer head!' He shoved his walker into Billie violently. The tray hit the floor and hot tea sprayed across Buddy's legs. Billie—their face white and confused—stared at Audrey, then Buddy.

'Sorry, sorry, Buddy, I—' Billie stammered.

'You're goddamn right you're sorry. Don't you know not to go searching through what doesn't belong to you?' Tears welled in Buddy's rheumy eyes. He yanked the zebra scarf from Billie's neck, held it to his chest.

'Billie, it's okay.' Audrey pulled the jacket from their shoulders and folded it carefully, plucked the hat from Billie's shaved head. 'Run these up to the attic where you found them. I'm going to make us all another—'

But Buddy was already wheeling his way through the door.

Audrey had picked up the broken tea tray and explained it must be adult troubles of some kind, to try not to mind, but Billie ignored her reassurances and left for home.

'I wreck everything,' Billie had said, and wouldn't be convinced that it wasn't true.

Audrey hadn't looked properly in the attic when she'd gone up there to store a box of old pots and pans, but she had grabbed that copy of *The Alchemist*, and she felt a wave of guilt for taking it without Buddy's permission. He owned the building, but she'd just assumed the collection of dusty boxes was the forgotten property of previous tenants. Obviously, that wasn't the case.

She gave Buddy a couple of hours on his own and finished cleaning the oven. Then she made up a new tray with aged cheddar, water crackers and a bowl of red seedless grapes, and walked back to the cabana. She heard his jazz as soon as she stepped outside the bakery, a song she didn't recognise, but the voice was Nina's. Audrey ducked her head. It was evening, and the wind was sharp. The coat Billie had worn earlier was a winter one, cheerful in a seventies way, a little swanky. Audrey hadn't had a chance to get a good look at the hat, but the zebra scarf had brought Buddy to tears. She walked down the scrubby path. She'd been so consumed with her own drama that she hadn't asked him anything about his life. He was a cartoonish old man to her. But how fair was it to think like that? He had a whole life behind him, but if he was lucky, he might have many years ahead too. He was older but he wasn't a caricature of himself any more than she was, and she scolded herself for thinking so. Everyone seemed to be dismissed with a label: a teenager was a troublemaker, a middle-aged woman was invisible, an old man, useless and resigned. That's all most people saw: the surface.

She knocked on his door. 'Can I come in?'

'Go away! Piss off!'

'I will, but I just want to check you're okay first.'

He was drunk, sitting in his recliner. With the gas heater on, the room had the sharp scent of misery and old age. Audrey perched on the couch and made up a couple of biscuits with wedges of crumbly cheddar. He stared at the turntable while

Nina Simone sang about being haunted by youth. Together they listened, saying nothing.

'I don't know this song,' Audrey said.

Buddy grunted.

Audrey set the plate in front of him. Still, he said nothing, and Nina carried on with her swinging anthem about being young, gifted and black. When the song finished its final upbeat chord, the record hissed on the player and Audrey stood to shut it off.

'Do you want me to do something for you, Buddy? Put on another record?' she asked quietly.

He took a long drink of bourbon from a dirty water glass. 'I was married, and she died. It was my fault.'

The room was silent, save for the low whoosh of warm air coming from the heater.

'I'm sorry. What was her name, Buddy?'

'It was . . .' His voice broke. Audrey handed him a paper napkin from the tray. 'Clara Jones. She was from America. She had this accent, it'd charm the pants off you.'

Audrey waited.

'She came here with another American nurse from Vietnam. I met her outside City Tatts.'

'That's the old club in the city?'

Buddy nodded. 'Real snooty place. City Tattersall Club. She wasn't allowed in on account of being black. Me and my mates were just walking by, and I flattened the doorman. Racist, he was. Bastard. But they were back then.'

'What did you do?'

'Invited her for a walk around Circular Quay, had fish and chips at the harbour. We stayed up all night, then I walked her back to her hotel. She was a real lady, Clara was.'

Audrey smiled. 'I can see you doing that.'

'We got married after the war. She gave up her family in America for me. We didn't have the money to go back to see them.' He took a drink from his bottle. 'We had a little place in Surry Hills.'

'It's trendy now,' Audrey said. 'So many cafés and startups.'

'Not back then. Just all of us thrown together. Dirt-poor Catholics, fancy boys and the people like us who didn't fit anywhere else. It was goddamn rough, but we were all in the same boat, there for each other.'

Audrey had trouble imagining that the swish, upmarket suburb was ever home to poverty and despair. It would cost several million now to buy in Surry Hills, and everyone loved it there. 'They were Clara's clothes. The nurse's hat?'

'She came from Saigon on furlough and spent her leave in Sydney. During the war, Qantas called them the champagne flights, they'd go from Saigon to Sydney and back again. Heaps of American military came here. But Clara was . . .' Buddy shook his head.

Audrey reached out and touched his hand. 'I'm so sorry. Her scarf looked lovely.' It was a stupid thing to say but she could think of nothing else.

Buddy took a long drink and wiped his eyes on his sleeve. 'We had a little girl.' He handed Audrey the photo album he kept beside his chair.

She opened the album's cracked spine, with the yellowed sheets of cellophane that stuck to the tacky backing of the square photos. A striking black woman in a nurse's uniform smiled at the camera, alongside a young Buddy with a full head of hair, brushed back. Then a baby in a knitted cardigan. She turned the page. Pictures in colour: the one she'd seen before of the woman leaning into the car, her face hidden. A little girl in a green dress with a short skirt and white sandals curtsied, her face shining, with a big gap-toothed grin. Another page: a tiny house, Buddy outside in a singlet waving a cigarette, Clara dressed for a party in a wildly patterned dress, hoop earrings, hair slicked back in a bun. She was gorgeous. Clara gripped the hand of their little girl.

Buddy's eyes filled with tears. 'Rotten kids called my daughter *monkey*, goddamn them. She was a beautiful little girl, all them big curls, prettier than her mama even. They bullied her.'

Audrey squeezed his arm. 'It was terrible back then. I hope it's better now, but from what Billie says, I'm guessing not a lot has changed.' She stared at Buddy and Clara's child, growing older as she flipped the pages. The pictures stopped suddenly when she was a teen. 'I'm sorry, Buddy. She's so pretty. What was her name?'

'Simone. Clara said it was either Nina or Simone, for a little girl who was going to be someone in this world.'

Audrey nodded. Waited. Held her breath. Buddy's pain, even remembered through the buffer of forty years, was so much greater than hers. An iceberg of pain, and all he showed anyone in the village was the grumpy, headstrong man forcing himself to take his morning constitutional, to keep going every single day, to breathe, live, drink, swim, even though he'd lost everything he loved. If he could live through that, surely she could rally? All she'd lost was a marriage and money. Money was nothing. She remembered Shez saying that Buddy had an insurance payout in the eighties, but she was sure he would give every cent of it to have his family back. Of course he would. And his isolation? His crankiness? He had a reason that the villagers didn't understand, so they ignored him.

'A taxi driver ran into them crossing the road. Reckless driving.

I wasn't even there. I was at the pub. Cops found me. I had a family, and then they were gone.'

Audrey held his hand while he cried. The clock ticked and the crackers grew soft, the cheddar hardening on the plate. Buddy drank deeply from his bottle and waved away the food. Finally, Audrey walked to the front door and opened it to the night air.

'Buddy, you need to sleep now. Let's get you up.'

'No! Staying here.'

She helped him to the couch, and he lay down. She covered him with the crocheted blanket on the back of the sofa and searched his room for something warmer. His bedroom smelled of sweat and old clothes, the bedroom of an elderly drunk who couldn't take care of himself. She'd left it untouched when she'd cleaned the cabana, but he needed help now.

Maybe Ruth was right; he could live in a retirement home and be cared for, clean and warm. Audrey had been irresponsible to assume that he was coping on his own. Tomorrow she'd come back with Lem and see if he needed help getting in the shower. Buddy would never get any younger; it was this until the end. His life couldn't get better, could it? She pulled the covers up and patted his shoulder. Maybe it could if she was there to help him.

'I'll be back in the morning, Buddy.'

She'd give him the copy of *The Alchemist* with the photos of his daughter. She hoped he'd be pleased to see them, and not saddened further. *To Clara, my treasure forever, Love Bernard*: it was Buddy's given name from a life before this, back when he was a family man and a father.

Tomorrow. There was always tomorrow, and sometimes it felt as unrelenting as a landslide, there with its problems, again, again.

CHAPTER 22

'Kylee says no can do. She wants her booth this weekend at the Speedway, and you can't have it.'

Shez handed Audrey a takeaway cup from the General Store and sat on the table in the middle of the kitchen. 'Robert said you take it white, two sugars. To me that's like drinking gummy bears.' Shez screwed up her nose. 'Anyway, you love what you love.'

Another roadblock. Audrey sighed. 'Are you sure?'

Shez wiggled her hips. 'God, my tights just want to crawl right down to my knees, it's what happens when you have thighs of steel like mine, I tell you. Bloody ThighMaster is a cracker! You should get one, Audrey. Plus possibly tend to those roots? We can talk business until Lem comes. I'll help you sort out your Plan C.'

Audrey touched the new silver in her hair, growing more noticeable every day. At first, she had too much on her mind to worry about it, but just this morning she'd pulled her hair back and squinted in surprise. Even on her—not a model, not feeling particularly empowered—she had to admit, the colour was pretty.

'Thanks for the coffee, Shez.' Coffee always helped, but probably not Robert's: lukewarm, way too sweet. Still, Audrey sipped gratefully and rubbed the back of her neck. What could she do now? She'd spent two days baking delicate, sugary macarons in the MX Goldbake and was just about to start on the fortune cookies. The oven had burnt her first three batches and almond flour wasn't cheap, but she'd finally managed to get the macaron feet to rise properly—the sea air was so humid that she'd had to adjust her drying time between piping the biscuits on the pans and letting them form their crust. After all that experimentation and money wasted, she'd had to turn down the oven temperature as well, which was tricky given the lack of digital controls. Then she'd sourced the flower petals for her fortune cookies. With Robert's blessing, she'd cut back the daisies growing in front of the General Store.

'Okay, on to Plan C,' Shez said.

'Don't you mean Plan B?'

'No, Plan C. For consciousness. Think, Audrey, think! I know you're almost a senior, but you've got to get a grip. You're building a business here!' Shez raised her stencilled eyebrows and spoke slowly, like she was explaining bedtime to a toddler. 'First you visualise using your conscious mind—your greatness, for example—then,' she slapped her hands together like a cymbal, 'you lock it in with your unconscious mind while you sleep. Then in the morning, you meditate for ten minutes—I set the timer on my phone so absolutely no cheating whatsoever. After that, you high five yourself in the bathroom mirror and say an "I-ffirmation" like *I am too much*. Then, you repeat a power mantra seven to thirteen times, like *I will launch my successful business at the Speedway, I will launch my—*'

Audrey cleared her throat. 'Maybe I should just call Kylee.'

Shez shrugged. 'Well, fine, if you want to go old school. Lem's out the front, gotta run!' She hopped off the table and tapped out a text with long burgundy nails. 'There. Kylee's number. They make sushi at the grocery store in town. We'll bring you some.'

Audrey closed the door behind Shez. Normally with a setback like this she'd have consulted with the team at the ad agency, but she didn't have that luxury now. If anything was going to happen, it was up to her. But she had Wyatt's voice in her head, mixed with that of her own ugly critic. Audrey stopped. Whenever she felt defeated and hopeless, her biggest argument was with herself: with a mean version of herself. Mean Audrey was the one who told her that her idea was too small. Mean Audrey brought up her age. Mean Audrey reminded her of her failings just like Wyatt did: that it was laughable, at her age, to think she was launching a *business* at a small-town speedway. A business! More like a cake stall. She was from the city, she had degrees—or, well, one Arts degree and the first semester of an MBA, which she would have finished if she hadn't married Wyatt.

She rubbed the base of her neck again where the headache was starting. Even if she managed to talk Kylee around, Saturday would just be a cake stall in a country town—nothing like the proper businesses she'd created marketing strategies for in her job at UDKE. They'd worked with the best brands, the biggest companies, putting products into the most exclusive retailers in the country. They'd handled global launches with startups like Wow Sunday!, the skincare brand owned by two young female founders that was selling its products worldwide in under two years. Or Canva. Now that was a business. She was just a middle-aged woman baking cookies in a derelict oven and trying to sell them at a stockcar racetrack in the country.

She glanced out the bay windows. There were no cars in front of the building, no people walking by, no anything. Audrey was living in the middle of nowhere. As soon as their house sold, she'd be facing a massive debt. She had no capital, no partners sharing her vision, absolutely nothing but her own two hands. There was no other way to start over, unless one of the agency jobs she'd applied for online came through, and so far, she'd had two flat-out rejections. Her business was ridiculous. She was ridiculous. Wasn't she?

She stopped herself. 'Nope,' she said out loud. 'Not today, Audrey.' The baking was all she had, and the money in her account was dwindling. She pulled the hair band from her ponytail and hitched up her grey and blonde curls into a messy bun that felt slightly more professional. 'I'm moving forward,' Audrey announced to the empty room. 'It's a leap of faith.' She picked up her phone and tapped in Kylee's number. She couldn't start any younger. She couldn't start any smarter, either. She could only start where she was.

The footlights ringing the Speedway were shining fluorescent and bright when Audrey pulled up with her carload of cinnamon buns, macarons and fortune cookies. She didn't have room for Billie, but Lem had promised them a lift so Billie could help sell biscuits. Buddy had refused to ride along for a night out at the races, and he hadn't stopped by the shop since their talk either. From her balcony, she'd watched him make his morning trek to the beach and she'd cajoled Billie to go over there with dinner twice—bubbling-hot chicken pot pie with golden puff pastry and a thick slice of spinach ricotta lasagne—along with instructions to be thoughtful and apologise. Billie said Buddy was drinking more than before and Audrey was worried about him. After all, she'd as good as given her word to Ruth Hickson and the rest of the village that she'd look out for him.

Dr Flood had dropped in at the bakery to see Buddy one day, and Audrey was relieved to see them chatting until he took a call that could have only been from a woman; he'd laughed in a charming way and said he'd pick her up for dinner, and that he'd been missing her. Overhearing the conversation gave Audrey a funny feeling in her chest, but really, it was none of her business. He was more of an acquaintance, wasn't he, someone who might one day be a friend? They seemed to share the same appreciation of the little town and the people who lived there.

'Looks good in here, Audrey,' Dr Flood had said, stepping in to the old bakery. 'You've done a great job. We need an experienced baker at Whitehaven. And maybe some decent coffee?'

'Thanks,' Audrey said weakly. A baker? She loved baking, but was that all he thought she was? He didn't know about her professional career or her life in the city; all her ad-agency accomplishments meant nothing at Whitehaven. And why would it matter if he did see her differently than just another holidaymaker who stayed on? She wasn't trying to impress him, was she? No. She wasn't. All the same, she found herself thinking of him more often than she should.

One morning at the laundromat, Shez suggested that Dr Flood was hogging most of the charisma at Whitehaven, but that the voices in *her* head were telling her to stick with a weak, silent type like Lem. Audrey had raised an eyebrow and kept on folding tea towels.

'Tawdry! Sorry I'm late,' said Billie, walking up to Audrey's stall at the Speedway. 'We had to wait for Shez to put on her make-up. It took forever. Apparently, you have to paint on the foundation in multiple coats.' Billie hitched up their huge jeans, which sagged as if they'd come from the Big and Tall section of a discount department store. 'Love what you've done with the place. It's like Traditional meets Old Lady. You needed me, obviously.'

Audrey glanced down at the baking stall she'd taken over from Kylee, which consisted of a wobbly portable plastic table set on the wet grass to the left of the canteen building. The canteen had a crowd of customers waiting for their hotdogs and beer, steak sandwiches, burgers and hot chips. Audrey's stall had no one but Audrey.

She'd used Lem's printer to make a stack of homemade business cards with Bittersweet Biscuits and her new website address printed on them, with COMING SOON written across the bottom. She'd been too busy baking to think about making the stall attractive, so she did the best she could quickly: a clean white paper tablecloth from the grocery store, an impromptu table runner made out of a navy silk scarf she rarely wore, and a vase with a bunch of deep purple tibouchina she'd snipped at the last minute from the blooming bush outside Robert's General Store. And her baking, displayed on the floral Royal Crown Derby plates, with her petal-studded fortune cookies on a fancy three-tiered tray she'd found at the op shop. Beside them sat a stack of brown paper lunch bags, white napkins from the grocery store and a plastic Tupperware container filled with the float that Audrey had borrowed from Robert earlier in the day. She knew her set-up was basic; her products would have to speak for themselves. Behind her on a smaller table, Audrey had stacked the assorted plastic containers holding her baking. She had no idea what she'd do with it all if it didn't sell.

Fortune cookies and macarons for two dollars, soft and warm cinnamon buns for three, and with a quick calculation Audrey thought she'd make enough for rent for two weeks if she sold it all. But more important than that, as Shez rightly pointed out, was the market research. Audrey knew everyone loved her macarons and cinnamon buns but she wondered if anyone would want to buy a freshly baked fortune cookie with flower petals pressed on the outside, and a handwritten fortune to make them laugh.

She'd cracked a few fortune cookies open and placed them in front of the tiered tray so customers could see what they might be getting. Most people weren't used to seeing these more austere biscuits unless they were paired with a Chinese restaurant bill, but Billie had helped her write the fortunes and some were hilarious. They'd re-used a few of the snarky comments that Audrey had written the night she'd gone home with Wyatt, and added some of Billie's mouthy sayings, plus a few positive affirmations on the advice of Shez, who snapped her gum loudly and said that our words create our reality. She insisted that some of the fortunes should be wildly optimistic for the manifesters and the woo-woo crowd.

As the sky darkened and the night grew colder, Audrey grew more worried. Customers wandered over with their burgers and drinks from the canteen, but it was mainly to take a look.

'No lamingtons? How much for the bickies?'

'Can I get a cinnamon roll? No, no, just the one—we'll share.'

'Is there an actual fortune inside this thing? Will it help me win the Lotto?'

A woman in tight jeans leaned against the table. Audrey smiled brightly at her. 'Got any melting moments?' she asked.

'Sorry,' Audrey said. 'I've got fresh cinnamon buns, and these fortune cookies—they're delicious—and the macarons.'

The woman shifted closer. 'I'll take one of them macaroons to try.'

Billie smiled through gritted teeth, popped a pistachio macaron in a paper bag and took the two-dollar coin. 'It's called a maca-*ron*, like *moron*? Here.'

'Pricey little beggars, ain't they?' The woman sniffed and shook her paper bag.

'They're handmade with almond flour and a butter filling,' Audrey said, 'and they normally retail for over three dollars each . . .' but the woman had drifted away.

Audrey looked despairingly at the stacks of baking in containers behind her and the table covered in Derby Posies plates piled with macarons, cinnamon buns and fortune cookies. None of this was going to sell, and she'd been stupid to even try. People wanted beer, burgers and fries, and all she'd done was waste hundreds of dollars on ingredients. Her shoulders slumped, and even Billie looked worried. She wondered if she could donate the baking to a shelter or a seniors' home, but probably not. There were food safety rules for that sort of thing.

The announcer's voice boomed from the loudspeaker. 'Modified Sedan Series! This is your five-minute warning.'

Lem and Shez walked over to the stall, his arm slung across her shoulders. 'Hi Audrey. This is the best race. Any modified sedan in New South Wales can enter,' Lem said.

'He'd do it if I let him.' Shez leaned in. 'God, Audrey, nothing's sold! What's the problem here?' She handed a cinnamon bun to Lem and gestured to the macarons. 'I'll take a dozen of those, plus this, Billie.'

'The announcer's doing the driver briefing,' Lem said, chewing his cinnamon bun. 'You probably don't know the rules, but some of the sedans look like they've got so much mud on them, drivers could've painted them brown. It's hard yakka, racing is—last time we came there was a crash.'

'Which is why you're not allowed,' Shez said, as she adjusted her tights beneath her denim miniskirt.

'Never say never, Shez.'

'Never, Lem.'

In a sombre voice that reminded Audrey of a preacher at a funeral, the announcer read out the duty of care statement, and everyone turned to the dusty track. 'It is my duty to advise you of the following: that motor racing can be dangerous; your equipment could be damaged or destroyed; and you may suffer serious personal injury or worse.'

Lem held his hand to his heart and nodded solemnly.

'Also,' the announcer continued, 'the Speedway Drug and Alcohol Policy is to be upheld and enforced. If you have any doubts as to your ability to pass a test with a negative or zero reading, you should withdraw from this race meeting *immediately*.'

Suddenly a low rumble came from the left of the field. People turned to stare. Audrey saw nothing but dust. But then, appearing through the haze, raced a stream of bikers on Harley-Davidsons. They crested the ridge in twos, some with helmets and some without, a tumble of leather jackets, denim vests, tattoos on bulging arms, long hair, shaved heads, handlebar moustaches, beards. A dozen or more Harleys roared up the road to the Speedway, then pulled up and idled beside the parked vehicles. The engines stopped.

The announcer raised two crossed flags, green and yellow.

'He's calling up the cars,' Lem explained. 'The Coffin Cheaters made it just in time.'

Three huge bikers, each of them more than six feet tall, ambled up to Audrey's table. The two on the outside wore leather vests open over beer bellies, and the man in the middle had a bald head and a long reddish-brown beard, earrings and tattoos.

'Hey, Tiny!' Billie said to the one in the middle. 'We're selling bickies!' Billie leaned closer to Audrey. 'It's the Creed Brothers. They're famous around here.' Billie grinned at Tiny. 'Your clubhouse is in town, right?'

'Yeah. Got busted during the week, though, cops came.' Tiny stuck out a thick, meaty hand and Audrey shook it. 'I'm Tiny. Pleased to meet ya. This here's my brother Stumpy . . .' He pointed a thumb to a brother, one of the leather-vested men who flanked him. This one had a grey buzzcut, blue eyes and forearms completely covered in tattoos '. . . and this is Smokey. Smokes, go get the beer.'

When the third brother ambled off towards the bar, Tiny leaned forward. 'Where's Kylee?'

Audrey smiled nervously. 'Kylee let me take over her stall tonight. She'll be back next weekend. I'm Audrey Sweetman. I'm here from the city.'

Tiny stared at the dainty china plates of macarons and fortune cookies. 'Got any gluten free?' he asked. 'I'm completely GF. Smokey's gone and turned vegan, so hell if I know what he eats anymore. He's doing a cleanse. But beer's okay because it's barley.'

'Easier when he was pescatarian,' Stumpy said, 'but then he watched the Mr Rogers movie and didn't want to eat anything with a mother. Like Mr Rogers said.' He smiled at Audrey, revealing surprisingly white upper teeth and a gold grid on the bottom ones.

Stumpy's teeth looked like they'd cost a fortune; she'd only ever seen that look on rappers in music videos. But customers were customers, and Audrey smiled at them gratefully.

'The macarons are gluten-free,' she said. 'They're made with almond flour.'

'Not selling much, are you?' Tiny shrugged. 'Are they any good?'

Audrey held up a tray. 'Try one on the house. Please. Take one of each.'

Stumpy chewed a biscuit. Audrey watched his stony face and gave a worried shiver. She waited while he considered his strawberry-pink macaron, and noticed his bicep bulging with a tattoo of a naked woman strategically wrapped in a python—or maybe it was a cobra? She wasn't sure and didn't want to stare. He brushed some crumbs off his leather vest and stuffed the second half of the macaron in his mouth. 'Mum used to say, *I don't care what the question is—cookies are the answer.*'

Tiny picked up a fortune cookie and cracked it in two with his huge hands. He bit into the flowery biscuit and chewed.

'Damn, Audrey! These are good. Light and crispy, just a hint of vanilla.' He waved it at his brother. 'Mum was right.' He pulled out the handwritten slip of paper and coughed until Audrey thought he might be choking. 'Stumps, listen to this: *Three can keep a secret . . . if you get rid of two.*' Tiny punched

Stumpy in the snaked-draped-naked-woman bicep and Stumpy slapped his brother's bald head.

'Thanks,' Audrey said, 'I wrote that one. Billie wrote some, too.'

'Damn straight,' Billie said. 'Mine are funnier.' Tiny gave Billie a fist bump, and they both grinned. Then he fist-bumped Audrey.

She felt something like . . . fun . . . bubbling up inside her for the first time in weeks. 'They're homemade, all original recipes, all natural ingredients,' she said.

'Mum would've loved these,' Tiny said, 'may she R.I.P.' Both men cast their eyes upward.

Audrey looked at Tiny's long red beard, and then at Stumpy. She'd never seen a biker in leather chaps and a Harley-Davidson t-shirt waving around a flower-petal cookie. 'Your mum was right. Cookies are the answer.'

'I'm addicted to your baking, Audrey,' Tiny said. He bought two dozen fortune cookies to take back to the clubhouse and a dozen macarons.

And that gave Audrey a very good idea.

CHAPTER 23

'I can't believe you got the Coffin Cheaters to walk around with your cookies. Holy crap, Tawd! They're a proper bikie gang; aren't you worried they're going to find out where you live and murder you?'

Billie pulled up a stool in the bakery kitchen. Empty containers littered the benchtop.

'I figured they might be persuasive.' Audrey glanced at the clock. Almost midnight and she was exhausted, but too wired to think about sleep.

'Hell, yeah! What would *you* do if a motorcycle gang asked you to buy a biscuit?' Billie shook the makeshift cash box. 'I bet you cleaned up tonight.'

Half an hour after Stumpy, Smokey and Tiny had walked around the Speedway grounds with Tupperware containers, handing out free samples, Audrey and Billie could barely keep up with the crowd at the stall. No doubt the Coffin Cheaters had a little to do with everyone's new enthusiasm for Audrey's biscuits, but all the same, once the locals had tried them, they came back to buy more. All the fortune cookies had sold, along with three-quarters of the macarons and half of the cinnamon buns. The fortune cookies were a clear winner. Customers bought them in multiples to share with friends the next day because they loved the snarky fortunes.

That was her market research done for outdoor events in country towns. Audrey packed the last of the half-empty containers in the bakery fridge. 'Not sure what I'll do with these leftovers. I need a freezer, so that should be the next thing, after the website and the marketing. Then I'll need to think about how to produce a higher volume if this is going to be viable, so that means a fortune-cookie machine. I looked online and they're ten grand from overseas, without delivery or installation.'

She handed over Billie's weekly pay in cash. 'You're so worth it, Billie. I wish I could pay you more. I could do an online transfer if that's better?'

'Nah, cash is good. Ruth checks my account to see what I'm buying. What's next, Tawd? Social media?'

Audrey ran water into the sink and began the washing up. 'After I finish the website—it's half done, so it won't take long—I have to figure out how to package the fortune cookies so they don't crush. That'll be my biggest expense, but we can talk marketing tomorrow after you've done your homework.' She inhaled sharply. She knew she should investigate applying for food safety certification, and a business licence too, but it all felt so permanent and the process was painfully detailed. She was worried it would involve a kitchen renovation that she definitely couldn't afford. Was she really ready to commit to a life at Whitehaven? It was too soon to tell. She pushed the thought from her mind and looked around the room, clean now, but still boasting the forest-green walls.

'Butt-ugly, isn't it?' Billie said. 'I hate this green, it's all gonna be China White. Maybe I can find someone to help me.'

Audrey pulled the larger notes out of the float and handed them to Billie. 'For the decorating supplies. Will this be enough?'

'Yep. Lem's going to the hardware in the morning, so he'll give me a lift. It'll look good in here, just you wait, Tawd.'

Billie's optimism was infectious, even if they couldn't see the problems. Audrey covered a yawn and stretched. 'Thanks for helping. With all of it.'

'You must be feeling better. It was a good night.' And Billie was gone.

Before Audrey creaked up the steps to her bed, she checked her phone. Three texts. One from Emma, effusive emojis, *good luck* plus *call me in the morning—I have news!!!* One from Kylee, wondering *Did Tiny ask about me or what??????* And one from Wyatt: *I have an update. Call ASAP.*

In the morning, Audrey heard the news from Emma: that she was heading to Vancouver to stay with a friend for a month, and they'd be taking an Alaskan cruise; Audrey could use her place in the city anytime. Next, she took a deep breath and called Wyatt. He'd found a real-estate agent who could put the house on the market in three weeks, and his lawyer would instruct her lawyer about the shared debt. They argued for over an hour about responsibility, liability and how he'd ruined them, until Audrey dissolved in furious tears.

'You know, Audrey,' he said, 'bankruptcy is your only option. I have a job. You don't.'

To which she responded in a voice she barely recognised: 'Yeah? Screw you.'

She told him he could contact her via her new lawyer, Danny Marshall. She'd met Danny last week, on the advice of Shez. Danny looked about seventeen, Audrey thought when she arrived at his office, which was in a tin shed next to the petrol station in town. Shez had recommended him as a budget lawyer who was good with details, and it turned out he was yet another one of her cousins. Danny told Audrey he'd graduated with a law degree from Wollongong University, where he'd specialised in conveyancing. But since he'd grown up in the area and knew how people carried on, he explained, he was positive he'd have a lot of divorce work and it was turning out to be absolutely true. His hourly rate was eighty percent lower than Eshana Patel's had been, so Audrey signed with him. Then she bought Shez the biggest box of chocolates she could find in the grocery store to thank her for having such a large and endlessly useful family.

At the other end of the phone, Wyatt cleared his throat. 'Charmaine's arranged for a mover to pack all your things. Where do you want them sent?'

She gave him Lem's address in town and hung up. Shez had mentioned that half of Lem's two-car garage was empty; he normally rented it to an importer of retro roller skates who had recently gone bust, and he'd said he would store Audrey's belongings if it came to that. Well, it had. Her life was slowly migrating down to the beach, all of it, in dregs and disasters. Was she somehow prejudicing her financial position by agreeing to move from their home? Danny would know. On Monday morning, Audrey gave him a call.

'Danny Marshall Lawyers,' he said. 'Get that damn dog outside! Sorry, hello?'

'Can I ask a quick question?' She told him about the conversation with Wyatt, and Danny outlined her options; when the house was sold, the legal fees paid and the divorce in motion, Audrey and Wyatt would have a shared debt and both of them would be liable for it. All Danny could offer were solutions that were dire: bankruptcy (no thank you, not without a fight) or a payment plan (although she might literally die before she paid the debt off, that's if the bank would accept her terms). Or, he suggested, she could get rich quick, maybe by playing the Lotto.

Audrey thanked Danny and hung up. She walked from the bay windows to the kitchen. Her head ached, and she knew this was the worst time to start a business. Didn't you need—as Shez reminded her regularly—some positive intentions? An angel investor? The vigour and self-confidence of youth? How could she possibly expect a cookie business to tackle a debt that size? But then she straightened her spine. She couldn't just sit and wait for a cavalry that wasn't coming. All she could do was the next right thing.

Buddy. She opened a can of Italian diced tomatoes and tipped the contents into a saucepan, poured in some chicken stock and a little heavy cream, along with a handful of freshly torn basil, and stirred until the soup bubbled and thickened. Then she set a bowl on a tray with a paper napkin and popped two slices of sourdough bread into the avocado-green toaster, another relic from the eighties. She texted Buddy to come over for lunch and some fresh air. It was time they talked. He needed her and she needed him, too.

When he settled in his chair in the corner of the bakery, she placed the tray on his lap. 'Missed you,' she said. 'I'm glad you're here.'

'What's this? Spag bol?' He stirred the soup. 'Where's the bloody pasta, Sweetman? Where's the meat?'

'It's homemade tomato soup. It's good for you.'

'Is it vegan flavoured? I don't need some goddamn woman telling me what's good for me,' Buddy said. 'And I know for sure you don't have anything to drink.' He took a flask from his jacket pocket and poured a little something into his soup, stirred it with his spoon. He slurped a spoonful, poured again from his flask, stirred, and started eating.

'How's it for you with the . . . you know?' he asked amiably.

Audrey sighed. 'Day twenty-four. It's a little easier this time because I'm busy, but I still think about it, oh, every twenty minutes. I get some help with recovery online.'

'That's the way they do it these days? No meetings in the town hall? Twelve steps to holy salvation, and all that?'

Audrey shrugged. 'There's still that, too, and it helps a lot of people. Connecting in person. But it's not always convenient when you need support so . . . online for me.' She squinted at Buddy. 'I could go with you to a meeti—'

'Nope.'

A bang startled them. Billie pushed a foot into the door and wedged themselves in sideways, balancing a huge flat parcel wrapped in brown paper in their arms.

'Hey you two old farts! Look what I did.' Billie set the package on the floor and tore back the paper to reveal a piece of art on an enormous black canvas. It was a complicated loop, a mobius, a jumble of lines in thick white strokes on top of blackboard paint. The white line on the black background seemed purposeful and deliberate, but meandering, wandering, searching, all at the same time. It ended where it had begun. It was beautiful, the sort of artwork that belonged in a loft in New York City, or a gallery in Surry Hills.

'I whipped this up for the wall over there. Whatcha think, Tawdry?'

Audrey inhaled and stared at the painting. So much talent and they didn't even know it. Billie couldn't see it in themselves.

'It's perfect.' Audrey gave them a hug. 'Does it have a title?'

Billie shrugged. 'No. What would you call it?'

'*A Goddamn Mess*,' Buddy said, and spooned up the last of his soup. 'All them squiggly lines leading nowhere.'

Audrey laughed. 'I'd call it *My Five-Year Plan*.'

Audrey spent the next three weeks finishing her website and sourcing cookie boxes and greaseproof paper from a supplier who was happy to sell his overstock at a deep discount. The boxes were different sizes and colours, mainly white but some red, hot pink, lilac and green. Audrey had the idea to mix and match the tops and bottoms of the boxes, so they made unique colour combinations. They looked fabulous, celebratory, fun. One overcast Saturday, she did a photo shoot on the beach with her iPhone in Portrait Mode: the flower-studded fortune cookies in their colourful boxes, then the cookies on their own, shot in close-up on the white sand, half-buried like little treasures, with a backdrop of sea and sky.

She weighed her products carefully and chose a market strategy she thought would work, then tweaked the weights to ensure the post office could deliver at a decent price and the fortune cookies would reach their destinations without being damaged. Since they were made of egg white, sugar and flour, they had a shelf life of four weeks. She'd need to bake fresh batches every two weeks to have enough stock on hand, but she thought she could just about manage it with the old MX Goldbake oven. She ordered a shrink-wrap machine for five hundred dollars, as well as a decent printer, and winced at the low number in her bank account.

Audrey spent hours in the evening designing logos for Bittersweet Biscuits. She worked on her laptop as a mini ad agency of one, and Billie encouraged her to set up all the social-media accounts: Instagram, Facebook, even TikTok. Audrey didn't love being in front of the camera, but Billie filmed her baking and chatting, and Audrey knew there was no other way to build a business but to begin. Small steps, move forward every day, try not to think too much about everything that could go wrong. She struggled to visualise her future; the key was to imagine it as a series of rolling hills, and try not to focus too much on the mountains or valleys.

She walked the beach every morning, in part to keep an eye on Buddy during his swims but also to feel the fresh start to the day, and try to gain some optimism and peace from inhaling the sea air. Some mornings she was early enough to see a distant Dr Flood running across the sand. He'd often stop to chat when their paths crossed.

'Nice to see that building being used,' he said one morning, his grey t-shirt sticking to his broad shoulders. 'Sorry for the sweat. Trying to stay fit. It takes more these days.'

Audrey laughed. 'Shez says as you get older, everything north just packs up and heads south.'

'Sherry's full of one-liners,' he said. 'I like the silver hair, by the way. Suits you. See you soon.' And then he was gone, leaving Audrey with a ridiculous smile that she would've been embarrassed about had anyone seen it.

Later that morning, Billie scooted across the floor, painting. They'd asked Buddy for permission to paint the worn timber floorboards white, which seemed like a bad idea to Audrey. Looking at it now, she had to admit that Billie had been right.

Billie looked up. 'I just know I'm going to get a splinter in my arse.'

In his chair in the corner, Buddy cackled until he coughed. 'Judge Judy'll have to take it out.'

'I wouldn't let Ruth near me with tweezers, would you? You better give me a raise for this, Tawdry.'

By midafternoon, Billie was finished, and the result was gorgeous: the wide sweep of whitewashed planks, with the white walls (the forest-green finally gone), high ceilings and huge bay windows, made the bakery look modern and clean, almost Scandinavian.

People from the village began to drop by. First Robert and Lem asked for a few cookies if she had any to spare, then Shez and her cleaner, Sal, arrived for morning tea.

'Do you mind if I get a coffee machine, Robert?' Audrey asked.

'Nah, course not!' Robert said. 'Don't be a bloody fool. You can sell whatever you want from here, so long as you stick to the baking and the coffee. I'll do the rest at the store, the groceries for the tourists when they start coming in a month's time.'

'That might be a little ambitious. For now, it's just to serve to friends,' Audrey said.

'Thanks, Bobbie,' Billie said. 'We'll set up a couple of tables and a few chairs, so people can have somewhere to sit.'

Audrey and Billie had already fixed up a cosy spot for Buddy in one of the bay windows, with a scratched table and a backgammon set pulled next to his leather chair. Every morning after his swim, he settled into his spot, waiting for anyone who was foolish enough to play him.

'All bloody sooks,' Buddy croaked, pocketing a fiver, 'specially you, Lem.'

'I'm getting better,' Lem said. 'I only cried the first time.'

Audrey bought a used coffee machine, and on Billie's advice, watched YouTube videos and practised until she could make a decent range of hot drinks. It wasn't long before she was serving cappuccinos, lattes and long blacks in floral teacups and saucers from the op shop. Soon most of the villagers had dropped by, especially on the days she made her classic three-tier carrot cake with its luscious cream cheese and butter frosting. Lem said it was the best he'd ever had, and he always took a slice to Shez.

One Wednesday Dr Flood parked his Mercedes convertible out the front and enjoyed an espresso and a game of backgammon, laughing and chatting with Buddy near the bay window. He ordered a box of fortune cookies as a gift and asked for pink packaging: a present for a woman, obviously. Audrey's heart gave an unreasonable twinge; she wasn't sure she wanted her fortune cookies to go to someone he was dating. But that was foolish. Business was business.

It was Lem who was the first to ask Audrey to bake a chocolate cake. This one was for Shez's birthday. She glazed it with a decadent drip-edged ganache made from melted couverture dark chocolate and decorated the top in fresh strawberry macarons and fortune cookies, making sure every fortune cookie was stuffed with a motivational quote chosen by Lem. Shez swore she loved it even more than date night hanky panky. Her unique endorsement was how word got out, and Audrey started baking a couple of date night hanky panky cakes a week.

The only villager who never dropped by was Ruth Hickson. When Audrey asked if Ruth was curious, Billie shrugged. 'Ruth wouldn't come in here unless she was dragged in, Tawdry.'

Every evening, exhausted in bed, Audrey ran through her to-do list. She'd need to order supplies and eventually find a fortune-cookie machine. She'd also have to read through the Food Authority website for hours on end and, when the kitchen was up to code, notify them, but she guiltily pushed the thought aside. There was too much to do, and too little cash to do it with. Renovating the kitchen to get it up to code was impossible. *Not yet*, she decided. *I'll cover all of that off when I'm sure I can make a go of things.* She was only just beginning to believe it might be possible to succeed. Her fledgling confidence couldn't stand another setback.

And then it was the beginning of August, the money from the Speedway was long gone, and Audrey was ready to launch her business online.

CHAPTER 24

It was a rookie mistake hoping that Bittersweet Biscuits would take off without a marketing budget. What had she been thinking? No business ever did; people couldn't buy what they couldn't see. Audrey launched her fortune-cookie offering to the sound of crickets. Every morning for a week, she checked and re-checked her website to ensure it was working properly. The analytics were atrocious. Even with the social-media posts and the videos Billie was putting up on YouTube, her tiny business was floundering.

Leaning against the island in the kitchen, Audrey tapped her pencil on a notepad, writing headline after headline to see if she could come up with an idea for a social-media campaign that had more wow than her current one, which consisted of beautiful, simple photos of her product or videos of herself chatting while baking. In her hot-pink apron, white t-shirt and white jeans, she looked like every other baker on Instagram, but older, with noticeably silver-blonde hair.

She could feature the beach—pristine, yes, and beautiful—but for Aussies, beaches were just a part of life, not a novelty. Even if the beach was as gorgeous as Whitehaven, with its white sand, sea eagles and kangaroos, pods of dolphins and whales, humpbacks to minkes and pilots depending on the season, all of that was normal. Beautiful, but everyday and expected. She needed a better idea to get some cut-through and create a buzz.

She sipped her coffee. She wanted her brand to be pretty, but a little edgy. Her fortune cookies tasted delicious, pure vanilla with a hint of bitter from the botanicals, light, with a satisfying crunch. The edible flowers pressed into them made the cookies completely unique, but none of those things were the key differentiator. It was the handwritten fortunes, sassy, tongue-in-cheek. Her fortune cookies told the truth! The fortunes were the key. So who would want sassy fortune cookies? What type of customer needed them? Who was the right spokesperson to sell something so irreverent and unique?

And that's when she remembered she still had Kylee's number. She dropped her pencil and reached for her phone.

The low rumble of Harley-Davidsons shook the glass in the bay windows. Buddy looked up from his backgammon and Billie whistled. Two Coffin Cheaters parked in front of the bakery, pulled off their leather riding gloves and removed their black helmets. One bald head, one silver brush cut.

'Holy crap, Tawd! They found you. The Coffin Cheaters are here! Tiny and Stumpy.'

Audrey untied her pink apron and walked to the door. 'I know,' she said over her shoulder. 'I invited them for morning tea.'

'Smells good in here. Audrey!' Tiny picked her up in a bear hug and set her back down on her feet. 'Sorry, had to do it. You remind me so much of my mum.'

'R.I.P.,' Stumpy said, his blue eyes flicking up to the ceiling. 'Choked on her steak. Very sad day.' Stumpy walked into the middle of the bakery. 'Nice place you got here. Sorry Smokey couldn't make it. It's Yoga Monday.'

'You boys know Billie, and this is Buddy Trask, my landlord.'

'G'day,' Buddy said. 'Nice bikes.'

'Take you for a ride, Gramps?' Tiny offered. 'Best way to see the open road.'

Audrey smiled. 'He'll probably take you up on it. I'll get the tea. Will you help me, Tiny? I made you some chicken pot pies and a chocolate cake.' The scent of golden puff pastry, dill and cream wafted through the bakery. Tiny inhaled and gave Audrey two thumbs up.

She waited, chatting about her recipes, until the brothers had eaten all the savoury pies and enjoyed a second serving of Shez's hanky panky cake before she made her pitch. She cleared her throat. 'So, I hope you don't mind my calling. I asked Kylee for your number because I have a favour to ask. I can only pay you in baking right now, but I'm hoping you'll model for me. I want you to be the face of a new ad campaign for Bittersweet Biscuits.'

'What? Tawdry! That's a bloody decent idea!' Billie said.

Stumpy rubbed his grey brush cut. 'Nah, you mean in print? We don't want our faces in any women's magazines. Anyway, we're so much more than how we look, Audrey.'

'Well, that's the thing, you see,' said Audrey, 'I knew you wouldn't want to be recognisable in the media. And I'm not trying to objectify you at all, but I wonder if we could use ... um ... parts of you in a campaign on social media?'

Tiny gestured at his lap. Billie howled.

'Uh, no. No, not those parts. Like for example,' Audrey started, grabbing her phone as she handed Stumpy a fortune cookie, 'if you held a cookie and crossed your arms, I could get a shot like this, with the cookie and your tattoos.' She took a quick photo and showed him the image.

Stumpy whistled. 'Freaking A, my biceps look good, Audrey.'

'Right?' she said and smiled at him. 'They do look good. And your tattoos make my fortune cookies look amazing.'

'So what would we have to do, exactly?' Tiny asked. 'Pose for you?'

'Just for a few photos, maybe a video or two. I'd make sure not to include your faces. I'd get you to approve every photo and sign a release form so you feel comfortable.'

'No cops. No faces?' Stumpy asked.

'No—but maybe we could include your motorcycles somehow, and have a few shots outdoors, on the beach in front of Buddy's cabana? I know it's a little bit illegal to drive down there, but—'

'We're good with illegal,' Tiny said. 'We find it's second nature. When do you want to do it?'

'Well, if you're finished eating, how about now?' Audrey said. 'We could go to the beach and get started.'

The photos on the beach were beautiful, but Audrey shot the best ones inside the bakery near one of the large bay windows. Tiny's long red beard, the tattoos, Stumpy's snake-draped arm, the leather vests: the photos were somehow authentic and tender. The delicate flower-studded cookies held in meaty biker palms were a paradox. Intriguing. Unique. After she had downloaded some to her laptop, Stumpy, Tiny and Billie stared at the photos on the screen. Even Audrey couldn't stop herself from looking at them.

She shot as many as she could with her phone and when the battery died, she switched to Billie's. She took videos where the brothers tossed fortune cookies at each other and smashed them with their fists (perfect for TikTok, Billie said), and then asked them to pose together for a video while Billie and Buddy threw fortune cookies in the air, raining down on the two bikers like confetti.

'Are we going to look like a couple?' Tiny asked. 'Because you could ask Craig and Guzza from the Cheaters. Their wedding was bloody awesome. They're what you might call diverse, like yourself, Billie.'

Buddy jutted his chin out. 'Our kid's more diverse than two gay blokes from a bikie gang.'

'You old fart, that's the nicest thing anyone's ever—' Billie stopped abruptly.

At that moment, Ruth Hickson opened the door of the bakery. She stared at them. The floor was littered with broken fortune cookies and Audrey lay at Tiny's feet, aiming Billie's phone towards the ceiling to capture the cookies raining down.

'What's going on? Billie? Why are you here?' Ruth's voice was sharp.

'We're uh, doing a . . .' Billie looked away.

Audrey hauled herself up and handed the phone to Billie. She dusted off her jeans. Her face reddened and her mouth felt dry. 'Ruth. I'd like you to meet Tiny and, um, Stumpy. They're helping me with, um . . .'

Tiny stuck out his hand, a ring on his fourth finger emblazoned with a skull, and Ruth recoiled. 'We're models,' he explained. 'For Audrey's business.'

'Male models,' Stumpy said, 'among other things. Tatts and biceps.'

'I see.' Ruth's mouth was a straight line.

Audrey reached up to tidy her hair, but it was covered in chunks of broken fortune cookies. She could only imagine what Ruth was thinking; she hadn't wanted to introduce her new business this way. She had to rely on the goodwill of the town until she got set up properly, and it was still early days. She'd planned to ask Ruth over for a coffee in a few weeks' time and mention how she'd like to trial Bittersweet Biscuits, possibly when the handsome Dr Flood was in, playing a game of backgammon with Buddy. Something in Ruth's sour expression made Audrey shrink like a little girl caught trying on her mother's make-up. She took a deep breath and tried to smile. 'We're just, you know, getting a few things done on the marketing end. I'm setting up a small business, well, just trying it out to see if it works. Market testing, if you will, before I set up formally. Everyone here was helping me.'

Ruth frowned. 'You need to come home now, Billie. I've hired you a new tutor. He's waiting at the house.'

Billie's eyes flashed. 'You can't just walk in and order me around, Ruth. I'm working. This is my part-time job.'

'Your what?'

'My job.' Billie glanced at Audrey.

Audrey's palms started to sweat. 'Ruth, I . . . it's not official, but I thought Billie might like some pocket money, so I hired them to help me out. I realise I should've asked you first. I—'

'You're employing my child?'

'It's only casual, a little design work, and helping around the place. I'm paying a proper wage for a junior. It's nothing formal, not yet—'

'So you're taking advantage of Billie? You're *exploiting* my child?' Ruth's voice was raised.

Audrey's face flushed. Had she taken advantage of Billie? She hadn't meant to; she thought it was like babysitting for any other teen, casual work for activities that Billie loved to do, and a way to help them feel useful and needed when they were struggling. She'd already planned to make it right with Billie if Bittersweet Biscuits turned into a proper business. She'd offer Billie a formal part-time job rather than pay in cash, and she intended to put them on her payroll with benefits the minute she decided to go ahead properly. There was no question, and Billie's work was exceptional. 'I'm paying Billie minimum wage and I'm planning to—'

'Without a contract? No superannuation, no sick leave or annual leave? That's illegal, and those motorcycles parked outside? You people are the Coffin Cheaters.' Ruth's face was crimson. 'I should phone the police. Billie, you're coming home. Now. They're part of a gang.'

'Well, I'd say it's more of a club than a gang, wouldn't you, Stumps?' Tiny said, and Stumpy nodded.

Buddy wheeled closer. 'Calm the farm, Judge Judy. Have a coffee. There's nothing going on here but a bit of morning tea for some hungry blokes who miss their own mum. Right, Audrey?'

'You!' Ruth crossed her arms. 'A mum? If you were, you'd never act like this. You're exploiting my child, and these are known criminals!'

'Well, we're not quite known,' Tiny said. 'Never been convicted.'

'Enough!' roared Ruth. 'I'm a former judge of the Federal Court. I know who you are. Billie, let's go.'

'Aw, mama, don't you think you're being a little rough on the kid?' Stumpy said. 'They were only—'

But Ruth grabbed Billie's arm and yanked them out the door.

CHAPTER 25

That night, sleepless as usual, Audrey questioned her own motives about Billie. She hadn't thought she was being unfair; everything in the business was unfolding like a startup, slowly and organically, and paying Billie in cash had felt appropriate. She decided she'd make it right as soon as she could, with backpay for superannuation and annual leave. But she was surprisingly calm about Ruth's indictment of her brand's affiliation with the Coffin Cheaters. In fact, the marketer in her knew that if she'd hit a nerve with Ruth, she'd also hit on something special, a campaign that customers would notice and share. And she was right.

Within days, the bikers and her biscuits went viral on Instagram and Facebook, and the TikTok with Stumpy and Tiny smashing fortune cookies with their fists to Fleetwood Mac's 'I Don't Want to Know' had over fifty thousand views. Bikers with biscuits on the beach, biscuit confetti, biscuits and tattoos, every image Audrey had shot so joyfully gained traction on social media. And that's when the orders started to arrive.

The first one was from a bar in Newtown, the main social hub of Sydney University. They wanted Bittersweet Biscuits for a student event in September. Then she received a message from a local gallery: they put in a modest order for the launch of a new artist who painted floral watercolours. Audrey's floral fortune cookies were very pretty, and they wondered if they could order them with a fortune-cookie message from the gallery itself? Audrey thanked them and said corporate branding may be possible in the future, but not at present; they'd have to take the cookies without knowing what sorts of fortunes they'd get. The gallery owner tittered nervously but agreed, and every marketing instinct in Audrey's body tingled. The owner had sounded a little excited, a little fearful and very, very intrigued. It was the perfect heady mix for a marketing storm.

Audrey knew from years of market research back in advertising that people loved introducing a small element of danger when they were planning a party. The behavioural heuristics were working beautifully: people craved the excitement of something unique and a little wild, of not knowing exactly what was going to happen at their event. Audrey's floral fortune cookies would deliver unpredictability. Excitement. Maybe even controversy. Variable, intermittent reinforcement was just as addictive as those hearts and likes on social media. Would the fortunes be appropriate? Would they cause offence? Everyone would want her fortune cookies: Bittersweet Biscuits, fortune cookies that—maybe a little worryingly—told the truth.

On the third morning after launching the campaign, Audrey opened an Instagram message from the Sydney socialite Imogen Hayes, swimwear model turned society wife—and daughter-in-law of the Hayes Corp chair.

I'm throwing a divorce party! Bye, bye, Matt Hayes. Can I get those fortune cookies?

The name made Audrey wince, as she remembered his boorish father and her pitching disaster on her last day at the ad agency. According to the papers, Matt Hayes Junior was the new CEO of Hayes Corp, and he was in the social pages as often as his soon-to-be ex-wife. Word would spread from the divorce party; other people would want what the rich and beautiful Imogen Hayes had. And they could have it, simply by buying a box of fortune cookies.

I want fifteen dozen, Imogen's message read. And in all caps: *MAKE THEM AS NASTY AS POSSIBLE.*

Audrey then got a garbled text from Tiny, who was excited to pick up his modelling payment, which consisted of seven dark chocolate cakes for the Coffin Cheaters' next meeting at their clubhouse. Kylee texted to say *omg Tiny looks amazing on Insta!!!* Emma texted to ask how business was tracking, and to say that she'd shown the Bittersweet Biscuits Facebook page to her Canadian friend, Louise, who thought the bikers were hilarious, and that she loved the photos of them on the beach. Wyatt texted to say they had an offer on the house and why wasn't she checking her email, the offer was better than expected, and he thought they should take it. She sent back a terse *Do it*, cc'd Danny, her lawyer, and that was all. After the sale, she'd have Danny help her negotiate the debt with the bank, but she couldn't think of that now. She had too much work to do.

Buddy helped her stick ingredients labels to the back of the fortune-cookie boxes, and Lem fixed the new shrink-wrap machine so it worked properly. Shez sat on a table swinging her legs and drinking coffee, offering very little in the way of hands-on help because of her new and extremely long fluoro-pink gel manicure—but a lot of what she called Critical Strategic Manifesting Advice for Female Entrepreneurs.

And Audrey baked.

She was up well before sunrise every day. Without a fortune-cookie machine, the batter for each cookie had to be poured on the cookie sheets, baked quickly, and then, while the cookie was hot, it had to be folded in half over a handwritten fortune—she'd ordered silicone gloves online after burning herself too often in the first week—and finally, crimped over the edge of a water glass. She'd found an app that turned her handwriting into a font so the fortunes retained the look of being handwritten but could be printed quickly in large quantities. The cost to print was almost nothing and Buddy cut the small strips of paper: handmade was the look she was creating, so it didn't matter if they weren't perfect, though she added 'paper guillotine' to her ever-growing supplies list. If only the balance of her bank account could match her needs!

Her back ached from standing and she barely had time to do her laundry. She opened tins of soup from Robert's General Store for herself and Buddy and worked harder than she'd ever worked in her life, before showering and falling into bed exhausted. But she got the orders out the door. There wasn't time to think about the city, Wyatt and Charmaine, or her former career at the agency. There was only now, and the need to respond quickly to new orders as they came through: to be professional and to direct her tiny but promising earnings into a new business bank account. She started to set aside the money she'd need for her business set-up and renovations to the kitchen to get her food safety certification, for tax and wages for Billie's part-time job.

Three days into the rush, Audrey sent a text to Billie but didn't get a response. That night, rolling around in her bed and unable to sleep, she turned on her bedside lamp and tried to read more of *The Alchemist* but had to start back at the beginning of the chapter. Buddy had said she could keep the book until she'd finished it. She closed it and sighed.

Ruth was right; Audrey hadn't thought of Billie as an underage child, as someone who needed to be protected from bikers or an employer who was asking them to work without a contract or superannuation or permission from their mother. She'd thought of Billie as almost an adult—so bright, articulate, able to take care of themselves, tough and independent—but of course that was wrong. Billie was a teenager, and vulnerable in so many ways, and Audrey had no right to interfere. There was no way around it: Audrey would have to apologise to Ruth and do her best to make it right.

A week later, with no Billie popping around, Audrey decided: she'd walk over to Ruth's that evening, take along some of Billie's favourite chocolate chip cookies, and apologise. She'd regretted ever asking Billie to take part in a casual work arrangement and wished she'd been more cautious about employing Ruth Hickson's child. She had the cookies ready, and she knew apologising to Ruth was the adult thing to do. But at the last minute, Audrey set the plate on the island in the bakery kitchen, put on her jacket and headed out to the beach instead.

Lights shone through the windows of Buddy's cabana, and Nina was singing 'My Baby Just Cares for Me', bouncy and joyful. She could stop by to check on him, but Buddy had seemed particularly cheerful that day after playing four games of backgammon with Dr Flood and fleecing him for fifty dollars. Audrey had been too busy to stop and chat, but she'd dropped off their coffees and watched Dr Flood shake his head when Buddy poured in the bourbon.

'Aw, Doc, it's medicine.'

'Well,' Dr Flood said, 'moderation, Buddy, like I told you. We want you around for a long time. Don't we, Audrey?' In spite of herself, she'd blushed and nodded, wondering just for a second what it might be like to be part of a 'we' with Justin Flood.

But tonight, Buddy could do without her, and a quick walk before she headed to Ruth's would calm her nervous energy. She found herself at the edge of the beach and eased off her shoes, then stuffed her socks inside them. The night breeze was unusually warm for winter; it hinted that spring was on its way. Overhead, a low-slung moon made the beach glow silver black.

Audrey stretched her arms up and took a deep breath. It seemed impossible that such a beautiful place was hers alone tonight: salty air, the sharp scent of seaweed, sky overloaded with a surfeit of stars, the waves calling, rolling relentlessly onward. She turned to her right, and looked down the length of the beach. To do the whole walk would take a little over an hour, but it was still early, and she could already feel the tension leaving her shoulders and neck. The fine sand, cold underfoot and packed tight from the tide, lay almost flat, a long pristine runway around the dark bay. She breathed in again, deeper, and felt that she was somehow walking with another version of herself, the little girl her mother had urged out to the beach at twilight, the girl who'd run so freely, arms pumping wildly, thin legs scissoring across the sand, calling out to Joyce in the growing darkness.

She wondered if the water was freezing, and asked herself how Buddy could stand it every morning when he swam. Audrey walked closer to the shoreline and gingerly stepped into the waves. Gasped.

Electric blue lightning shot from her footstep in the sand through the water, bolts of neon light, spreading. Again, she stepped. More lightning. She reached down and cupped the ocean water in two hands: a magical potion of bright blue in the black water. She kept walking; it kept happening. Blue lightning, a deep blue glow as she stirred the water.

Bioluminescence.

She laughed like a girl, like a sorceress, and ran straight into the electric blue. Her jeans were heavy and cold, wet to the thighs. She leaped, splashed, sang out. She flung her arms wide and sang one long, high G, like an opera soprano performing the 'Queen of the Night' aria from *The Magic Flute*. The water answered her, waves rolling, and with every step, she leaped into electric blue. Audrey twirled then, weaving on the sloshy shore like a figure skater, lightning shooting from her bare feet. The night was a gift she hadn't even dreamt of asking for. She didn't know the ocean could be this beautiful, magical. She'd heard of bioluminescence vaguely, but to be in it, alone, in this huge starry night, the black sea filled with impossible blue?

It was a miracle. A gift. Maybe even a sign from the universe or whoever was in charge that she'd be a success.

And then she saw someone in the distance. Stop. Raise a hand hello.

She held her breath.

Oh, she didn't want to share! She didn't want to break this moment, to make this memory with another person! She wanted it to be hers alone. Audrey triumphant, all the versions of herself she'd ever been, like a Russian doll, on a magical beach that gifted her one of the wonders of the world. Her feelings were selfish, but true.

The person walked towards her, churning electric blue water in the night. They would've seen everything, heard her crazy witch-like song. They were twenty metres from her, then fifteen, then ten. She forced down her disappointment and gulped a breath of cold beach air. Of course, she could share this miracle. For goodness' sake, the earth didn't have favourites—this wasn't a benediction chosen for her!

Audrey's shoulders tightened; her mind prepared to launch into her usual people-pleasing banter. *Hello! Fabulous night, so lucky, nice to see you* . . . when the man stopped. With the hint of a smile on his handsome face, he saluted her. 'Beautiful night for dancing, Audrey.' He started to walk away, but something made him turn back. He looked at her and shrugged. 'But then . . . you seem to make everything beautiful.' He turned and strode up the beach towards the path leading to Buddy's cabana.

Audrey's face flushed under the silvery sky. She watched the retreating back of Dr Justin Flood, leaving her with herself, to revel in the magic.

When Billie opened the Hicksons' front door two hours later, Audrey stood breathless. She felt huge, incandescent, different. Taller.

'Hi Tawd.' Billie took the plate of cookies, loaded with chocolate chips and sprinkled with sea salt, and Audrey stepped inside.

Billie looked well enough, and Audrey resisted an urge to hug them. 'How are you?'

'Tortured. Death by homework. My new tutor's a ball breaker, and he doesn't even know if I have them.' Billie winked, and Audrey laughed.

'I'm here to apologise to your mum. I miss you. We all miss you. I'm hoping I can explain to Ruth about hiring you.'

'Naw, Tawd, it's fine—'

'No, it wasn't fair. I know you enjoyed it, and I paid you, but I should've set it up better.'

'I was good at it.'

Audrey pointed at Billie's hoodie. 'You're better than good. The bakery is beautiful thanks to you.'

'And I did it all with nothing.' Billie laughed. 'Imagine what I could do if I had a decent budget, Tawd.'

'I wonder if . . . just thinking ahead . . . you'd accept a proper part-time job with superannuation and a contract. If you wanted to. You could work around your homeschooling. Might be useful on a resume, how you designed the space and—'

'I think not.' Ruth Hickson walked into the foyer as she spoke. 'Billie, time for Maths. Your tutor wants it emailed by ten-thirty.'

Audrey smiled at Billie encouragingly, but they slouched down the hallway. She turned to face Ruth. 'I wanted to apologise. I shouldn't've hired Billie without speaking to you first.'

'You might as well come in and discuss it,' Ruth said, and Audrey felt the magic drain out of her, along with all her resolve.

Ruth poured a Scotch and held it out. Audrey politely shook her head. *Day sixty-one.* She forced herself to look Ruth in the eyes. 'No thanks, I'm not drinking right now.'

'Oh.' Ruth arched an eyebrow and gestured to the sofa. 'Addiction? I've heard that's difficult.'

Audrey exhaled. Ruth had a talent for saying horrible things. It was obvious why Billie was unhappy. 'Ruth, listen. I wanted to tell you you're welcome at the bakery. So is Billie. I hope you're okay if they drop by.'

Ruth took a sip from the crystal glass and set it on the coffee table between them. She picked up a box of matches and lit three candles. The scent of vanilla drifted up, cloying and sweet.

'Audrey, you aren't a mother, so you don't understand. Billie needs to study.' Ruth picked up the glass and swirled her Scotch. 'They don't need a part-time job hanging around a derelict building with questionable people.'

Audrey stared past Ruth at the piece of art behind her. It looked like a Margaret Olley original: gorgeous though a little droopy, a jug of snowcap daisies, orange honeysuckle and Chinese lanterns on a muted blue background. The daisy petals reminded Audrey of her fortune cookies. She'd worked so hard to get this far, and there was still so much to do before she could even begin to think of being financially stable or secure. Her business, her tiny group of new friends, her new beginning: Billie was a big part of it. Audrey needed their laughter and wisecracking, their naïve belief in what was possible, more than she wanted to admit. Billie was pure energy, a jump, a leap and a dive. Audrey saw who they were inside, and if the outsides were a little teenagery, still shifting, Audrey knew Billie would become an incredible adult one day.

'Well?' Ruth added, as if she were speaking to a child. 'Can I assume you understand?'

Audrey met Ruth's gaze. She cleared her throat. 'Billie needs someone to see their talent and appreciate them. Not expect them to be different.'

'I beg your pardon?'

'They love working at the bakery. Part-time jobs are good for teens.'

'What gives you the right to think you know what's best?' Ruth pursed her lips and took a sip of Scotch. 'Can you even trust yourself?'

Audrey frowned. 'This isn't about me, Ruth. Billie needs to figure out who they are, what they want—'

Ruth's eyes were hard, grey, accusing. 'Like you are? Figuring it out? An unemployed middle-aged woman in a neglected rental with bikers on your premises? Those people are criminals. And Buddy is a drunk, but you'd get that.'

Audrey took a deep breath and kept her voice calm, though her hands in her lap were shaking. 'We're talking about Billie, not me,' she repeated.

'You're acting like their mother,' Ruth said. 'It's laughable.'

Audrey clasped her hands together. How dare Ruth Hickson behave like this? She'd helped Billie more in a month than Ruth's parenting would help in a year. Homeschooling because of some fake glandular fever? A raft of tutors when Billie was obviously smart as a whip? Audrey had offered friendship and acceptance, and good old-fashioned purpose and pride from hard work in a casual, part-time job. Billie had achieved something in the bakery; the two of them were a team.

'Well, you're not acting like their mother, and somebody has to,' Audrey said.

Ruth slammed her crystal glass on the coffee table and stood. 'That's it. Enough! You're not a mother at all, Audrey, so what would you know? Billie told me all about you. You're an alcoholic. Your husband left you, and you've lost your job. You're not someone who can tell *me* how to raise *my child*.' Audrey felt anger radiating from Ruth's body like an electrical current. 'You think you're a people-pleaser, but actually? You're a manipulator.'

Audrey stared at the ugly twist to Ruth's mouth. Her stomach rolled over. Yes, she tried to help people! Yes, she wanted to please them. Why not? That didn't make her manipulative, did it?

'I'm only trying to—'

'Help?' Ruth laughed. 'Please. You're a mess. Can you see that about yourself? How blind are you, Audrey? We don't need your help—you need to get your life together and leave us alone. It's time for you to leave Whitehaven Bay.'

CHAPTER 26

Audrey walked out of the Hicksons' front door on legs so shaky she thought she might faint. When Ruth closed it behind her, her knees sagged, and she leaned against the house. She wanted a drink. Needed one. Every cell in her body screamed for comfort, and it went by the name of *shiraz chardonnay vodka gin*. It was the thing clawing inside her; it needed to get out and give her some relief. No one talked about this in regular life, in the office or at a dinner party. But in the undercurrent, where women on their recovery journeys found each other online, rolling beneath waves, tumbling and churning inside their pain—those women, yes, mostly women—were talking and pulling each other from the riptide. She could reach out in a second, through an app or a website. Send a message. Someone in the world, awake somewhere, would answer her and help. She knew this.

But.

Her brain reared up and fought against her. No one talked about the lack of alcohol being the problem, but it was! *Not having it* was the problem! When she could use a drink like a pacifier or a buffer, she was fine. Absolutely okay, able to handle anything. She wasn't a drunk; she just slept better when she'd had a few glasses of wine, maybe with a too-early bedtime and a headache in the morning, but still. Wine worked. It did the job. It dulled the pain. It was a simple fix.

Until it wasn't.

Until she needed more to fall asleep. Then more again.

She could get in her car right now and find a drink somewhere, but it was too late, the liquor store in town was shut. She could go to Buddy's and casually ask for a little top-up in a cup of tea, shrug gamely; he'd let her. Drive to a hotel, walk into the bar, but everything shut so early midweek and where could she— *Don't go there.* She stepped around Ruth and Billie's house and trudged mechanically to the beach. *One hour, one minute at a time.*

It was only this bad after confrontations. When Audrey was busy, she didn't crave it. But right now she just wanted the relief on her tongue, burning her throat and warming her belly, and then the escape of sleep. Other people took drugs for that, sleeping pills, or drowned themselves in chocolate or sex or fast food or Tim Tams or online shopping or so many other tempting things. Was this so different? She didn't really need to *drink*; it wasn't the alcohol, it was the sleep she wanted, the forgetting. All of it was the same in the end, a way to forget, but people like Ruth judged alcohol as being so much worse than other temptations. *You're an alcoholic. An addict.*

The label did not help.

This dark neighbourhood of Audrey's mind was dangerous, and she'd walked it before a hundred thousand times. The beach confronted her, pitch black. There might be kangaroos, and yes, deep in the churning waves, sharks—but the real enemy was inside her. Her own stupid self. Weak, ill-prepared to handle what life was throwing her, a disaster in the middle of her life, everything changing and caving in, dominoes that fell on top of dominoes, whizzing past too fast, her life, her mistakes, all the things she hadn't done and hadn't built and hadn't managed. Her career. Wyatt. Motherhood. A stupid homemade biscuit business.

You're an unsuccessful middle-aged woman. Nobody sees you.

Audrey stood on the beach in the darkness, her back to the Hicksons' house, its lamps glowing with Ruth and Billie's family life. She forced herself to plod forward through loose sand to the edge of the water, hoping for the bioluminescent magic she knew was long gone. It only ever lasted a couple of hours, that's what Google had said earlier, when she was at home reading about the miracle she'd just witnessed, trembling in her underwear, pulling off her wet jeans before getting ready to go and see Ruth. Now, she glanced down and squinted in the dark. Someone had written a message ringed in driftwood, shells and a few feathers. Beach graffiti. Billie. The words were drawn with a stick on the sand.

Question everything . . . and keep going.

'You were up late.' Buddy settled into his chair and pulled out the backgammon.

'Guess you were, too.' Audrey set down his coffee and a plate of spicy and warm orange cardamom biscuits. Baked golden brown and sprinkled with sugar, they smelled earthy, sweet, and reminded her of her mother, the amber perfume from the chemist shop that Joyce used to spray all around her in a cloud before she went to work at the salon. 'Did you see my light on?'

Buddy nodded as he chewed, then took a sip of coffee. 'So damn good, Sweetman.' He sighed. 'Let me guess. Battling the demon drink.'

Audrey sighed. 'Have you ever . . . ?'

'I tried, Sweetman, ten years back. But everyone I care about is gone. Nobody here gives a damn. Why would I stop now?'

She knew there was no good answer. But maybe you could make a family out of whatever was left, even if you didn't have the real thing. Maybe a patchwork family was better than nothing at all. She reached out and touched his arm. 'Because of me? Because I need you to try with me?'

'You?'

Audrey tucked a strand of silver and blonde hair behind her ear. 'I'm around the age Simone would've been, Buddy, and I'm still here. What if I need you?'

He stared out the bay window towards the street, his eyes watery. Audrey handed him a napkin.

'Goddamn women,' he said.

A buzz in the kitchen made Audrey leap up. She pulled on her silicone gloves and took out a tray of biscuits, placed the fortunes inside them, folded each one quickly and hooked them in a ring around the lip of a glass bowl. She'd learned this was easier than using multiple water glasses, and her system was getting faster, but still, it was far too inefficient for a real business. She'd need the fortune-cookie machine if Bittersweet Biscuits ever really took off. She couldn't keep baking tray by tray, with only one of her folding the hot discs in two, but it was the best she could do for now.

She piped another tray of batter, slid it in the oven and clicked the page she'd bookmarked on her laptop. She winced at the costs on the high-tech Asian website. She scanned the specs on two fortune-cookie machine models, trying to work out features and delivery costs when an email pinged. She glanced down; it was junk mail from a major women's magazine ... but wait. No—there was an editor's name on the email. Tamara O'Hara. She clicked it open. The magazine was running a feature on female entrepreneurs opening businesses in their second act; would Audrey like to be interviewed about Bittersweet Biscuits? *The Sydney Morning Herald* had mentioned her fortune cookies when they wrote about Imogen Hayes' divorce party in the Private Sydney column (trashy, compulsively readable, Audrey knew because she couldn't stop herself from wondering about the lives of the elite even though it was embarrassing), and Tamara O'Hara had tracked Audrey down. Would the bikers in her social-media campaign be available for the photo shoot? Was Audrey willing to be a spokesperson for launching a business in midlife? Imogen Hayes was willing to provide a quote about her cookies, and had agreed to release the photos from her party on Instagram; had Audrey seen them?

The oven timer buzzed; she ignored it, and soon the scent of burning cookies flooded the bakery. Free publicity directed at the right demographic could catapult her business into public awareness and then ... well, she could prove to investors that she had a strong market. She needed the capital an investor would bring. It was only one article, but it would be a feature, and in a magazine with a huge circulation that targeted women—who, after all, were the people typically responsible for planning parties.

'Sweetman! What the hell are you doing in there! Cookies are burning!' Buddy trundled into the kitchen with his walker. 'Why are you sitting there like a dummy?'

'It's starting, Buddy. I got some good news.' She handed him her reading glasses and he peered at the screen over her shoulder.

'Kissed on the arse by the good luck fairy,' he said. 'Well, it's about goddamn time.'

Though she only had a week to prepare for the interview, online orders kept arriving and left Audrey little time to worry about the article. She called Tiny but as she suspected, the Coffin Cheaters declined to be in the feature on account of the publicity they were already dealing with, after the new signage for the minigolf course in town was changed from Puttsville to Buttsville, and CCTV cameras had recorded their exuberant, drunken signwriting.

Shez said it was a good thing, those blokes were too photogenic, and Audrey would never shine with her half grey-half blonde hair if she had to pose next to bikies in leather chaps and tatts. She also suggested a girls' spa day at Curl Up and Dye, with a gel manicure and some aggressive Brazilian bikini waxing, so Audrey would look and feel her best when she met the journalist, but Audrey had refused under the guise of being too busy with work. On the morning of the interview, she'd pulled on her signature white t-shirt and white jeans, with a hot-pink cotton apron tied neatly around her waist, her silvering hair twisted up in a bun. At the last minute, she put on the heart necklace from Emma, who'd texted that she was loving her Canadian holiday and wanted a full report about the journalist from Sydney. *Absolutely—I'll tell all! xxx* Audrey had texted back.

Audrey fussed with the fortune cookies on the Royal Crown Derby plates as she and Buddy waited for the journalist to arrive.

She'd set a stack of colourful, mismatched boxes—lilac with a green top, pink with red, blue with orange, all with her Bittersweet Biscuits labels—on the table beside the cookies. She'd send them back to Sydney as a thank you to the team from the magazine.

'Billie's here,' Buddy called from his table in the window.

Billie opened the door carrying a long plank of recycled timber, their white hoodie covered in blood on one shoulder, dripping down the front, splattered across the sleeves.

'Jesus, Kid! You look like a wreck,' Buddy said.

Billie tapped the top of Buddy's balding head. 'You too, you old fart. I almost gave Ruth a heart attack. I bought this online—cool silk-screening, hey?—and then I wore it in the kitchen carrying an axe with tomato sauce on it. Ruth nearly died.' Billie laughed. 'Hey, brought you a present, Tawdry. Shez told me about the photo shoot.'

Audrey wiped her hands on a dish towel. 'I was wondering if you'd drop by.'

'Hitting the books, Tawd. Trying to see things from Ruth's point of view, but it's tough to get my head that far up my own arse.'

Buddy snorted. 'Judge Judy is a killer, Kid. You're brave for living with her.'

'Show me quickly,' Audrey said. 'Your mum says you're not to hang around here.'

Billie turned around the recycled board. It was painted a lovely deep charcoal, with simple white lettering in all caps: *BITTERSWEET BAKERY CAFÉ*. Underneath, in smaller letters, Billie had painted *AUDREY SWEETMAN, FOUNDER*.

'For the photo shoot.' Billie shrugged. 'We can nail it up over the door, so they know where to find you.'

'I love it,' Audrey said. 'But it isn't a café, Billie. It's barely a bakery.'

'It isn't a café yet. You need to dream bigger, Tawdry, and keep going. That's what you're always telling me, maybe not, you know, in so many words but—'

Audrey squished the tall, slim body to her heart.

Half an hour later, after Buddy had declared he was tired of goddamn no-show journos and was leaving to take a swim, the bakery door swung open, and the journalist, a slim older woman, stepped inside, followed by a tall, boyish photographer. Audrey blinked at the journalist's shiny black vinyl jumpsuit, red stilettos and wide, feathered belt. Her hair was cut into an asymmetrical black bob with a sharp fringe and chunky white highlights. Somehow it had the look of sitting slightly askew on her tiny head. A wig? Hair extensions? Audrey couldn't tell, but the overall effect was channelling a well-groomed crow. She made a mental note to tell Shez, who would surely love to hear about it.

'Tamara O'Hara, from the *Weekly*,' the journalist said in a crisp English accent, and held out red almond-shaped fingertips. 'Via thirty-one years in London at *British Vogue*.'

'Audrey Sweetman.' Audrey's hand knocked against the feathered belt.

'Careful,' Tamara said. 'Authentic emu. Dreadfully rare, but I managed to snatch some from a farmer in the Southern Highlands.' She patted the belt. 'Upcycled vintage Hermès. It took so much glue.'

'It's . . . uh . . . wow,' Audrey said. 'Very . . . bold.'

'I know.' Tamara adjusted her wig and waved a hand at the photographer. 'Martin, set up over there.' She glanced around the empty bakery. 'So, this is the business Imogen Hayes was raving about? Her divorce party was sublime, by the way. Nobody divorces like Imogen.'

'You were there?' Audrey asked.

Tamara frowned as if Audrey were just the tiniest bit stupid. 'All three times she's done it. I'm Tamara O'Hara. I go to every party in Vaucluse. I was the one who tipped off the journalist at *The Sydney Morning Herald.*'

'Of course,' Audrey said. She gestured to the table of sweets. 'Would either of you like a coffee or some biscuits?'

The photographer headed to the table, but Tamara raised her thin eyebrows to decline.

'Shall we sit and begin?' Tamara clicked record on her mobile phone and pulled a leopard-print notebook from her handbag. 'Tell me your origin story, Audrey. Starting a baking business at your age, in the middle of nowhere? Do you find it a cliché? Somewhat gendered? A life implosion perhaps, that made you race back into sexist gender roles, straight into the kitchen in a remote beachside town?'

Audrey exhaled. She knew exactly what Tamara was thinking—a midlife woman and a baking business: very Mrs Fields Cookies from 1975. What was so interesting about that? She also knew that articles had to be sensational, and these days, most entrepreneurs were happy to reveal their innermost struggles publicly. The struggle was often more newsworthy than the truth—like the billionaire Sydney tech group that boasted about starting up in a garage, but neglected to mention they were financed by their parents' platinum credit cards. Audrey wasn't that type of entrepreneur, desperate for clicks and recognition. In fact, she'd been relieved when she'd come up with the strategy to ask the Coffin Cheaters to be brand ambassadors for Bittersweet Biscuits. It was fun and fresh and didn't involve her own predictable story: a middle-aged woman retrenched and wronged, creating what she could with her own two hands. She knew her life implosion would help sell magazines—and cookies—if she were willing to tell all. A cheating husband. His personal assistant. Lies and outrage. Fortune cookies that told the freaking truth. A woman's fury transformed into a business empire. Magicking beauty out of nothing, like many women before her: for Audrey it was flower petals, bits of paper and the kind of snarky wisdom women had always traded over a coffee and a chat.

When her life had upended, she'd added sugar and butter, and turned up the heat.

'Very quiet here in your business, Audrey.' Tamara squinted at her, black and white striped bob cocked to the side. 'Is it doing well?'

The question was extremely pointed, but Audrey knew how to answer it. 'It's quiet this morning, but my orders are mainly online. I ship to all the major centres.' Audrey raised her chin. 'Whitehaven Bay is a vibrant community. So many lovely people. And the business is reclaiming a dream I had when I was younger.' She described her cookie cart in university, her decades-long advertising career and her spontaneous sea change. She apologised that her bikie brand ambassadors weren't available for a photo. She left out the cheating husband and her financial disaster. 'I wanted to build a business that brought people joy, and I started baking fortune cookies because they were my late mother's favourite. She believed in the fortunes, but I always found them a little . . . disappointing. I thought, why not make fortune cookies that tell the truth?'

Tamara tugged at her wig. 'They're a bit bonkers, I'll give you that. Great for a laugh at a party. And very pretty with those botanicals. Imogen Hayes adored them. But living out here? Thinking you could pull off a startup in a tiny little place like Whitehaven Bay?' She sniffed. 'It must be difficult being so very far away from culture. Do you spend time with the locals?'

'I work long hours, but the community here is . . .' Audrey wondered how to describe them. Nosy? Opinionated? Always in her space, dropping in unannounced for coffee and a chat, but somehow chewing her out and cheering her on, encouraging her to have a go no matter how often she had to course correct and begin again? Audrey glanced around the bakery, and remembered all the teamwork it had taken to come this far. Billie and Buddy. Shez with her ridiculous entrepreneurial advice. Robert and his terrible coffee. Finally, she shrugged at Tamara. 'They're a lot like family.'

The bakery door swung open. 'Sweetman! Forgot my goddamn keys!'

In all his naked, shrivelled glory, Buddy stood in the doorway, faded striped towel draped over one shoulder, fedora on his head, wrinkled hands inching his red walker forward step by jiggly step. 'Oh, there, on the table.' He trundled over to where Martin the photographer sat gaping. 'Don't mind me,' he waved at Tamara, 'just heading out for a swim. Carry on with your journalling.' Buddy bent to pick up his keys and glanced over his shoulder at Tamara's vinyl jumpsuit. 'Unless you want to take a dip?'

Tamara shuddered. 'These are dark times, but . . . not that dark.'

Buddy wheeled around and stared at her. 'What's that? Some kind of philosophy woo-woo? You one of them yogi types from the city?'

'Excuse me?' Tamara crinkled her nose as if something smelled a little off. 'Would you like a minute to deal with this, Audrey?'

Audrey flushed and straightened her spine. Buddy owned the building and had been nothing but helpful. Eccentric, yes, and difficult, but he had his reasons. She wouldn't let him be disrespected, naked or not. 'Tamara, I'd like you to meet my landlord, Buddy Trask.' Buddy rolled towards Tamara, who flinched as he shook her hand. Her sour expression made Audrey suppress a giggle. 'Buddy's also a good friend. Incredibly helpful here,' Audrey said. 'Loves to swim.'

'Damn right I do. You tell Tamarama all about your business, Sweetman. Greatest biscuits on the eastern seaboard.' He waggled a crooked finger at the biscuit table. 'You should eat a few. You're a bit scrawny for my taste. You could beef up a little.'

Tamara raised her eyebrows.

'I'm late for my constitutional,' Buddy said. 'Best way to manage constipation.' He rolled past Tamara, white buttocks jiggling, and walked out the door.

Tamara coughed. 'I think I've seen enough,' she said. 'Just one last question, Audrey. You gave up a corporate career to bake biscuits in a seaside town. Asking for our readers: do you feel too old to start over?'

Audrey held Tamara's gaze and took a deep breath. 'I don't think anyone's too old to start over. But I think everyone's too old to keep on doing something that isn't working for them.'

CHAPTER 27

Kneeling outside the General Store, Audrey snipped heads off Robert's daisies, imagining the bobbly stems were the necks of oh, Summer from the ad agency. Snip! Wyatt and Charmaine. Hack. Hack. Poor Robert's flower beds were becoming increasingly depleted the more fortune cookies she sold. Though Tamara O'Hara's magazine article hadn't exactly transformed her business overnight, online orders had improved so much that Audrey had asked Buddy if she could plant daisies in the weed-filled flower beds around the bakery.

Planting daisies: one more job for her extremely long to-do list. She wondered what would happen if a woman ever made a to-don't list. To-don't: don't waste any time worrying about your husband since he'll be unfaithful if he wants to. Don't ignore your joint mortgage account. Don't assume your boss is happy with you. Don't believe that excellence at work will protect you from ageism. Don't forget to have sex for six months when you're menopausal and drowning in night sweats, and definitely don't imagine it's an accomplishment when you do. Don't forget to keep three steps ahead of any potential problems: chardonnay, chocolate, people-pleasing, ambitious colleagues. Don't give up your dreams in case you need to resurrect them to feed yourself.

Robert opened the door. 'Coffee?'

'No, thanks, Robert. But I'm taking all your daisies.'

'Take away!' he said, and went back inside.

Audrey pushed back her damp curls with a dirty gardening glove. After the magazine feature, she'd received an email from an executive at the country's largest grocery store chain, asking if she was available for a video call to discuss the possibility of supplying stores country-wide with Bittersweet Biscuits—just a trial to see if the general public had any appetite for her fortune cookies. The exec was worried they might be more of a novelty item than a cookie people would enjoy eating. Audrey explained about the botanicals that made her fortune cookies beautiful and unique, and told her brand story of how the name 'bittersweet' had originated . . . partly by sheer luck, renting a flat above a disused building that used to be the Bittersweet Bakery, and of course because of her surname, Sweetman. As she chatted, she wove a more acceptable version of the real story of how her business had come to be, leaving out her debt, her broken heart, the reason for the snarky fortunes and her philandering husband. In short: she lied a little. But origin stories always sold, and she didn't want to be a dissected frog on a laboratory table. She was stronger and wiser than that.

She'd held her breath when the executive named the estimated size of an initial order. The final number, he explained, would depend on whether he could get head office to agree on the pricing and volume discounts. But if all went well, the ongoing order would be so large that it would be impossible to supply with any consistency unless she had a fortune-cookie machine and an employee or two. Audrey thanked him for his interest and said she'd be in touch as soon as she worked out the details of her business expansion, and to please keep Bittersweet Biscuits in mind—she'd love to consider next steps and keep talking! So exciting!

She knew from her work at the ad agency that corporate dances like this happened all the time. Maybe it would eventuate in a deal, but more likely not. Still, it was an exciting lead, but the production problems were enormous; first, she'd have to find an angel investor, spend weeks creating a brilliant and convincing pitch for them, and then receive an offer for funding without signing over too much equity in her company. After securing funding (extremely hard, probably impossible), she'd need to order the machinery from overseas, and have it trucked to the beach and installed in the Bittersweet Biscuits kitchen. But she was getting ahead of herself; she hadn't formally rented the bakery yet. Her stomach rolled over and she brushed the thought aside. She made dinners for Buddy several times a week, but when she offered to pay him rent for the downstairs as well as the apartment, he'd waved it off. Surely that was the first thing she needed to do? Then she'd apply for all the proper set-up with the Food Authority and a business licence and she'd be ready to launch properly. She felt a pang of guilt; she knew she had to take the plunge and set up her business, but she didn't have the money for a kitchen renovation yet.

There was no way she wanted to take advantage of Buddy's kindness or be the sort of person who cared for an older person only to gain from it. No, she was a friend. A friend to Buddy. And a friend to Billie, not a mother-figure—she would make sure of that after Ruth's ugly accusations, and step very carefully around Billie's wild enthusiasms. Billie was welcome anytime, but Ruth had deliberately been keeping them busy with tutoring these past few weeks. Audrey sighed. Everyone loved seeing Billie race through the door with their shaved head and scarily silk-screened hoodies. Even Buddy missed Billie's wisecracking.

Audrey picked up her pruning shears and started again. Ruth Hickson's neck—snip! She'd never act like Ruth. Bullying everyone, expecting them to do what she thought was best. She straightened and picked up the wicker basket filled with daisy heads. She'd found the basket in the attic and had asked Buddy for his permission to use it. It had been Clara's, so she lined it with a clean tea towel and treated it with care. No, Audrey was completely unlike Ruth. She might be a people-pleaser, helping others and stuffing down her own feelings, but she would never attempt to make anyone do what they didn't want to—she stopped. Was people-pleasing a kind of manipulation? Could Ruth be right?

The door of the General Store opened, and Billie walked out.

'What's wrong, Tawdry? You look like you just ate a piece of your own B.S.' Billie bit into a Fruit and Nut bar and chewed loudly. 'Love these. The latest is, Ruth says no sugar, on account of it affects my brain. She suspects I've got ADHD, plus my other regular letters, so I guess that means your baking's out, huh?' They waved the purple foil-wrapped family-size bar in Audrey's direction. 'Want some?'

'No thanks.' She fiddled with the pruning shears. 'Billie, do you think I'm a people-pleaser?'

'Nah.'

Audrey exhaled.

'You're a liar. All people-pleasers are. You're super nice about everything, Tawdry, but you should just let rip with the truth.

And a lot of the time?' Billie raised a shoulder. 'You don't. But we love you anyway.' Billie chewed happily. 'Everybody's got baggage. Me? I'm as lazy as the day is long and wasting all my potential. You? You lie to be nice. You need to tell the truth.'

Audrey set her shears inside Clara's basket and blinked twice.

Billie laughed. 'Aw, Tawdry, come on. You know we like you. But hey . . . you could pay us back for being so nice to you. Throw a party. We haven't had any fun around here in a long time.'

'What would Ruth say?'

'Don't invite her! Just invite the fun people. She's going to be in the city next Saturday, for some awards dinner or something. It's your party, Tawd. Celebrate your sixtieth! You'll get great gifts. The big six-oh.'

Audrey cleared her throat. 'I'm fifty-three. And it's not my birthday.'

'Well, whatev, you youngster!' Billie ruffled Audrey's silver-blonde hair. 'I'll do the decorations, and Shez's got a cousin with a band. Old timey, country? Banjos?'

From inside the General Store, Lem slid open his office window. 'Congrats,' he said. 'Happy sixtieth, Audrey. Hey, you could do a fancy-dress theme like Beanies and Bikinis. Or wait—how about Barbarians and Librarians?'

Billie snorted. 'Yeah, maybe not the library theme, Lem. I'll talk to Shez and see what she comes up with. She's good with parties.'

Audrey straightened her shoulders. 'Wait—I'm good with parties!'

Billie's eyes rolled back farther than any teenager's Audrey had ever seen. 'Sure, Tawdry, you bet. You're party central, just like Ruth. I'm gonna find Shez. See ya later.'

Shez decided a sixties party was the way to go, what with Audrey being a 1968 baby. Shez would handle the party planning herself. She dropped by the bakery after work and handed Audrey a brown paper package, practically strangled with layers of packing tape.

'Don't you love your invite?' Shez waved her phone at Audrey. The invitation featured a massive silver '60'.

'Doesn't it look like I'm *turning* sixty?'

Shez shrugged. 'Whoopsie, already on Facebook.' She rubbed her neon-green gel nails together as if she were Dolly Parton playing the opening bars of '9 to 5'. 'Plus, with your grey hair and all that, people assume you're a bit aged.'

'What about you, Shez?'

Shez waved a hand like she was shooing a fly. 'My age is just a number that changes depending on who's asking. Hey, though, about the grey hair: I have this cousin who's taking a hairdressing course at the community college. She could do a balayage; you could keep those long grey roots and go, say, black or copper on the bottom. Copper tips! Let me see if I can get you in. Or we could go to Curl Up and Dye. Get a seasoned pro.'

Audrey tucked her hair behind her ears. It was softer now where the colour was natural silver. She hadn't decided to grow it out, but her roots seemed to have a mind of their own. As they got longer, Audrey watched another version of herself being revealed. Her silver hair reminded her of the models she'd cast for Love Your Age; it somehow suited her skin tone far better than blonde had. In fact, she almost liked it. And it was easy—so easy to be released from the relentless colouring. It felt healthier, silky, like it had when she was a child. Just this morning, she'd squinted at herself in the mirror and admitted it made her look a little older, but also somehow better, too.

'Thanks for the offer, Shez. I'm fine, but would she cut Buddy's?'

'Sure. I'll give Trin a call. You know, Audrey, all my local cousins are coming to the party. Our names all end in E. That's a family tradition passed down from our Catholic parents.' Shez held up a green nail for each. 'Trinity, Harmony, Liberty, Mimi, Livy. Sally and Kylee, they'll all be there. Oh, and the twins, Hailey and Mary. And Rosary.'

Audrey's eyebrows shot up.

Shez leaned in to explain. 'We were named in simpler times. But we're all strictly sacrilegious.'

'Don't you mean *religious*?' Audrey asked.

Shez frowned and tapped her phone. 'Whatever you say, Audrey. Oh, and Danny's coming. He just texted. He makes eleven.'

'My lawyer's invited to my birthday party?'

'Well, how many people do you know, Audrey? It's embarrassing if there isn't a crowd. Danny's in the band. Look, trust me on the party thing. Here, open your gift. Resistance is fertile.'

Audrey tore at the bulky package, but it wouldn't budge due to all the packing tape. Finally, she found the kitchen shears and cut it open. Shiny white Gogo boots fell onto her lap. She flipped one over. It was exactly her size. They smelled like the inside of a factory and the pleather crinkled joyfully when she held them up. She hadn't worn anything like them in years, but their chunky heels managed to look sexy and comfortable at the same time.

'Hot-babe boots, Audrey! I got myself something similar. You're an eight, right?'

Audrey couldn't stop herself from smiling. The Gogo boots were outrageous and exactly the kind of thing she'd have worn to a fancy-dress party in university, before Wyatt and before becoming so proper and constrained. She reached out and squeezed Shez's thin, orange-coloured arm. 'Thank you, Shez. I love them.'

'I thought they looked like you. Now all you've got to do is find a dress. Oh, and bake yourself a birthday cake. We need it to feed, oh, let's say . . . eighty.'

'*Eighty* people?'

Shez shrugged. 'You're right. More like ninety. Lem'll pull his barbie around the side and do a sausage sizzle, Kylee's making lamingtons, and we'll do BYO drinks so that's us all set for Saturday. Plus, on Facebook I said bring a veggie plate. Like one of those hard-as-a-rock cheese balls, you know, or meat pies or chicken on a stick. We'll use your oven. And Billie's on decorations.' She gazed at her neon-green nails. 'Gotta get these babies changed to white. Lem and I are going as the good-looking half of ABBA. The cute ones, not the daggy ones.'

'ABBA was the seventies, Shez.'

'Whatever! It's a party, Audrey. Plus, I look great in a blonde wig, and I sing some.' Shez peered over Audrey's shoulder. 'Wait! Maybe I'll be Dolly Parton. I'm a good sexy Dolly. I love her. All those bosoms overflowing with . . .' Shez twirled her hands. 'Joy! Joyful bosoms. I think that was a song from catechism class when I was a kid. Something about the joyful bosom of Jesus. Or God. Jesus or God, one of those two. Definitely not the Virgin Mary. Do you know it?'

Audrey shook her head, bewildered.

'Okay. Not a believer. That's fine, Audrey. No one's forcing you. Whatcha doing?'

Audrey held up her phone. Ninety people coming to an impromptu party she was responsible for hosting, and Shez had planned the whole thing? What on earth could go wrong? She shook her head. 'Putting cake for ninety and a costume on my to-do list,' she said. There was no stopping it now, so she moved her worries and concerns to her to-don't list.

The morning of the party was slightly overcast. Audrey took her coffee to the balcony and watched Buddy trundle naked to the beach, his butt cheeks cheerfully jiggling. She had to get the birthday cakes in the oven. Surely she wouldn't need ninety slices, but it was always better to over-cater than under. She'd decided to bake several dark chocolate cakes with her signature chocolate ganache, like the one she'd made for Shez's birthday. She'd bake a large pan of gluten-free brownies, too, and a lemon and Greek yogurt rosemary cake, her personal favourite; it was a simple recipe to whip up quickly. The cake made the room smell like a special kind of joy whenever she made it, rubbing fresh rosemary and lemon zest into the sugar until it was damp and fragrant. She'd found a cake stand in the attic, and another at the op shop. She planned to put three cakes on her floral plates on a table, then two on the proper cake stands, and the third on a crystal plate she'd glued to a glass bowl to make another cake stand. Audrey smiled. That sort of thing was exactly what her mother would've done. The gluten-free brownies would be arranged on her old-fashioned three-tiered tray, with some fortune cookies. The cake table would be simple but pretty, and for the sixties vibe, she'd strew it with flowers from Robert's purple tibouchina bush.

The cakes were out of the oven, cooled and decorated by the time Billie barged through the bakery door.

'Ruth just left for the city,' Billie said. Their hoodie was light blue, completely plain, their face excited and bright. 'Smells amazing in here. Like you dipped the place in melted chocolate.'

'Coast is clear, huh?' Audrey asked. 'You ready to party?'

'You're gonna love the decorations, Tawd. Danny and I planned something special for out front, but you'll have to wait until tonight to see it. Dr Flood paid for it!' Billie proceeded to throw down several large sixes and zeroes cut from silver construction paper and a dozen packages of balloons. 'I'm going to blow these up and leave them all over the floor. We'll be knee deep in balloons. Cheap and cheerful, Shez said. Good for dancing. Where do you want the numbers, Tawd? I figure on the side walls.'

After Billie had finished with the balloons, Shez arrived with a young woman sporting pink hair extensions.

'Love the decorations,' Shez said. 'This is Trin.'

'Happy sixtieth,' Trinity said.

Audrey raised her eyebrows at Shez.

'Did you tell Buddy we were coming?' Shez asked.

'I didn't dare.'

'Don't blame you. He'll go off like a frog in a sock. Let's go shave his scraggly facial hair, Trin. Oh, and he told Lem to go into the attic to find one of his old suits, so make sure Lem does that when he brings the barbie around.'

'Buddy's wearing a costume?' Audrey asked.

'Of course, Audrey, everyone is. That's what makes it a party.'

CHAPTER 28

Audrey was in the shower when she heard the drums and electric guitar. When the first 'Testing, one, two . . .' boomed through an amp, she towelled herself off and slid into her bra and underpants, then into the yellow dress. Thanks to all her hours of rushing around baking and the long walks on the beach, the dress fastened easily. Its heavy satin lining felt luxurious and almost bespoke; clothes were made so beautifully in the sixties. She dried her hair as straight as she could, flipped up the ends, tied on a yellow scarf as a headband, and added enormous hoop earrings she'd found online. When she zipped up the white pleather hot-babe boots from Shez, she grinned.

While she did her make-up, Audrey ticked off the items from her to-do list: cakes done, baking sheets loaded with tiny meat pies, coffee and tea supplies ready to go. Even though Billie was still on L plates, they insisted on getting the ice from the petrol station in town, and Lem had ridden along as the chaperoning driver. Audrey rubbed cucumber face cream into her skin and added contour and blush, then a pearly white sixties eyeshadow and a black flick of eyeliner on each lid. She swept on two coats of mascara and put in contacts. Then she stood back to contemplate her outfit in the tiny bathroom mirror.

The yellow dress had a sixties vibe, but it wasn't skimpy or inappropriate, and—she tipped her head and smiled at herself—she looked festive. She was short enough that the vintage dress hit just above the knee, and the white boots had chunky, comfortable heels and tall tops that left only a bit of leg showing. Still, Wyatt's disapproving voice popped into her head. Shouldn't she be wearing tights? But she hated how they crept down as much as Shez did. She decided to go with bare legs. Whatever. It was a fancy-dress party, and she was at the beach; Wyatt wasn't there to squint at her and suggest she should wear something a little less *cheerful*. He had a talent for making comments exactly the way his own mother did, a series of innocent questions that sounded suspiciously like veiled criticisms. But tonight, there was no Wyatt, no friends from her old life in the city, not even Emma, who was happily texting Audrey a million pictures of her Alaskan cruise.

Tonight was Audrey on her own, celebrating with the people of the village, the new friends who had been so good to her as she launched her business. She'd made party bags for everyone, filled with an assortment of fortune cookies and macarons, and stashed them in an empty laundry basket in her little kitchen. She planned to put them out on the cake table later in the evening as a tiny thank you for being so welcoming and making her feel at home in Whitehaven.

The opening chords to 'Bad Moon Rising' rose through the floor and Audrey thought she heard someone call her name. The echo of car doors slamming, and the scent of sausages on the barbecue, floated through the bay windows. She tugged down her dress and slicked on some pale pink lip gloss. It was time to go downstairs and host her first party alone.

The laughing and music got louder as Audrey walked down the steps into the bakery kitchen. The bakery was packed with people in costume, milling around the floor in front of the band. They'd set up in one of the bay windows, cords and amps and equipment plugged in to a multi-plug splitter from the single wall socket at the front of the room. Danny, Audrey's teen-lookalike lawyer, strummed the lead guitar in a denim shirt with the sleeves cut off, a red bandana keeping back his long hair. He looked like Bruce Springsteen from the eighties, during his 'Born in the USA' days. He'd got the decades slightly mixed up, like a lot of the guests—but his costume looked more comfortable than what the rest of the band was wearing. The male drummer was poured into shiny pleather pants, a woman on keys had come as Marilyn Monroe in a white dress, with what must have been inflatable boobs (or possibly not), and a bass player wore a black suit and skinny tie reminiscent of the early Beatles.

Audrey pushed through the crowd towards Billie as the band launched into the opening bars of 'Oh, Pretty Woman'.

'Billie!' Audrey shouted. 'You're not old enough to drink!'

Billie held up a beer and did a twirl. They were dressed in navy and white striped bellbottoms, with a fringed leather vest over a floral shirt. Their long black wig was tied back with a floral headband, and they wore Beatles-esque round sunglasses, the lenses tinted pink.

'Happy sixtieth, Tawd!' Billie shouted back. 'It's just one beer. Relax. Well, maybe two. Aw, look at the old geezer.' Billie pointed a bottle in the direction of the door. Buddy had squeezed himself into a red seventies leisure suit, his wide shirt collar spread across the lapels. His hair was cut neatly, and his beard was trimmed; he looked healthier than ever, and he grinned when he saw them. An Olivia Newton John from *Grease*—in a sexy black leather strapless jumpsuit—handed Buddy a stubbie and he raised it to Audrey in a silent toast.

Billie grabbed Audrey's hand. 'You gotta see the outside decorations, Tawd!'

On the usually silent street in front of the bakery, cars pulled up. Hippies stepped out carrying foil-wrapped plates and cases of beer, bottles of bourbon and soft drinks. A minivan parked and out poured a stream of people in costumes: Elvis, Batman, a grim reaper and three fairies in pink tutus. There was a man riding an inflatable T-rex walking beside a girl in a tie-dyed dress. The girl turned to the dinosaur-rider. 'Who's turning sixty?' she asked as she waved a large white envelope.

'See?' Audrey exclaimed.

Billie laughed and dragged Audrey towards a yellow Volkswagen Beetle parked in front of the bakery, and Audrey caught her breath. The car literally bloomed, a joyous billboard for the party. Its open front overflowed with pots and pots of yellow chrysanthemums and purple pansies. Long branches of greenery poured out the windows. It was stunning, and it must've taken hours to put together. Audrey shook her head; it was the most creative thing she'd ever seen. Billie was a marvel. They'd stuck huge white construction paper daisies on the sides of the car, and on its hood, among spilling flowers, stood a carefully hand-lettered sign read *Happy 60th Tawdry Hepburn*.

It was beautiful.

Audrey hugged them. 'I love it so, so much.'

'It's Danny's. It was his mum's car from the seventies, but this was my idea. Mostly free, except for the flowers. Dr Flood paid for those. He told me he wanted to help out and make it special for you. I hacked the branches from Ruth's garden. Do you really love it?'

Audrey nodded. 'You're incredible, Billie. You'd be brilliant working at an ad agency.'

'Yeah?' Billie said. 'Not too weird?'

Audrey turned and straightened Billie's wig, then smiled. 'Nope. Not too weird at all. You might be the most creative person I've ever met. Something to keep in mind after you graduate.'

'But first we party, Tawdry.'

Billie tugged Audrey back inside the crammed bakery. Shez stood at the mic. She was Dolly Parton, dressed in a cowgirl outfit that barely covered her rear, her long brown legs gleaming, dancing in pink sequined cowboy boots. From the side of the makeshift stage, Lem, dressed discreetly as Dolly's husband, Carl, beamed at her proudly.

'Let's wish Audrey a happy sixtieth!' Shez called into the mic. The crowd sent up a roar. Then the drummer and bass guitar launched into '9 to 5'. Shez took a deep breath and sang the first line in a perfect imitation of Dolly, her Aussie accent miraculously turned southern. The walls in the building rocked and the bay windows shook. Buddy, nestled in his favourite chair at the side of the room, nodded in time with a male hippie in a leather vest, bellbottoms and white shirt. He had a paisley headband tied in his grey hair, and Audrey smiled when she recognised him. Dr Flood saluted Audrey and smiled. His blue eyes seemed to divide her in two, and her insides wobbled, a feeling she hadn't had in years.

Then Billie grabbed her hand, and Audrey danced.

Warm steak pies were passed on platters, sausages were eaten sizzling from the barbie in buttered white bread piled with fried onions and dripping with spicy-sweet barbecue sauce. Hippies and superheroes danced holding bottles of beer above their heads. Inside the bakery, the floor became sticky underfoot, and still Audrey kept on dancing. She danced with Lem and Billie, with Shez, even a little with Buddy, with strangers in costumes and finally, on her own in the joyful crowd.

Suddenly the roar of Harleys drowned out Fleetwood Mac. The bikes got louder. The crowd stamped in time to a drum solo and the walls shook as the Coffin Cheaters burst through the door. Tiny was first, dressed as the Pope, his long red beard matching the red cross on his robes. The room erupted with screaming. He held up his staff.

'God bless the Catholics,' he shouted, 'but not you goddamn heathens!'

'Yasssssssss!' Billie screamed back at him, holding up a beer.

Tiny lifted Audrey in a bear hug. He handed her a mixed bouquet of droopy petrol station flowers in a cellophane sleeve. 'Happy Birthday, mama,' he said.

Shez leaned into the mic. 'Audrey Sweetman looks damn good for SIXTY!'

The room cheered and the band launched into 'These Boots Are Made For Walkin'. Shez shimmied into the crowd and grabbed Audrey's left hand. Billie lifted her right one and the three of them danced near the band, Shez's and Audrey's boots stomping together. Then someone twirled her around. It was Dr Flood. He laughed and shifted her to the front of a conga line and stepped in behind her, holding her waist in a firm grip. Audrey danced forward and the line grew longer, snaking around the floor of the bakery. She led the line past the kitchen, past the cake table, past Buddy, who smiled at her and yelled something she couldn't hear.

'Best. Party. Ever!' Billie screamed. 'Happy birthday, Tawd!'

Nobody partied like Aussies did. And the drink? It was all around her, but Audrey didn't even want it. She just wanted to dance like this, sweat pouring from her, boots stomping, laughing, handing her guests chocolate chip sea salt cookies and chunks of decadent brownies. It was simple food for the people who had been so good to her in the tiny town, a community that had grabbed her in their arms and hadn't let her fall. Instead, they'd welcomed her home.

Shez sang another verse of 'These Boots Are Made For Walkin', and Harleys roared up and down the street well past midnight—a street that was normally silent and starlit but tonight, throbbing with music and dancing. Audrey snaked the conga line next to Buddy and he held up his red plastic cup in a mock toast. Billie tapped him on his bald head, and Dr Flood laughed behind Audrey. 'Having fun?' he yelled.

She turned and smiled at him as a young woman in a black and white checkered mini dress stepped closer. 'Dance?' she asked, and Dr Flood peeled away with her into a makeshift jive. Audrey shrugged off her disappointment. Maybe this was the Lucinda she'd overheard him talking to? That sort of thing was everywhere—Wyatt, Dr Flood, Ruth Hickson's husband—tonight it didn't matter. Maybe all middle-aged men wanted younger women. Who cared? Dr Flood was an attractive man, cordial to her and kind, but Audrey had her friends; she had the bakery and her fledgling business. So what if she never had a partner again? She was fifty-three; she'd already had a husband and honestly, it wasn't so great. Was it such a big loss, or was this, the laughter and the dancing and the baking and the sheer life of it, was this what she had been missing all along? Tonight Wyatt would've been a bore, snickering at the villagers, a fastidious weight tied to her white plastic boots. He'd have wanted to leave early. He'd have sat in a chair and refused to dance.

Shez belted out her Nancy Sinatra impression in a final husky call to the dancers, when the rest of the Coffin Cheaters piled through the door, not in fancy dress but looking just as celebratory in their biker-gang leathers and tattoos as the others did in costume. Audrey swivelled her hips in her yellow dress and kept walking as Shez directed them to, stomping her white Gogo boots while the floor shook, and the music boomed and—

'What is going on?'

The shriek echoed from the door: Ruth stood rigid, red-faced and incredulous. 'Billie, you're drinking! *Audrey Sweetman*. There are noise restrictions! I'm calling the police. Billie, we're leaving. Now.'

The lead guitarist played a final twang, and the music vibrated to a stop.

The Pope handed Ruth a beer. 'Aw, mama, calm down,' Tiny said. 'Have a drink! You look like you could use a sausage too.'

The bikers screamed with laughter.

Shez yelled to the band. 'Let's do "Only the Good Die Young"!'

'I'm calling the police.' Ruth dug her phone from her handbag.

'Nooooooo!' the crowd called, along with a few other words.

'Screw you!' Billie yelled drunkenly. Audrey squeezed their hand and held them back from charging at their mother. It wasn't good to upset Ruth, Billie was right—Ruth had a talent for making everyone hate her. Billie tugged against Audrey's firm grip.

'I'm calling now!' Ruth screeched.

Danny pulled off his bandana and took a swig from his beer. He leaned into his mic and cleared his throat. 'As a legal professional, I should inform you she has the right to call the cops. It's after midnight and we're loud as hell.'

'You're a conveyancing lawyer, Danny!' someone shouted. 'Dan-ny! Dan-ny! Law-yer! Law-yer!'

'Drop it, Judge Judy,' called Buddy. 'What's yer problem, you old killjoy!'

Ruth's face flushed. 'My underage child is drinking alcohol. That's a ten-thousand-dollar fine. And you—' she pointed to Audrey, 'are responsible! Billie told me you don't even have the licences you need to run this place.'

Audrey's stomach rolled over. Ruth knew, and she'd never overlook it. Beside Audrey, Billie screamed in what sounded like frustration or wounded pride. 'Ruth, just leave, why don't you? C'mon Shez, let's sing.' Audrey caught the look on Billie's face: trapped bird, nowhere to fly. Desperate.

Ruth crossed the floor and yanked Billie's arm. 'You're going to the city to live with your father, and back to your old school. Tomorrow.'

'No! I won't!' Hard and fast, Billie shoved Ruth backwards.

The Pope caught Ruth before she fell. Billie pushed through the crowd to the kitchen and pounded up the stairs to Audrey's flat. Audrey followed, tripping over her own boots, but Billie was faster. By the time Audrey reached the top of the internal steps, Billie had already raced through the tiny kitchen and out the balcony door. They slid down the back stairs and jumped.

Audrey was too slow. She clattered down the steps and caught a glimpse of Billie vanishing down the side of the building. When she ran to the side, she saw Billie climb into the driver's seat of her car. They revved the engine.

'Billie, no!' Audrey screamed.

The car backed out, screeching into the street, and sped away, too fast, crookedly, up the road away from the village.

Audrey covered her face with her hands. Billie was drunk. A sixteen-year-old without a full driver's licence had taken her car. She turned around, panicking. She'd have to find someone, anyone, but who could help and how? Loud voices spilled from the bakery; the lights had been turned up and people were milling around outside. Audrey glanced wildly at the open door to her flat. Shez? Lem? Dr Flood? Maybe they could chase Billie down, but that might make it worse. No. She had to tell Ruth and try to fix her terrible mistake. She ran inside, her teeth chattering.

'Billie took my car.'

Shez walked to the mic. 'Party's over. Let's clear out,' she said.

Ruth's face was grey. She pulled out her phone.

'Wait, Ruth,' Dr Flood said. 'That might make it worse if the police chased them. Trying to pull Billie over might cause an accident. Let's think for a minute.'

Buddy wheeled over. 'Billie'll be right. They'll pull over and sleep it off. They're not stupid.'

Ruth screamed. 'Billie is a child, you fool! Of course they're stupid!'

They stood in a silent circle. Audrey thought she might be sick. 'Billie had maybe three beers,' she said, her voice wobbly. 'That's what I saw. Dr Flood is right. They might be safer if they're not hunted down while they're upset.'

'What do you know?' Ruth spat the words. 'You could be responsible for killing my child! For my child killing someone else!'

The remaining partygoers left drunkenly, and in the silent bakery the final few revellers—Audrey, Dr Flood, Buddy, Shez and Lem—looked away from each other.

'I'm calling the police,' Ruth said.

Dr Flood nodded. 'Ruth, I think you should go home and wait there. Talk to the police if you like. Sherry and Lem will drive you. Does anyone know if Billie took a phone?' He glanced at Audrey, an inscrutable look she couldn't decipher. She shook her head and felt herself getting sicker, bile rising. Buddy reached over and squeezed her hand.

'I'll go look for Billie,' Audrey said.

'I'd like to help. We can take my car,' Dr Flood said.

In the kitchen, a phone pinged. Audrey ran to pick it up, her hands fumbling so it nearly fell off the benchtop.

'Is it Billie?' Ruth screeched.

Audrey gripped her phone with a shaky hand and swayed on her feet. A text from Wyatt stared back at her.

Charmaine is pregnant. I thought you should know.

CHAPTER 29

Wyatt was going to be a father. Audrey's forehead pounded, and she tried to breathe. He would hold his own baby, and she'd never know what that felt like.

'What is it, Audrey?' Ruth shrieked. 'Is it Billie?'

Billie. Billie was drunk and alone in a car and shouldn't be driving. It mattered so much more right now than this. Audrey shook her head. She felt wobbly, like she might faint. 'It's not Billie. It's from . . . someone else.'

'Audrey?' Dr Flood called. 'We should go.'

'Yes.' Her voice was a strangled whisper. She moved through the bakery, past Ruth and the others, without seeing anything at all. What had she been thinking? Billie was underage and a guest at her party. Audrey was responsible—she should've stopped Billie from drinking, not ignored it. It was a good thing she'd never been a mother; she didn't deserve to be. And now Wyatt and Charmaine were having . . . but there was no time to think about that.

She yanked open the passenger door of Dr Flood's car. In her thin yellow dress, bare legs and boots, Audrey trembled on the cold leather seat.

'Where should we start?' Dr Flood pulled onto the highway. He clicked on her seat warmer, dialled up the heat.

'Town. I have an idea.'

He accelerated on the empty road and glanced over. 'The gift's for you. I thought it'd get broken if I took it inside.' Nestled between their seats was the most beautiful luminous blue glass baking bowl, tied with a thick white ribbon. She shifted it over and read the simple white tag where he'd scrawled, 'Thanks for baking up the joy. Justin.'

She'd never called him that, not on the beach, not when he'd been in the bakery with Buddy. No one but Ruth did. 'It's beautiful. Thank you.'

'It's the colour of bioluminescence,' he said. 'I saw it in a kitchen shop and thought you'd like it.'

She flushed, remembering that night on the beach and his thoughtfulness, the inside jokes about coffee, how easy he was with everyone, how ready to help. Even if she'd had her car, she wouldn't've been calm enough to drive. Fear whooshed through her. Billie was alone and angry, driving drunk. Audrey should've taken their beer away. She, of all people, should've been careful with alcohol, especially when a minor was doing the drinking. She never should have thrown a party in the first place! What had she been thinking?

The interior of the Mercedes was clean and smelled of aftershave, something conservative, lemons and cedarwood. Bluetooth picked up Dr Flood's—Justin's—phone, and suddenly music unfurled. Dusty Springfield. He turned it down a little.

Audrey hadn't heard the song in years. As Dusty sang, Audrey knew the lyrics described exactly what Billie had done, taken a piece of Audrey's heart, wormed their way into her life and made a home there, whether Ruth wanted them to or not.

He glanced at her. 'You didn't want to tell Ruth where you think Billie is?'

Audrey crossed her arms tightly against her chest. She wondered briefly what it would be like to talk about all her problems and challenges with Justin. He'd offer sensible advice, but he'd also listen to her. She had the feeling she could trust him, no matter what. 'I might know. I didn't want to say in front of Ruth. I thought I had a better chance of helping Billie. I've seen them fight.'

'How bad?' He cleared his throat. 'Professional ethics, I have to ask. Want to ask.'

'I'm not sure. I'm not a mother.' Audrey hugged herself. 'But . . . pushing and screaming. A lot of frustration. Billie said it doesn't get out of hand.' She remembered Ruth twisting Billie's wrist, the sound of Ruth's scream in her apartment, the look on Ruth's face when Billie pushed her. It hadn't been a look of surprise.

He nodded. 'Not good, though.'

'No.' Audrey rubbed her temples. 'Do you think they'll be okay to drive?'

'I've seen Billie worse off than tonight,' he said carefully. 'The roads aren't busy, but I want to find them before the police do.'

'Let's try the op shop. Billie knows how to break in.'

Dr Flood reached over and turned up the stereo. The soothing opening chords of 'Cry to Me' began to play. He tapped a finger in time on the steering wheel, and Audrey exhaled. The night was dark, the highway empty. It would be fine; it had to be. Audrey's hands shook. Billie had driven before, sensibly, in Audrey's car. They hadn't had too many drinks during the party, not that she'd seen, and on an empty road they'd be okay. She willed it to be true. Dr Flood accelerated up a hill, and Audrey looked at the dark sky loaded with stars. Her body was warming now from the heated seat, and the slow beat of the music made her feel a little glimmer of hope. She glanced at him, his profile. He was good in a crisis; it was part of the profession. What would it feel like to be in a relationship with a man like him? Her stomach flipped over. Wyatt. A baby at last. Then they crested the hill and Audrey gasped.

Jumbled like a toy, upside down on the highway, sat her small white car.

'Billie.' Her voice was thin, strangled.

Dr Flood pulled over. He reached an arm across Audrey. His eyes were calm, and his forearm felt strong. 'Audrey. Call an ambulance.' Then he was out and running.

Her phone lay in her lap, but her fingers were frozen, unworkable. Triple zero. Wait. Wait. Wait. Finally, the recorded voice started, too friendly. 'You have dialled Emergency Triple Zero. Your call is being connected.'

She yanked opened her door, then started walking on shaky legs. She would go to Billie, whatever she found there. The night air was freezing. Her teeth chattered and wouldn't stop.

'Billie?' Dr Flood called, his reassuring voice echoing into the silence and the dark.

'Police, ambulance or fire?'

'Ambulance! Police!' Audrey shouted into her phone.

'What's your location?'

'The highway near the turn-off to Whitehaven Bay, at the bottom of the first hill.'

'Has there been an accident?'

'Yes.' She stumbled towards the overturned car, its roof crushed on the pavement. The road gave off the sharp tang of rubber and smoke.

'Ma'am, stay where you are. We'll use your location and be there as soon as possible. Don't move any victims. Do you know CPR?'

'I'm with a doctor,' Audrey whispered. She said it again, louder. 'A doctor is here.' She couldn't seem to move. Dizziness swept over her, and she wanted to drop to her knees and crawl. She called out, but it was a croak, a whisper. She couldn't see anyone behind the car. She tried again and stumbled forward.

Her knees buckled. Billie wasn't dead. They couldn't be! They were dancing at the party thirty minutes ago. The accident was a mistake. Audrey could press the undo key like she did on a computer, set the car upright, make Billie open the door and step out unharmed. Billie had to be fine. Undo, undo.

'Billie? Justin?' she croaked.

'Here,' Dr Flood called.

'Billie?' Audrey pushed past the smoking car. It tilted on the roof, one headlight shining forward in the darkness, the seatbelt buzzer dinging.

'Billie!' Audrey whispered.

Dr Flood crouched in front of a dark shape. Audrey could only see Billie's legs; they were still and twisted at an odd angle. Dr Flood turned, his face white in the beam of the headlights. 'It's okay, Audrey.' He shifted aside.

Billie crouched on the ground crying, blood smeared across their face, their shaved head sticky with it. In their arms slumped a young wallaby, its furry body motionless.

'I killed it.'

Audrey dropped to her knees. 'It was an accident. It wasn't your fault.'

Billie rubbed a thin hand across their eyes. More blood. 'It's my fault, Tawd. Everything's my fault.'

'No, Billie, you're okay. It's okay,' Audrey crooned.

Dr Flood leaned down. 'Let's get you warm.' He unbuttoned his hippie shirt and draped it around Billie's shoulders. He felt Billie's face and arms, then their legs. 'Any pain here?'

'No.' Billie rocked the limp body.

The fur brushed against Audrey's hand. It reminded her of the larger grey kangaroos she'd seen near the beach. The wind was cold, biting in the late-winter night, and her legs shook. She inhaled to stop her teeth from chattering.

'Did I tell you what happened when I shaved my head? The first time?'

'It's okay,' Audrey said. 'You're in shock. The ambulance is coming.' Audrey put an arm around Billie's shoulder, rubbing it, willing them to get warm, all the while her mind sending up the best prayer she knew. *Thank you, thank you, thank you, thank you . . .*

'I was thirteen. I shaved it off in my bathroom and cut my neck. By a-ac-ccident. Maybe. Maybe not. I was bleeding. I needed to look . . . different.' Billie exhaled, a ragged breath. 'Ruth walked in. She cleaned up and didn't say anything. Hair and blood in a white towel. She stuck on Band-Aids. Then she locked me in my room.'

Audrey squeezed Billie's hand in the cold night air. A siren blared in the distance.

'It was Christmas. My cousins were there, my aunt and uncle. Ruth said she wanted to talk to them first. *Warn them* before they saw me, as if I was some kind of monster.' Billie wiped angrily at tears. Their hands left streaks of blood.

'I'm sorry, Billie.' Audrey's eyes filled.

'I'm bad, Tawd,' Billie whispered. 'I hate her. I hate my own mother. She ruined our family.'

Audrey turned Billie's face to her own. 'Look at me. You're not bad. There's nothing wrong with you.'

'I don't know who I am,' Billie said. 'Not for sure.'

Audrey nodded. Maybe no one did. Maybe everyone, all their lives, were just trying to figure it out. 'You're going to be okay, Billie. You'll do—'

'Something amazing? Like a Hickson?' Billie's voice was high-pitched. 'Maybe I can't.' Billie hugged the wallaby. 'You know what Ruth says? *Be somebody, Billie*! Be a lawyer and represent your people! Like there're two kinds of people, my kind, the messed-up ones, or her kind.' Billie took a deep breath. 'I want to be like you, Tawd—I want to do something that makes me happy, and if it doesn't work, so what? I don't care.'

The siren was louder now. Dr Flood walked over.

'Ruth and Sherry are on the way.' He kneeled at Billie's feet. 'Can I take it, Billie? I'll lay him down.' Justin lifted the wallaby from Billie's arms. 'Are you hurting anywhere?'

'My shoulder.'

Audrey squeezed Billie's hands, holding space, holding on. Billie wanted to be like her. How could she explain to a sixteen-year-old about life choices, that even the very best plans may not work? Audrey gazed into Billie's teary eyes. And how could she tell a child that shaving their head on Christmas Day might have felt enormously aggressive to their mother, who had to explain it to a room full of relatives waiting for dinner? No. She couldn't. She'd sound exactly like a retired judge of the Federal Court of Australia. But Ruth's fears about Billie were also true.

Billie looked up at her. Trusting her. A child in front of you, expecting you to be heroic when you didn't feel that way at all—this was the part of parenting Audrey hadn't understood before. They looked at you like this, with love and fear and hope and worry, and wondered if you could say anything to take away their pain. And they knew whether you were lying or telling the truth.

The siren was deafening now, red-blue lights swirling at the top of the hill. Audrey took a deep breath. 'Billie. You're so, so loved by all of us. And that includes your mum, even if you can't see it.' The ambulance pulled up and cut its siren. Silence in the dark night. Another car pulled up, screeched, stopped.

Billie lifted a bloody face to her, tremulous, hopeful. Trusting. True. 'Let me move in with you. I don't want to go back to school. *Please*, Audrey?'

She heard car doors slamming, running feet. It was the first time Billie had ever called her by her name.

'I want to live with you,' Billie whispered.

Audrey's throat ached. It was impossible. She wasn't able to take care of a child, and she wasn't strong enough to fight against Ruth Hickson. But Billie's eyes were filled with so much pain, and so much hope. She couldn't lie, not to Billie. Audrey shook her head slowly. 'I'm sorry. I can't. It won't work, Billie.'

It was after three in the morning when they pulled up in front of the bakery.

'Do you need anything, Audrey?' Justin Flood asked. 'Should I come inside and wait?'

She shook her head and opened the car door. If only it were that simple, inviting him in and sharing the worry. The problems somehow halved when you had a partner, but Justin was only a friend. Images of Billie, bloody and crying, made her squeeze her eyes shut, but when she did, she remembered Wyatt's text. Her chest ached. She climbed out of the car. The wintry night was cold and starless. The sea rumbled behind the bakery, waves rolling over relentlessly in the dark.

Justin opened his door and walked around to meet her. 'They'll keep Billie overnight in the hospital, just to make sure everything's fine. Minor injuries, mostly shock. Nothing serious.' He walked with her to the bakery. 'I'm more than happy to stay and clean up a bit. You need some sleep.'

She turned to him. 'I . . . no, but thank you. I'll do it in the morning. Shez'll help. I'm just glad Billie's okay.'

'Of course,' he said. 'And Audrey? It's not your fault. This didn't happen because of you.'

She nodded, but it was impossible to believe him. The party had happened because of her, and she hadn't stopped Billie from drinking. After saying goodnight to him, Audrey let herself into the bakery and smelled the stale, sharp pang of spilled beer. She climbed upstairs and stood in the shower, washing off the wallaby's blood, and Billie's. She pulled on grey trackpants and a sweatshirt, trying to warm up, and tottered downstairs. Her legs were wobbly, her head throbbing. The birthday cakes had dried on the table, uncut. She opened a black garbage bag and tipped in uneaten food, collected the red plastic cups for recycling, poured warm beer out of bottles by the side of the building. The foamy stink made her gag. She didn't want a drink. Foolishly, she wanted her mother. What would Joyce do?

Clean up. Start over.

Audrey ran bucket after bucket of steamy water, and got on her knees and scrubbed, the knees of her trackpants soaking through. A movie montage played in her head of what could have been: Billie's body broken, Billie holding a dead person from another car, instead of a wallaby. Billie paralysed, or on fire in the small car. It had looked so flimsy, overturned on the road. Audrey could've taken the safe, huge Volvo all those months ago, why hadn't she? Because it had reminded her of Charmaine.

Pregnant. A baby.

She leaned over her bucket and vomited, long strings of nothing . . . water, bile, then chunks of spinach pie. She deserved this. Everything was a mess. Billie could've died. She stood on trembling legs, carried the bucket to the toilet, emptied it. Began again.

By five-thirty, it was finished. The Bittersweet Bakery smelled of bleach and sea air. She showered once more, scrubbed at herself as if she were floorboards that had never been cleaned. She sat in the bakery at a rickety table in jeans and a grey jumper that reached her knees. Her wet hair dripped down her back. Her laptop was propped open, her phone resting beside a cup of cold coffee. She stared outside at the empty street. A currawong sang like a baby crying, plaintive warbling.

Wyatt would be a father and Audrey would be alone.

Billie's face had been full of pain and disbelief when Audrey had said no. But there was no way she could take Billie in and offer them a proper home; Ruth would never agree, and even if she did, Audrey barely had the resources to take care of herself. She couldn't interfere in another family, could she? It wasn't right to take in someone else's child without a parent's permission, was it? Billie needed her, but Billie had a mother and a home. Two parents. Two homes.

Someone knocked on her door. Audrey's knees wobbled as she walked to open it. It was Ruth. Her lined face looked older than Audrey had ever seen it.

'My child could be dead because of you.'

Audrey felt light-headed, as if she might faint, but no. This was her doing. Ruth was right. She hadn't taken care of Billie properly.

'Ruth. I'm so, so sorry.'

'I've left instructions at the nurse's station not to let you in. I'm taking Billie to live with their father in the city. Back to school.'

'Ruth, I—'

'I've already notified the rest of the council that you're running a business without a licence. In fact, I did it two weeks ago, as soon as Billie let it slip. Billie begged me not to do anything, but you'll be served a ten-thousand-dollar fine. The police will also charge Buddy for serving alcohol to a minor on his premises. Another ten.'

Audrey flinched. 'I'll pay Buddy's. It's my fault.'

Ruth turned to leave. Audrey reached out to touch her but thought better of it. She dropped her hand to her side. 'I'm sorry, Ruth. I know it's complicated with Billie.'

Ruth stared at her, incredulous. 'You? You're not a mother. You don't know anything.'

CHAPTER 30

Billie didn't return to the bakery.

On the third day after the party, Shez handed Audrey an envelope she'd taken from the mailbox. 'I saw Billie at the beach.'

'Did they seem okay?' Audrey asked, frowning.

'No. They're leaving for the city today.'

Audrey tore open the letter and read it: it was the fine from the Department of Trading. Ruth had really meant it then. Ten thousand dollars for operating a business without a licence. She could apply for a licence once the fine was paid in full, but until then she'd have to cease trading. She had thirty days to pay. Her head throbbed; it was impossible.

'Failure's only market research,' Shez said, twisting a silver hoop earring.

'It's not that simple.'

'It is. Entrepreneurs don't stay in bed unless they make money in bed.'

'Pardon me?'

'Think, Audrey! Passive income! Jeez, I have so much to teach you. I'll give you my mini course. Sit your butt down.' Shez then launched into a lecture on sales funnels and Facebook ads. Finally she was finished, although she carried on giving advice about how to get free publicity doing TikTok dances in revealing clothing as she made her way out. She paused in the doorway. 'On second thought, you might need a friend to do that for you. Okay, bye!'

Audrey opened her laptop and logged in to her website. The photos of her biscuits, of the Coffin Cheaters and their tattoos, the sea, the inside of the bakery where she sat now, alone and defeated—all those images looked so cheerful and optimistic, as if business were booming. But social media was a lie. She clicked the disable button and shut down her site, took a sip of coffee and reread the letter outlining the fine. The way forward was obvious; she should do the sensible thing. Return to the city, stay at Emma's while she was still travelling in the Pacific Northwest, find a job, restart her career, pay her fine and Buddy's, and forget about the beach. Forget about Bittersweet Biscuits. The pain in her chest caught her off guard. She was meant to be an employee, not an entrepreneur. Wyatt was right. What had she been thinking?

Why hadn't she applied for a business licence right from the start? It was on her list, of course, but she thought she'd have time to test the market first. How had she been so stupid as to *wait*? One tiny step forward had become another, a sort of a stab at a business, and Audrey had wanted to see if Bittersweet Biscuits was viable before she had to commit. She gazed out the front window of the bakery. That wasn't the whole truth, and she'd been lying to herself; Audrey had suspected all along that she'd have to do kitchen renovations before getting the Food Safety certificate she'd need for the licence, so she carried on and took the risk—trying to stay ahead of disaster. And now she'd ruined everything. She could picture Wyatt shaking his head at her execution as if she were a toddler learning to walk and failing at taking her first step. Why hadn't she believed in herself enough to formalise the business? Why hadn't she asked Emma for a loan?

Audrey sighed. And then there were Billie and Ruth. Ruth felt like the real problem, not the licence, though Audrey had no idea where she'd find twenty thousand dollars for the fines. Ruth Hickson was a roadblock, and probably always would be. She wanted Audrey to leave, but the village had started to feel more like home than the city. Audrey's stomach flipped. She forced herself to take a sip of coffee, now cold. Ruth was right; Audrey should have stopped Billie from drinking at her party. But then, Ruth knew better than anyone how headstrong teenagers were. They had agency, they could make their own decisions, and drinking a few beers at a party was normal for a sixteen-year-old. Taking a car, driving without a full licence? That was rash and stupid, but it was also normal, wasn't it, to run away when you were so angry and frustrated and cornered, publicly humiliated? Isn't that what teenagers did? Isn't that what she had done herself?

Audrey couldn't forget the look on Billie's face when she told them they couldn't live with her. Pain and disbelief. But she couldn't just take another woman's child when that woman was a good-enough mother. Billie hadn't understood. They'd pushed her away and climbed into the ambulance. Now their relationship was gone, and in its place, a screaming silence.

Ruth Hickson would never know the favour Audrey had done her. She stared at her phone, wondering what to say to Billie, how to make it right. She avoided Wyatt's text, unanswered but impossible to ignore. A baby. What they'd always wanted together, Wyatt had got without her. A message pinged from Emma, exuberant as always. *Alaska is amazing! Can you talk?* But Audrey didn't have the energy to explain everything that had happened. She was careful to leave the message unread. She walked through the empty bakery that smelled too optimistically of sea air and drained the dregs of her cold coffee down the chipped, ancient sink.

She could see no other way forward than moving back to the city.

A chicken pie with puff pastry bubbled fragrant in the oven while Audrey washed the dishes. The pie would feed Buddy for a few days. The other five individual pies she'd cover and freeze so he could reheat them for healthy meals when she wasn't there to help. She shook her head: five days of dinners, what was that worth? What had she done for him, for any of them? Almost nothing. Through her kitchen window, the sun glinted on the sea, sparkling water, a spectacular day. Spring was coming and with it, the tourists. She could do a roaring trade if she had the capital to get set up as a café, but all of that was beyond her, surely: hiring staff, running it all? She had no capital even to get Bittersweet Biscuits back on its feet, let alone to expand. She had to pay off the fines and source equipment, get all the licences and pass the inspections. And after the mortgage fiasco, she'd never get a business loan from a bank. People like her—in the middle of their lives—were considered too old for a loan. It was grossly unfair, probably a hangover from the times when life expectancy was sixty-seven, but there it was: modern banking. She scrubbed a frying pan and lifted it from the suds, remembering Wyatt ignoring her when she was a young woman looking through her recipe books, nodding absentmindedly while she talked about which street in their suburb would be perfect for a bakery, which old building would house it beautifully. She'd believed in herself back then, when she was fresh out of uni, but not enough to follow through with the Audrey's Cookies cart.

She glanced out the kitchen window. A police officer strode across the lawn and knocked sharply on the door of the cabana, and when Buddy opened it, disappeared inside. She gave a worried frown, pulled the hot chicken pie from the oven and trod carefully down the back steps. She opened Buddy's door with one hand.

'Hi! I'm here with your dinner.'

'What the hell. It's three in the afternoon, Sweetman. Can't you tell the time?' Buddy sniffed at the pie. 'This here's young Skiffy Broughton. He's giving me a lecture.'

'G'day,' the officer said. 'Smells good.'

'She's the best baker in town, aren't you Sweetman?'

'The only baker. Is there a problem, Officer?'

'Nope,' Buddy said. 'Skiffy's threatening to give me a ten-thousand-dollar fine for letting Billie drink in my building. Judge Judy sent him to harass me.'

'It was my responsibility,' Audrey said quickly. 'I hosted the party and I rent the building from Buddy.'

'Sweetman's lying. She rents the flat upstairs. And you can fine me all you want, but I won't pay you, Skiffy. I used to watch you hoon up and down these roads ten years ago, you almost ran me over in your ute when you were sixteen. You were probably on the piss yourself.'

'No one's fining you, Buddy, not yet. It's a warning,' Officer Broughton said. 'But Ruth is mad—'

'Mad as a hatter! Judge Judy ruins every damn thing.' Buddy shook his head, disgusted.

Audrey reached out and squeezed Buddy's arm. She exhaled carefully and let go of some of the tension she'd been carrying. She had one less fine to pay, and somehow ten thousand dollars felt a little more manageable. 'I was just wondering,' Audrey said, 'did you, uh, hear anything about what happened to Billie Hickson after the accident?' Officer Broughton wasn't likely to tell her, but she was desperate to know if Billie had been charged with driving under the influence.

The police officer cleared his throat.

'Come on, Skiffy. You're among mates,' Buddy said. 'Spill the beans.'

'Probably shouldn't say, but it was just a fine and double demerit points. I think it means they're suspended from driving for twelve months. They already had some demerits, so this pushed it over the limit. Lucky, though. Only some wildlife got run over.' Officer Broughton coughed. 'Ruth Hickson asked us to, uh, delay. Well . . . we didn't have time to breathalyse Billie before the ambulance arrived.'

Audrey relaxed her shoulders. 'Can I give you a piece of chicken pie? I'm just about to cut Buddy a slice.'

'Sure. I'll take one to go.'

She handed him a slice of warm chicken pie in a takeaway container, and he left them with a warning after Audrey promised him that underage drinking in the bakery would never happen again.

'You can stay as long as you want, rent-free, Sweetman.' Buddy waved a fork at her. 'You'll find a way around Judge Judy. She tortures that kid. But Billie shouldn'ta stolen your car. Drunk driving. Stupid!' Buddy chewed a mouthful of pie, ignoring the knife she'd given him and hacking at the piece on his plate with his fork. 'We should raise that kid better. You and me. Judge Judy sure as hell isn't going to do it, so that leaves us.'

'Buddy, we can't interfere. And anyway, Billie's gone to the city.'

'That won't take. Billie hates it there. And sometimes strangers know better than family, Sweetman.'

Audrey straightened the newspapers on the coffee table. She didn't have the heart to tell him that she was leaving, but she had to do it all the same. She wondered what her mother would have thought of Buddy. Joyce would have told her to help him, she knew. She took a breath and began to explain about the fine, and how the business would have to close until she paid it. 'I can't stay, Buddy. I love it here, but I have to find a regular job. This was just . . . a holiday. An experiment. And it didn't work. I've hurt people. I've hurt Billie.'

'What the hell, Sweetman? You're going to leave with everything in a muddle?' He took a long drink of beer. 'You got people counting on you. You got to find a way to make it right.' He looked at her without blinking, as if he were certain she would do it. 'You're a big city advertising woman. Figure it out.'

CHAPTER 31

'Okay, time for some strategic business advice. Enough of your moping, Audrey. Sit your plump rear down on this chair.'

Shez hopped on the table opposite Audrey and crossed her self-tanned legs. 'Normally my rate for mentoring entrepreneurs is three hundred dollars an hour, and my online course will cost, let's say twenty-five hundred when I get around to creating it, but . . .' She pulled her denim skirt down until it met the tail of the scorpion tattoo crawling up her thigh, 'you don't have time for that. So for you, my fellow-CEO and entrepreneur, it's free. Now listen.'

'Okay.' Audrey took a sip of coffee.

'It's been four days since you were fined. I always say, never wrestle with a pig: you both get dirty, and the pig likes it.'

'Okay?' Audrey squinted. 'And that means . . .'

'Think, Audrey, think! That means you're going at this the wrong way!'

'You're saying that I—'

'Never interrupt your enemy when he's making a mistake. That's Napoleon.' Shez raised her drawn-on eyebrows.

'Okay, but I've been—'

'And plus,' Shez said, 'you need to innovate. Think different than everybody else. Be like Steve Jobs. And remember Warren Buffett and his millionaire mindset: only when the tide goes out do you discover who's been swimming naked.'

Audrey stared at her. She imagined introducing Emma and Shez; the thought of the two of them having dinner together made her smile despite her current problems. Small town meets big city, and with enough self-belief between the two of them to win a presidential campaign. They'd absolutely adore each other.

'The universe gave you a sign, Audrey! It's hanging right over there.' Shez fluttered her bright blue nails at the bay window where the Bittersweet Bakery Café sign was nailed, crookedly. The orange five o'clock sun glinted on the empty street. 'What are you waiting for? A sign-ier sign?'

'Billie gave me the sign, Shez.'

'No, the universe gave you that sign. The Y-O-Universe. There's a you in universe, Audrey! This place is meant to be a café eventually, so you need to do it. Find a way! Visualise. Use a mantra. Set your intentions! I have a cousin who could work here. Teri. She's a good waitress when she isn't having one of her angoraphobia attacks. It's being around all those people in wool. Hard for her, especially in winter.' Shez shook her head sadly and hopped off the table. 'Okay, well, you need to get cracking, Audrey. You don't even know how many years you have left! You're getting on, aren't you? But don't worry. I'll be back to help you make a vision board after date night. Lem is so keen!'

THE BITTERSWEET BAKERY CAFÉ

The door slammed, and Audrey sighed. Whatever happened to all those upbeat ideas she'd had at the ad agency about loving her age? She was fifty-three, for goodness' sake, and Shez was right; she didn't know how much time she had left. She'd heard somewhere that eighty-three years was the average life expectancy for a woman. Audrey picked up her phone and idly tapped the numbers into the calculator app—30,295 days. She tapped again. At fifty-three, she'd spent 19,345 of those. She had 10,950 left, more if she took good care of herself. More than ten thousand days.

She leaned back in her chair. A person could do a lot with ten thousand days, but what would she do? Work to build someone else's dream? Find a mid-level agency job and help launch other people's businesses? Take macarons to the office and give them to people who didn't care about her? Or be a bat-shit crazy CEO like Shez?

Audrey stood up, then strode across the creaky floorboards of the bakery, scrubbed clean and smelling of bleach and sea air. The room was bathed in the glow of twilight coming through the bay windows. She knew in her bones she could run an e-commerce business and, eventually, a bakery café. She could make it work somehow. All she needed was capital from somewhere to get over this glitch and fund the initial set-up.

She glanced at the stack of cards the party guests had left on the table against the wall. She hadn't had the heart to open them. She picked them up now and flipped through until a large pink envelope caught her eye. *To Tawdry Hepburn* was scrawled on the front in loopy handwriting. Billie had drawn a simple outline of Audrey Hepburn in the beehive hairdo from

Breakfast at Tiffany's, her arms in black gloves, with an impossibly long cigarette holder in her hand and ropes of pearls around her neck. It was a similar drawing to the one Audrey had left on her thank you note months ago, the night she'd been Billie and Ruth's house guest. She slid her finger under the envelope seal and pulled out a homemade card. On the front, Billie had printed:

Happy 60th
Another year older,
another year closer to wearing orthopaedic shoes
and peeing yourself when you sneeze.

Inside, they'd scrawled the quintessential Audrey Hepburn quote:

To Tawdry,
Life is a party. Dress like it!
Love, Billie.

Underneath was a drawing of a cookie stand with the Bittersweet Biscuits logo, and a sign that said *$3 each.*

'What the hell kind of stupid idea is that, Sweetman? In the city?'

Buddy shoved aside the green beans and coleslaw on his plate and sliced off a piece of the lamb chop she'd seared in butter, sea salt and rosemary. In the background, bouncy and low, Nina sang 'Mood Indigo', and Audrey impatiently tapped her foot in time to it, energised by the jazz piano and her own wild, almost impossible idea.

'Yep. Selling in train stations. Rush hour commuters. I'm pretty sure it could work. Well, it's possibly just a tiny bit unorthodox—'

'You mean illegal.' Buddy speared another piece of lamb.

'Hmmmmm, not comfortable with that word at the moment, Buddy, and I'm not one hundred percent sure, but I think in three days I could make enough to pay off the fine.' Audrey ignored the pounding of her own heart. What choice did she have? She pulled the clip from her silvery hair, scrunched it up in a messy bun, and clipped it back. 'I'd only do it for as long as I needed to. A few days. I could worry about taxes later; I don't need to pay those now, just record the income and track it. Five thousand biscuits at two or three dollars each . . . it would give me breathing room. Plus, it would be good market research. It would look like a marketing promotion to customers in the city, so it would build my brand as well.'

Buddy chewed. 'Keep going.'

She told him about the church community in America who'd come up with an ingenious idea during the Global Financial Crisis in 2008. When the bank called the mortgage on their building, the congregation had baked butter cookies and sold them for two dollars each at train stations during rush hour. In a month, they'd paid off their entire loan, something like sixty thousand dollars. Audrey had read about it in the *New York Times*. It had given her comfort that somehow cookies could win—even against huge financial disasters like bank failures and mortgage foreclosures. Wyatt had pursed his lips and said it was ridiculous, but Audrey found the story charming, inspiring even: a victory for people who were willing to fight for what they needed, armed with nothing more than butter and flour, sugar and hope.

Maybe she could be as brave as the parishioners had been. She only needed enough for the fine, ten thousand dollars, and this was the quickest way she could think of to get it. She didn't have anything worth selling; her car was still in the shop being fixed by the insurance company after Billie's accident. It would fetch next to nothing, even when it was repaired. But bake and sell quickly? Rush hour twice a day in a major train station was a way to do it. All she had to do was take a chance.

'You'll need a team, Sweetman.' Buddy pushed his plate aside, leaving the coleslaw untouched.

'I know. I was thinking Lem and Shez. They'd have to take time off work, but I was hoping they could help. And you could come along if you like. We'll have a headquarters at my friend Emma's house. She's still overseas and said I could use her place in the city. You could stay there and help with packaging. What do you think?'

'I think it's worth a shot,' he said. 'Want a—' He held up the bottle of bourbon.

'Day ninety-seven. You know I can't, Buddy. Not ever. Please don't keep offering.'

'Still saying no, one sixty-five-hour day at a time, hey? Well, good on ya, Sweetman.' Buddy poured himself a drink. 'Too bad the Kid couldn't help us. They'd love selling biscuits. Scare everybody away! Put on their ugliest hoodie for the train station. The blood-stained one.'

'The severed hand.' Audrey smiled sadly.

'The dead roach!' Buddy snorted. 'Judge Judy hated that one.'

'The red one with the axe and the chainsaw. I know.' Audrey sighed. 'I can't believe they're gone. I feel like something's missing when I'm in the bakery, and it's Billie.' Audrey gathered up Buddy's plate and cutlery. She'd composed a dozen texts to Billie and had sent none. The last thing she wanted to do was bother them when they were trying to settle back into school, living with a family who didn't accept them. Audrey breathed in, remembering Billie's face when they asked to move in with her.

'What's wrong?' Buddy asked.

'The night of the accident Billie asked to stay with me, but I said no.'

'Well, you couldn't take in Judge Judy's kid. She'd never let it happen.'

Audrey blinked quickly, remembering the pain on Billie's face. The shock. The look of betrayal. 'Billie was too upset to understand that. But . . . I'll give them a couple of weeks to settle in at their dad's, and then I'll call. I'll tell them I'm trying to find a way to build a life here. That's something, at least.'

'You sure, Sweetman?' Buddy asked, his voice even. 'If this crackpot idea pays your fine, you're staying for good?'

'Well, I've already got a bakery I can rent from a miserable landlord old enough to be my father, and a mentor who's a CEO of some holiday flats. What more could I want?'

'Not a goddamn thing. Everything you need is right here.'

But Buddy was wrong. She didn't have everything she needed. There was one thing missing: a teenager with multiple piercings and a sharp tongue who believed she was as special as Audrey Hepburn.

CHAPTER 32

Audrey slid egg whites and vanilla into her bioluminescent-blue baking bowl. Dr Flood had been a rock the night of the party—so calm, so kind—and he'd stopped by the bakery twice since to see how she was getting on. Both times he reminded her that she'd done her best to help Billie, and that everyone in the village knew it. Audrey had been a good friend to them all, he said, and she mustn't blame herself. Audrey sighed as she thought of his words. She beat the egg whites into a froth, then sifted flour, sugar and salt through a fine-mesh sieve. She mixed the fortune-cookie batter into a paste, then added water a tablespoon at a time until it was smooth and fell in ribbons when she raised her spatula. It looked like crêpe batter, silky, creamy white. She inhaled the scent of vanilla and sugar. The batter looked perfect in the beautiful bowl.

She popped in her earbuds and clicked play on the Bittersweet Bakery playlist she'd made. Lately, on the advice of Shez, she'd been listening to country music. It was completely unusual for her, but the zippy riffs from Caroline Jones' guitar made her feel more positive. The title of the song—'Come In (But Don't Make Yourself Comfortable)'—made her smile, and Audrey clomped around her kitchen in Ugg boots, not exactly like her hot-babe boots from Shez, but they'd do. Making the biscuits was always the easy part. The old MX Goldbake oven was humming, it wasn't yet dawn, and Audrey thumped around the bakery kitchen, setting out trays and cooling racks. Damn! The flowers. She grabbed pruning shears and a plastic bowl and crept outside.

In the chilly pre-dawn, everything was silent save for a few maniacal cackling frogs. So noisy, as Shez said, that you wanted to trap them and dump them in an enemy's garden to keep them awake at night. She thought of Wyatt, probably sleeping now, curled around the pregnant Charmaine. She tested the thought for pain like it was a broken tooth. He'd recently moved to an apartment nearer the city, close to Chinatown and Central Station. Surely he would be classified as her enemy.

Her stomach churned. She was furious every time she thought about how he'd ruined their mortgage and lost their savings, and she was humiliated that her marriage was over, a failure after twenty-five years, but . . . was that the same as missing Wyatt? She'd been so busy with her beach life and all the shenanigans in the village. Surprisingly, village life was more eventful than her sophisticated routine in the city had been. In the city she'd had Emma, but most of her days had consisted of getting up early and heading into the agency, a Friday night dinner out with Wyatt, and a weekend at home. Would she trade chats with Shez, Buddy's jokes, the gorgeous beach and her baking for twelve-hour ad-agency workdays with Colin and the horrible Summer, occasional trips to the Opera House and a few dinners in restaurants? She could see now that the only real good in that life, the only constant, had been Emma. But she'd always have Emma, no matter where they both lived.

The streetlights cast a low glow in the cool morning air, and the street was empty. She crouched in front of Robert's nearly depleted bed of daisies and took what she could without leaving it too bedraggled, then snipped a couple of heads off his marigolds and four bright pink dahlia blossoms. She hurried across the road to liberate a few stalks from the lavender bushes lining the driveway. Better to beg for forgiveness than ask for permission, and it was only flowers. She silently added flower-stealer to her list of personal recriminations, along with irresponsible party host, unpromotable advertising executive, deceived soon-to-be ex-wife and stymied business owner. But none of those women were small-hearted, were they? No. She was an overcomer; she was trying to keep going despite every setback. She walked to the bakery and found herself humming.

While she baked, Audrey scrawled a list on a notepad: cellophane bags, ribbon, tags printed with her Bittersweet Biscuits logo and website address, hole punch. By noon, her legs and feet ached from standing. She checked her baking supplies; she had a bulk supply of chocolate chips she'd bought for the party and hadn't used. It would be a good idea to take along a quick classic to sell, as well as the fortune cookies. She'd make as many as she could of Billie's favourite cookies, and she would use the name they had given them: Chip, Chip, Hooray! She stopped and sent up a silent wish for Billie: to reconnect with friends at school, to feel loved, to be okay.

On the benchtop, her phone buzzed. It was a text from Emma. Audrey shoved another tray of fortune cookies in the oven, touched the speaker button and dialled. Emma answered, breathless, from a cruise ship in the Inside Passage, and chattered about the islands and orcas, the blue-grey water in the Pacific Northwest. Audrey added the appropriate exclamations of girlfriend-support whenever Emma paused for breath.

'Miss you, Sweetie! All these cryptic texts. I need to know how you are.'

'Me too. How much time do you have?'

'Ten minutes till we dock.'

Audrey gave her a quick overview—the party, Billie's accident, the mistake with her business licence, and ended with the plan to sell biscuits at rush hour. 'I'd like to use your place as a home base for three days. Would it be okay to bring a couple of friends?'

Emma squealed. 'Ohhhhh, the doctor? Justin-what's-his-name?'

'You're getting ahead of yourself, Em. Anyway, he was dancing with someone at my party. I assume he's dating her.' Audrey took a tray from the oven and folded hot cookies over her fortunes. Justin had been amazing with Billie, and that was all that mattered. 'Besides, I'm not interested in finding a man.'

'Never say never. You know where the key is, Sweetie. Let yourself in. There's nothing in the fridge but you can do an online shop and have it delivered.' Emma paused for a second. 'I wish I was there to help you.'

'I know. Me too, but I'll let you know how it goes.'

Three whistles trilled, and Emma said the ship was pulling in. They said a quick goodbye and Audrey readied another tray of cookie batter for the oven. She was getting faster, but the thought of the fortune-cookie machine and some sort of production process was always on her mind. But first: paying the fine, building the business up and somehow financing the necessary outlay. She could apply for a grant for female founders? Maybe pitch for a spot in a business accelerator program? But she doubted that any of that would work since her startup was so simple; she wasn't reducing global plastic use or starting a design company or selling a personal coaching program to large corporates. She was a middle-aged woman, not some young entrepreneur. She was baking cookies, for goodness' sake!

Audrey spooned more batter onto the tray and stopped her negative self-talk. Mean Audrey always sounded suspiciously like Wyatt, when he went on about risk and said a corporate career was best for her, which was ironic, considering his own high-stakes investments. Where were her limiting beliefs coming from, if not from him? She wiped the benchtop and forced herself to think it through. Her mother had been supportive, a consistent cheerleader, and she'd had no real childhood trauma aside from not being able to afford much. She'd bounced into her first degree, clueless, and in her first semester of her MBA she'd got pregnant. She married Wyatt. She lost the first baby. The second. Then . . . more. Audrey set the dishcloth down and hugged herself, remembering the cramping and the despair of staring down at her own blood. She blinked back tears and leaned against the benchtop. It was after the last miscarriage that she'd turned to wine to cope. But even when she eventually found the strength to quit, she'd never found the courage to reinvent her life. She'd continued working in the city in a slightly less than satisfying career, building other people's businesses, their marketing campaigns, sales strategies, websites. With every year, her dreams had fallen away. Was it the patriarchy, like Shez said, that made her think so little of herself? Was it that she'd accepted what her boss at the ad agency thought—that younger people had so much more to offer than she did?

But wait—*did* they? Not always.

She thought of Charmaine, twenty-five and foolish, sleeping with her boss—a married man. Was Charmaine smarter than Audrey? Was Summer smarter: conniving to get ahead in the office, talking about other women, sabotaging their projects, actively working against them? No.

Shez was younger, too, but she was an original. Totally herself, unapologetic. Probably closer to forty than thirty, and able to go all in and act like a CEO not just of the holiday flats, but in all things: CEO of her life, of her relationship with Lem, who was dying to marry her but seemed too afraid to ask. Shez had verve and a kind of energy, from her crazy optimism right down to her sparkly fingernails. And she believed in Audrey.

Audrey pressed marigold petals and lavender blossom into her fortune cookies and slid another tray in the oven. Flecked with orange and purple blossoms, her biscuits were beautiful, completely unique. She'd never seen anything like them, and from the reaction she got online and in person, neither had anyone else. Her idea for the biscuits was simple but fun, different, a showstopper. Yes, they were just cookies. But even cookies could be amazing if you took the time to make them special. Nothing or something, plain or unique. Just another treat, or meaningful, beautiful like hers. Hers. Her idea. She was also an original. It didn't matter that she was starting over in the middle of her life.

She shoved the next tray in the oven and walked through the bakery, glancing at the white walls and floors, the huge piece of art Billie had painted. The wobbly lines, snaking around, finding their way back to where they started. Buddy's armchair in the corner, the backgammon table. Audrey felt the flutter of excitement she always got when she came up with a new ad campaign; she squinted and imagined what the bakery could be like in summer, with Buddy's jazz humming through the café, her serving coffee and afternoon tea to tourists in colourful swimmers, the grit of sand and happiness dusting the floor. Tables arranged on the footpath with striped blue and white umbrellas. Maybe a simple breakfast menu, continental only, with *pain au chocolat* and warm croissants, fresh sourdough toast, coffees, pressed juices. Local jam? Audrey loved baking bread but had stopped when Wyatt complained about the carbs. She could imagine a couple of staff in hot-pink aprons, white t-shirts with the Bittersweet Biscuits logo and denim shorts. A festive party in December for the whole community. Old-fashioned bulb lights strung outside the bakery. A range of gift baskets. Her online orders all sent out with a Happy Holidays card. Her first product, Bittersweet Biscuits: floral fortune cookies that told the truth. Her second product, Chip, Chip, Hooray! chocolate chip cookies. And her third? It could be anything. Lavender biscuits, cinnamon buns with edible rose petals mixed in with the brown sugar and butter filling or . . .

Audrey's heart beat faster. She had ten thousand days left if she was lucky, maybe even a few thousand more. She would use them, all of them, for her dreams.

The door opened and Shez walked in, waving a plastic bag from the two-dollar shop.

'What's up? Your face looks like Ruth Hickson's, all sort of . . .' Shez twirled her silver nails, 'frenzied preacher meets pissed-off judge.'

'I have a plan, Shez.'

She outlined her idea for the train stations and Shez whistled. 'Jeez, Louise, seriously? You think you can do ten grand in three days?'

'I'll need some help, but yes, I want to leave tomorrow afternoon. I have to take this chance. Buddy's coming. Are you in?'

Shez set the bag of supplies on the benchtop. 'My consultancy rate is normally one sixty-five an hour, but if you give me an afternoon off to shop, plus accommodation, then I'll do it for free.' She picked up her phone and tried to frown. 'I'll book in my preventative Botox—my forehead is smoother than a baby's buttocks, but I go four times a year anyway. Too late for you, Audrey, but then again . . .' Shez lifted a shoulder. '"It's never too late to be what you might have been!" Boy George.'

'I think you mean George Eliot? The British author?'

Shez shrugged in Audrey's direction. 'If you say so. Anyway, I love a good business trip. Botox can be a tax write-off.'

'For selling cookies at a train station?'

'That's just one of my responsibilities. But also, I'll be doing customer retaliation research. I'll give you the whole package, my entire brains trust. God, those chocolate chip cookies look amazing, Audrey.' Shez picked up a fortune cookie and nibbled the end. 'But these are the diet ones, right? Zero calorie?'

'Uh, not exactly. Billie called the chocolate chip ones Chip, Chip, Hooray!'

Shez sighed. 'We could see Billie while we're in the city. They could help us after school.'

Audrey had already argued with herself about this until she'd had trouble falling asleep. Billie living with a stepmother who hated them, Billie at a private school they couldn't stand, Billie banished to the city in part because of her. Audrey hoped they were settling in, but she didn't think it was likely. 'I don't know, Shez. I don't think it's fair to ask. Billie's probably still furious with me, and Ruth would never give me permission, so . . . no, I don't think so.'

'Buddy can't sell biscuits.' Shez chewed the last of her fortune cookie and pinched the little slip of paper between two silver fingernails. 'Oh, I got a Billie one: *Don't play leapfrog with a unicorn*. God, I miss that kid.'

'Me too,' Audrey said. 'Do you have any cousins who could help?'

'Nah. Kylee and Sally are busy, and Trin's doing half days at the salon now. All the Sydney cousins work full-time. Sorry.' Shez smoothed out her fortune and stuck it in her wallet. 'I'll go ask Lem if he'll look after the holiday flats for me. He always says yes, plus it's slow midweek until summer. I'm sure you'll think of something.'

The following afternoon they packed both Audrey's car and Shez's with huge plastic storage tubs filled with biscuits in cellophane bags. Lem's friend owned the local crash repair, and thankfully insurance had covered the cost of fixing Audrey's car due to wildlife having caused the accident. She closed Buddy's passenger door and slid into the driver's seat, massaging the back of her neck. It hurt from baking for two days straight, but Audrey cranked up the stereo and tried to ignore it. Next to her, in the passenger seat, Buddy adjusted his ancient aviator sunnies and nodded along to Wilson Pickett crooning 'Mustang Sally'.

'Been a while since you've been in the city, Buddy?' Audrey patted his knee. 'You can relax at Emma's on the balcony during the day, and then at night I'll make us a nice di—'

'No can do, Sweetman. I'm meeting the boys at Harry's Singapore Chilli Crab tonight, so you can drop me on the way.'

Audrey stared at him.

'Watch the bleeding road, Sweetman! What's wrong with you? Think you can drive looking at me?' Buddy reached over and turned up the volume. 'You need to get a move on! I have to be at Harry's by seven. Don't wait up for me, either.'

Buddy turned on the air conditioning, and cold air blew in Audrey's face. She adjusted her vent. 'Will one of your friends drive you back after dinner?' She frowned, thinking of Buddy's walker.

'Them bludgers? Nah. I got the Yuber on my phone, and Lem showed me how to call a driver.' Buddy took a flask from the pocket of his tweed jacket and unscrewed the tarnished silver top. 'Works a treat, apparently.'

'I thought you were coming to help me package the biscuits.'

'Sweetman, you don't need me. You got yourself into this mess, and it's time to get yourself out.'

CHAPTER 33

Early the next morning, Audrey and Shez lugged four tubs filled with cookies into Central Station in the heart of Sydney's CBD. The station held the sharp scent of dawn, stale beer and neglect. Beside the entrance, someone lay curled on the wet concrete, snoring.

'Oh! That's not good,' Shez said.

Audrey's heart tugged as she stepped closer to the sleeping figure. It was a woman, grey hair, lined face, lying on the damp concrete in a brown shapeless winter jacket, an empty litre bottle of cooking wine beside her. Audrey set down her containers, pulled out a cellophane-wrapped fortune cookie and opened her wallet. The fortune she'd saved from the restaurant with Wyatt was stuck against a fifty-dollar bill. *Love will come back to you.* She should've thrown it away, but somehow she couldn't bring herself to do it. She moved the fortune into her coin purse, tucked the fifty-dollar note under the ribbon of the cellophane bag and slid it quickly into the woman's gaping jacket pocket. Then she picked up her tubs and hurried inside the station to catch up with

Shez. Despite the commuters, Shez was easy to spot in her gold boots, black leggings and red leather motorcycle jacket.

'Was she okay?' Shez asked.

'I think so.' Audrey hoped the fortune in the woman's cookie was encouraging, and that the money would be spent on a big breakfast: bacon, eggs, a side of avocado, buttered sourdough toast and raspberry jam, a steaming hot latte. She knew how it went, how it felt sometimes. Not like that exactly, she'd never dipped down so far with her drinking as to lose her way or hit rock bottom, but still, life wasn't easy for anyone. Sometimes drinking felt like an answer. People had their reasons for coping as they did, and you never knew the dragons someone else was trying to slay.

Audrey and Shez positioned themselves in Central Station with the hope of catching the most foot traffic. Yesterday Audrey had dropped Buddy at the restaurant to meet his mates, and she and Shez had picked up sushi, then driven to an office supply store for tap-and-go cashless terminals, then on to a discount department store for hot-pink t-shirts and DIY transfers that she'd run through Emma's printer. While Shez had eaten sushi on Emma's balcony, Audrey had ironed the Bittersweet Biscuits logos on the shirts. If Shez was curious about the extras Audrey had purchased in the largest size she could find, women's 2XL, she didn't mention it.

'Coffee?' Shez yawned. 'God, it's so early.'

'Love one. I'll set up.' Audrey positioned the stacked tubs and lifted the lid of the top one. The Bittersweet Biscuits logo taped to the side of each tub was printed on plain paper; she hadn't had time to do anything more. She had no idea what the early-morning commuters would think of her business, or if they'd even want a cookie so early. And it was a risk to sell goods at a station, but at the very worst, she'd only be told by the staff to stop. She felt the adrenaline rush through her, similar to how she'd felt before a big pitch at the agency, but far more panicky. Here she had real stakes. But what else could she do? What more did she have to lose? She felt a wall of cold air hit her in her pink t-shirt and jeans, and pulled her jacket tighter. Shez handed her a coffee.

'"Fail early, fail often, fail forward."' Shez took a sip. 'Bloody hot. I burnt my tongue. John C. Maxwell. Or maybe it was Dolly. No. I think Dolly was "Never, ever, ever give up." Oh, and "If I have one more facelift, I'll have a beard."'

Audrey choked on her coffee and Shez laughed. Audrey gave silent thanks that Shez was with her, buoying her spirits, but it didn't stop a tension headache from creeping up the base of her neck. She hadn't slept long enough; she'd been worried about Buddy remembering the address after his night out and getting to Emma's in an Uber. He had done it in the end, and when he hammered on the door after midnight, she wasn't anywhere near falling asleep. He was full of stories about his mates, the Singapore chilli crab they'd shared, and his plans for the morning. She'd lain in bed for hours, finally drifting off around three, then was up again by five-thirty. Shez had used most of the hot water and Audrey barely had time to slick on some lipstick and mascara, but they were here now. It was time to save her business.

A country train pulled up with a long screech and the platform smelled of creosote, the pungent stench of diesel mixed with coal. Commuters spilled from the open doors, hurrying towards the entrance of the station and out into the workday world. Shez, who had set up ten metres or so away from Audrey, waved her arms over her head.

'Good morning, people!' she yelled. 'We have the *best* homemade fortune cookies you'll ever eat. And they're funny, too! Handmade. Three bucks! You're going to love them. But these fortune cookies? They tell the *freaking truth*.'

Audrey gaped at her.

'What?' Shez cried. 'I'm going in, boots and all.'

A woman in leather pants and a long grey cardigan stepped up to Audrey. 'How much?'

'Three dollars each.'

'Can I pay by card? I'll get twenty for the office.'

The woman tapped and Audrey slid ten cello bags into a white paper gift bag. 'Thanks! Enjoy your Bittersweet Biscuits.'

'It's like playing shops!' Shez called from across the hall. 'How are you going, Audrey?'

Audrey waved and kept selling. The next train pulled in and soon she had a crowd standing in a queue in front of her. Customers bought fortune cookies in multiples to share in the office, and chocolate chip cookies singly, probably to eat with a coffee. She didn't have time to look over at Shez, and with the crowds, she couldn't see how Shez's stock was faring anyway. And then it was nine-thirty, the commuters were gone to their offices, rush hour was over, and though the trains kept coming, there were only a few passengers getting off.

Audrey put the lids back on her two tubs. There were a handful of chocolate chip cookies left in the bottom of one. The floral fortune cookies had all sold. She walked over to Shez.

'Sell much?' Audrey asked, her heart in her throat.

'It's all gone except for these! Holy crap, Audrey. I think we did it.'

'Same for me.' Audrey smiled. 'Breakfast to celebrate?'

'I could murder some avocado toast but it's probably twenty-five bucks,' Shez said. 'Isn't that what everybody eats in the city?'

'It is, and I'm buying. There's a cute café near Emma's. We can take a break before this afternoon.'

'Good. We'll have to photocopy ourselves to do this in three days. We need more people selling,' Shez said.

'Wait until this afternoon. I've got it covered.'

Shez frowned, but Audrey refused to say a word.

At first, the afternoon rush was not quite as busy as Audrey had hoped, and they were a little less organised. It took Shez half an hour to find a parking spot—she was late due to her Botox appointment—and by the time she rocked up with her red, dotty forehead and refilled cookie tubs, Audrey was already selling. The commuters were interested, but a little less so since they were heading home. There weren't nearly as many multiple sales. A few people asked if they'd be back in the morning, and Audrey said she wasn't sure; they may be moving to another train station. Scarcity marketing, but it was true all the same.

'Audrey *Sweetman*!' The yell came from somewhere behind the wall of commuters.

She jumped up on her toes and waved an arm. 'Over here!'

'What the . . .' Shez said as Tiny and Stumpy appeared on cue in their leather chaps and motorcycle jackets, each holding a helmet with *Coffin Cheaters* on the side.

Tiny lifted Audrey in a bear hug, and Stumpy gave Shez a fist bump.

'We need the t-shirts, Audrey. It looks more professional,' Tiny said.

They changed in front of the crowd, which Audrey privately thought was anything but professional as she watched them pull their t-shirts on over beer bellies, hairy chests and tattoos. But it was only a few seconds until they were strutting the platform in their new hot-pink Bittersweet Biscuit shirts. Shez giggled, and Audrey hoped she wouldn't mention the shirts were from the women's section.

'Where should we stand?' Tiny asked.

'Just, um, over here . . . your job is more to attract attention than anything else.'

'Like models,' said Stumpy.

'Brand ambassadors,' Shez called. 'Don't you know anything about business?'

'Hey! You're the bikie dudes from TikTok!' A young man in jeans and a grey hoodie shifted his backpack to his other shoulder. 'You're the guys who smash the cookies. Smash one.'

Tiny did a demo. 'You gotta buy the next one, mate.'

'Will if you crush it, dude.'

'Audrey!' Tiny called across the heads of the crowd he'd gathered. 'Let's go for vegan after. I'm thinking Korean fried chicken.'

'Uh, I don't think chicken is vegan—'

'It can be if you cook it right. I know a place,' Tiny said, and Audrey was too busy selling cookies to argue. The Coffin Cheaters knew how to work as a team, and Audrey was grateful. Between doing demos, chatting with the commuters, laughing and calling out, they gave the station a party atmosphere that

Audrey couldn't've done on her own. By three-thirty, groups of teens in various school uniforms thronged the platform.

'Surprised they have money for this,' Shez yelled. 'None of them look like they work.'

A girl in a navy plaid kilt and white blouse, her school hat slung low over her ponytail, sneered. 'We're not deaf you know. We're standing right here. We can hear you.'

And then Shez screamed. A thin body pushed through the pack; it belonged to a teen in charcoal wool trousers, white shirt, skinny tie and a jacket with the same logo as the girl's. Audrey glimpsed a shaved head, two slim wrists. She breathed in sharply.

'Billllllllllie! You got my text!' Shez pulled Billie into her arms.

'Hey! Tiny, Stumpy.'

Billie wouldn't look at Audrey. Their eyes were shadowed, with dark smudges underneath, the left one marked with a purplish bruise. The earrings were gone, leaving gaping red holes at the top of their ears. The school uniform was too big and made them look young, fragile, and far too thin. The new black school shoes in the middle of a term marked Billie as vulnerable, out of place. Audrey tried to concentrate on the customer in front of her, then sold three packages of cookies to an older woman in a black cardigan.

'So, you guys are selling on the street now, Shez?' Billie said.

Audrey smiled at Billie, her heart pinching. 'It's so good to see you. Can you stay until we fin—'

'FREAK!'

There was a high-pitched laugh from a group of teens in uniforms identical to Billie's. They jostled each other, a trio of beefy boys flanking a tall girl with blonde hair. The girl laughed and pointed. 'She's a FREAK.'

A boy laughed. 'Nah, he's a SHIM. She-him!'

'Freak!'

Billie stood motionless, glowering, their face bright red.

'What the hell,' Shez yelled. 'You arseholes!'

'Freak! Shim!' The mob bounced together on the platform tiles, chanting. 'Shim, shim, shim! Freeeeeak!'

Audrey shoved the tap-and-go terminal into Shez's arms and grabbed the lid from the plastic tub. She didn't stop, couldn't think. She charged headfirst at the students, waving the lid of the plastic tub at them as if they were pigeons she could shoo.

'Billie's a FREAK!' one of the boys yelled.

Audrey lifted the plastic lid and smacked him across the chest as hard as she could, then again. '*Shut up!*' she yelled, and kept on hitting. The boy stumbled backwards, his face shocked. Audrey whacked his arms with the plastic lid.

'It's assault!' the blonde girl called. 'Video her!'

'You stupid brats can video my bare arse,' Tiny roared, flipping them the bird and hauling Audrey back. 'Little private school arseholes! Get outta here!' Students scattered down the platform, the blonde girl shouting as she ran.

A small crowd had gathered to stare at them. Audrey dropped her arms to her side, hobbled back to Billie and set down the lid. She was shaking with adrenaline, her breath coming in gasps. 'Nice school you go to.'

Billie took a shaky breath and shrugged. 'Very elite, Tawd. All the best people go there. Three generations of Hicksons.'

'I think we're done here.' Audrey clicked the lid on the plastic storage tub and turned around. Billie looked so terribly thin in uniform. How could they have changed so much since they'd left the beach? It had been no time at all. She touched Billie's shoulder. 'We're going back to my friend's place. Will you join us?'

'Come,' Shez said.

'What about the vegan fried chicken?' Tiny asked. 'Ya gotta celebrate after a bust-up. You killed it, Audrey. You beat those little arseholes into the ground.'

Audrey reclipped the strands of grey hair that had loosened as she ran. 'They deserved it,' she said. 'First, vegan chicken, then Emma's. Will you come, Billie?'

CHAPTER 34

After searching in vain for the restaurant where Tiny had once eaten vegan Korean fried chicken—he insisted he'd been there with the city branch of the Coffin Cheaters, but they'd been having a piss-up at the time—Audrey led them to Happy Lucky Go-Go in Chinatown. She wanted a happier memory of the bustling restaurant than her last dinner with Wyatt.

They crowded together at a round table with a wobbly carousel in the centre. Audrey ordered for everyone and poured hot jasmine tea all around. Billie and Audrey picked at the food, but Tiny and Stumpy ate enough for all of them. Shez sipped her gin and tonic and peppered Billie with questions about their father and Debra, the school, whether Billie missed the beach and if they planned to come home on weekends. Audrey watched Billie's face carefully, trying to decide how she could help.

'Are those kids like that all the time, Billie?' Shez asked.

'Yep, the school motto is We Eat Our Young. But in Latin.' Billie speared a dumpling with a chopstick. 'Ruth loves the old alma mater. She was Head Girl and I'm School Loser.'

Audrey was careful to keep her voice even. 'Billie, look . . . did those kids hit you? That black eye isn't from the car accident.'

Billie was silent. Tiny patted their shoulder kindly. 'We've missed ya, kid.' He waved the server over. 'More pork dumplings and another beer, mate.'

'Love the pink,' the server said. 'Great colour on you boys.'

Tiny sighed. 'We think it's slimming.'

Billie snorted, and Audrey squeezed their hand. 'Did those kids hurt you?' she asked again.

'Don't really want to talk about it, Tawdry. And you don't have to worry about it anyway. I'm Dad's problem now. Ruth loves me making his life hell.' Billie lifted a dumpling and pointed it at her. 'But enough about me, folks. Are you and Shez business partners? You're hawking cookies in train stations?'

Shez waved her sparkly manicured hand. 'I'm Audrey's business advisor. Train stations are a temporary strategy on account of the ten-thousand-dollar fine Ruth got the council to give her for operating a business without a licence.'

'What the *hell*, Tawdry? I can't believe she actually did it.'

'Don't worry. I'm sorting it out. It's okay,' Audrey said, and, eyes narrowed, Billie nodded.

By the time they finished, the table was littered with empty plates and the debris of crushed fortune cookies. Audrey slipped off to pay the bill. Tiny and Stumpy left to collect their Harleys, promising to meet them in the morning back at Central Station, and Billie stood to leave. Audrey touched their arm.

'I wanted to call after the accident. To explain. Ruth would never let you live with me, Billie. There's just no way—'

'Don't, Tawdry. I get it. You don't have to say it.'

'I do have to say it. I'm so sorry.' Audrey waited.

Finally, Billie met her gaze. 'Well, if I ever need a geriatric bodyguard with a plastic lid, I'll let you know.'

Audrey let out her breath. 'Anytime. Can I drive you home?'

'Nah. Uber. Hooked up to Dad's credit card, so whatev.' Billie shrugged. 'Tawd? I'm sorry, too. It was a mistake when I told Ruth about the licence thing. It just slipped out. Are you mad?'

Audrey shook her head and squeezed Billie's shoulder. 'No, I'm not mad. You were telling the truth, and it was my responsibility. It's not your fault, Billie. I'm just happy you're here.'

Buddy was waiting for them at Emma's. He'd spent the afternoon at the races and had come back early to sleep it off.

'How'd you go with the cash?' he asked.

Audrey did the sums; the sales from their first day were pretty average, and Tiny and Stumpy would help them get through the next morning's queues faster. She hadn't the heart to tell Shez and Buddy that the takings weren't as good as she'd hoped. The cookies had sold well in the morning, but with Billie being attacked, they'd left before the real evening rush hour had started. She'd need at least four more days to pay the fine, and maybe earn a little extra to invest in the business and save for machinery. She'd have to ask Buddy and Shez to stay on in Sydney longer than they'd planned.

Audrey settled into the guest room while Shez and Buddy laughed together in the lounge, the sound of the television making it almost impossible to hear herself think. She tried to imagine what it was like for Billie at a school with students who would scream names like that, and wondered how long they'd stay before running away again. Anything else was too terrible to think about, and Billie was stronger than that, Audrey was sure of it. But her dreams, when they came at last, were full of Volkswagen Beetles filled with flowers, shaved heads and the blood of a dead wallaby.

Dawn arrived too early, and with it, a thunderstorm crashing overhead, with wild spring rain pelting down on the slick pavement. Audrey and Shez ran from the parking garage through the green outside Central Station with their plastic tubs, getting thoroughly soaked while the thunder boomed. Audrey knew it wouldn't be a good day. People would work from home in weather like this if they could, and no one was in a generous mood when it was dark and wet; why would they want to carry a soggy bag of cookies into the cold, dreary office?

She was right. By the end of the morning rush hour, more than half their morning's stock was unsold. Tiny and Stumpy left for home, since it was obvious that they couldn't do much to attract a crowd that wasn't there. When Audrey and Shez stopped for lunch at a diner, Shez flicked through her social-media feed and picked at her salad.

'Shez, why don't you go shopping? I can handle the afternoon crowds myself. I'll make us a nice dinner at Emma's. I'll do dessert, the chocolate cake from your birthday.'

'Thanks, if you're sure!' Shez hopped up and hustled out the door before Audrey had time to take another sip of her coffee.

The afternoon stretched in front of her, grey and cold. Audrey pulled a notepad out of her handbag and made yet another list. What could she do if this didn't work? She didn't feel right imposing so much on her friends; they were helpful, but they didn't work for her, and they should've been paid for their efforts, but she had no capital. She thought of Wyatt in his office just blocks away, and wondered if Charmaine still reported to him or how long she'd continue to work being pregnant. A baby, a fresh start, the feeling of a real family. Audrey's stomach clenched. All of that was too late for her now; it was a different kind of life, and one she'd never have.

Her phone pinged with a text from Billie. *Good luck with the cookies . . . you can do it Tawdry.*

Audrey gazed at the rain, slackening a little, and straightened her shoulders. She had friends, and her own two hands. Good health for now. More time. Possibly ten thousand days. She wrote down all her hurdles: pay the fine, get a business licence, buy machinery, and find an employee, at least part-time. Invest in more ads on social media, send sample products to catering companies and event planners. Audrey ordered another coffee and a slice of lemon tart, and kept working in the quiet diner. The obvious places to pitch for funding would be investors, and she was, technically, a startup—if a rather old-fashioned one—so that meant she was eligible to enter pitch competitions. Her idea was traditional, non-tech, and she doubted she'd win, but maybe it was worth a try.

She used her phone to search for angel investors, pitch competitions, startup programs and ultra-high net worth family offices. Every lead went on the list. She tucked her now mostly silver hair behind her ears, remembering Matthew Hayes' rude comments about the models she'd featured in her Love Your Age campaign. Someone like that would never back a business with a middle-aged female founder. Was it only a few months ago? It felt like a lifetime.

When it was time to head back to the station for afternoon rush hour, the rain had lifted, and the sky was the cold grey of spring. The Bittersweet Biscuits signs she'd taped to the containers the day before were still damp from the rain. Audrey set down the plastic tubs. She wanted a hot bath and a cup of tea; maybe tonight she'd order in dinner instead of cooking. She was sure Shez and Buddy would understand.

A woman in a red jacket hurried towards her, her hair frizzy from the rain. 'Can I get two dozen cookies?' she asked. 'I need them for my daughter's preschool class. The Parents and Friends Association say homemade only, labelled for food intolerances.' She sighed and grabbed her phone. 'What's in them?'

Audrey rattled off the ingredients and threw in a couple of extra packages. 'Listen, just take them out of the individual bags and put them on a plate with some cellophane. Bend a few so they look like you made them.'

The woman thanked her with a tired smile. A few other commuters wandered up, and Audrey imagined how a silver-haired woman in a pink t-shirt standing beside two plastic containers of cookies would look to passers-by. Tired. Bedraggled. Hawking her wares.

That's when she saw them walking towards her. In his trench coat, the expensive Burberry one she'd given him last Christmas, Wyatt strode closer, his arm draped around Charmaine.

There was nowhere to run.

Audrey stood alone on the platform. She stared at Charmaine's belly, rounded now, a cute baby bump underneath her tight knit dress. Her blonde head tilted up to Wyatt's, and she laughed. She looked young and glamorous, with a designer handbag and matching heels, an elegant low ponytail at the nape of her slim neck. A deep, cramp-like pain lodged in Audrey's stomach, and she could barely breathe. Charmaine and Wyatt looked happy. They looked like a couple in love.

Audrey stood, shaking. She could leave her cookies—leave everything—but she'd be running ahead of Wyatt and Charmaine, and they were too close now. His eyes widened as he caught sight of her. Dizziness swept over her, but she stood her ground, paralysed.

'Audrey? What are you . . .'

He read her t-shirt, stared at the flimsy Bittersweet Biscuits signs on the plastic tubs stacked beside her. Her business. Her failure. All he could see of her new life was here on a cold platform, stacked in front of him. He couldn't see her renovated apartment, the feature article in the national women's magazine, the small frenzy generated by her social-media posts, her fifty thousand followers on TikTok. He couldn't see the humble beginnings of a real business, with a product that customers had just started to know and love. He didn't know that one of the most prominent members of Sydney society, Imogen Hayes, had praised Audrey's originality and posted divorce-party pictures with her floral fortune cookies. He couldn't see her professional Bittersweet Biscuits website, now disabled, or understand her need to scrounge together money for a fine when she'd have had that money in the bank if he hadn't ruined their financial life with his shoddy investments.

No.

All he saw was this. Audrey alone.

'Oh my God!' Charmaine stared at her, her lip-glossed mouth a perfect O.

A train pulled up. It stopped with a high-pitched squeal and the stink of diesel. Audrey's heart hammered and her mind catapulted forward: what would Wyatt say, and how would she answer him? He could say whatever he wanted! She would stand up for herself. She would tell him about her business, her worth, her plans. She would tell him exactly what she was building, and what she thought of him and his lies. She'd tell him he'd almost ruined her, but that in the end she'd survived. Thrived!

Wyatt opened his mouth, then looked away. He took Charmaine's hand and led her around his wife.

Audrey stood alone on the cold concrete platform.

She was invisible.

CHAPTER 35

Students walked past her, staring at her strangely: a middle-aged woman with silver hair, crouched on a platform at the train station. Still, Audrey didn't move. Her knees had turned to rubber, and she couldn't seem to get up. Images of her beautiful suburban home crashed through her mind, of Wyatt's garden after she'd destroyed it, of Charmaine hammering on her yellow front door. Of the debt she was facing now, the likelihood of bankruptcy unless she could buy the time to make Bittersweet Biscuits a success. That was so unlikely that it was laughable. She was a joke.

'Tawdry?' Billie barrelled across the platform and kneeled in front of her, school tie dangling next to Audrey's hands, their white face concerned. 'Tawdry! What's wrong? Are you sick?'

It was too humiliating to explain. Her normally reliable sentences, her way of convincing people and making sense of things, being there for everyone else, being the helper, had completely deserted her. Despite how hard she'd fought for women like her to be seen, somehow she, Audrey Sweetman—senior executive at a major ad agency, wife of twenty-five years, homeowner, responsible taxpayer and money-earner—had become nothing in the eyes of Wyatt. No. She was nothing in the eyes of the world.

'I can't keep going, Billie.' Her shoulders shook. 'I can't do it.' Audrey felt sick with the weight of failure. Billie would never understand. They were too young; they still believed that everything would work out eventually. But maybe they wouldn't. Maybe it was too late for Audrey and all her ridiculous dreams. The bank wanted money for the debt; the local council had demanded she pay the business fine. And every day, as Danny worked to find a way to help her stave off bankruptcy, his legal fees were mounting.

'You can, Tawd.' Billie pulled Audrey to her feet and shook her shoulders sharply.

'I can't.' Audrey looked away.

'Don't you dare give up on you. I'm not giving up on you!'

But Wyatt had, and so had Colin, and the stupid sexist, ageist Matthew Hayes, chair of Hayes Corp. They'd all given up on her, hadn't they? Maybe they were right. Audrey had always thought she'd find her way through, and Billie believed she could, but maybe she couldn't. She was so, so tired. She wiped her face with the back of a hand.

'Why do you believe in me, Billie? Why?'

Billie's yell echoed from the cavernous metal ceiling of the train station. 'Because you're Tawdry freaking Hepburn! Because life is a party. Dress like it!'

It took the long drive through rush-hour traffic to make up her mind.

Billie said nothing, just turned on some Stevie Wonder and left Audrey alone with her thoughts. 'For Once in My Life' bounced in the background. It was the song Audrey's mum had played the night she'd announced her engagement to Michael, the fiancé they both believed would be Audrey's new father. They'd done the dad dance together, little Audrey two-stepping to Motown on top of her mother's feet. But a week later, Michael had disappeared without an explanation. Audrey and her mum had gone to the op shop, where Joyce had found a chipped rose quartz crystal the size of a human heart. For years after Michael had gone, they'd moved the crystal from apartment to apartment, coffee table to coffee table. The resolve she felt now was what her mother must've felt then, Audrey thought: a stone in her heart. Rose quartz. Solid and unbreakable. Making her little family safe, no matter what.

Audrey gripped the steering wheel. She was the second generation of independent women, wasn't she? Joyce had been the first; she'd shown her daughter how. Audrey stared out at the rain-soaked streets. Joyce had lived with joy, despite her teenage pregnancy in the sixties and her parents' disapproval. Despite everything. And like her mother, Audrey could build a future, whatever it took. She refused to walk meekly into bankruptcy without a fight.

She pulled her car into Emma's tiny garage and Buddy opened the front door. Audrey strode into Emma's home. 'Buddy, put on some jazz. Billie, text your dad and tell him you're staying overnight at a friend's. Please.' She dumped her handbag and phone on the kitchen table. 'Let's get moving. Shez, I need a coffee.'

They stared at her.

'Holy hell, Audrey,' Shez said. 'What happened to you?'

'I woke up. Buddy! Music!'

'Kid, show me how to use this speaker thing.' With Billie's help, Buddy soon had 'Mack the Knife' bopping through the room.

Audrey flipped open her laptop. 'Coffee pods are in the right-hand cupboard, Shez. No sugar. No milk.'

'But you always take two sug—'

'No. I don't, Shez. I drink it black.'

Halfway through the song, Shez slid a hot coffee across the counter to Audrey. 'What are you doing?'

Audrey flicked through the list she'd made of pitch competitions in the city. There were seventeen opportunities for founders. She scanned the page for tomorrow's date, and there it was: a pitch competition at Workmates on York Street. First prize, fifty thousand dollars. It was a long shot, but it was worth it.

'Saving my business, Shez. We're pitching Bittersweet Biscuits at a startup competition tomorrow. Billie, can you take a half-day off school?'

'If someone calls to say I have a doctor's appointment.'

'Shez, you do it,' Audrey said.

'Has Sweetman finally lost her marbles, Kid?' Buddy asked in a stage whisper.

'Actually, I think she found them,' Billie whispered back, and Audrey nodded.

Cortisol flushed through her body. She wouldn't give Wyatt or anyone the power to make her feel invisible. Not anymore. She handed her phone to Billie. 'Call Workmates and say you're the executive assistant for Bittersweet Biscuits. Get a pitching slot for me, Billie. They'll say we didn't submit our application on time. Tell them it's in their inbox. Don't take no for an answer. I'll send it through as soon as I can.'

Billie blinked. 'What should I say—'

'Anything to get a yes, Billie.'

Shez leaned over Audrey's shoulder. 'What is this?'

'A pitch deck for startup funding. Can you look up the Byron Bay Cookie Company? I need you to find their financials in their annual report. Text me their growth rate for the last three financial years. I'll cite them as proof of what we can do with a cookie company. If they did it, I can.'

Shez tapped her phone with bright green nails. 'Uh, I don't know what to do.'

Audrey grabbed Shez's phone. A minute later she handed it back. 'If you find any good quotes about market sizing or distribution and reach, copy them into a Word doc. Then skim the financials at the end. You're looking for profit margin and price to sales.'

Shez nodded. 'Okay, but . . . I'm not sure?'

'Grab whatever you think is good. I'll review it.' Audrey kept typing. 'Buddy! Can you take an Uber to the shopping centre? You need chinos and a button-down. Decent leather shoes, reading glasses. An outfit that looks expensive, but not a suit. Investors go casual. And one more pink t-shirt for Billie. We're going in as a team.'

'Sure, Sweetman, if you give me the cash.'

'The money from the cookies. Take it all.'

Shez stared at her. 'What happened to you, Audrey? Are you okay?'

Was it a switch that Wyatt had flicked? Was it simply time to see herself as the capable, experienced woman she truly was? Did she want to prove that Billie was right to believe in her? She wasn't sure. But something had changed.

Billie got the appointment at the startup competition, a fifteen-minute time slot the following morning at eleven-thirty. Buddy brought back three new t-shirts, in case Shez and Audrey needed fresh ones too, and another package of iron-on transfers. Shez printed the Bittersweet Biscuits logos and did the ironing while Billie set the table on the verandah and waited for the pizza delivery. Buddy modelled what he called his business clothes: a pair of chinos, a button-down shirt, brown leather shoes and a navy cashmere vest. When he handed her the receipt, Audrey sucked in her breath. She knew they only had a slim chance of winning the fifty-thousand-dollar first prize, but second place was ten thousand. Anything would help.

'The pizza's crappy here,' Billie said, and served themselves a second slice. 'I miss Livio's from town.'

Audrey nodded and gazed at Emma's filtered view of the sea. Billie was right. A lot of things were better at Whitehaven Bay. For one thing, she'd never find or afford an ocean view like it in the city. She picked up her phone and snapped a photo of the four of them, toasting each other with mineral water. She texted it to Emma, with multiple emojis thanking her for letting them use her home.

I'm moving to the beach, Emma. For good.

What??? What's happening??? She could feel Emma's alarm creeping through her text.

I'm starting over.

Around two in the morning, Audrey finished her pitch deck and crawled into bed. Still, it was impossible to sleep. Every time she closed her eyes she saw Wyatt's incredulous face, watched him step around her without speaking, as if she were an embarrassing homeless person he couldn't bear to acknowledge. A stranger. She wondered what allowed men to be like that, to ignore their own history and family and everything that had come before, and simply waltz off into a new future. Wyatt did it because he believed he could; he had a job and a young woman who was willing to run away with him.

But her? Why did women her age become invisible? Were they too quiet? Did they need to learn to fight? And invisible to *whom*, anyway? That was the real question. Not to themselves, and not to their friends. Maybe they were only invisible to men. But so what? What if they just stopped giving men the power to decide? Audrey shut her eyes, rolled over and luxuriated in the extra width of the bed. She was proud of what she'd built from absolutely nothing, despite everything Wyatt had done. Her business was her own, and it was wholly unique.

She was not a victim or a survivor; she was a warrior, just like every other woman she knew. Warriors might be tired, and scarred, and a little beaten up by life—or even a lot—but they weren't invisible.

In her dreams that night, she crashed through floors, falling. But she flailed her arms and caught herself, made herself wake up before she hit the ground.

CHAPTER 36

'Time to get up!' Audrey stood in Emma's living room, dressed in her pink Bittersweet Biscuits t-shirt and white jeans.

'What the hell, Tawd . . .' Stretched out on the sofa, Billie pulled a pillow over their head.

'We need to get a move on. We're leaving in an hour.'

Audrey had printed copies of her slide deck for her team to review. She'd be the one presenting, but she needed them with her. Yes, they would look like a motley crew, possibly even unprofessional. But they weren't. She smiled at Billie, who'd wriggled back under the blankets. Billie had street smarts and wit, so much talent and creativity. Buddy and Shez—with their unfailing, dogged loyalty—they counted as much as anyone else, and so did she.

This was only the first pitching competition she'd try. If she failed, she'd try again, and keep on going. She'd get Danny to figure out how long they could stall the bank, or if they could work out a payment plan for her debt until her business flourished.

A long line of female entrepreneurs lit the way for her: Sara Blakely with Spanx, Lorna Jane with her athletic and leisurewear, even Mrs Fields with her cookie business. Other women had done it. It wasn't easy for anyone, but if they could achieve millions and even billions in turnover, Audrey could build a solid business to support herself. All she needed was to get an investor interested and buy herself some time.

And if all her pitches failed, well, she might be forced to go the traditional route and pitch to friends, family and fools, asking everyone she knew to back her. She'd head back to the beach and work hard and pivot until she succeeded because that was how you built a business. But today, she'd make her pitch as compelling as she could. She'd give it everything she had. All her life she'd played it safe. She'd left her good ideas crouching inside her because she didn't have the self-belief to plant them, kneel on the ground, get her hands in the dirt, work and wait. She'd been too afraid to start because she might fail . . . so she failed in advance by never trying.

She sighed: all those wasted years, the wasted dreams, the fear of what somebody else might think. But who could judge her, or stop her? No one, unless she let them. Wyatt and Ruth and even Colin and Summer from the agency—*Audrey* had set them up as judges at her judges' table. *She* was the one who had invited them into her brain and accepted their opinions as truth.

No more. She was done. It was time to listen to herself.

'Coffee?' Shez handed her a long black.

Audrey took a sip. 'I'd like to introduce you as my head of business development, Shez. Billie, will you be my executive assistant? Buddy, I'm hoping you'll pose as an investor and shareholder. All you need to do is say you have financial confidence in Bittersweet Biscuits. You've got zero online presence so you're perfect. They can't google you.'

'You're saying he has to lie?' Billie asked.

'Not exactly. You do believe in me, don't you, Buddy?'

From across the room, Buddy grunted.

Audrey smiled at her team. 'Don't worry. It's going to be fine. And no drinking today, okay, Buddy? We have to make this work.'

The Workmates head office was located on the third floor of an historic office block in York Street, across from the iconic Queen Victoria building. When the Bittersweet Biscuits team arrived, the ground-floor lobby was crowded with a queue waiting for the lifts. Audrey stepped past two young women dressed in matching black t-shirts with huge red hearts emblazoned with HugCo. Two teen boys in hoodies carried a black vinyl bag containing what looked like a pull-up sign. There were twin brothers who looked mid-twenties in chef uniforms with Skytable logos on their hats, and a thin, nervous-looking couple, the woman clutching a toddler wearing a t-shirt branded with PottyNet: internet connectivity from your potty!

'Shez, could you wait for the lifts with Buddy? Billie and I will take the stairs.'

'Tough competition from the baby,' Billie said. 'You're gonna have to be a killer, Tawd.'

Audrey nodded and pushed open the door on Level 3. A young woman with dreadlocks leaned against a glass reception desk. A wall running the length of the open-plan office was filled floor to ceiling with plants around a neon sign: We're Workmates! The middle of the room was dominated by table tennis and shuffleboard, the two tables surrounded by white leather bean bag chairs scattered in groups, and low navy velvet sofas. At the far end of the room was a fully stocked café.

'Hey! Come in and chill,' the receptionist said.

'This is Audrey Sweetman, founder of Bittersweet Biscuits. I'm her EA, Billie.' Billie's tone was surprisingly officious, as if they'd been an executive assistant for years. Once a Hickson, Audrey thought.

'Billie! Cool t-shirt. Love! And Audrey, wow, your hair! I'm gonna go full-on silver one day. Kombucha on tap over there, organic herbal teas, GF, DF and vegan snacks, help yourselves. You have to pay for the alcohol in that fridge. You're up at eleven thirty, but we're running late, and we've got four groups ahead of you. You're pitching to . . .' she looked down at her tablet, 'Hayes Corp, that's the angel investor sponsoring this round. If you win, it's fifty K, yay!'

Audrey's face paled.

'Something wrong, Tawd?' Billie whispered.

She shook her head. There was no way she'd tell her team about Hayes Corp and its shocking chair. There was no point replaying the history: the pitch she'd delivered so unsuccessfully, and how Matthew Hayes Senior had rubbished her Love Your Age idea. She was here with another idea, a solid business, and that was all that mattered, wasn't it? Still, she felt her confidence draining, and the memory of Wyatt and Charmaine stepping around her and her wet and bedraggled cookies flooded back. His face. Her failure.

She inhaled deeply. Water. Coffee. Either of those would help. The elevator door opened behind them, and Shez and Buddy rolled in. Shez spun around and whistled. She clacked over to the wide island in front of a well-stocked kitchen with drinks fridges and a deluxe coffee machine, the stiletto heels of her snakeskin boots striking the wide expanse of polished concrete floor.

'Free food! But no biscuits. Think, Audrey! Yours would be perfect here. You've got the samples? We can leave them after the pitch. Marketing.'

Audrey nodded as she sat down and opened her laptop. She knew the nine stages of her pitch by heart: problem, solution, market, product, traction, her team, financials, investment amount needed and what she'd do with it. Her deck was simple but beautiful, and she'd incorporated video clips of the Coffin Cheaters smashing cookies on the beach, the gorgeous images of her floral fortune cookies, a shot of the bakery, white and minimalist in the morning sun, then wild and rocking with people dancing during her party. Billie had managed to catch a photo of Audrey in her yellow dress and white boots, holding a fortune cookie above her head. And of course, she had samples to hand around, but she hadn't had the time to make new biscuits with carefully selected fortunes. She'd just have to see what the investors got and hope for the best—if they were intrigued enough to crack them open. But from her experience, she knew that an unopened fortune cookie was like an unopened present: no one could resist for long.

After checking out the snack bar, the others joined her on the comfortable couch. And soon, the two young women in the HugCo t-shirts sat down across from them.

'Hi! We haven't seen you at any pitches before.'

'It's our first one. I'm Audrey. Bittersweet Biscuits.'

'We're a hug company. You can send hugs to anyone in the world, well, eventually that's the plan. We're operating in two cities now, but the idea is to expand. You know how isolated everyone is these days? Facetime just doesn't cut it, and Covid was so rough. People need real hugs. That's where we come in.'

Shez stared, incredulous, at the girl who was speaking. 'Pay for hugs? Just the hugs, or—'

'Great idea,' Audrey cut in. 'I like it.'

The young woman adjusted her heavy-framed black glasses. 'There's a lot of research to back it up. You'd be surprised. We like to think of ourselves as subbing in for loving friends and family. It's especially good for older people like you,' she said, looking at Audrey and Buddy in turn.

Audrey squinted at her. Didn't everyone need connection? And what was old? Fifty? Ninety?

Buddy snorted. 'Pay for hugs? Sounds like a load of crap to me.'

'Excuse me?' The woman took off her glasses. 'Hugs are popular for the elderly. We're meeting a real need in aged care. What do you do?'

'I make floral fortune cookies,' Audrey said.

'Oh. Isn't that . . . cultural appropriation?'

Billie scowled. 'Ever make a lamb roast? You don't exactly sound like a Kiwi.'

The woman laughed. 'I guess you're right. We're assuming older people need hugs, but we're not there yet ourselves. Hey, Audrey, we should interview you for market research.'

'She's not that elderly,' Shez said. 'It's mainly her grey roots. Aged care is at least a decade away.'

Audrey raised her eyebrows and handed the HugCo founder a fortune cookie.

'Ohhh! These are pretty.' The HugCo founder cracked it open and pulled out her fortune. '*You're doing better than you think you are.* I'm keeping this. It's a good omen for today.'

'They're handmade, with funny or uplifting fortunes and edible flower petals,' said Audrey. 'Perfect for parties, and delicious, too. Sweet with a hint of bitter from the botanicals.'

'We could order these for our Christmas hampers.'

Audrey gave her a card, hoping she'd still be in business at Christmas. Three months was a long time for a startup. 'That'd be great. I'll give you a special rate.'

'Thanks, Audrey.'

HugCo was called first. The toddler from PottyNet ran around hiding snacks underneath chairs and asking his father to read *Bluey*. Skytable was up next, and Audrey overheard them telling the parents with the toddler that they hosted dinner parties in unique locations on platforms suspended by cranes. Shez leaned closer to Audrey. 'Total failure! Think of the cost of that one!'

Skytable was followed by the two teens in hoodies, who spoke in whispers and didn't reveal anything about their pitch to the others. By the time PottyNet was called, the mother's hair was frizzy, with strands escaping from her sagging ponytail, the toddler had eaten five packets of snacks, spilled juice near Audrey's handbag and used the demo potty. The family walked from the pitch room looking relieved to be done, and resettled themselves behind Audrey's team.

'Bittersweet Biscuits! You're on!'

Audrey took a deep breath.

'Ready?' She squeezed Shez's hand, then Billie's, and nodded to Buddy who was looking distinguished and aloof, already in character for his role as investor. She walked to the door and opened it, bracing herself to say hello to Matthew Hayes Senior.

He wasn't there. A man in a navy suit and crisp white shirt sat at the head of the table. Matt Hayes Junior. Audrey sent up a prayer of gratitude, until she heard a woman's voice.

CHAPTER 37

Summer laughed. 'Audrey? You're pitching a startup?'

Audrey's instinct was to turn and walk out the door.

'I'm surprised to see you, Audrey,' Summer said. 'I moved from the ad agency to Hayes Corp a month ago. I'm the new head of community and brand. Have you met Matt Hayes? You do know his father. Remember? The day I got promoted and your pitch failed?'

Summer, with her perfectly wavy hair and black suit sat next to the new CEO of Hayes Corp. Audrey stared at them, her chest tight. Her heart beat faster, and a feeling of dread washed through her. It would be hard enough to pitch her business to a member of the Hayes family, but to pitch to Summer as well? To know, while she was talking, that Summer would be judging her? Her eyes flew to Matt Hayes Junior, who stared at his phone, his long hair gelled back from his tanned face. Maybe he'd be more open to her ideas, but she doubted it. He looked like he came from generations of aristocracy, which he had, if aristocracy meant money and lots of it.

Summer leaned towards Matt. 'Audrey would've reported to me at the ad agency, but she was let go.'

Audrey stared at Summer. It was an outright lie; she'd resigned precisely because she couldn't report to someone like her.

Shez coughed and tugged down her leopard-print miniskirt. Audrey noticed too late she'd tied the new huge pink Bittersweet Biscuits t-shirt in a jaunty knot at her ribcage. The effect was celebratory rather than professional, to put it kindly. Shez nudged Audrey's foot with her snakeskin boot. Audrey tried to breathe. How could this be happening? It was a repeat of her terrible final day at the agency.

'Audrey's CEO of her own business now,' Shez said. 'Bittersweet Biscuits. I'm Sherry, head of business development, this is Billie, Audrey's EA, and this is Buddy Trask.'

'I'm an investor with a . . . with a . . . a wealth of experience,' Buddy started.

Audrey tried to clear her throat, which felt blocked up tight. She'd backed herself this far, and she had to keep going. Despite every horrible thing that had happened to her, she hadn't quit. That counted for something. Her stomach rolled over, and she forced herself to walk further into the room and stand in front of Summer.

'Hello, Matt. Summer.' With a hand she willed not to tremble, Audrey placed two packages of fortune cookies on the table in front of them. She opened her laptop and pressed AirPlay. The Bittersweet Biscuits logo filled the big screen.

'Let me start with a story.' Audrey clicked the first slide and there she was, dancing in her yellow dress, holding a fortune cookie above her head.

'Once there was a woman who needed to host a party and have some fun. But actually, she needed to *be more fun*, and rediscover herself. And what does every party need?'

'Young people?' Summer asked. 'Alcohol?'

'No. Every party needs something sweet. Why? Because that's what all of us have been taught as children: good news is sweet. Baking is a party. Always, in almost every culture. As Ina Garten, the Barefoot Contessa, says—' the screen flashed up a large quote: 'You can never be miserable while you're eating a cookie.'

Matt Hayes grinned at her. 'True.'

'A cookie is a party you hold in your hand.' Audrey clicked to an image of Tiny, tattoos and leather, holding a cookie at Whitehaven Bay.

'But Bittersweet Biscuits is different. What we offer is even better than a regular cookie. We make cookies beautiful, like our signature floral fortune cookies.'

Another slide, this one featuring a row of fortune cookies on the sugar-white sand at Whitehaven Bay, their daisy and marigold petals glowing purple and yellow, illuminated by sunshine.

'And inside?' Audrey continued. 'Inside is what makes Bittersweet Biscuits truly special. Our floral fortune cookies don't just hold tired old fortunes. They contain modern fortunes, handwritten, surprising and inspiring. Sometimes quirky and a little bit risqué, but always unique. My fortunes don't sugarcoat it; they tell the truth.'

She clicked to a close-up image of Billie's fortune about playing leapfrog with unicorns. Shez laughed, and Matt Hayes snorted. Summer looked bored.

'They tell the truth about people.' Audrey paused. 'Young people, and who they are inside.' A shot of Billie in their blood-splattered hoodie and piercings filled the screen, holding a fortune cookie and laughing, eyes squeezed shut.

'Old people.'

Suddenly there was Buddy, incognito from behind: Audrey had snapped the photo from her balcony, his naked butt jiggling on his way to the beach with his walker, the striped towel slung over his shoulder.

Matt chuckled. 'Love it! That's a great shot.'

'Fun people.'

There was an image of Shez sitting on a table in the bakery, a fortune cookie pinched between her rainbow-manicured nails, her arm filled with jingly bracelets, a huge aquamarine cocktail ring on her index finger.

Matt Hayes smiled.

'These are modern biscuits for modern times. Customers love them. They bring people together. It's a simple idea, but it's valuable because it reminds all of us . . .' she took a big breath, 'to grab the joy that life has to offer. To eat a cookie and be less miserable. To celebrate life. To live a little. As Audrey Hepburn famously said . . .' she clicked on to the next slide. 'Life is a party. We should dress like it.'

Summer yawned and reached for her phone. Audrey raised her voice. 'Every person lives their life. But whether or not you enjoy it? That's up to you.'

It was exactly what she'd been trying to do all along with her baking: to bring the joy. It was her way of loving life, like her mother had before her. Joyce had managed to back herself through teen pregnancy and a lifetime as a solo parent, through a career filled with hard work standing for hours every day in a hair salon, listening to clients' worries and troubles. She'd filled

Audrey's life with abundance and love. 'That's why I started Bittersweet Biscuits. To bring some joy.'

Matt Hayes nodded. 'I like it, Audrey. It's catchy and your market positioning is great. But it's non-tech and old-school. Why should we invest?'

Audrey took a deep breath. Could she tell him the truth? That she desperately needed a win? That she needed capital to keep going? That she was trying so hard to throw some good back into the world, when all she'd received in the past few months was bad news? No. She had to back herself with confidence, and trust that Matt Hayes would see the value in her business.

'I have twenty years of experience in advertising, and a lifelong passion for baking. And that makes me an expert at two things: how to bake cookies that people love, and how to sell them.' She smiled at Matt. 'But here's the real reason you should invest. I've learned a lot in my life, and I know one thing for sure: everybody needs love. Cookies are love, and people love cookies. That's why they'll never stop selling.'

She clicked to the final image, another one from her party: the conga line with partygoers holding firm to each other's waists, the laughter, the guests eating her cookies. Billie grinning, Shez dressed as Dolly with a microphone in her hands and her blonde wig slightly askew, Buddy in his red leisure suit, Justin Flood behind Audrey, dancing. The bikers and a belly dancer, hippies and superheroes, the man in the inflatable T-Rex—all of them, together, living life, loving her biscuits. Underneath Audrey had typed in bold letters: *Bittersweet Biscuits: Life Is What You Bake It.*

'Thanks, Audrey,' Matt said. 'Leave us a copy of your financials. We'll make our decision soon.'

As the door closed, Audrey heard Summer laugh and murmur something about 'old-school clichés'.

Shez gave her a squeeze. 'You were good, Audrey. Never mind that stupid cow. Let's go get some chocolate, hey?'

'The photos were amazing, Tawdry,' Billie said. 'You killed it. I almost cried.'

Buddy wheeled himself over to the kitchen island and loaded up a plate from the tray of sushi. 'Sweetman! Can I have a beer? Wait, it's six bucks, and I don't carry cash.'

'Here.' She rummaged inside her bag and pulled out her wallet. Inside her change purse, folded on one corner but still legible, lay the fortune she'd saved from Happy Lucky Go-Go. *Love will come back to you.* She handed Buddy three gold coins and looked at her team: Billie and Shez in their matching pink t-shirts, Buddy with his plateful of sushi, all three of them here for her when she needed them most. It was true; love had come back to her, but in a way she'd never expected.

Shez stared up at the circular staircase leading to the open-plan upper floor. 'This place screams CEO. You could rent an office here.'

Audrey looked around the room, the wall of plants, the groovy artwork and polished concrete floors. 'Maybe, but it doesn't feel like home.'

'You think we've got a shot at winning, Tawd?' Billie asked.

Did they have a chance? She wasn't sure. Pitching competitions were never meritocracies, and often the most ridiculous ideas with the unlikeliest founders got the investment dollars. But she wasn't ready to teach Billie that hard lesson just yet.

'I hope so. Let's wait and see.'

Audrey settled back into a chair between Billie and Shez. The PottyNet toddler was now asleep in the pram, the parents sipping tea from Workmates mugs. They looked exhausted. On the other side of the room, the young women from HugCo snapped selfies in front of the Workmates logo and recorded a video for social media.

Summer opened the door and walked with Matt Hayes to the centre of the room.

'Everyone,' Summer said, throwing her arms wide, 'thank you for pitching. On behalf of Hayes Corp, and our fabulous CEO, I'd like to say it was a tough decision. Steve Jobs proved that an idea is only as good as its founder. We look for businesses that will perform long term and create the equity and returns we need at Hayes Corp. We want vibrant founders who are dynamic and purposeful—who have their fingers on the pulse of the community. Founders who matter. Leaders who can move the dial and connect with a wide demographic, bring people together and make a difference.'

Billie leaned in. 'That's you, Tawdry. Hundred percent.'

Shez gripped Audrey's hand.

'Which is why we're pleased to have Matt Hayes announce the winner of the first prize, a fifty-thousand-dollar grant for business development.'

Audrey held her breath. Fifty thousand dollars would buy her precious time: she could pay the fine and reimburse her friends for working for her these past few days. She could buy her fortune-cookie machine, install it, and start making payments on her debt. If she was careful, the funding could carry Bittersweet Biscuits into the new year. She could open the café before Christmas, host a holiday party, serve the summer tourists and send gift hampers to local businesses. She'd provide trays of complimentary biscuits at Shez's holiday flats and Robert's General Store.

Shez nudged her. 'I have a good feeling about this,' she whispered. 'Sign from the universe. He's wearing a steel ring like you.'

'I'm not wearing a steel ring, Shez.'

'Think, Audrey! Not a ring. A backbone. You have a steel backbone.'

'. . . and that's how Hayes Corp started, with my great-great-grandfather and a good idea. So, we're pleased to announce the first-place grant of fifty thousand dollars will go to . . .' Matt Hayes paused, and looked across the room. 'HugCo! Congratulations.'

Audrey exhaled and clapped. She blinked twice and clapped harder. The young women screamed and ran up the front of the room, videoing themselves. They snapped selfies with Summer and Matt Hayes.

'Bloody hell,' Buddy said. 'Don't buy me any hugs, Sweetman.'

Billie slung an arm around Audrey's shoulder. 'There's still second. That's ten grand.'

'Second place,' Summer said, 'is for a business with real potential to meet a need that's incredibly important in our communities. Love, acceptance, a feel-good startup. The grant for second place, ten thousand dollars, goes to . . . PottyNet! No more trying to keep bored toddlers still while they learn to do their business.' She laughed gaily. 'Congratulations! Communities everywhere need you.'

The young couple kissed and pushed their pram with their sleeping toddler to the front of the room. They held up the certificate and posed for a photo.

Audrey clapped along with her team, her face a smiling mask. Her easy fix, the quick result she wanted was gone. She wasn't sure what she'd say to Shez, Buddy and Billie in the lobby, other than thank you for believing in her, and for helping so generously.

'Time to go,' she whispered. 'I'm taking us for lunch—'

Matt Hayes stepped up. 'Today, we added one last prize. A mentorship for a new founder who needs help. Advice so valuable you can't put a price on it. This founder gets eight hours of online coaching with our own Summer Hollis. And the mentoring is awarded to . . . Audrey Sweetman from Bittersweet Biscuits!'

Audrey stared at him. The attendees clapped. As the words sunk in, Audrey felt her confidence rising, stronger than it had ever been. She walked to the front of the room and shook Matt Hayes' hand. She smiled back at her team, their faces filled with worry and love.

'Thank you,' Audrey said as she turned to Summer, 'but I don't need you. I'll run Bittersweet Biscuits my way.'

CHAPTER 38

'Did you see Summer's face? Jeez, Tawd, she must hate you. She looked like she ate a lemon when you turned her down.'

Audrey nodded. Her heart was still pumping from the absolute pleasure of saying no to Summer, and seeing the sour look on her face. But still, she'd lost her chance at an easy solution, and now she'd have to figure out how to keep going.

Billie's phone rang. They shuffled over on the footpath and answered it. 'Dad. I know. Yep. I know! I will. I said I will. You can tell him I will!' Billie hung up and looked at them glumly. 'The headmaster called my dad. I have to go back to school. I hate it.'

Audrey put her hand on Billie's slim shoulder. Their purple eye had not yet healed, and Audrey knew she had no right to interfere. She wasn't Billie's mother. But Billie's parents weren't protecting their own child, and if Billie was being bullied, she wouldn't leave them to cope on their own. Not again. Even if she was interfering, even if Ruth insisted Billie stay at school, even if Audrey had to petition the courts and become Billie's guardian, she would do it.

'Billie, tell me right now: are you okay? If you need to come home, I'll call Ruth and we'll make it happen.'

Buddy rolled his walker closer and put an arm around Billie's shoulder. 'Tell her, Kid. Sweetman will stick up for you. She's tough as guts.'

Billie took a deep breath. Their eyes filled. 'I'm okay.'

'Don't lie to me, Billie.' Audrey held their sleeve.

Billie's body shook. They took a deep breath and wouldn't meet Audrey's eyes. 'They cornered me in the bathroom yesterday, four of them, and tried to pull my pants down . . . but I got away.'

Audrey's stomach rolled over. As long as she had breath, she'd make sure Billie was safe. It didn't matter what it cost her, or how much she'd have to fight. Every child deserved to feel loved, to be safe in a school and be okay. 'That's it. I'm taking you home. We're calling your mum.'

Billie stared at Audrey, wary as a cat. 'But what if she kicks me out and if I have to live with you, Tawd? Like if we need a court order to make you my person? Will you do it?'

Audrey lifted her chin. 'If it comes to that, I won't let you down. I promise. But let's give your mum a chance. She might surprise you.'

They huddled together on the busy footpath while Billie made the call.

'It's me. Yeah. Listen. No, listen! Audrey's bringing me home.' A worried look crossed Billie's face. 'I don't want to fight. I'm coming home. No. I am!' A pause. Audrey stepped closer. 'She's right here.' Billie scowled. 'Tawdry? Ruth wants to talk to you.'

And so it began. Audrey took Billie's phone.

When they pulled up at Ruth's front door, it was close to midnight. Audrey had talked to Ruth on the phone for forty-five minutes, then taken Billie for an early dinner while Ruth called Billie's father and the headmaster. The conversation with Ruth had been exhausting, but when Audrey had explained about Billie being attacked in the bathroom, the black eye, the train station and the horrible names, Ruth had finally agreed Billie should come home.

While Shez and Buddy tidied up at Emma's, Audrey and Billie drove to Billie's dad's place and picked up their belongings. Debra, ecstatic at the change in living arrangements, helped pack their clothes and laundry into garbage bags. Billie hugged the baby the longest, as Audrey knew they would.

'Bye, Version 2.0,' she heard Billie whisper. 'Good luck with Dad.' Billie's father had texted from the office but hadn't made it home in time to say goodbye.

Audrey glanced at Billie now, in the car. They were snoring quietly, their shaved head pressed against the passenger window. She touched their shoulder. 'You're home.'

The porch light snapped on, and Ruth stood at the door in grey tracksuit bottoms and a blue cardigan. When Billie reached the porch, she hugged them stiffly. 'Go on up,' she said. 'Your bedroom's ready for you. I'll talk with Audrey.'

Billie nodded and trudged up the stairs. Audrey followed Ruth into the kitchen, a chilly room with stainless steel appliances and white tiles. A small potted succulent sat on the benchtop. Otherwise, everything was as pale and clean as she remembered from the night she first arrived at the beach and was Ruth's reluctant house guest.

Ruth turned on the kettle. 'Please, sit,' she said, and Audrey sank down onto a leather kitchen chair. It was surprisingly comfortable. Her entire body ached from the driving, and she wanted more than anything to wash off her make-up, slather on some face cream and crawl into her own bed.

Ruth swirled a ginger and lemon tea bag in a teacup and handed it to Audrey.

'Did Billie tell you what happened when they decided to leave school last year?' Ruth asked. Her voice was strained.

Audrey looked up. 'No.'

'They ran away. The police brought Billie home. Then Billie cut themselves in my bathroom. I found them, blood everywhere, panicking at what they'd done.' Ruth cleared her throat, her voice stronger. 'Billie didn't even give me a chance. Assumed I wouldn't have helped if they asked.' Ruth didn't meet Audrey's eyes. 'I still have nightmares about it.'

'That must've been terrible.' Audrey gripped her teacup. She willed herself to be compassionate to Ruth, to imagine what Ruth went through that night, finding Billie, but Billie was all she could think of. Billie and blood. Black eyes. Billie feeling like no one—not even their parents—would listen to how bad things were at school. Audrey shivered. She wasn't a mother, but she couldn't imagine sending Billie back to a school that caused them to harm themselves. 'But you made Billie go back.' It was an accusation, yet Audrey couldn't stop herself.

'The headmaster assured me the bullying wouldn't happen again. He put policies in place. He promised to watch Billie.' Ruth cleared her throat. 'I know what you all think of me. But the truth is . . .' she paused and stared at the wall behind Audrey,

'Billie can't afford to be left behind. Without a good education and powerful friends—and that private school does produce the people who will run the country eventually—Billie could fail. I knew it was a risk, but I had to fight for their future. You're not a mother so you won't understand.' Ruth set her cup down into the saucer.

'I wouldn't have done it,' Audrey said.

Ruth shrugged. 'No. We're different. I have expectations for Billie.'

Audrey exhaled. Ruth was wrong, but she couldn't see it. How would intolerance and bullying and fear ever give Billie the space to grow up and find themselves? The best thing for Billie was to be with people who accepted them. Audrey's head ached, and she'd barely slept for the past three days—or maybe even for the past three months. Nothing was the same as it had been when she'd arrived at Whitehaven in June. It was as if a giant had tipped her upside down and shaken her until everything she owned had fallen out of her pockets: her marriage, her home, her bank account, her job, even her identity. The only things that remained were insecure and new, but they were what she loved: Billie and Buddy, Shez, the beach, her business, the village. And yet she felt lucky, lighter, clean somehow, as if whomever had shaken her had known what she really needed, and it wasn't the life she'd had.

'Surely you won't send Billie back, Ruth? Not now.'

Ruth shook her head. She looked older in the harsh light of the kitchen, softer somehow. 'It was a mistake.'

'I'm glad you've realised it,' Audrey said. 'It's good to know you care.'

Ruth sighed. 'You won't believe this, Audrey, but Billie's not the only person I worry about. I care about everyone in the village.'

Audrey stared at her.

Ruth's laugh sounded tired. 'Oh, fair enough, I don't really care about you, but I do care about the rest. Buddy, that cantankerous old fool. Robert. Justin. Sherry and Lem. You're a bother, always poking around into everything, making changes, thinking you can fix things up with cookies and a lick of paint. But you look after Buddy, so it's one less person for me to think about. He's being fed hot meals now. You'll call Justin if Buddy needs help. That's something.' Ruth picked up a linen napkin and refolded it. 'I know Billie likes you, Audrey. They think you're so much fun. But you aren't responsible for Billie's life. You think Billie should do what they love, even if that means—I don't know—not graduating from high school. Doing art or mooching around. But I need Billie to think about their future. To buckle down and put things in place so that they don't wind up middle-aged and regretting their decisions like—'

'Like you think I have?' Audrey glanced at her teacup, the thin and tasteless ginger tea growing cold.

'You're starting over with nothing. I'm surprised you're not bitter.'

Audrey set down her cup. She could've become bitter, she almost had a right to be, but she would never let herself go there. Once you did, you were lost, and life was fifty-fifty for everyone, no matter what they seemed to have. She looked at Ruth's new kitchen; her house was lovely, but it didn't feel like a home. Money, success, a child—Ruth had it all, but none of it magically made her life easy. In comparison, Audrey had nothing, only what she might build with her own two hands. That wasn't easy either. *It doesn't matter who you are or what you have*, she thought, *everything is bittersweet*.

'I always knew life could be a challenge. I didn't come from a family like yours, Ruth.'

Ruth raised a bony shoulder. 'You're making an assumption, but yes. My mother was a researcher at Sydney University. She had a science degree. My father was a professor of physics. His father owned a medical practice in Macquarie Street. The building's still there. Heritage listed, I made sure of it.'

Audrey nodded. 'My mum was a hairdresser. She worked in a shopping centre all her life. We lived in rented flats.'

'Like you do now.' Ruth pulled her cardigan closer. 'But you seem happy enough.'

Audrey remembered what it was like to be hugged by Joyce, to come home to her. The smell of hairspray and cheap perfume, the strong hands, how she always wore yellow, hummed to herself while she was working. The joy she brought to her clients, the love. Remembering birthdays and names of children, keeping track of who was getting married or divorced. Decorating their dingy apartments with treasures from the op shop, making magic with a can of silver spray paint and fairy lights, baking Audrey's pink frosted birthday cakes and serving them on someone else's discarded china. The rose quartz crystal the size of a human heart she'd bought after being betrayed by a man she loved. Audrey was the one who had given her mother the most faithful love she'd ever had. Not a man.

'My mum was full of joy. That's how she described herself. Full of joy, full of ideas, but not much cash to make them happen.'

Audrey smiled at the memory of her. 'I guess you're right. Maybe I am following in her footsteps.'

'Maybe.' Ruth stood, and so did Audrey. 'But that might not be a bad thing. I've spent my career judging human nature, and I have a feeling you're going to make it.' Audrey followed Ruth to the front door. The rolling tumble of waves grew louder as she stepped outside. 'Thank you for bringing Billie home,' Ruth said.

Audrey nodded. 'You know where to find me if you need me, Ruth.' Even if Ruth was not the kind of person she'd choose as a friend, it was best for women to stick together.

CHAPTER 39

Audrey woke at dawn to kookaburras chortling. For a moment, she was at peace; Billie was safe at home, and Audrey could relax. The sun streamed through the sheer curtains in the bay windows. She'd have a hot shower and her first coffee of the day.

She rolled over and the weight of her financial commitments flooded in. She'd have to decide about Bittersweet Biscuits. After just two days selling cookies at Central Station, they had raised nowhere near enough money to pay the fine, let alone cover the licensing and all the other expenses of setting back up in earnest. There was no other way forward but to find a job. Audrey pulled herself from bed, threw on her tracksuit and drank a glass of water at the kitchen sink. As usual, Buddy was rolling his way down to the beach for his morning swim, his striped towel thrown over his shoulder. She wondered what he did in tourist season and made a mental note to discuss it with him. She'd pick up a pair of boardshorts with an elasticised waist, easy to pull on and off . . . but then, she'd have to convince him to wear them. She smiled, thinking how that conversation would go. She turned on her oven to preheat for muffins and headed down the back steps. Her days at the beach were so different than they had been in the city. Being back there—the traffic, the rain, the crowds—she hadn't loved it. And then there was Wyatt. Her stomach pinched thinking of him, but it was pain and embarrassment, that was all, not longing or love. Certainly not regret. No, she didn't miss Wyatt, not anymore.

At the shoreline, the sun tinted the clouds magenta, mauve, mandarin orange. The tide crept out, and the sand lay white and damp at the rim of the bay before her. She raised an arm at Buddy, saluting him, but he kept up a slow breaststroke and didn't see her. Audrey started walking. Far down the beach she saw a man in the distance. As he made his way closer, he waved.

'Okay, Audrey?' Justin Flood called. His grey t-shirt was plastered to his chest.

'It's a beautiful day.' What could she tell him? That she was facing financial ruin?

'Sure is.' He ran closer and jogged in place. 'I've been wondering how you are. I've missed Buddy. I usually keep an eye on him in the mornings, just in case. I stopped by the bakery, but neither of you were there. Robert said you'd gone to the city.'

'Yes, but only for a few days.'

'Welcome home. It's good to see you back.' He smiled and was off. Audrey watched him run down the beach and head up the path after Buddy, who was wheeling back towards the cabana. Justin Flood had been timing his runs with Buddy's early morning swims, and she'd never known. She smiled, remembering him dancing at her party, starting the conga line, putting her first. Playing backgammon with Buddy, being kind to Ruth even though he was dating someone, tending to

Audrey when she fell down the steps all those months ago. Helping her find Billie. Carrying the wallaby to the side of the road in strong, capable arms. The images stayed with her and wouldn't go away. She'd never met a man so easy in his own skin, relaxed and not critical, not demanding people be perfect, or something they weren't. Not expecting the worst of someone, but the best.

Audrey's phone buzzed in her pocket: it was Shez, wondering if Audrey might be ready to make her breakfast and a coffee, and also checking in to see if Audrey was okay. And in a way, she was. Though nothing was resolved in her own life, she would make the most of the day spreading out in front of her. She'd bake blueberry muffins for Shez, take some toasted and slathered with butter to Buddy for his breakfast, then head back down to the bakery, open her laptop and make a plan.

'Tawdry! Smells good in here.' Billie stood at the bakery door around eleven, wearing an enormous Grateful Dead t-shirt and tattered black jeans.

Audrey pushed a plate of blueberry muffins towards Billie. 'You're just happy you're not in school.'

'Damn straight. Whatcha doing?'

'Searching for more pitch competitions. Applying for business loans with not a hope of getting one and trying to find work on freelancer.com that actually has reasonable pay. You?'

'Slept in as long as possible and talked to Ruth for two hours. Pretty sure my morning's been worse than yours.'

'What did your mum say?'

Billie shrugged and rubbed a shoe along the painted timber floorboards. 'She has an idea that doesn't completely suck. It's a boarding school. In America.'

Audrey looked up, startled, and searched Billie's face. How could she help Billie if they were in America? If there was bullying, she'd have no way of knowing and no money to get there. And a boarding school? Surely that couldn't be good. 'It's so far away, Billie.'

'Yeah.' Billie nodded. 'But this one's different. It's kind of famous, so Ruth freaking loves that part, but it's got this new all-gender dorm, and the website says the school is committed to inclusivity so . . .'

'So?'

Billie's eyes rolled back. 'Yeah, Tawd, so there will be other people like me, and according to the website we'll be—quote unquote—"fully supported in our chosen gender identity".' Billie shrugged as if they didn't care at all, but there was an excitement in their eyes Audrey hadn't seen before.

'It might be worth a shot,' Audrey said casually. 'You'd get to know friends whose lives have been more like yours. And if you hate it, well, you could always chuck a wobbly and come home.'

'Exactly.' Billie bit into a muffin and chewed. 'You'd miss me, though. And what would the old fart do without me hanging around his cabana and dropping off his dinner?'

Audrey scanned Billie's face. Her heart squeezed in her chest—life without Billie around the village would be so different—but then, Billie would have the chance to finish high school and be somewhere genuinely committed to safety and inclusion. Everyone there would love Billie; how could they not? Their wisecracking and the constant optimism underneath those mouthy teenage jokes? Their beautiful, trusting heart? Audrey smiled in a way she hoped looked encouraging. 'We'll all miss you terribly, but I'll take care of Buddy. And we could Facetime whenever you want. Plus, American Christmas vacation is in what, three months?'

'That's what Ruth said.'

'So, what do you think?' Audrey sipped her coffee and waited.

'I think I might say yes.'

A week later, Audrey said goodbye to Billie. She'd promised herself she wouldn't cry, but she did anyway, mascara and tears streaming.

'Calm the farm, Tawdry,' Billie said, and hugged her, but she could tell Billie liked the attention. She handed Billie a container of cookies for the plane and promised that the Bittersweet Bakery Café would be open when Billie came home for the holidays. She had no idea how she'd keep her promise, but she'd try.

Ruth and Billie climbed into Lem's car, their suitcases loaded in the back. Lem had offered to drive them both to the airport, on account of Shez saying it would put them in Ruth's good books. Ruth planned to settle Billie at the school in New York, and no doubt make an impression on the principal. Buddy rolled his walker to the car and knocked on Billie's window. When they lowered it, he stuffed the zebra fur scarf into their hands: Clara's, the one Billie had found in the attic months ago.

'Good luck, Kid,' he said. 'Cold enough to freeze your bollocks off in New York. You might need this. We'll be here when you come back home.'

'Thanks, old fart.' Billie held on to his gnarled hand.

'Make sure you watch your driving, Lem!' Shez said as he climbed into the car. 'I want you back here by seven. Date night. We're doing Greek yogurt facials.'

'Rightio,' Lem said.

Shez tugged down the hem of her leopard-print miniskirt and handed Audrey a tissue. They watched Lem drive up the hill, away from the bakery. Shez patted Audrey's arm. 'How about you make me a nice cuppa? That'll do you a world of good.'

Audrey's phone buzzed: unknown number. She braced herself for more bad news. She'd been expecting divorce papers from Wyatt, and while Danny had instructed that calls from the bank's collections department go to him, she was certain they had her number. She took a breath and tried to be positive as she answered. It could be a freelancing job, although that thought didn't make her feel much better.

'Hello, Audrey speaking.'

'Are you the fortune-cookie person? Bittersweet Biscuits?'

'Yes. Can I help you?'

'I'm Imogen Stanton, formerly Hayes? You supplied my divorce party.'

'Right! I saw your posts on Instagram. Thanks, Imogen—the photos were amazing.'

'Yeah, listen: I have like five secs before my massage. Talked to Matt yesterday, we were discussing our divorce settlement and how he basically hid the existence of an entire yacht, which I found out about and was so pissed. We're still friends, but barely. He owes me half that boat. Anyway. He told me about these fortune cookies that made him laugh and I knew they were yours. He said you pitched for funding.'

'I did. We didn't win.'

'I know. He said his new person, what's her name? Skye?'
'Summer.'
'That's right. She hated your idea. Matt loved it, but he was too dumb to back you. He said he thought you were onto a vibe. Anyway, he's not the only one with capital. I told him I want to invest.'

Audrey sucked in her breath and told herself to remain calm. She shifted the phone to her other ear. 'You've got good timing. I'm approaching investors now.'

'You should come see my investment guy. I'll have my EA set up a meeting.' Imogen called out to someone, and Audrey heard kids splashing in a pool. 'But in general, how does, I don't know, fifty percent equity for fifty grand sound?' Imogen asked.

Audrey straightened her shoulders and told herself to stay calm. Investors always expected way too much equity. It was a mistake to jump at the money and give away that much of her company. Imogen was suggesting the same amount as the pitch competition, but if Bittersweet Biscuits was going to thrive, she needed more than what Imogen was offering to set up properly and scale. And this was her chance to negotiate.

'I'd be excited to partner with you, Imogen, but this is what I'm looking for.' She thought of a number, took a deep breath, and doubled it. Women always underestimated what they were worth, but she would never do that to herself again. Her voice wobbled, and she forced herself to speak slowly. What would it take to find another investor as interested as Imogen Hayes? It would be almost impossible. This was her shot, and she had to make the most of it. 'For two hundred and fifty thousand, I could offer you ten percent of the company.'

'Hmmm. For that much, I'd want twenty-five.'

Audrey flushed and gripped the phone tighter, her hands shaking. The cash injection would give her the runway she needed. Her mind jumped ahead: a local factory for the fortune cookies, staff to run the bakery café, kitchen renovations, new packaging, branding, a proper budget for advertising. And best of all, some capital to start paying down her portion of the debt from Wyatt's failed investments.

'If you'll agree to fifteen percent, we've got a deal, Imogen. And I'll build an amazing business.' Audrey held her breath. Waiting without speaking was more powerful than trying to convince someone. The pause got uncomfortably long, but Audrey held her ground.

'Deal,' Imogen said finally. 'My investment guy will call you. Let's meet later next week and oh—' Imogen yelled again at the swimming kids; Audrey heard them shout in response '—bring me six dozen fortune cookies, Audrey. We'll courier them to Matt's office, just to piss off what's-her-name. Skye.'

'Summer. Absolutely.'

Imogen laughed. 'She's probably after him, but poor thing—he's not worth the trouble. Anyway, I've told my friend Marissa about your biscuits, Audrey. She wants you to supply their nightclubs. They've got three here in the city, and another three in Singapore, plus one in Dubai. That's your first overseas deal when you're ready.'

'Great,' Audrey said, exhaling carefully. 'I'll get on it.'

'Lovely doing business with you, Audrey. Bye!'

Audrey hung up the phone and resisted the urge to scream.

'Who was that?' Shez asked. 'You look like Miley Cyrus accepting her first Grammy, but without the hot bod.'

'That,' Audrey said, 'was a miracle. And we need to celebrate.'

They walked with Buddy back to the cabana, and she told them her news. She put on the kettle, and Buddy clicked on the turntable, then settled into his chair. The singer belted out 'Just One Look', and Shez bopped around the coffee table singing. She grabbed Audrey's hands and twirled her around in a makeshift jive.

Somebody knocked at the door. Shez raised two stencilled eyebrows at Audrey.

'Buddy? You home?' A man's voice.

'Doc! In here!'

Justin Flood walked in with a woman. She was beautiful: fresh-faced and athletic, and Audrey remembered her black and white checkered mini dress from the party. The young woman had a pleasant look about her, outgoing and friendly, completely unlike Charmaine. They'd be about the same age, Audrey calculated, though this woman didn't seem as clingy with Justin as Charmaine had been with Wyatt.

'Thought we might find you in here,' Justin said.

Audrey nodded and smiled. Older men, younger women: what was the point in worrying about it? She had her friends and her business, and she'd just heard some brilliant news. She was on her way to building a new life, even if she was starting from scratch.

'This is Lucinda. Lucy, this is Buddy, Sherry and Audrey.'

Lucinda stared at Buddy's albums. 'Wow, great record collection.' She held out a slim hand to him, and then to Audrey. 'You look like you're celebrating. You probably don't remember me, but I crashed your party when I was home from uni. Dad said you were the kind of person who welcomed everybody.'

Audrey looked up. Warmth spread across her chest and into her face.

'I didn't think you'd mind, and I wanted to show Lucinda your bakery.' Justin shrugged and grinned at her.

Handsome, that's what he was. And just possibly . . . patient. She smiled back at him. *The best is yet to come*, Joyce used to say. She had always believed that luck would find them both, and now that Joyce was gone, maybe all her luck would go to Audrey.

Shez gave Audrey a squeeze. 'We're celebrating, but now that I think of it, we really could use a cake around here.' Shez shrugged. 'But anyway, Audrey's landed an investor for Bittersweet Biscuits, thanks to following my business advice.' Shez pointed a fluoro-orange fingernail at Audrey. 'She doesn't even need my new online course. I've niched it down to appeal to everyone: it's called How to Communicate Telepathically with Yourself.'

'You're a lunatic, Shez,' Buddy said.

Justin Flood smiled at Audrey. 'It's good news about the investor. Does it mean you're staying?'

CHAPTER 40

Beside the open door of the Bittersweet Bakery Café, gardenias bloomed waxy and fragrant from two sandstone pots. Paper daisies grew lush and green in the garden beds in front of the café. Inside, Audrey balanced on a ladder, looping strands of silver jingle bells from the ceiling. Near Buddy's chair, a Christmas tree she'd found on the beach twinkled with white lights. She'd made it from a driftwood branch bleached silver by the sun, and decorated it with delicate aqua baubles. On the door, she'd hung a simple homemade wreath of white cockatoo feathers and seashells. Everything was ready for a warm Australian Christmas.

The buttery scent of freshly baked croissants and *pain au chocolat* drifted through the café. Three young backpackers laughed together around a wooden table outside, enjoying the shade of a blue and white striped beach umbrella. Michael Bublé crooned Christmas jazz from the vintage timber stereo Lem had installed in the café two months earlier; Buddy had insisted they find an old-fashioned stereo with a turntable, and he'd moved hundreds of his albums over from the cabana. Buddy's records and his selection of music were an instant drawcard for anyone who stepped into the café. So many tourists flipped carefully through Buddy's vintage albums that Audrey had suggested sourcing albums to sell. Buddy was excellent at curating them, and Lem had taught him how to use eBay. Every morning after his naked swim, he rolled to the café for coffee and breakfast. He was permanently in charge of music and backgammon.

A stack of gold fortune-cookie boxes sat on the old timber table in the kitchen, waiting for the delivery van driver to pick them up. Thanks to Christmas party season, Bittersweet Biscuits orders had doubled this past month, and the fortune-cookie machine had been a godsend.

A young mother with a pram hesitated in the door. 'Any tables free?'

Audrey glanced at the heaving café and climbed down the ladder. 'Cute baby,' she said. The baby kicked its fat little feet. 'I think table five is leaving. Let me help.' She settled the young mum, then perched on the arm of Buddy's leather chair and handed him her phone.

'Can you believe Billie posted this?'

'What's that, Sweetman?'

It was a video of Billie and two friends dancing in the falling snow to 'All I Want For Christmas Is You'. They wore black suit jackets and cherry-red tulle skirts, red feather boas and top hats, but wound around Billie's neck was the zebra fur scarf from Buddy.

'They're dancing. Billie looks like they're going to fall on the ice, but this one's holding them up by the back of their jacket. And this one has a t-shirt that says . . .' Audrey peered at her phone, 'I think it's *Ask me my pronouns*. But I need my glasses.'

'We just went to the pub and drank beer when I was in high school,' Buddy said.

Audrey laughed. 'They probably do that, too. But it's so good to know they have friends their own age, and not just us.'

'You'll be happy to see them.'

Audrey nodded. 'Billie gets home on Thursday. Did you hear they placed third in Industrial Tech?'

Buddy cut into his muffin and buttered it. 'What the hell is that?'

'Woodwork and metalwork class. Billie made a metal safe for Ruth's Christmas gift and it weighs three hundred kilos. They want to ship it here from America. Ruth says she doesn't need a homemade present that costs ten thousand dollars to ship, and Billie says what else is money for?'

'Kid still knows how to irritate the bejesus out of Judge Judy.'

'Like a pro.'

Shez pushed her way into the bakery with Lem at her heels. 'Seasonal greetings, Audrey. Great decorations.' Her jingle bell earrings jangled as she twirled around. 'Coffee, thanks. I'm parched. Listen, Audrey, we need to do more promotion for your surprise Christmas party. I put it on Facebook and there's a hundred and seventy-five yeses, so we need a theme.' Shez perched on a table and swung her legs in the air. The startled pensioner sitting there scowled up at her. 'Don't get your knickers in a twist, mister,' Shez said. 'I'm only staying three seconds. Eat your eggs.'

Audrey coughed. 'My surprise party is on Facebook?'

'Yes, but it turns out I didn't have to promote it. Everyone's coming because it's yours, and they loved the last one. Dress as a Christmas carol was Lem's idea. He wanted to come as Round

John Virgin, but I said it's just not *you*, Lem. It was almost as terrible as his first idea: My Big Fat Christmas Wedding.' Shez waved her diamante-studded nails in his direction. 'No offence, Lem, you know I love you. But I think we should go for something more traditional, like . . .' she threw her arms wide, 'Christmas in Vegas! What do you think?'

'Hmmm. Vegas doesn't scream Christmas to me,' Audrey said.

Lem nodded. 'See, Shez? I knew she wouldn't like it. What about my other one? Christmas Carol-oke! We get a huge karaoke machine and—'

'Audrey's already a mile down the motorway ahead of you, Lem. Anyway, we'll have the band.'

'Santa's Ho-ho-hoedown? All of us in cowboy boots and Western gear—'

'Think, Lem, *think*! Can you imagine how my cousins would dress? You couldn't move for the busty elves and sexy reindeer.'

'How about White Christmas?' Across the café, Justin Flood set down a tray of dishes. He wiped his hands on a pink Bittersweet Biscuits apron and handed Audrey a cup of coffee, steaming hot and black, just the way she liked it. 'We could hang paper snowflakes from the ceiling. Everyone has something white to wear. Easy and beautiful, old school. "I'm Dreaming of a Whitehaven Christmas". What do you think, boss?'

'If the white runs out, I'll drink the red,' Buddy said.

They turned to Audrey and waited. She smiled at them. Her business. Her people. How could she say anything but yes?

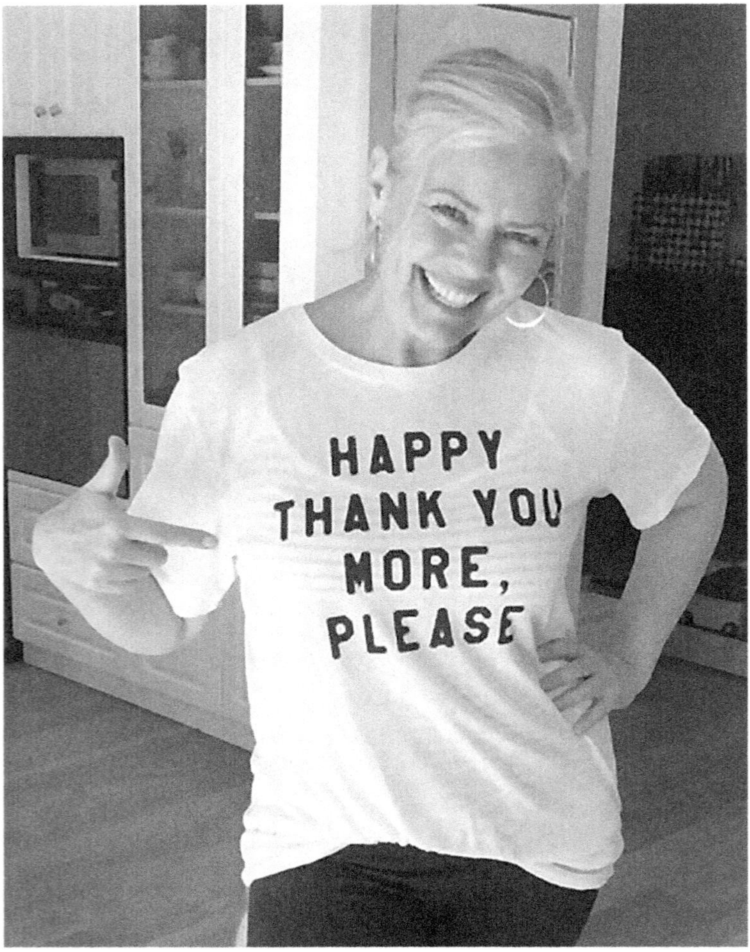
HAPPY
THANK YOU
MORE,
PLEASE

Recipes from the Bittersweet Bakery Café

Hello to my readers and friends! I hope that reading my book has inspired you to try some of the recipes from Audrey's Bittersweet Bakery Café. They're all family favourites—made with love for the past twenty-five years.

You might want to start with Shez's Dark Chocolate Birthday Cake; it's the cake I bake for every family birthday, and I can guarantee that it's the best! (The secret ingredients are olive oil, balsamic vinegar and coffee.) The classic Carrot Cake is another easy favourite, compliments of my dear friend, Tammy, and the Chip, Chip, Hooray cookies are from my talented big sis, Sheila, the best baker I know. And since I was raised by a family of bakers and farmers in Canada, I'll often mix a batch of Cinnamon Buns in the evening, leave the covered bowl of dough to rise on the benchtop overnight, and bake them fresh for my sons or house guests in the morning. Absolutely delicious!

If we had the chance to be friends in real life, there would be a chair at my kitchen table for you, along with a slice of cake, hot coffee just the way you like it, and a listening ear. I hope you enjoyed reading *The Bittersweet Bakery Café* as much as I loved writing it. As the Irish proverb says, 'When I count my blessings, I count you twice.'

I'd love to have you join me for my weekly newsletter at catherinegreer.com.au.

Catherine x

Spicy Orange Cardamom Biscuits

Audrey's mum said if you spice it with love, it'll please every palate.

Ingredients

375 grams (2½ cups) plain flour
2 teaspoons baking powder
1 tablespoon ground ginger
1 teaspoon ground nutmeg
2 teaspoons ground cardamom
250 grams (1 cup) butter, softened
330 grams (1½ cups) brown sugar
3 teaspoons brandy or vanilla extract
Finely grated zest of 1 orange
1 egg white for glazing and raw sugar for sprinkling

Method

- Line two baking trays with baking paper or silicone mats.
- Preheat the oven to 180°C, fan forced.
- Sift the flour, baking powder, ginger, nutmeg and cardamom into a bowl.
- Using your mixer, beat the butter and brown sugar in a separate bowl until pale and creamy. Add the brandy or vanilla extract, along with the orange zest.
- Fold in the dry ingredients and mix thoroughly.
- Roll the dough into a large rectangle, 5 mm thick.
- Cut into 3 × 6 cm rectangles.
- Brush with the beaten egg white and sprinkle with sugar.
- Place the biscuits on a tray and bake for 10–12 minutes, until lightly browned.
- Cool on a wire rack and serve. Makes 40 biscuits.

Audrey's Cinnamon Buns with Cream Cheese Frosting

When your life upends, add sugar and butter and turn up the heat.

INGREDIENTS

Dough

60 ml (¼ cup) warm water
1 tablespoon instant yeast
250 ml (1 cup) warm milk
125 ml (½ cup) olive oil
110 grams (½ cup) white sugar
1 teaspoon salt
600 grams (4 cups) plain flour
2 eggs

Filling

90 grams (6 tablespoons) butter, softened
110 grams (½ cup) white sugar
110 grams (½ cup) brown sugar
2 teaspoons ground cinnamon

Frosting

125 grams (1 small package) cream cheese
60 grams (4 tablespoons) butter, softened
150 grams (1 cup) icing sugar
1 teaspoon vanilla extract

Method

- In a small glass bowl, place the warm water and yeast. Stir to dissolve and let stand for 5 minutes or until frothy.
- Pour the warm milk into a large mixing bowl. Add the oil, eggs, sugar, yeast mixture and salt. Mix in 1 cup of the flour. Add the remaining flour 1 cup at a time, mixing to make a soft dough.
- Turn onto a floured surface and knead dough until smooth and elastic. Cover and let rest while you wash the mixing bowl.
- Lightly oil the bowl and replace dough. Cover with a damp tea towel and let rise in a warm place until doubled in bulk (usually 1 to 1½ hours).
- Line a 30 × 45 cm baking tin with baking paper.
- Punch the dough, then roll it out into a rectangle (50 × 35 cm) on a floured surface. Spread with the 90 grams of softened butter.
- Mix the brown sugar, white sugar and cinnamon, and sprinkle over the rectangle of dough.
- Starting on the long side, roll up the dough into a log.
- Mark the centre with a knife, and then make 12 evenly spaced marks each side of the centre, for a total of 24 rolls.
- Slice into 24 pieces with a strand of dental floss: simply slide it under the log and crisscross to cut (or use a sharp knife).
- Place the rolls tightly together in the baking tin.
- Cover with a damp tea towel and let rise again for 30 minutes, until doubled in size.
- Preheat the oven to 200°C, fan forced.
- Bake for 12 minutes, until just lightly browned.
- While baking, make the frosting. Using a mixer, beat the cream cheese, butter, icing sugar and vanilla until fluffy.
- Frost the cinnamon buns while still warm and serve immediately.

Billie's Chip, Chip, Hooray Cookies

The best chocolate chip cookies in Whitehaven Bay.

INGREDIENTS

250 grams (1 cup) butter, softened
220 grams (1 cup) white sugar
220 grams (1 cup) brown sugar
2 eggs
400 grams (3 cups) plain flour
1 teaspoon baking soda
1 teaspoon baking powder
1 teaspoon vanilla extract
½ teaspoon sea salt, plus more for sprinkling
200 grams (approx. 1 generous cup) dark chocolate chips

METHOD

- Preheat the oven to 160°C, fan forced.
- In a mixer, cream the butter, brown sugar and white sugar.
- Mix in the eggs and vanilla.
- Add the flour, baking soda, baking powder and salt. Mix well.
- Stir in the chocolate chips.
- Roll the dough into 2 cm balls (or drop by spoonful) and place on baking trays. Leave enough space for the cookies to spread out as they cook.
- Sprinkle with sea salt.
- Bake for 10–12 minutes and serve warm. Makes 36 cookies.

Raspberry Shortbread Cookies with White Chocolate

You can't be miserable while you eat a cookie.

INGREDIENTS

Dough

250 grams (1 cup) butter, softened
145 grams (⅔ cup) white sugar
½ teaspoon almond extract
300 grams (2 cups) plain flour

Filling

Small jar (approx. 1 cup) of raspberry jam

Drizzle

250 grams (1⅔ cups) white chocolate melts, melted

METHOD

- Line baking trays with baking paper or silicone mats.
- Preheat the oven to 180°C, fan forced.
- Using a mixer, cream the butter and sugar until fluffy.
- Beat in the almond extract, add the flour and mix.
- Roll into 2 cm balls and place on the baking trays.
- Make an indentation in the centre of each ball and fill with jam. You can pipe this in or use a spoon.
- Bake for 10–12 minutes, depending on your oven.
- Cool and drizzle with melted white chocolate. You can use a sandwich bag and snip the corner, or drizzle using a fork.
- Let cool completely and serve. Makes 30 cookies.

Classic Two-tier Carrot Cake

Sugar, flour, butter, love.

INGREDIENTS

Cake

300 grams (2 cups) plain flour
2 teaspoons baking powder
2 teaspoons baking soda
1 teaspoon salt
2 teaspoons ground cinnamon
330 grams (1½ cups) white sugar
4 eggs
155 ml (½ cup plus 2 tablespoons) olive oil
310 grams (approx. 2 cups) grated fresh carrot
432 grams (approx. 2 cups) crushed pineapple, strained
60 grams (½ cup) chopped walnuts

Frosting

250 grams (1 large package) cream cheese, softened
125 grams (½ cup) butter, softened
500 grams (3⅓ cups) icing sugar
2 teaspoons vanilla extract

METHOD

- Preheat the oven to 180°C, fan forced.
- Place all the dry ingredients for the cake in a bowl.
- Add the eggs and olive oil.
- Stir in the grated carrot, crushed pineapple and walnuts.
- Grease and line the bottom of two 20 cm cake tins.

- ❋ Pour in the batter and bake for 30 minutes.
- ❋ Cool the cake layers on a wire rack.
- ❋ To make the frosting, use a mixer to beat the cream cheese and butter until smooth. Mix in the icing sugar and the vanilla extract.
- ❋ When the cake has cooled, lay the first layer on a cake plate. Add a layer of frosting and top with the second layer.
- ❋ Frost the outside of the cake, sides first and the top last. Serve chilled.

Shez's Dark Chocolate Birthday Cake

Shez loves it even more than date night hanky panky.

INGREDIENTS

Cake

225 grams (1½ cups) plain flour
275 grams (1¼ cups) caster sugar
50 grams (½ cup) baking cocoa—use dark for best results
1¼ teaspoons baking soda
½ teaspoon salt
80 ml (approx. ⅓ cup) olive oil
1 tablespoon balsamic vinegar
3 teaspoons vanilla extract
375 ml (1½ cups) cooled coffee

Chocolate ganache

125 grams (½ cup) butter, melted
150 grams (just under 1 cup) dark chocolate, coarsely chopped
2 tablespoons olive oil

METHOD

- Preheat the oven to 170°C, fan forced.
- Grease and line the bottom of one 20 cm cake tin.
- Sift the flour, sugar, cocoa, baking soda and salt into a mixing bowl.
- Mix with a whisk to combine.
- Add the olive oil, balsamic vinegar, vanilla and cooled coffee and mix.
- Pour the batter into the cake tin.

- ❄ Bake for 35 minutes. Cool completely on a wire rack.
- ❄ Make the ganache: add the butter, chocolate and olive oil to a bowl or glass measuring cup.
- ❄ Melt the mixture (microwave is fine but watch it carefully). Stir until smooth.
- ❄ Wait until the ganache has thickened slightly. Drizzle cooled ganache over the cake, allowing it to drip down the sides.

Macarons with Fresh Buttercream

The Coffin Cheaters think they're delicious.

Ingredients

Macarons

130 grams egg whites (use 4–5 large eggs), at room temperature
85 grams (5½ tablespoons) caster sugar
3 drops gel food colour of your choice
155 grams (approx. 1½ cups) almond flour
235 grams (approx. 1½ cups) icing sugar

Buttercream filling

110 grams (approx. 7 tablespoons) butter, softened
190 grams (approx. 1⅓ cups) icing sugar

Method

- Line three baking trays with baking paper or use silicone macaron baking mats.
- Whisk room temperature egg whites to glossy peaks, adding the caster sugar gradually.
- Add the gel food colour and mix.
- Into a separate bowl, sift the almond flour with the icing sugar. Mix with a whisk.
- Incorporate the beaten egg whites into the dry ingredients with a large spatula. Mix well.
- *Macaronage*: use a flat scraper to mix and press out air from the batter. Stop when the batter can flow off the spatula in an unbroken 'figure 8'.
- Preheat the oven to 160°C, fan forced.

- ❊ Transfer the mixture to a piping bag and pipe rounds onto the baking trays about 2 cm apart. Let set for 30 minutes. Touch the tops of the macarons—they should be dry to the touch before baking.
- ❊ Bake for 10–12 minutes. Cool. Peel carefully from the baking paper.
- ❊ Whip the buttercream filling ingredients using a mixer until smooth and fluffy.
- ❊ Match the macaron tops and bottoms and use a piping bag to sandwich with buttercream. Press together.

Billie's Blueberry Muffins

For every kid who needs an extra serving of love.

INGREDIENTS

225 grams (1½ cups) plain flour, spooned and levelled

165 grams (¾ cup) white sugar, plus more for muffin tops

¼ teaspoon sea salt

2 teaspoons baking powder

80 ml (approx. ⅓ cup) vegetable oil

1 large egg

80 ml (approx. ⅓ cup) milk

1½ teaspoons vanilla extract

200 grams (approx. 1 generous cup) fresh or frozen blueberries

METHOD

- Preheat the oven to 180°C, fan forced.
- Line muffin trays with paper cases. You will need around 10 cases.
- Whisk the flour, sugar, salt and baking powder in a bowl.
- Choose a glass measuring jug that holds more than 250 ml. Add the oil, then crack in the egg, and pour in enough milk to reach the 1 cup line on the jug. Add the vanilla extract and whisk together.
- Add the wet ingredients to the bowl with the dry ingredients, and stir until the batter comes together. It will be thick. Try not to overmix.
- Gently fold in the blueberries.
- Divide the batter between the muffin cups. Sprinkle the tops with additional sugar.
- Depending on your oven, bake for around 15 minutes.

Emma's Blackberry Afternoon Tea Cake

Darling, a heart won't stay bruised and broken forever.

INGREDIENTS

4 eggs, separated
165 grams (¾ cup) caster sugar, plus 35 grams (approx. 2 tablespoons) extra
110 grams (¾ cup) plain flour
80 grams (approx. ⅓ cup) butter, melted
200 grams (approx. 1 generous cup) fresh or frozen blackberries
Icing sugar for dusting

METHOD

- Preheat the oven to 160°C, fan forced.
- Line a 20 cm springform cake tin with baking paper.
- Whisk the egg yolks with the 165 grams sugar until thick and pale.
- In a separate bowl (using a stand mixer is best), whisk the egg whites to soft peaks. Add the 35 grams caster sugar and whisk until smooth.
- Fold a third of the egg white mixture into the yolk mixture, gently stir in the flour and butter, then gently fold in the remaining egg white. Pour the batter into the cake tin.
- Scatter the blackberries onto the cake, and using a skewer, press some blackberries down into the batter.
- Bake for 40 minutes, dust with icing sugar and serve warm.

Buddy's Warm Cinnamon Apple Cake

A lady on the beach gave Buddy the whole goddamn cake.

Ingredients

125 grams (½ cup) butter, softened
1 teaspoon vanilla extract
165 grams (¾ cup) caster sugar
1 teaspoon ground cinnamon
2 eggs
125 ml (½ cup) milk
225 grams (1½ cups) self-raising flour
3 medium-sized apples, cored, peeled and very thinly sliced
Raw sugar for sprinkling

Method

- Line a 22 cm springform cake tin with baking paper.
- Preheat the oven to 160°C, fan forced.
- Using a mixer, beat the butter, caster sugar, cinnamon and vanilla until smooth and creamy.
- Add the eggs and milk and beat until combined.
- Pour half the mixture into the tin. Add a layer of apple using half the sliced apples.
- Pour over the remaining cake mixture and top with the remaining half of the sliced apples.
- Sprinkle with raw sugar.
- Bake for 40–45 minutes. Serve warm.

Rosemary, Greek Yogurt and Olive Oil Cake

The perfect not-too-sweet cake for friends.

INGREDIENTS

2 tablespoons fresh rosemary, chopped
2 lemons, zest and juice
220 grams (1 cup) white sugar
2 eggs
230 grams (1 cup) Greek yogurt
250 ml (1 cup) olive oil
300 grams (2 cups) self-raising flour
Icing sugar for dusting

METHOD

- Line a 20 cm springform cake tin with baking paper.
- Preheat the oven to 170°C, fan forced.
- In a bowl, mix the rosemary, lemon zest and sugar. Rub the mixture with your hands to release the rosemary aroma and flavour.
- Add the eggs and beat with a whisk until pale and thick.
- Mix in the Greek yogurt, lemon juice and olive oil.
- Sift in the flour. Gently fold it all together.
- Pour into the cake tin.
- Bake for 45 minutes. Cool slightly.
- Dust with icing sugar and serve warm.

Audrey's Bittersweet Biscuits

Life is what you bake it.

INGREDIENTS

60 grams egg whites (use 2 large eggs)
½ teaspoon vanilla extract
75 grams (½ cup) plain flour
110 grams (½ cup) caster sugar
1 pinch of salt
3 tablespoons water
Edible flower petals: marigold, pansy and daisy (optional)

METHOD

- For the fortune cookies, write your own fortunes on strips of paper.
- Preheat the oven to 220°C, fan forced.
- Beat the egg whites and vanilla in a mixing bowl until frothy (about 1 minute).
- Sift in the flour, sugar and salt, and using a spatula, gently mix until the batter is paste-like.
- Add the water, one tablespoon at a time, until the batter is smooth and falls in ribbons.
- Place 1 tablespoon of batter onto a silicone baking tray and spread into a 7 cm circle. Repeat. You may be able to fit 4 cookies on one silicone sheet.
- If you want to make floral fortune cookies, gently place edible fresh flower petals on top.
- Bake for 8 minutes until the edges are golden.
- Working quickly, remove the cookies from the baking tray.

- ❀ Add a fortune across the middle, fold in half into a semi-circle shape, then bend the flat edge over the rim of a cup.
- ❀ To help the fortune cookies retain their shape, cool each one in a muffin tin. *(Note: fortune cookies are tricky to perfect, so please be patient with yourself.)*

Acknowledgements

I'm so grateful to the people who shared their love, insights and expertise to help me bring this story to readers. Thank you to Kristin Gill, my amazing agent-friend, skilled interlocutor, consultant and founding partner of Northern Books. You are an inspiration in all things, Kristin. Life is a party, and we both dress like it! Thank you to my brilliant team at Allen & Unwin, including Annette Barlow, Greer Gamble, Samantha Ryan, Shannon Edwards, the sales team and those working behind the scenes. Thank you to the Novelry's Tash Barsby and Emylia Hall for your early insights and support. And to booksellers and readers everywhere, thank you.

To my incredible reading team in Australia, England, Ireland, America and Canada—thank you for your enthusiasm, warmth and unstoppable cheerleading. To be on the receiving end of women supporting other women is humbling and essential. I am so, so grateful to each of you: Carolyn Anderson-Fermann, Leslie Bishop, Rebecca Blair, Chari, Rose Faulkner, Teri G., Heather Getz, Ann Grix, Marg Hagey, Dorothy Hawes, Jean Ives, Judy,

Catherine Greer

Jan Kelly, Hemmie Martin, Cheryll Meredith, June Myles, Claire Mulae, Katrina Nahikian, Harriet Newbold, Kate O., Tracy Palmer, Yvette P., Adele Poier, Marci Poier, Lu-Ann Procter, Tara Ray, Heather Remo, Juls Rollnik, Katie S. Rushing, Cheryl Shurtliffe, Wendy and Fiona Wedding.

To my mother and sisters in Canada—Katie Greer, Sheila Eskdale, Darlene Nast, Rena Mazer—the love and the baking come from you. Thank you to Claire, Dani, Heather, Jenny, Jules, Marg, Merilyn and Wenxi. It's always a good idea for women to stick together. And to Glenn and Adele Poier, thank you for being our family; we love hitting the dance floor with the two of you.

Writers are often told to write the book they want to read, and that's exactly what I did with *The Bittersweet Bakery Café*. This book is for me, and I love it, and if it's for you, too, then I'm happy you found it. Shout-out to Shez, fictional CEO and entrepreneur, who introduced her glorious self to me on the page and made me laugh every time I sat down to write. A couple of Shez's best malapropisms are thanks to my brilliant husband, Luther, partner in all things, including my writing life.

When I wrote *The Bittersweet Bakery Café*, I needed more grit and determination. I also needed to learn to love my age . . . and so, like I've always done, I wrote about life's challenges to understand how to face them. And though I'm not in recovery like Audrey, I was inspired by teaching a writing class to recovery coaches with Jean McCarthy, author, podcaster, soul sister and cousin. If anything rings untrue about recovery in this novel, the mistakes are entirely mine. And if anyone needs support, it's there just as Audrey found it—quietly, online, from generous people who share their time, experiences and resources. As these women taught me, *we're all in recovery from something*. I believe this to be true.

Thank you to my colleagues at our dynamic Sydney and Melbourne offices, where inclusion, not ageism, is the norm. We've had a frenetic and fulfilling year, and you've made it possible for me to balance my career as an author and a copywriter. Thank you. I appreciate you.

Finally, and forever, I want to thank my family: Luther, Luke and Elijah Poier. You're the ones I treasure on this Australian adventure.

Music from the Bittersweet Bakery Café

Lizzo, 'Good as Hell'
Julie London, 'Cry Me a River'
Nina Simone, 'Little Girl Blue'
Nina Simone, 'Nobody Knows You When You're Down and Out'
Charlie Dée, 'A Case of You'
The Beatles, 'Here Comes the Sun'
Nina Simone, 'Love Me or Leave Me'
Nina Simone, 'To Be Young, Gifted and Black'
Fleetwood Mac, 'I Don't Want to Know'
Nina Simone, 'My Baby Just Cares for Me'
Creedence Clearwater Revival, 'Bad Moon Rising'
Pomplamoose, 'Oh, Pretty Woman'
Dolly Parton, '9 to 5'
Nancy Sinatra, 'These Boots Are Made for Walkin'
Dusty Springfield, 'Take Another Little Piece of My Heart'
Solomon Burke, 'Cry to Me'
Nina Simone, 'Mood Indigo'
Billy Joel, 'Only the Good Die Young'
Caroline Jones, 'Come In (But Don't Make Yourself Comfortable)'
Wilson Pickett, 'Mustang Sally'
Stevie Wonder, 'For Once in My Life'
Bobby Darin, 'Mack the Knife'
Doris Troy, 'Just One Look'
Mariah Carey, 'All I Want for Christmas Is You'
Michael Bublé (with Shania Twain), 'White Christmas'

Printed in Great Britain
by Amazon